Praise for The Betrayal of Lincoln Crockett

"A captivating story of humor, strive and tragedy during the socially turbulent 1960s in a small southern town. George Scott captures the persona of small-town characters struggling to adapt to the social changes of the civil rights era and exposes the bigotry and class system that existed for hundreds of years before the transition to the "New South." A great read that will make you laugh and make you cry while riveting you to the flow of the story."
—Rollin K. McKean, President Delta Literary Group

"This book took me on a journey through a small town in East Tennessee during the mid-1960s. It was a time of civil unrest; a time which included the recently passed federal Civil Rights Act of 1964, moonshine, small town politics, racism, the Vietnam war, heroes, villains, and a complete roller coaster ride of good times and bad times. Each time when I was getting comfortable with the story, I was presented with yet another twist or turn. A must read! You will definitely enjoy it!"
—Greg R. Hossbach, Ed.D.

The Betrayal of
Lincoln Crockett

The Betrayal of Lincoln Crockett

G.W. Scott

Crippled Beagle Publishing
Knoxville, Tennessee
dyer.cbpublishing@gmail.com

Cover and book design by Rhonda Day, Hart Graphics.
www.hartgraphics.com

Epitaph scripture taken from The Holy Bible, King James Version

ISBN softcover 978-1-970037-23-4

Other publications by G.W. Scott: *Where Roads May Lead*, Second
Edition

"And ye shall know the truth, and the truth shall make you free." John 8:32 (KJV)

Chapter 1

April, 1965

It was early evening when the black Cadillac limo rolled to a stop under the awning-covered entrance at the Lacy Hotel. Smoke-black windows concealed the identity of its passengers, but only physically. Everyone knew to whom the car belonged; there was only one other like it in town, but that one was a different color. The black-clad chauffeur swung the curbside doors open and stood at attention while the occupants disembarked.

The first to emerge from the car's plush, dimly lit interior were Emerson Armstrong and Leland Longworth followed by their wives Victoria and Cora Sue, respectively. From the rear seat climbed the Longworths' nineteen-year-old son Montgomery, along with the Armstrongs' daughter Ashley, an eighteen-year-old high school senior. All fashionably attired, they had arrived on time for their dinner reservations at the hotel's restaurant to celebrate Mr. Longworth's birthday.

The Armstrongs and Longworths were the two most powerful families in the county. Between the Armstrong Textile Mill and Longworth Furniture Manufacturing Company, they comprised the primary sources of employment in Jackson County, Tennessee. In fact, with Jackson County being the smallest county in the state, their mills offered the only option for long-term, sustainable employment (much of it hard, dirty work at low pay), thus controlling the economic well-being of the community. As a result, Messrs. Armstrong and Longworth wielded considerable influence over local politics (not to mention the politicians that made up the small county government), as well as holding inroads into the state political machinery. They were powerful and wealthy individuals.

Likewise, with the husbands holding such prestigious positions of leadership, their wives were looked upon as the "first ladies" of local society. As might be expected, their offspring, each an only child and sole heir to the family fortunes, were not only being groomed to assume roles of responsibility in the generations-old family businesses, but also in the area of social leadership.

The party lingered on the sidewalk and waited for Mr. Armstrong, who was lagging behind giving instructions to the chauffeur, to join them. An impatient Victoria suggested (her suggestions were more like orders) that they wait in the comfort of the hotel lobby. As they approached the lobby entrance, the door suddenly swung open.

"Welcome to the Lacy," came a courteous greeting from a quite handsome young man. He was tall with an athletic build and dressed in black slacks, shiny black shoes, a starched white shirt, and a red jacket trimmed with gold cords. Mrs. Armstrong, ignoring the young man's greeting, proceeded to march through the open doorway into the lobby while dragging her daughter Ashley along by the arm. The Longworths followed her lead with the young bellman following behind.

Even though it was one of his duties to welcome guests, there was one member of this party in particular that the bellman had a personal interest in greeting.

"Good evening Montgomery...Ashley," smiled Lincoln Crockett, exposing a row of gleaming white teeth that stood out in contrast to his suntanned complexion and mop of black, curly hair.

Montgomery nodded back, smiling.

"Good evening," Ashley courteously replied.

"You look nice this evening Ashley," the bellman shyly complemented to the Nancy Sinatra lookalike. She was dressed in a Jackie Kennedy-inspired tailored suit. Lincoln had always admired the blonde from afar; always from afar, for she was way out of his league. It was not only because of her looks that he held her in such high esteem. She wasn't like the other society girls from The Ridge (snobbish, stuck-up, and self-centered). On the contrary, she was down-to-earth, personable, and friendly toward everyone.

"Thank you, Lincoln," she acknowledged with a slight smile, "so do you in your bellman's uniform."

Victoria Armstrong flashed a frown in her daughter's direction, then stared indignantly at Lincoln.

"This way to the Piano Room," he said, gesturing toward the restaurant.

"That will be all young man," Victoria snapped.

"We'll require no mo'uh of yo'uh services," she added, shooing him away with a flick of her hand.

"Yes ma'am," nodded the bellman as he excused himself.

"Mama! That was rude! Lincoln was just trying to be nice," scolded Ashley.

Her mother frowned at her with raised eyebrows and responded through clenched teeth as coldhearted as a cast-iron commode. "I know that boy. I know where he's *from*, what he *is*!"

"No, you don't know him Mama. You know he's from Milltown, that he's a 'Millie' as you call people from there."

"But that's all a 'Ridger' needs to know, isn't it?" she added sarcastically, trying to keep her voice low.

"Don't be impuh-tinent," rebuked her mother. "We'll have no mo'uh talk of this sort, and if you know what's good fo'uh you young lady, you'll stay away from his kind."

"Well, he's a nice boy. Don't you think so Montgomery?" added Ashley, looking in Montgomery's direction.

Montgomery nodded in agreement, "Yes, old Lincoln's an okay chap."

Montgomery's parents observed him questioningly but said nothing as they heard Emerson Armstrong's voice.

Emerson Armstrong, catching up to the group, had just caught the tail end of the conversation and noticed the look of displeasure on his wife's face and the frown on his daughter's.

"Is there some problem?" he asked.

"You'd best have a talk with yo'uh daughta about the facts of life he'uh in Coldwata," ordered his wife discretely. "She's apparently forgettin' who she is and becomin' too familiar with some *undesirables*."

Emerson looked quizzically, first at his wife, then at his daughter who just shrugged her shoulders as if to say, "What?" Saying nothing more, the party followed Emerson's lead to the restaurant (which was currently only half full) where he informed the maître d' of their reservation. They were promptly seated at a table next to a window overlooking the hotel's well-manicured, lighted grounds.

The Lacy was a grand old hotel offering all the conveniences and amenities of a modern-day guesthouse while maintaining the traditional grace and charm of a rustic southern inn. In addition to being a four-star hotel, the Lacy was also home to the area's premier restaurant.

Inside the restaurant, a four-star establishment in its own right, was the Piano Room, named for the solid white grand piano that sat on a black, velvet-draped, slowly rotating carousel in the center of the room. On Friday and Saturday evenings, a pianist fitted in white tuxedo, top hat, and cane made his entrance and tickled the ivories while diners satisfied their pallets with generous servings of succulent New York steaks and savory southern-fried catfish.

After giving the waiter their orders, the group settled into friendly chit-chat while the parents shared a toast, clinking their wine glasses together. Although Jackson County was officially dry, the only drink of the alcohol variety that could be imbibed at the Lacy Hotel was wine, legally, that is. Moonshine could be had if one knew where to find it and how to get it.

Over salads, the ladies discussed upcoming events on the social calendar as well as an item or two of gossip making its way across the grapevine telegraph. The gentlemen's exchange focused mostly on the current situation in Southeast Asia where, just two weeks earlier, the first large-scale U.S. Army ground units had arrived in South Vietnam. The two businessmen's primary concern with the whole foreign conflict was the effect escalating U.S. involvement may have on the country's economy in general and specifically on their own businesses. Young Montgomery's worry was of a more personal nature. He was of draft age.

"Don't worry, Montgomery," assured Emerson, "you're in college now and have a military deferment."

"That's right son," added his father, "you won't have to get involved in that mess over there. We'll send all the Millies and Darkies over there to do the fightin' if it comes to that."

Emerson Armstrong and Leland Longworth were an odd pair to have become social friends. But, more times than not, similar business and political interests have often served to make strange bedfellows in spite of many personal differences. A well-dressed, middle-aged, trim figure of a man, Armstrong was the progeny of a longstanding southern family that could trace its lineage back to Colonial times. Ivy League educated and of somewhat moderate views in matters of politics, he was the third-generation owner of the family textile business. A charitable man, he was widely respected in the community.

In contrast, Leland Longworth (a few years Emerson's senior) was an overweight, balding fellow who always, to some extent, looked disheveled in his clothing. Born and bred in the South, the alumnus of a well-known southern university had been a dyed-in-the-wool, old-school conservative from day one and would be as long as he was alive and kicking. As owner of Longworth Furniture Manufacturing, a business he inherited from his father, and him from his father, he was a shrewd, and some would say unscrupulous, businessman. He was self-centered and as tight with a dollar as the rusted lug nuts on a '47 Ford. In summary, Armstrong might be described as a tennis and martini man and Longworth more of a football and beer man.

After the waiter had served Delmonico steaks all around except for Ashley (a vegetarian who ordered a pasta salad), Victoria, who was always on some high and mighty crusade, resurrected the earlier conversation in the lobby; one of her ignoble lectures: burning Millies in effigy like Christ on the cross.

"I do wish they would hire suitable employees he'uh in the hotel and restaurant," offered Victoria indignantly.

"What do you mean dear?" questioned Cora Sue, taking a sip of wine.

"Well, fuh instance, that boy we met at the do'uh. He's just not the *kind* one should hav'ta encoun'ta in genteel places where proper people go. You know, people educated in tha proprieties and correct social decorum."

"She means a Millie, mother," interjected Montgomery bluntly, carving a large portion of pink flesh from his steak.

"I think I know where you'uh going with this Victoria," said Leland, heartily chowing down on a mouthful of meat, "but, as Ashley said, he was just doing his job."

"But he did have the audacity to practically flirt with Ashley right in front of us!" interjected Cora Sue defensively, as though they had witnessed some obscene act, "...and being so informal with Montgomery...calling him *Monty*! I understand what you mean, Victoria. A respectable young lady shouldn't have to be exposed to that type of roughish behavior."

"Oh, Cora Sue, everyone *does* call Montgomery *Monty* now, don't they?" teased Victoria, toying with her potato.

"He was not flirting!" snapped Ashley, "We're classmates...and friends. He was simply being polite and complimentary."

"Friends!" retorted Victoria, red-faced, her voice trailing off.

"What?" echoed her husband, as astonished as if hearing she was pregnant. "Just how good of 'friends' do you mean?"

"She means just what she said... *friends*," added Montgomery, coming to Ashley's aid. "Lincoln and I are also friends. We've worked on class projects together...talked in the halls. So what?"

"So what?" echoed Cora Sue and Leland Longworth in chorus, as taken aback as were the Armstrongs. "It means a lot, *so what*," added Leland.

Patting his mouth with his napkin, in a gesture for calmness Emerson waved his arms at the group, whose voices were escalating.

After a few moments of silence, Emerson resumed where he had left off before the interruption.

"Look, Ashley. And you, too, Montgomery. You come into contact with different kinds of people, like at school, and you have to treat people right. But, you also have to remember that people live in different worlds and when it comes to forming friendships and relationships. You must keep in mind which world you live in; there are dictates of society to be followed and a status quo to be maintained."

"That's right," agreed Leland. "In short, oil and water don't mix. Neither do Ridgers and Millies. I agree with Victoria; I don't care a tinker's damn for that white trash!" he added unceremoniously and to the point, lacking the diplomacy and civil sensitivity of an Emerson Armstrong towards those considered to be one's social inferiors.

"Yes, *that's right!*" bawled Ashley, much like Alice in *Alice in Wonderland*, confused and amazed at the world around her. Jumping to her feet, tears trickling from her eyes, she said, "No one mixes with the social snobs around here; not Millies, Negros, Jews, or anyone else who doesn't have a pedigree that can be traced through a lineage back to some rich old Colonial who made a fortune either working slaves to death in a cotton field or being paid off for political patronage." Throwing her napkin down in disgust and overturning a water glass, she did an about face, and stormed out of the restaurant, through the lobby, and out of the hotel.

"Excuse me. I'll go after her and see that she's alright," offered Montgomery, scurrying after Ashley, leaving the two sets of parents sitting there flabbergasted at the outburst and embarrassed amidst a room full of glaring eyes.

Montgomery met Lincoln in the lobby.

"Did you see Ashley?'

"Yeah, she went through here like a bat outta hell!"

"Which way did she go?"

"She hopped a cab that was leaving the hotel. It headed north, up The Ridge. What happened?"

"Oh, she just got upset. North, huh? I think I may know where she's headed, probably to her friend Peggy's house."

"Want me to call you a cab?"

"Yes, please do. Thanks, Lincoln."

Lincoln skipped out to the curb and hailed the only cab available at the taxicab stand across the street. They watched as the yellow, 1960 Dodge U-turned across the two lanes of Depot Street and pulled under the red awning where the two young men waited.

"At your service Mr. Crockett," greeted the old cabbie.

"Evenin' Dutch, gotta fare for you."

"My friend here's in a hurry. Can you get him where he needs to go fast?"

"Faster'n a deacon in a whorehouse!" chuckled Dutch. "Just point me in the right direction."

Shortly after Montgomery's departure, the Armstrongs and Longworths made their own hasty retreat from the restaurant. Lincoln, anticipating their forthcoming exit, had waited in the lobby to hold the door for their departure. He was anxious to see if he might discern some clue from them that would account for Ashley's rapid flight from the premises.

Leland Longworth stopped and with a wave of his hand demanded snobbishly, "Stand aside Millie, we require no assistance from you."

Lincoln, not surprised by the stark orders, complied with the man's request. As the quartet of patrons filed by single file into the night, each glared as if he were some malefactor who had committed a grievous sacrilege.

Even though he had grown up with it, every time he heard the term "Millie" personally directed at him, it cut like a knife. He marveled at how such systems of labeling developed and how the labels themselves could convey contempt even when unspoken. But, at times even he couldn't, resist the temptation to use one of those labels himself in retaliation.

"Have a good evening," he called out, adding under his breath, "Ridgers."

Lincoln watched the black limo as it careened onto Main Street and quickly vanished from sight as if spirited away like Cinderella's carriage fleeing the ball. Inside the car, its four occupants yelled obscenities at anyone and everyone they could think of being responsible for the social humiliation to which they had just been subjected. In the mind of Victoria Armstrong, there was only one source; the same source she generally blamed for all the ills of society: Millies. But more specifically she found that the Millies' faults were embodied in one young man: Lincoln Crockett.

Chapter 2

Lincoln walked out onto the veranda, leaned against the banister, and, gazing upward, stared intently at the star-laden sky. All was quiet as he studied the night lights all about him, and from his vantage point at that moment in time and space, the place he lived appeared so peaceful, pleasant, and disarming. Nestled in the foothills of the Smoky Mountains, a first-time visitor to this charming little community of five thousand would see little evidence, on the surface at least, to lead one to believe that there existed barriers designed to separate the classes. But, Lincoln knew better. This was his home. He had lived here all his life. In reality, beneath a façade of harmony and tranquility there beat the heart of a town divided socially, economically, and geographically, and where one lived geographically had a direct bearing on the other two.

The affluent of Coldwater society, like birds of a feather, flocked together in the high-rent district known as The Ridge, a prime piece of real estate that stretched along most of the two-mile length of the city limits. Known to outsiders as "Ridgers," these mostly "old money," upper class families occupying large, old Victorian homes are the descendants of wealthy forebears holding firmly to the conviction that all are duty bound to march quietly along like cheerful robots in deference to that sacred cow, the generations-old status quo.

Standing in stark contrast to The Ridge is Milltown, a collection of manufacturing mills that lies in a river plane between The Ridge and Little River, whose dominating feature is toxin-puffing smokestacks. Located on the "other side of the tracks," blue collar families who labor in the mills live in company-owned, low-rent mill houses jammed side-by-side on dirty streets that meander around the mills in helter-skelter fashion, reminiscent of scenes from a Charles Dickens novel.

Few Millies are able to overcome the economic and social barriers necessary to break the cycle of child following parent, generation after generation, into the mills to work for forty-hour, minimum wage, weekly paychecks.

But, this is the 1960s, and winds of change are sweeping the land. Forces like the Civil Rights movement, Supreme Court rulings on prayer in schools, separation of church and state, and abortion; the war in Vietnam, the Cold War with its threat of nuclear annihilation, and the "hippie" generation with their "if it feels good, do it" philosophy all contribute to an uneasy atmosphere. In such an atmosphere, undefined change fans the winds of transformation and even revolution that seek to alter the American political, religious, and social landscapes with reforms that, to many, represent liberation and equality (e.g., the Millies), but, to others, signal a threat to longstanding values and ways of life (e.g. the Ridgers).

This is as true for a generation of young people in Coldwater as any other place in the country. It is especially true for one like eighteen-year-old Lincoln Crockett who, on one hand, is a product of Milltown, but on the other hand, is a dreamer and idealist trying to make sense of a chaotic world and an uncertain future.

What a difference a year makes! Last year at this time, Lincoln Crockett was on top of the world. Before high school graduation, he had it all in his hands. Not just a dream, but a future; a future with a bus ticket out of Milltown, out of Coldwater, and a full-ride basketball scholarship to a big-time school and big-time basketball in his hip pocket. But, then, in a moment of time, it had all slipped away like sand through a sieve.

Lincoln had been blessed with the ability to shoot a basketball and to do it better than most. A shoo-in for all-state honors, he was being recruited by several large colleges. That was until the final game of the season when he and another player collided and both went sprawling across the floor in a tangle of arms and legs. He never played another game. A shattered right knee took care of that. It also took care of the scholarship that was to have been his saving grace.

He had been fortunate in one respect, however. After his basketball career fouled out, Miss Jessica Wingo, owner of the Lacy Hotel, hired him to work full time at the hotel. But, where could he go from there? Any kind of future in Coldwater was faced with a degree of uncertainty.

Although Fate had slammed a door in his face, Lincoln still had hopes and dreams; not just fantasies, but real ones that didn't include trudging through the turnstiles at one of Milltown's mills like a wooden pony on a carousel.

The sun was now sinking near the horizon and Lincoln turned his attention to the glowing western skies. The skies, painted with an array of blazing colors as if splashed there by the hand of some mad artist, reminded him of a fire storm raging on the distant horizon or the doors to some great abyss flung open wide to expose the very fires of hell. He watched intently as the sun slipped slowly through that tiny seam in space where earth and sky meet and the fiery sphere dissolves into black, velvety darkness. And with that, another day in the small southern town of Coldwater, Tennessee, came to a close, and with it, another day in the life of Lincoln Crockett. For both, each day was much like the one before it, and the one before it, and so on.

But, on this Friday evening in April, 1965, Lincoln Crockett could not have imagined that in the coming months his life would become entangled with the lives of two Ridger families, the Armstrongs and Longworths, his social superiors, and that all their futures would be forever and unalterably changed—especially his and Ashley Armstrong's. The courses of their lives would take new directions much like the country itself, directions in which fate would sweep them through a series of events and experiences that would prove to have tragic consequences when their two very different worlds would collide. This is Lincoln Crockett's story; this is Lincoln Crockett's life.

Chapter 3

The old grandfather clock in the hotel lobby chimed nine times as Lincoln bounded down the back steps of the veranda, clearing every other one like a rock skipping across water, and rounded the hotel onto Main Street. It was his usual practice after work in the evenings to take the shortcut home through the back streets down to Town Creek, cross the log footbridge, and walk through the furniture factory's parking lot into Milltown.

With the exception of Ashley Armstrong's outburst in the restaurant and her party's rude exit, the day had been an uneventful one. So, tonight, he decided to take the longer route through town and see what was happening (if anything) on Main Street.

All the stores on the main drag were now closed and dark. The only light on the sidewalks came from old flashing neon signs above the store fronts and the dim, yellowing light of dirty streetlamps. Together, their reflections in the stores' windows cast a confusion of grotesque, shadowy figures dancing eerily about that seemed to beckon admittance into spooky carnival side shows.

Lincoln shoved his hands deep into the tight pockets of faded Levi's for warmth against the dogwood winter chill and squeezed his sleeveless arms close against his body both for additional warmth and to appear inconspicuous to the "spooks" lurking in the doorways.

Main Street itself was alive with its usual parade of Friday night cruisers; a continuous procession of highschoolers prowling back and forth and up and down between Mickey D's on the east side of town and the A&W Root Beer joint on the west side. This carousel of hotrods and muscle cars would continue for most of the evening and stop only at one hangout or the other long enough to slurp a mug or munch some fries. That is, until the lucky ones hooked a "pickup" to lock lips with in the back seat at one of the local "lover's lanes."

But, this was not Lincoln's scene; this was not Lincoln's crowd. He didn't have a ride, frequent social events, or have a girlfriend (except for the one he could only dream about). Then, out of the corner of his eye, he saw it, the solid white, '56 T-Bird. The car, whose driver's identity was betrayed by a blonde mane periodically illuminated in the hardtop's porthole by passing headlights and streetlamps. Stopping, his eyes followed it for as long as the car was visible, the one car and driver that stood out from all the rest, the one that everyone knew by sight, the one driven by Ashley Armstrong. Apparently, Ashley hadn't gone to her friend Peggy's house after she fled from the Lacy as Montgomery Longworth had surmised.

With images of the blonde dancing through his head, he hurried along, speeding up his gait from a stride to a fast walk. He glanced up toward The Ridge. The lights in the houses seemed to twinkle like stars playing peek-a-boo through the trees' foliage.

No! This wasn't Lincoln's neighborhood by a longshot; it was, however, Ashley Armstrong's. Lincoln lived on the opposite side of Main Street. From Milltown to Little River and the bluffs beyond were Lincoln's stomping grounds. Main Street was like the Berlin Wall of Coldwater. As the crow flies, it was but a stone's throw from Milltown to The Ridge. But in reality, anyway you cared to slice it , economically, socially, or figuratively, Milltown was a long way from The Ridge.

As Lincoln approached Mill Street (the main entrance into the mills), he heard a rumbling sound knocking in his brain. He immediately recognized the signature heartbeat of Tyler Justice's old Indian motorcycle coming down Main Street behind him. Tyler pulled up to the curb beside Lincoln and silenced the two-wheeler's engine.

"My man Linc!"

"What's happening brother Rats?" (No one called Tyler by his name. Everyone called him "Rats" because he was always saying, "Aw, rats!")

"Headin' home?" asked Rats.

"Yeah. And you?"

"Yep! Me too."

"Say, it's not that late. Wanna stop by Joe's and get a bite?" asked Rats.

"Sure, why not?" answered his friend.

Lincoln hopped on the Indian behind Rats and they motored a few blocks farther down Main, hung a right on Blue Tick Lane into Milltown, and a block later, Rats steered the cycle to a stop in front of the Come-On-In Cafe. The Come-On-In was a little mom-and-pop, greasy spoon with a long counter in the front with a dozen stools attached and a half-dozen, four-person booths at one end. At the opposite end of the booth area stood an old Wurlitzer juke box that blared out George Jones and Patsy Cline crying-in-your-beer songs at ten cents a pop or, triple your pleasure, three for a quarter.

Joe and Mavis Stinnett had run the place for as long as Lincoln and Rats could remember, serving up a midday, blue plate special, with breakfast, burgers, and fries and such from six in the morning until closing around ten that night. Mavis took the orders and Joe cooked them up.

Mavis, a reasonably attractive lady in her forties, sauntered over to the counter where the fellows had parked themselves on stools to take their orders.

"Ooo, Ooo, you lookin' good tonight girl," flirted the nineteen-year-old Rats, winking at Mavis.

Mavis leaned over the counter and said coyly, "Tyler, you wouldn't know what to do with this much woman."

"Oh, ho!" laughed Lincoln, "What say you to that, brother Rats?"

Rats just blushed.

"Anyway, I'm old enough to be your mama, and besides, I'm a married woman."

"And I'll come across this here counter and whup your butt fer flirtin' with my wife," scowled Joe, turning around from the grill, pointing his spatula at Rats.

Lincoln put his arm around Rats' shoulder and warned, "I think you best leave this woman alone!"

"Aw, rats!"

Then the four of them had a laugh all around. Joe and Mavis had known the two since they were little squirts.

"What can I git fer the two best looking young fellers in Milltown?" the biscuit shooter asked with a playful wink.

"Now you know our second favorite sweet thing, don't you Mav?" reminded Lincoln.

"Gimmee two grilled hunnies'n cream, Joe," ordered Mavis.

"Comin' up!" acknowledged the chef.

Now Joe made the world's best grilled honey buns topped with ice cream in the world. It was a little slice of heaven, at least as far as Lincoln and Rats determined.

The boys were best friends, having grown up together in Milltown. They were like a couple of Huck Finns; palling around and usually getting into mischief. Yet, they were as different as salt and pepper. Rats, an academic procrastinator, took things at face value. He approached life one day at a time with a swaggering confidence. He was daring, ready to take on a challenge any time, any place; however, those same attributes that, for the most part, served him well could also be his Achilles' heel; they tended, from time to time, to get him into trouble.

Lincoln, on the other hand, while not an academic scholar, was an above-average student who relished literature, and by the age of sixteen, had read the complete works of William Shakespeare, Edgar Allen Poe, Mark Twain, and Charles Dickens. Intelligent and deep-thinking, he had never been satisfied with simply learning facts; he questioned the "whys" behind the facts. This was a valuable attribute for learning, but one that tended to make him more cautious and calculating in addressing situations that called for immediate action.

A good-looking young man and, although outwardly friendly and likable, Lincoln was basically shy, private, and prone to mood swings that often caused him to be seen as unsociable by others. But, unknown to those around him (and perhaps even himself), beneath that good-natured exterior lay a seething pressure cooker of anger held at bay only by a fog of deep depression that enveloped him much of the time—a well of melancholy that someday would gush forth like the black liquid of a new oil strike bursting from the bowels of earth.

They moved to one of the booths for privacy where they lapped up their buns and cream, washed down with a glass of cold milk. After feeding the juke box a few coins, they kicked back and began to discuss their love life.

"How's your main squeeze?" asked Lincoln.

"Bonnie? Oh, she's doing good…we're doing good."

"That's good!"

"Yeah, she's a sweet girl."

"You gotta skirt on the line yet or you still moon-eyed over that blonde-haired society girl?"

Lincoln just smiled and took a big swig of the cherry Coke he had just ordered.

"Man, you gotta get over Ashley Armstrong. She's a Ridger. She's untouchable. There's no way that's gonna happen! You might as well be in love with Raquel Welch!"

"I know. You're right. I guess I'm like that Ray Charles song, 'I Can't Stop Loving You.' You have to admit that she's a fox."

Rats rolled his eyes in disbelief, slipped a comb out of his jeans pocket, and smoothed back the sides of his ducktail.

"You spend too much time book bustin'. You're a hopeless romantic."

"Might do you some good to read a book now and then," challenged Lincoln.

"I don't have time…I have a girlfriend!"

"You taking Bonnie to the prom?" questioned Lincoln.

"I didn't go last year when I graduated and Bonnie's graduating this year…so…yeah! Why not? It's a once-in-a-lifetime deal—something to remember."

"You?" asked Rats.

"Well, since I'm an alumnus now, no girl's asked me to escort her."

"Why don't you ask *Ashley*?" teased Rats.

"Right! The odds on that happening are about as good as finding bird crap in a cuckoo clock,"
responded Lincoln, arching his eyebrows.

"Well, you ready to bug out?" Rats asked, looking at his watch, "I have to go to work in the morning."

"Yeah, guess we better. It's later than I thought," answered Lincoln, "but before we leave, I need to check out the plumbing."

After ponying up for their tab and saying goodbye to Joe and Mavis, they let the screen door slam softly behind them as they stepped into the parking lot and headed for the two-wheeler.

"Hey, you put a new paint job on the Chief," noticed Lincoln. "Looks good!"

"Yeah, the Chief's beautiful," said Rats proudly.

"Well, I don't know that I'd go that far. It's still an old motorcycle," joked Lincoln.

"I guess beauty is in the eyes of the beholder," quipped his friend.

"Say, do you know how fast this thing will go?" asked Lincoln.

"Not exactly…don't have a speedometer."

[16]

"But, do you know how fast a scalded dog can run?" Rats asked in return.

"Not exactly," answered Lincoln, "guess I never really thought about it."

"Neither do I," said Rats, "but that's how fast the Chief can go."

Lincoln just shook his head and laughed.

The old Indian had belonged to Rats' uncle in a nearby town who had died a few years ago. The motorcycle had gotten covered up by junk in his garage and forgotten about until one day when Rats was visiting his aunt and uncovered it while cleaning out her garage. His aunt had told him he could have it if he could get it running. Rats had gotten to be a pretty fair mechanic since having a fulltime job at Mr. DeLaney's Texaco service station, and after working on that machine for months, he'd finally got it into good running condition and looking pretty good, too.

They straddled the bike and headed back down Main Street, took a left on Mill Street, and a block later, hung a right onto MacAnally Flats. He came to a stop in front of a little weather-worn, oyster-white mill house where the Crocketts lived. Lincoln's heart sank at the sight of the house. He didn't want to be home. He slid reluctantly off the back of the seat.

"See you later Mr. Lincoln."

"Take care King Rats."

They shook hands and Lincoln watched Rats ride off into the distance until the Indian's taillight faded out of sight; he wished that he, too, could just disappear into the night.

Turning toward the house, a barrage of thoughts flooded his mind, "This House! This damned house! I hate this place! I hate *them*! I wish I could be a thousand miles from here. I wish I never had to see this place, or them, again.

Chapter 4

Late that night

The mill house that the Crocketts lived in was a cookie-cutter copy of all the others; a wood-frame dwelling consisting of a bathroom sandwiched between two bedrooms with a living room and kitchen divided by a small dining area.

Entering through the kitchen from the back porch, Lincoln found his father, Clovis, in the living room stretched out in his recliner staring bug-eyed at the television. His mother, Anna Mae, was in her bedroom, swaying gently back and forth in her favorite rocking chair sewing. Slipping unnoticed into his own sleeping quarters, he wondered what their moods were like, having no knowledge of what interactions may have transpired between the two of them during the evening. Bedtime would tell the tale and according to the clock on his nightstand, that time would soon be forthcoming.

He stretched out on his bed and began thumbing through a back issue of *Popular Science*. The only sound to be heard was that of the television before which his father camped out every night to admire the He-Man heroes of *Bonanza* and other Hollywood-manufactured horse operas. Then came the moment of truth: the deafening "click" that silenced the television. It was 10:00 p.m. His father's bedtime had arrived. Lincoln tensed up in anticipation of what he feared the next few minutes would bring.

Right on cue, Anna Mae emerged from her hideaway into the hallway as if timing her path to intentionally cross her husband's, who was now on his way from the living room to the hall bathroom.

Why does she do it? Lincoln thought to himself, *She seems to delight in provoking him, like a mischievous kid goading a snarling dog with a stick. Why can't she just ignore him and let him go on to bed? A small, frail, weak thing like her can't stand up to him anymore than I can! I don't understand! It scares the hell out of me.*

The physical size and stature of Clovis Crockett's fifty-five-year-old body belied the exceptional strength that coursed through muscles hardened by years of backbreaking work at the sawmill. He was tougher than the back end of a shootin' gallery and could out work any two men half his age. But, what Lincoln feared most about his father was his bad temper.

Life had never turned out to be what Clovis Crockett had hoped it would be. He had never been really happy and was, in some ways, a troubled man. Most of the time he was a decent enough fellow, going to church, living a moral life, and providing for his family the best he could. But, sometimes, something seemed to possess him and the dark side of his Jekyll and Hyde personality emerged, the side that Lincoln feared.

Lincoln had felt the wrath of that Mr. Hyde persona more than once, either in the form of a backhand to the face that sent him staggering across the floor or in lashings across the back from a big, black leather belt, and so had his mother.

He whispered, "Please, God, don't let the fighting start tonight. Just let them go quietly to bed."

But no such luck this night. The first telltale signs appear: a bump in the night, some mumbled words, a curse, a shout, a scuffle in the hallway. The bell rings and the fight is on; only there's no referee in this bout. No rules, no bounds, no sportsmanship. This is not sport, not a game. This is no-holds-barred, kick-him-in-the-balls, down-and-dirty fighting. This is home; this is family; this is marriage; this is life, which was life at its dirtiest. Lincoln closed his eyes as the life seemed to drain from his body like air escaping from a balloon.

"How many replays of this night have there been?" he asked himself rhetorically. He'd lost count. "How many more will there be?" he shook his head in wonderment. The walls closed in on him. A straitjacket of suffocating anxiety squeezed tighter and tighter around his chest.

Lincoln believed in his own mind that, sooner or later, on some night like this, his father would lose total control and a violent blow from his huge right hand would smash his mother's head like a pumpkin and, in a blind frenzy, would also kill him. He'd seen the rage that could emerge and possess his father's body to the point of uncontrollable trembling, heard the venomous language that could spew forth between clenched teeth, and seen the wild, unfocused stare in those dark-eyed windows into the soul of a demon. He had to escape from that bedroom and get out of the house.

In the hallway, he found the combatants engaged like two alley cats spitting and clawing at each other.

He pushed his way past them into the kitchen and reached for the doorknob on the kitchen door. Déjà vu!

How many times had he been there before as a kid, holding that doorknob in a death grip, trembling from head to toe, scared out of his wits, knowing that if push came to shove, he'd open that door and run? But where to? A neighbor's house? The police station? He didn't know. He just knew he'd have to *run*. Now, he was nineteen years old and no weakling, but he was still no match for his father, especially in a crazed state of mind.

The shouting and name calling continued for what seemed an eternity. Lincoln never paid much attention to what their arguments and fights were about and didn't really care; he just wanted it to stop. He turned back from the door and ventured part way toward the opponents and pleaded with them, as he had before, to stop their quarrelling.

Clovis turned to his son in rebuke, "Oh, shud up. We ain't botherin' you!"

The young man was stunned by his father's incredible reprimand! Retreating to the back porch, he fumed.

How could he say such a thing? Are they so blinded by their own self-absorbed agendas that they think the world only revolves around them, or do they just plain not give a damn? the young man pondered in disbelief.

Pulling away from her husband into the dining room, Anna Mae, tears streaming down her face, suddenly grabbed a cup off the dining table, turned, and slung it furiously in Clovis' direction, striking a glancing blow off the side of his head.

In retaliation, Clovis angrily seized Anna Mae by the arm, slammed her against the dining room wall and, with her throat in the clutches of both hands, screamed at her nose-to-nose, "You ever do that agin an I'll kill you, ya stringy-headed bitch!" He stormed off toward the bathroom.

In the half-open kitchen door stood Lincoln, trembling with anger, screaming, "Stop it, damn you, stop it!"

Suddenly, a streak of light from the street pierced the darkness and lit up the back porch. Startled, Lincoln whirled around and peered into the night, shielding his eyes from the laser-like beam.

"Is everything okay Lincoln?" came the voice of an obscure figure on the sidewalk, shrouded in shadows being cast by a full moon.

Lincoln let out sigh of relief! He recognized first the voice and then the familiar face of Deputy Clay Cassidy who came into view as the law officer drew closer to the porch with his oversized flashlight in hand. Clay Cassidy, a young man in his mid-twenties, a graduate of the Atlanta Police Academy, and one third of the county's police force, was the more congenial of Sheriff Buford Coker's two deputies. Lincoln didn't care much for Lester Odom, Cassidy's counterpart. He was sullen and ill-mannered and catered to the whims of the boastful and brash Coker.

"Yeah, everything's okay" he called out, "...I hope," he added under his breath.

"Got a call from a neighbor that things were sounding pretty rough over here," reported Clay. "Your parents fightin' again?"

"Yeah."

"Must have been pretty bad for the neighbors to hear."

"Yeah, I guess it was."

"Does it ever get violent?"

"Sometimes."

"Did it tonight?"

"Yeah...could have been worse though."

"What happened?"

"The parents got into a big argument and mom hit'im in the head with somethin'. He threatened to kill her and a bunch of hollering and stuff...the usual."

"Maybe I should go in and talk to them."

"No...don't. Not now. They'll think I got you to," argued Lincoln. "Besides, it's all quiet now. I think they've gone to bed."

"I didn't know Mr. Crockett was like that. He's always seemed like a pretty good fellow to me...what little I know him anyway," concluded the deputy.

"That's what a lot of people think," replied Lincoln. "He's a different person in public than at home. He's got a terrible temper and you've not seen what he's like when he loses control. It's scary!"

"Okay Lincoln. If you're sure everything's okay, I'll be on my way. Look, if things ever get bad again, you give me a call, okay?"

"Okay" replied Lincoln, nodding his head.

When the police cruiser pulled away around 11:00 p.m., Lincoln realized that he'd been left standing alone in the dark. Unsettled, he stole quietly through the house back to his bedroom, closed the door, and slipped under the covers still dressed. He could never get used to the fighting; it was driving him crazy. But, for now, his only recourse was to try and block it out, escape from the reality of life and bide his time. Lying there in the darkness he could, in his mind's eye, voyage to worlds in another time, another place…with Ashley Armstrong.

When Lincoln Crockett finally drifted off to sleep, it was one of restless, nightmarish slumber.

Chapter 5

May, 1965

A blanket of fog hung lazily over Town Creek, filtering the light of the morning sun which was pushing its way into the dove gray sky above the Great Smoky Mountains, giving it an eerie glow. Lincoln had been up at first light, wanting to make an early getaway in order to avoid any fallout that might be remaining from last evening's conflict. But, it didn't matter. Lincoln enjoyed walking in the tranquility of the early morning and didn't need an excuse to do so.

He didn't mind being a bit ahead of schedule, for he liked his job at the Lacy as janitor, bellhop, and personal errand boy for the hotel's owner and manager. The job not only provided him with an income, but the hotel's lively environment afforded him the opportunity to meet a wide variety of interesting people; it also gave him the opportunity to be away from home for extended periods of time.

Coldwater is a pretty typical small southern town where life is generally lived at a slow, easy pace, is somewhat clannish, and doesn't attract much new blood or encourage it. It does, however, get its share of traffic. Located in the foothills of the Smokies near the Tennessee/North Carolina border, it's a jumping off point on a federal highway running north and south that carries a fair amount of commerce through its streets. In addition, Greyhound Buses and Southern Railroad trains, carrying both passengers and freight, make regularly scheduled stops.

Aside from the mills, the hub-bub of activity in town is the Lacy, a shining jewel in an otherwise unremarkable downtown district. With buses, trains, and taxis ferrying businessmen about drawn by the mills, along with other travelers, the hotel is a beehive of activity.

Guest rooms in the four-story structure are comfortably and tastefully furnished and decorated in a southern colonial motif complete with period furnishings and wall murals. The showcase room, however, is the hotel lobby, a toast to the Victorian era.

Large French doors open into a spacious gathering area furnished with groupings of medallion-backed sofas and wingback chairs. Persian area rugs scattered about the polished hardwood floor accent the furnishings while wallpaper in floral patterns add a splash of color to the walls. A large crystal chandelier hanging from the center of the ceiling illuminates the entire area. One anomaly to the motif, however, is an ornately hand carved mahogany bar retrieved from an old western saloon. The bar serves as the check-in counter.

A private elevator behind the check-in counter leads to a mezzanine where the manager's office and living quarters are located (along with a few "special" rooms) and a balcony overlooking the lobby. A public elevator along with mirror image, crescent-shaped stairways provide access to the upper floors.

Most Saturday mornings there is, in the rear of the Piano Room, called into session a "meeting of the minds." Although this group claims no official membership role, it's made up primarily of the town's "powers that be." A roll call (if taken) would reveal such notables as the Sheriff, perhaps one of his deputies, the mayor, a few elected officials, some businessmen, perhaps a man of the cloth or two, and any other Tom, Dick, or Harry who might care to join in.

This assemblage of pseudo philosophers spends the better part of the morning feeding their faces from the breakfast buffet and emptying a few pots of black java while spinning their cracker-barrel philosophy in an attempt to impress one another with their knowledge (or lack thereof) on a variety of subjects. They discuss, argue, fuss, cuss, and sometimes digress into shouting matches over everything from how to cast a fly rod, to the content of President Johnson's news conference, to the second coming of Jesus.

That is, except when it comes to matters of the heart relative to the status quo of the southern way of life, in which case they are, in traditional, old-school conservative fashion, of one mind and one accord with few exceptions. The exceptions are most likely to come from Deputy Clay Cassidy, who has seen more of the outside world than most of them; Mayor McKean, a Champagne Socialist who advocates moderate reform while consuming the best in life; and the pastors who provide some spiritual perspective on the issues, although somewhat skewed at times to accommodate their personal agendas.

On this particular Saturday, the topic for discussion had turned to the world of sports, more specifically, to the game of basketball. Abe Hornish and John Henry Johnson had gotten into a heated debate over which was the most memorable moment in the annals of

Coldwater basketball: Big John's hook shot at the buzzer to beat their heated rival Carson City to clinch an undefeated regular season in 1922 or Abe's twenty-five point game in 1933 to knock off Cumberland High, the number-one ranked team in the state at the time.

At any rate, Deputy Cassidy reminded them both that their heroic efforts combined couldn't begin to compare to the monumental feat of Philadelphia Warriors' center Wilt Chamberlain's feat of scoring a record one hundred points in a game against the New York Knicks back in March of 1962. As several of these former high school bench jockeys were each providing their own expert opinions on how such an achievement could be accomplished (racial slurs aside) while reliving their own "glory days" on the hardwood, they were suddenly and pleasantly interrupted by the sound of a silky smooth, female voice tipped with a slow southern twang.

"Good mawnin' boys. What hot topics are you learn-ed scha'las chewin' on this week?"

All eyes turned toward the sound of the voice and total silence ensued; it was quiet enough to hear snowflakes falling on cotton. There, posed at the head of the table, her right arm propped against her right hip and a little Shih Tzu dog cradled in the crook of her left arm, stood Jessica Wingo, better known as Miss Jessie, the proprietor of the Lacy Hotel.

Jessica Wingo, a tall, slender lady of forty packed into a twenty-five-year-old body, lingered there for a minute as if posing for the cover of *Vogue* magazine. A peaches-and-cream complexion and green eyes stood out against the backdrop of a crop of long, red hair that flowed down across ivory shoulders, framing a mother-of-pearl pendant nestled in the crevice of firm, ivory breasts. A knee-length, green dress that hugged her hourglass figure matched the pair of green, patent leather pumps at the end of a pair of long, shapely legs.

Miss Jessie, a clothes horse who took great pleasure in dressing fashionably no matter what the time of day, was never seen in anything but her glad rags. One couldn't really say whether the clothes made her or she made the clothes, but in either case, she was a feast to gaze upon. At least, that is in the eyes of all the males in town from the age of sixteen to a hundred and six. As far as the women were concerned, they either envied her or despised her.

As Miss Jessie broke her pose and began walking toward the band of stupefied men babbling like a gaggle of geese, the Sheriff shuffled ahead to meet her.

"Miss Jessie, I need to talk with ya. It is of the greatest importance."

"Now Sheriff Coka, what could be so important this early in the mawnin'? But, if you insist, pull up'a chair he'ah at my table."

Buford Coker, a middle-aged, boisterous man (who'd sat too close to the dinner table for too long) fancies himself in the bold likeness of the famous Tennessee Sheriff Buford Pusser. But in the public presence of Jessica Wingo, he's more like an apologetic schoolboy asking his schoolteacher permission to go to the restroom.

"No, no, Miss Jessie. Let's go to yo'ah office please," begged the Sheriff, rolling his hat through his fingers by the brim. "We need ta speak in private."

"Okay, follow me," agreed Jessica with a long breath.

"See ya latta boys," smiled Miss Jessie, waving to the breakfast group as she and Buford turned to leave the restaurant.

Just as they were approaching Miss Jessie's office, they met Lincoln in the hallway.

"Good mawnin' Lincoln," said Miss Jessie, "I hadn't seen you this mawnin'."

"Good morning Miss Jessie."

Good morning Sheriff," replied Lincoln.

Sheriff Coker just grunted and nodded.

Lincoln's eyes shifted past Miss Jessie and the Sherriff to the big black man standing behind them. Lincoln shaped the fist and fingers of his right hand into the form of a make-believe pistol which he pointed at the big man, winked, and "shot" silently. The big man, known as "Bam Bam," mirrored the same gesture back at Lincoln. This was their way of greeting one another. Bam Bam was Miss Jessie's bodyguard, chauffer, and man Friday. Anywhere Miss Jessie was, you could be sure Bam Bam would be lurking somewhere nearby.

"I've been outside cleaning up some things on the grounds," said Lincoln as he faced Miss Jessie, "and I just now came inside."

"Say, are you okay?" inquired Miss Jessie. "You don't look like ya feel well."

"Oh, I just have a headache ma'am."

[26]

"Another one of those bad ones? Well, go'ta tha kitchen and get some brekfest; maybe that'll help," answered Miss Jessie,

"When you've finished eatin', run on ova to tha clinic and pick up a prescription Doc has fah me and ask him ta give you sump'n for that headache. Drop tha script off at Long's Drug Store an go on home 'til you feel betta."

"Okay, thank you ma'am," nodded Lincoln, turning and heading toward the kitchen.

As Miss Jessie led the Sheriff up to the mezzanine, Buford chided, "Why the Sam Hill do'ya mollycoddle that Millie so?"

"Oh! Fer heaven's sake, Bufud! I don't *mollycoddle* anybody. I jus try to be nice to people. Why don't ya give it a try? People might like you a little more!"

"Bullshit!"

"B'sides, he's a nice young man, deserves a break. I worry 'bout him. He has a'lot of bad headaches."

Reaching her office and unlocking the door, Miss Jessie asked,

"So, Bufud, what's so important we have ta talk in private about it?"

"Miss Jessie, we got us a problem," said the Sherriff with a worried look on his face,

"a *big* problim!"

Chapter 6

Jessica Wingo gave her office door a shove and it closed with a "click" behind her. She left Bam Bam outside with orders that she and the Sheriff weren't to be disturbed. The alluring redhead leaned back in her burgundy leather office chair, swung her legs across the glass-topped antique desk, and crossed them.

"Now, what's this prob'lim of yours Bufud?"

The Sheriff, who stood staring at the two nylon-clad gams, swallowed hard, looked up at Jessica, who had a mischievous smile on her face (she loved to tease the old boy), and began with a stammer.

"Huh… huh…as I say'id, we have a prob'lim Miss Jessie, a *big* prob'lim!" began Buford, sitting down on the cushion's edge of a wingback chair, resting his arms on his knees and staring at the floor.

"And what prob'lim would that be? Do you an I have a prob'lim Bufud?" she asked coyly.

"Not personally, but *we* means mo'uh than jus tha two of us, Jessica," answered the Sheriff looking up. "It means several people, includin' one of yo *girls*."

"Wha'da ya mean, 'one of my *girls*'?"

Buford jumped to his feet.

"Dammit Jessica Wingo, don't play games with me. Ya know damn well what I mean."

The two of them just stared at each other for a long moment knowing that each other understood what the Sheriff was referring to.

Only a select few individuals had knowledge of three special rooms, referred to by the doors' colors and located on the same level as Miss Jessie's office. When out-of-town businessmen sought gratification for their manly cravings via a discrete encounter with a member of the opposite sex, Miss Jessie could provide (for a price, of course) both the playground and the playmate. Several local gentlemen (some prominent figures included) have also been known to have satisfied their own carnal appetites from the menu of sensual pleasures served behind the red, blue, and green doors.

The lady's "black book" catalogs a list of local females, noting their physical characteristics and "specialties," who are on call to render their services. Her "girls" range from young to mature, from working girls to society dames. Some do it for the money, some out of boredom, some for the excitement, and, some, just for the hell of it.

Jessica slid her legs off the desk onto the floor, pulled her chair up close to the desk, and leaned forward, forearms resting on the desk with fingers intertwined. She looked at Buford with a serious look.

"Okay, Bufud, cut to the chase. Just what *is* the prob'lim?" inquired Jessica, breaking the silence.

"You've hud tha sayin' 'bout stickin' yo'ah nose where it don't b'long an gettin' it cut off?"

"Of co'us."

"Well, that's what's happened with one of yo girls. She's stuck huh nose where it don't b'long, prob'ly by accident, but it's still there. She's seen things, heard things, and now knows things she shouldn't."

"So, what does that have ta'do with me?" asked Jessica concerned.

Buford stood up and leaned forward, placing his hands palms down in front of Jessica's, and looked her in the eye.

"In the fust place, Jessica, don't fuhget Jackson's a dry county. Ya want tha wine ya serve in this high-falutin' joint ta keep flowin' frum tha source that provides it, an the special dispensation ya have frum tha powers that be to serve it to remain in place, don't ya?"

Buford spit the words out with a menacing tone.

Jessica didn't say anything.

"And, in the secon' place, these rooms ya have back here fer 'special' guests! Even though they benefit both you an ya business partners, ya could take tha biggest fall if'n their purpose become public knowledge. So if'n I was you, Jessica, I'd not look a gift horse in tha mouth," he added.

"Okay, so, wha'da ya want me ta'do?"

"Well, she's yo 'associate' an ya betta hav'a talk with huh 'bout losin' huh memry or there's gonna be consequences."

Jessica stood up and moved around the desk to face her adversary.

"What kind'a consequences Bufud?"

"Not good ones, Jessica, *not good ones!*"

"Fa who?"

"Fa *her* dammit, an maybe fa *you* if'n ya don't get ya whores under control!" screamed the Sheriff grabbing her by the shoulders.

In his fit of temper, Buford had failed to hear the office door open and the big man who had been standing guard over his benefactor enter and approach him from behind; he did, however, feel the large muscular hands of Bam Bam as they closed in a vice-like grip around his throat.

Bam Bam, who got his nickname because his favorite cartoon character is Bam Bam of the Flintstones, is a huge, muscular man, well over six feet in stature, weighing in at some two-hundred and fifty pounds. He has been loyally devoted to Miss Jessie after she helped him avoid some serious trouble down in New Orleans some years back.

"All right!" fumed Jessica, "Tell me who she is an I'll do what ya ask. But, don't ya eva come in he'ah agin (poking a finger in his chest) threatenin' me ya half-assed little Dudley Do-Right. If it's consequences ya want, consequences you'll get! I'll not stop Bam Bam frum shuvin' that tin star up yo fat redneck ass! Bam Bam, show the man out!"

Chapter 7

Meanwhile

By the time Lincoln had made a visit to Doc Simpson's office and dropped off the prescription at Long's Drug Store, he had become too sick from the migraine to walk home. Deciding that he could spare four bits for a cab ride, he flagged down Patrick McNally who he just happened to see passing by in his taxi. On the way to Lincoln's house, "Dutch" refused Lincoln's fare, insisting that he'd give him a ride "on the house" since he was on a call that was just a few blocks from where he lived anyway. As sick as he was, Lincoln didn't feel much like putting up an argument with old Dutch, so he just said, "Thanks!"

With the money he made at the hotel, Lincoln bought his own clothes, pocketed some for spending money, and squirreled away as much as possible in a savings account at the bank. He also helped his mother (who was in poor health) pay for the medications she required. His father, who had never been sick a day in his life, had no comprehension of what it was like, lacked all compassion for those who suffered, and begrudged every dollar he had to spend on his wife's illness.

It was noon by the time Dutch dropped Lincoln off at his house, but again refused the four bit fare. He thanked the cabbie and walked dizzily toward the house from the pain that swirled in his head. His father had their old '52 Plymouth pulled up in the yard with the hood up.

"Well, wha-cha doin' home in tha middle of tha day?" said his father looking up from under the hood.

"Thangs slow at 'Madam' Jessie's taday?" he added with emphasis on the "Madam."

His father had never approved of Lincoln working at the hotel. Not because of the money he made (that was a help to him), but because of the evils of the world he thought his son was being exposed to. Like many of the self-righteous do-gooders in town (both Ridgers and Millies), he believed the rumors about "Madam" Jessie and the Lacy "brothel" that had been spread around town for years, although none of the accusers had been able to actually produce any hard evidence to the fact. The one thing his father did know for a fact, however, was that they sold that "devil's brew" in the restaurant there.

"Tunin' her up?" answered Lincoln with a question, ignoring the sarcastic reference to Miss Jessie.

"Naw, she's just needin' some new plugs."

Lincoln nodded to indicate understanding and added, "Got a headache...need to lie down."

Lincoln stumbled up the back porch steps where his mother sat stringing and breaking a bucket full of fresh green beans she was going to cook for supper.

"Hi, mom."

"Hello son. Say, you gotta 'nother one of them bad headaches?"

"Yes, ma'am. Doc Simpson gave me some medicine. Told me to take it and go to bed."

"You been having more 'n more of them thangs," replied his mother with a concerned look. "Okay, go ta bed 'n try ta sleep it off. Holler if you need anythang."

Lincoln opened the small white envelope Doc Simpson had given him and out rolled two large capsules onto the kitchen counter. For the past couple of years, Lincoln had been plagued with skull-splitting headaches, nightmares, and bouts of depression.

After swallowing the pills, he walked gingerly to his bedroom; with every step, his head pounded. Drawing the drapes to block out the pain-intensifying light, he lay down slowly across the bed without throwing back the covers. Easing a pillow gently beneath his head, he lay as still as possible in the darkness and closed his eyes.

Spots and starbursts swirled in the darkness behind his clinched eyelids; flashing, strobe-like beams of light bombarded his eye socket until tears trickled down his cheeks; laser beams of pain that jabbed, twisted, and turned like an ice pick pierced his temples. He gagged and heaved at the nausea that welled up in his stomach and throat. The pain was excruciating; it felt as if his head would literally split open.

He lay there, enduring torment, for what seemed like hours as he waited for the drugs to do their work. Finally, when the pain had reached its apex, a warm, narcotic-induced fuzziness dulled the sharp-edged lightning bolts of throbbing pain as dilated blood vessels became gorged with blood and numbed nerves lost their sensation. The aching began a downward spiral and dissipated into lightness, as light as light itself, and enveloped his body. The pains of torture that had racked his brain were transformed into waves of sensual pleasure.

Soon, Lincoln drifted off into a world of pain-free, euphoric sleep.

Chapter 8

The Next Morning

Lincoln woke to the smells of breakfast in the air: bacon and eggs sizzling in the skillet, hot biscuits fresh from the oven, and the aroma of steaming-hot coffee brewing on the stove. He also heard sounds of muted conversation and shuffling about coming from the kitchen. It must be Sunday morning! When there were lulls in the fighting, hard feelings were smoothed over, and things were well between his parents, they always cooked breakfast on Sunday morning. That also meant he must have been zonked out for about eighteen hours.

He slipped on his clothes, stumbled groggy-headed down the hallway, and slumped down in a chair at the dining table. He rubbed his eyes trying to clear the cobwebs from his head.

"Good mornin' Lincoln," greeted his mother, "you slep a long time."

"Good mornin' Mama. Yes, I surely did."

"Mornin' son, ready for some chow?" asked his father.

"Yeah, I'm hungry."

Shortly, the three of them were seated at the dining room table and sharing a quite breakfast. The bright morning sun streamed through the open curtains, flooding the room with the warmness of spring. Lincoln paused and looked about, relishing the atmosphere of the moment. He wished it could always be this way, but he knew it wouldn't last… it never did. As he observed them, he marveled at how their relationship could vacillate back and forth between one of such venomous hostilities and such congeniality with seeming regularity and ease.

"How's that headache this mornin' son?" inquired his mother.

"It's much better, thank you. I feel a little groggy still."

"What does ole Doc Simpson say 'bout 'em?" asked his father.

"He calls them migraines. Says they don't know what causes them. I just know they hurt like the dickens and make me sick as a dog."

When they had had their fill of the morning's fare and were casually sipping a last cup of coffee, Anna Mae raised the question of a possible summer trip with her husband.

"Clovis, ya know my sister Lucy'n her family moved down ta Daytona Beach a few years back. Well, I ain't seed her in a long time, an I wuz'a wondering if we could…maybe…take a trip down there to visit with'um this summer."

"I dunno. That's a long trip ya'know…an the money."

"I talked ta her an she said we could stay with them."

"Well…I dunno."

"Ya'know, Lincoln's never seed tha ocean…none of us has! It'd be a good chance."

"We'll see, we'll see."

"Right now, it's time we'uz gettin' ready fer church service," declared Clovis.

"Dad, I don't know if I'll go today. I'm feeling a little hung over from that headache," said Lincoln, massaging his temples.

"Nonsense! The Lord ain't pleased with us a'layin' outta church. It's Sunday and we're Christians, and Christians go to church on Sunday!" replied his father. "B'sides, a little dose of the Spirit might just perk ye up!"

Lincoln had had a Damascus Road experience at a Billy Graham Crusade down in Atlanta a few years back while attending a youth rally. But, so far, his religious experience had not measured up to his understanding of what Christianity is all about. Becoming skeptical, it seemed to him the church was more a place of condemnation than absolution; Christianity more a display of emotional fervor than a demonstration of love; and most church members more hypocrite than genuine.

Later that morning

By 11:30 a.m. the worship service at the River Street Gospel Tabernacle in Milltown was in full swing. People were standing, swaying back and forth and clapping their hands to the beat of drums and guitars backing up Ms. Lola Albright pounding out hymns on the ivories on her pumping piano with great enthusiasm. Mr. Albert Hayes, the choir director, his arms flailing like windmills in a storm, was urging his vocalists onward and upward to melodious heights the like they had never known as they belted out the words of that great old gospel song "I'll Fly Away" with animated exultation.

[35]

As the choir launched into the second verse, the congregation joined in. It was now one big happy-clappy singalong, punctuated from time to time with an *aman* or *halleluiah* emanating from somewhere in the throng. On the third verse, the worshipers began streaming into the aisles and alter area, and as if transformed into some hypnotic trance dance, began engaging in varying forms of ecstatic behavior. Some, with arms reaching heavenward, rocked back and forth, several ladies fluttered about on tippy toes like butterflies while others jumped and shouted. A few even fainted and fell out on the floor in a spiritual stupor.

Lincoln, who sat on one of the back pews with a few of his friends, including Rats, wondered at this spectacle he witnessed week-in, week-out. What made the scene even more of a curiosity was the sight of his parents' open participation in this public display of religious fervor. Watching them weave about as if lost in a drug-induced haze was rather bizarre and so contrary to their everyday demeanors.

After the singing of all verses and several iterations of the chorus had wrung all the life out of the old song it had to give, the exhausted devotees began filing back to their seats with the fulfilled look of having just consumed a hearty and satisfying meal. The surreal atmosphere that had been holding the meeting house hostage for the past several minutes slowly dissipated, returning to its former state of worship character.

A hush fell over the congregation as Reverend Clifton Nutter rose from his seat, a big black Bible with tattered pages in hand, and slowly made his way to the podium. The Reverend was a tall slender man, getting on in years, dressed in a faded black suit and a somewhat wrinkled white shirt with a red tie twisted about the neck. The jackleg preacher called to mind a modern-day beardless Abraham Lincoln.

But the man's age and physical demeanor belied a fiery enthusiasm within for preaching the Gospel. For the better part of the next hour he strutted back and forth across the stage denouncing the evils of dancing, playing cards, and watching moving picture shows. Energized by amens from the Amen Corner (including one seat occupied by Lincoln's father), he slapped that Bible and railed against demon rum, adultery, and fornicating; sweaty-faced and hyperventilating, he condemned the demonic forces behind rock-n-roll music, warned of the horrors of hell, and extolled the delights of heaven.

At the conclusion of the sermon and in response to the beckoning call of Reverend Nutter, the altar was soon filled with sinners, backsliders and guilt-ridden Christians, all seeking redemption from the sins they had done, could have done, might have done, or had thought about doing. There followed another episode of euphoric rejoicing over those repentant ones, culminating with the close of the service.

Lincoln lingered near the family car in its parking space near the curb waiting for his parents who were socializing with friends. He massaged his temples in an effort to sooth away the lingering effects of yesterday's headache which the loud music in the service seemed to have resurrected. A few feet away, an elderly black man passing by on the sidewalk looked his way. Lincoln smiled, nodded his head, and said, "Hello" to which the man returned a smile and nod of the head.

As the old man continued on his way, Lincoln overheard two church members nearby talking.

"Look at that! What's that Darky doing around here on Sunday morning?" said one.

"Yeah, don't they know their place is in Johnnytown!" said the other.

They watched the old man until he was out of sight, discussing the evils of the civil rights movement and mixing of the races. Then, their conversation turned back to more immediate concerns.

"Man, wasn't that a great service today?" observed the first.

"It certainly was. Great singing! Great preaching! Great Spirit! What more could you want?" commented the second, puffing up his chest.

"Yes, makes you feel so heavenly don't it?" added the first.

Lincoln studied the two men thoughtfully. He marveled at the hypocrisy in using the doors of the church as a line of demarcation between God and people, between love and hate, between Sunday religious ritual and weekly worldly living. Gazing out the back seat window of the old Plymouth, he rode home in silent meditation.

What ever happened to the idea of "love thy neighbor? he pondered.

Chapter 9

That afternoon

Across town on The Ridge, services at the First Church of The Trinity had concluded at 12:00 noon sharp as usual, and the Armstrongs were serving Sunday brunch on their veranda to a select group of guests. Included among the invitees were the Longworths, the pastor of the church, Reverend Dr. Andrew Priestly, and his wife Eleanor, along with State Representative Charles Rodman and his wife Loretta, who were in town for the weekend.

The members of the group casually engaged in trivial chin music as they filled their plates from a buffet of eggs Benedict, Canadian bacon, and strawberry crepes, while the maid served cappuccino in floral-decorated China cups.

"My, isn't it a lovely day today?" swooned Eleanor Priestly, inhaling a breath of fresh spring air.

"You have such a lovely view from here."

"Yes, it is nice isn't it?" said Emerson modestly with a half bow. "We enjoy it very much."

"We're so glad you could join us today," said their hostess.

"Oh, we're so glad you invited us," said the pastor.

"And Victoria, you've done it again!" bragged Leland Longworth. "The brunch is wonderful."

"Oh, Leland! As long as it's food, to you it's wonderful," laughed his wife Cora Sue with a comical wave of her hand.

"Dr. Priestly, that was such a lovely sermon you presented this morning. I enjoyed it so much," said Victoria flatteringly, taking the pastor by his arm.

"Well, thank you very much for those kind words," responded the pastor patting her hand.

"By the way, pastor, have you had a chance to talk with Senator Rodman?" asked Victoria, leading the pastor to where her husband, Leland Longworth, and the senator were engaged in conversation.

"Pardon me, gentlemen," she interrupted.

The men turned their attention to Victoria and the gentleman on her arm.

"Senator Rodman, have you and Dr. Priestly had a chance to get acquainted?"

"Dr. Priestly, Senator Rodman represents our district in the State Legislature."

Victoria Armstrong, who could be calculating and ruthless to a fault, came from old-stock southern society whose manners and standards of etiquette had been refined at a prestigious finishing school for young ladies of class. Her two ambitions in life were to advance her position in the social circles to which her husband's coattails would carry her and to preserve the status quo of the traditional southern way of life.

After the two men had shaken hands and exchanged pleasantries, the senator was rejoined by his wife. Loretta Rodman had just successfully extricated herself from the company of Mrs. Priestly and Mrs. Longworth where Cora Sue had been grilling her about the goings on in the Nashville social circles.

Cora Sue Longworth, a chatterbox, had come from a middle class family unable to afford college. She had met Leland through a mutual friend and enjoyed the society queen lifestyle her marriage had afforded her. She played the role to the hilt, dropping designer label names and showing off her latest piece of jewelry at any moment of opportunity. Less refined socially and lacking the elegant "southernese" of Victoria Armstrong, both her best friend and nemesis, Cora Sue resented playing second fiddle to the pompous Victoria who, by word or look, could make her feel small and unimportant.

The two young people found a spot to themselves on the edge of the veranda where they could observe the social game-playing and imagine how much different the people's conversations would be later on when each had gone their own way and compared notes on the afternoon's charade.

When brunch had been concluded and everyone was lounging about in the shade sharing personal antidotes, chatting about church matters, and debating political issues, Ashley, who had been in private conversation with Montgomery, approached the group of adults.

"I have something to say to my parents and the Longworths. I promised mama and daddy that I would apologize for an incident at the Lacy Hotel the other night, but I don't mind our other guests hearing it also. So, I'm sorry for the disturbance I made and for any embarrassment it might have caused y'all; however, I do not apologize for having or expressing the feelings I have about certain things."

"Thank you my dear," said her mother.

"Bravo, Ashley," spoke up Leland, "Apology accepted."

Turning her attention to the pastor she asked, "Dr. Priestly, may I ask you a question?"

"Certainly, my dear! What is it you wish to ask?" cordially replied the theologian who held advanced degrees from two well-known southern seminaries.

"Well, sir, you preach about how God created all people and loves all people and wants us to love all people."

"Yes, that's right my dear."

"Does that mean just people who are like us or all people everywhere?"

"Ashley, God wants us to love all people, regardless of who they are."

"Then why do some people, even in the church, feel they are superior to certain other people and harbor contempt for them, simply because they have attained a higher level of financial and social privilege, like the Ridgers, for example?"

Everyone suddenly snapped to attention and froze as if struck by lightning. The only sounds that broke the silence were those of a soft breeze rustling through the trees and the chirping of a songbird somewhere overhead.

Ashley continued, "Why do they believe certain people should be ostracized from society like lepers simply because of who they are, such as the Millies?"

"Ashley, this is not the time or place to be bothering the pastor with these socialist ideas," chided her father. "This whole civil rights movement business has got the whole country in an uproar."

"Yes, you see what it's doing to the young people," added Leland, "with the chattering classes up north putting all kinds of liberal ideas into their heads!"

"I don't know the answer to all these problems," confessed the pastor, "it's just the way the world is."

"That's funny! I thought you gave me the answer to these problems with your answer to my first two questions. Why don't you preach about that?" challenged Ashley.

Everyone was aghast at Ashley's challenge to the pastor.

"*Ashley*! You apologize to Dr. Priestly this instant," scolded her mother. But, before the words had cleared her mother's lips, Ashley was already exiting the veranda through the French doors into the library.

Montgomery, who was taking in the whole scene from his vantage point off to one side of the veranda, thought to himself, "Well, Ashley, you've done it again!"

Meanwhile

After his family had finished a lunch of fried chicken and mashed potatoes, Lincoln needed some time alone. He wandered across the vacant field next to their house, down to where Town Creek disappears into the woods. Just inside the tree line where a big flat rock juts out of the ground near the base of a large oak tree, was a place he liked to go to get away and meditate on things. Lying there on that rock, he could look up through a large opening in the canopy of trees and see the sky. At times, he would loll about on that stone and lounge for what seemed like hours, envisioning whimsical characters peeking from their hiding places in the clouds or dreaming of passages to Shangri La and other such exotic lands far from Milltown. But, this afternoon was different. Even the sun-filled, powder-blue sky above him and the colors and sounds of nature all around, which normally gave him solace, could not displace the cloak of melancholy wrapped about him, body, and soul.

Today, more serious thoughts pervaded his mind; thoughts that kept carrying him back to the morning church service. He wondered how people could profess to be such ardent examples of righteousness on Sunday, yet live lives of such a contradictory manner the rest of the week; appear so spiritually connected on one hand, while being coldhearted on the other. Although Lincoln found this to be apparently true of many, he was most acutely aware of it in the lives of his own parents. None of it made sense to him. Surely there must be some piece to this religion/world puzzle that eluded his search for understanding. But, what was that piece? Where was that piece to be found? How was he to find the answer to his dilemma? Lincoln Crockett was a troubled young man in both mind and soul.

Chapter 10

It was already late when Lincoln and Rats entered Big Al's Pool Hall located on a dirty side street a block off Main. The dimly lit hall reeked of tobacco smoke and chalk dust. They eyeballed the hazy background for familiar faces as they walked gingerly across the creaking wood floor. Spotting none to which they could lay claim as a personal acquaintance, they staked out a table midway through the building.

Big Al's was neither an exclusive establishment frequented by the elite billiards enthusiasts nor a place of reputation that would be endeared to the churchgoing crowd. On the contrary. As pool halls go, Big Al's was a hole-in-the-wall, backstreet dive, typical of most small-town pool parlors, where the majority of its patrons (a motley mixture of two-bit gamblers, ramblers, and drinkers) played for bragging rights in penny ante games of eight-ball. Albert "Big Al" Coffey, so known for his size (he had played tackle on a Division III college football team in his younger days), did keep things on the up-and-up and was intolerant of any rowdiness.

Most tables were in poor condition, the faded green felt chicken-pecked with grooves worn along the side rails. There was, however, one exception. A fancy table in the back under covers was reserved for special games and special shooters. It wasn't used very often.

Although not habitual players at Big Al's gaming tables, the boys were on quite good speaking terms with the proprietor.

"Evenin', fellers! Ain't seen you guys 'round fer a while," said Big Al in his gravelly voice, chomping down on the stub of a cigar that almost disappeared between the lips of his fat, round face. He pushed a rack and tray of balls across the counter to Rats.

"Jus been busy with work," replied Rats.

Lincoln gave the man a wave from across the room as he retrieved cue sticks from the wall rack.

"Howdy! Mr. Coffey, how ya doin'?" called Lincoln. "What we playing?"

"Straight pool, okay?" asked Rats.

"Okey dokey," agreed Lincoln, "rack 'em up!"

The two comrades had just settled into their game when a commotion arose at the front door.

"Hey! Do you guys smell somethin' bad in here?"

Silence fell throughout the pool hall.

"It's Miss Jessie's little errand boy and a rat!"

Lincoln and Rats didn't have to look up; they recognized the voices.

"Aw Rats!" snarled Rats.

Looking around, there were the snickering faces of trouble; trouble in the form of three ne'er-do-wells named Billy Ray Coker and his bookend cronies, Edgar McBee and Sammy Stoner.

Billy Ray (a.k.a. BR), the offspring of Sheriff Buford Coker, was captain of the football team and now, with a scholarship in his back pocket, was playing at Mountain State Junior College. That was the problem. His athlete's ego along with his sense of privilege due to his father's position of authority, had transformed him into an egocentric, loudmouthed bully in the image of his forebear. In fact, a lot of people, including his daddy, referred to him as "Little Buford."

In truth, he played the role of bully quite well, as long as his two buddies were nearby to back him up. Edgar and Sammy were gorilla-sized teammates of BR's (riding his jersey tail to Mountain State) who follow him around like obedient lap dogs to feed on the crumbs that fall from his table of privilege.

"That's what it 'tis. Thought I smelled a Millie," answered BR, sniffing like a dog as they approached the boys' table.

"What are you Ridgers doin' down here? You lost or something?" asked Rats.

"Yeah! Better watch your language. You're on the wrong side of town now," added Lincoln.

"Oh, we just out slummin' a little," whispered Billy Ray up close to the boys with a smirk.

Lincoln and Rats bowed up but decided the three were just troublemakers looking for a fight, so they let it go.

The bookends just grinned as the trio moved on past them.

Billy Ray, dressed in black cowboy boots and hat like his dad, swaggered on down the aisle, followed by his companions and strolled up to the counter and Big Al.

"Eve'nin Big Man," said Billy Ray.

[44]

"Little Man," answered Big Al with a nod, blowing a puff of cigar smoke Billy Ray's way.

"Your daddy know you're down here? You a long way from Main Street, so ta speak."

"My daddy don't have to know everywhere I go or everything I do."

"Okay. So whatta ya want?"

"To play the best you got in some nine-ball for a few bucks," waving a roll of bills.

"Ha!" chimed in Lincoln who had been listening in on their conversation along with Rats.

"You think you're some kind of nine-ball whiz or something Billy Ray?" asked Rats sarcastically.

"Billy Ray, I bet you couldn't even beat…huh…even ole 'Stick' over there," stammered Lincoln looking around, then pointing to a fellow standing in the shadows and winking at Big Al.

Big Al got the message and nodded and winked back.

"Yeah, I'll bet you dollars to doughnuts you can't," bragged Rats.

"Stick, you wanna play this man?" asked Big Al.

"I'm game," said Johnny Mack Brown, leaning against a cue stick planted on the floor.

Stepping out of the corner shadows was a tall, lanky kid with a moustache and goatee the same color as the long, unkempt red hair that fell to his shoulders. A white T-shirt hung out of a pair of tattered jeans strapped to his small waist with an old black belt, sporting a huge silver horseshoe buckle. A pair of sandals and a Red Sox baseball cap, the bill pulled down to almost cover his pale blue eyes from view, completed the attire of this scarecrow of a young man in his early twenties.

When the Ridger boys saw this would-be challenger, they tried to stifle a laugh.

"What's this? He looks like a cue stick! Is this really the best ya got?" chuckled Billy Ray.

"You asked for a shootta…you got a shootta." said Big Al, "You gonna play the man or not?"

"Okay, okay," said Billy Ray, "this should be some experience."

"Yep! I'd bet on it," said Big Al.

"Well, the name fits. Okay, Stick! Let's play pool," said Billy Ray.

Billy Ray didn't realize at the time that a word can have more than one meaning.

Big Al pulled the cover off the "special" table and racked a triangle of balls. Lincoln and Rats moved up with the crowd that had gathered around to get a closer view.

Al stated the rules: ten game minimum, five dollars a game, winner of each game has the next break. Billy Ray would break first.

In the first five games, Billy Ray played pretty well, winning four games to Stick's one who played like an amateur. They had also raised the ante to ten dollars a game after game two and Billy Ray was ahead moneywise thirty dollars to ten. At this point, Billy Ray, who was on a roll, agreed to raising the ante to twenty dollars. Big Al winked at Stick. The trap was set. Billy Ray slammed the cue ball into the triangle of nine pool balls, scattering them helter-skelter across the table, but not one found its way into one of the six pockets. The door was open for Stick.

Johnny Mack Brown, a twenty-one-year-old product of Milltown and a grammar school dropout, had never found anything in his young life that he was good at or cared about except shooting pool. He had a natural-born talent for the game and could shoot with the best of them, regardless of age. And that's how he made his living; traveling from town to town hustling pool.

With a Lucky Strike hanging between his lips, Stick proceeded to run five racks of balls. Billy Ray realized that he had been hustled and that Big Al and those two Millie boys had set him up. He was fuming mad and wound up tighter than an eight-day clock.

"Accordin' to my 'rithmetic, that's 'bout seventy George Washington's ya owe the Stick," quipped Big Al, to the laughter of those who had been watching the fiasco now returning to their own business.

"You mean tha games I got hustled," accused Billy Ray.

"Look boy, you the one come lookin' to play, wantin' to play the best," answered Big Al, "so now it's time to pay up."

Billy Ray picked up his small roll of money and began to count off bills until all he had in his hands were on the table.

"Uh, looks like I'm a little short," confessed Billy Ray.

Big Al stepped up to Billy Ray face to face while Stick sandwiched him in from behind. At this, the bookends reacted and moved quickly toward their comrade in his defense before their progress was abruptly halted by a flash of light across their path.

The flash was the reflection of the overhead lights off the gleaming steel blade of Stick's switchblade weaving menacingly back and forth in the direction of Edgar and Sammy. The big boys backed away. Stick turned back to Billy Ray, reached around him from behind, and laid the stiletto next to Billy Ray's throat.

"Don't ya know there's consequences if you play the game when ya can't cover the bet?" said Stick in a low, threatening voice.

"I...I...I'll get the money...tomorrow...I swear...I'll pay ya tomorrow," pleaded Billy Ray.

"Tomorrow noon and don't make us hafta come and collect. After noon, there'll be interest due."

"Yes sir, I'll have it...here."

Lincoln and Rats had returned to their table and were leaning against it watching with considerable pleasure, the three Ridgers slinking down the center aisle toward the front door like three whimpering pups with their tails between their legs.

"Just wait, we'll get you scumbags for this," scowled Billy Ray, pointing a finger at Lincoln and Rats.

"Payback's comin'," threatened Edgar and Sammy.

"Now don't go away mad boys," pleaded Rats sarcastically.

"No, just go away," added Lincoln as they both laughed.

A minute later, when Lincoln and Rats had turned to gather up their cue sticks and balls, a cue ball skipped across their table, glanced off Lincoln's forearm, and struck Rats in the back.

"Ouch!" bellowed Rats, "What the...." He grabbed the cue ball off the floor.

There was Billy Ray looking straight at them giving them the finger.

"Yeah, well take this ya son of a bitch!" shouted an angry Rats.

Grasping the cue ball like a baseball, Rats wound up and cut loose a fast ball Bob Feller would have been proud of.

Billy Ray grabbed Edgar McBee and jerked him into the line of fire in front of him. The cue ball was on target and cleaned ole Edgar's clock. Edgar hit the floor like he'd been shot with a .45 and was bleeding like a stuck pig where that ball had smashed his nose back into his face.

"Oh, that'll make your eyeteeth hurt," grimaced Big Al.

Lincoln had grabbed a pool que and was sprinting toward their rivals wielding it like a baseball bat but came to a sudden stop when he saw Edgar hit the deck.

For a moment, the pool hall became as quiet as a church on Monday morning.

"Shit, Rats…you've…killed him!" stammered Lincoln, breaking the silence.

"Let's get the hell outta here," Lincoln yelled pulling the dumbfounded Rats by the arm toward the front door.

"Ole Sheriff Buford'll be here any minute and he'll be after us for sure!"

"I didn't think I could even hit'im," confessed Rats in disbelief, stumbling along behind Lincoln, whose heart was pounding in his chest like a bass drum.

Once out of the building, they split up heading in different directions. Billy Ray and Sammy also fled the scene like rats from a sinking ship. They left their buddy Edgar to his own fate.

Chapter 11

It was just two days before the high school senior prom and Lincoln had to stop by the J.C. Penney store to buy a new shirt and tie to go with the only suit he had, which was now at the dry cleaners. After picking up the clothes, it was on to Sweet's Barber Shop for a haircut. In fact, he was going to get the works: shampoo, haircut, shave...the works, because Amanda Cross had asked him to be her escort to the prom. They had known each other since they were kids and had, in fact, dated on a few occasions. So, he was glad Amanda had asked him; he had missed his own senior prom last year due to the basketball injury that sidelined him. He glanced at his watch: 12:00 noon.

While shopping at Penney's, he noticed an attractive, middle-aged lady with short blonde hair browsing through the aisles of men's shirts, who had, for whatever reason, also noticed him. They exchanged smiles. While a salesclerk assisted him with a tie selection, he endeavored to keep an eye out for the whereabouts of the captivating woman.

The formfitting white dress with matching accessories made her easy to spot as she continued to linger nearby. What intrigued him most was that every time he looked her way, she seemed to be looking his, her body language saying "hello." Naturally, he would return her a "hello, there" smile. It became a sort of game they were playing with each other and it gave him an excitedly funny feeling inside.

When he had completed his purchase and was leaving, he looked around the store for the mysterious lady, hoping for one last opportunity to play their flirting game. Disappointed, he was unable to spot her anywhere. Turning to go, he stopped dead still almost bumping into someone. It was her! He was so close to her he could smell her perfume. Walking casually by and ignoring his presence, she nonchalantly dropped her checkbook which fell at his feet. Lincoln picked it up, and without speaking, handed it to her. She took it with her left hand and offered her right for a handshake. Lincoln reached out and took her hand.

"Thank you," she said in a soft voice and flashed him a wink.

With the touch of her warm, soft hand, the flash of her blue eyes, and the sound of her silky voice, Lincoln's body flushed hot from head to toe. He swallowed and choked out the words, "You're most welcome ma'am."

With that, she turned away and continued casually down the aisle stopping at counters along the way and pretending interest in miscellaneous items.

Lincoln, somewhat taken aback by the experience, was out on the sidewalk before he thought about the small folded piece of paper she had slipped to him when they shook hands. He unfolded the paper and there was written a telephone number. He assumed it to be her number, but what was she saying? It opened up many questions…and possibilities.

He refolded the paper and tucked it away in his wallet for safe keeping. His steps got lighter as his thoughts shifted into fantasy mode.

It was mid-afternoon by the time Lincoln walked into Warren Sweet's barber shop. Mr. Sweet told Lincoln to take a seat and that he was next in line. Lincoln had known the barber all of his life, for the man had been cutting his hair since he was so little a board had to be placed across the arms of the barber chair for Lincoln to sit on so Sweet could cut his hair.

The barber shop itself was as much a place for patrons to chew the fat on whatever kind of fat anybody cared to chew. Folks also offered opinions on limitless subjects as they got their ears lowered. In that respect, it was much like the breakfast club meetings at the Lacy Hotel; the difference was that the breakfast club only held forth on Saturday mornings while the barber shop crowd was in session every day of the week, except Sundays, of course.

"Looks like you've been shopping for clothes," speculated Mr. Sweet when Lincoln finally took his place in the chair.

"And now I'm getting the works at the barber shop," added Lincoln.

"Say! You wouldn't be getting all duded up for some special occasion, would you?"

"Could be."

"Yeah, here it is the end of May and the big prom and graduation are coming up this weekend," smiled Mr. Sweet. "Going to the dance?"

"Yeah."

"Who you taking?"

"Oh! No one special. Just a friend who asked me to escort her."

During their conversation, Mr. Sweet and Lincoln both had become aware of one old fellow that had been lingering quietly near the chair, glancing about here and there, as if standing on a street corner waiting for a bus.

"Huh, do you need us to talk a little louder so you can hear better Joe?" asked Mr. Sweet, momentarily pausing his clipping.

"Oh! No, Warren. I wasn't eavesdropping. I just didn't want to interrupt," said old Joe Clark.

"No. I just wanted to ask young Crockett something."

"Okay, go ahead," obliged Warren.

"Say, Crockett, wondered if you might could shed some light on'a rumor that's going 'round?"

"I dunno," answered Lincoln suspiciously, sliding around in his seat, wondering what was coming.

"Rumor has it there was a fight over at Big Al's the other night. Certain names been tossed 'round as being involved. Wouldn't know anything 'bout that would you?"

"Huh, no," lied Lincoln, "why would you ask me about that anyway?"

"Like I said, certain *names* was mentioned, on both sides of tha fight," said the old man.

"Sorry I can't help you...I...I don't know anything about it," stuttered Lincoln. "Think there'll be any trouble over it?" he added.

"Naw, don't think there's much chance of that," said the old fellow, scratching his head. "Would like to know who them boys was though," he went on, "might have sumpin' for one of'em."

When Mr. Sweet had completed "the works" on his customer, Lincoln gathered up his things and started for the front door. As soon as he was outside on the sidewalk, the old man who had questioned him about the fight caught him by the shoulder.

"Mr. Crockett, if you happen ta run inta one of them fellers, give'em this! They might like'ta have it for a souvenir," and pushed an object in Lincoln's hand. "You have fun at your dance," said the old man who turned away and went back inside the barber shop.

Lincoln opened his hand and stared at the object for a minute. He looked back through the shop window at the old man sitting there pretending to be reading a newspaper. They looked at each other for a moment, then the old man nodded; Lincoln nodded back with a slight grin.

There in his hand lay a white cue ball with the words *Big Al's* tattooed on one side.

Chapter 12

With the Temptations vocalizing the lyrics to "My Girl" on the car radio and "his girl" Bonnie O'Dell snuggled next to him with her arm draped across his shoulders, Rats was on top of the world, tooling down Main Street in his dad's mint-condition, blue '55 Chevy. Decked out in a black suit and tie borrowed from his older brother and Bonnie in a dress that matched the color of the Chevy, they were out for the biggest night of their lives.

In the back seat, seated at arm's length, were Lincoln and his prom date Amanda Cross, who was a mutual friend with Rats and Amanda. They, too, were decked out in prom attire and the two couples were on their way to Coldwater High School and the senior prom. For the girls, it was their last school dance before their graduation the next day. Approaching the school, they all, except for Lincoln, chatted excitedly. He had remained somewhat nervously subdued for most of the trip. He had things on his mind, as usual.

Inside, the school gymnasium was festively decorated in the school colors with the usual assortment of faculty members, school officials, and parental chaperones manning food tables laden with the usual assortment of finger foods and bowls of red and green-colored punch. A local band of amateur musicians, who could play loud, if not well, provided musical entertainment. On the polished hardwood floor of the dimly lit arena, a throng of teenagers gyrated (to the chagrin of the adults) to the loud, pulsating rhythms being pounded out by the band's renditions of the top rock-and-roll and country hits of the day.

Around the perimeter of the dance floor, students gathered in small groups munching goodies and sipping punch from paper cups while they reminisced over school memories, shared plans for the future, and signed year books. A few "wallflowers" and dateless individuals lingered in the shadows trying to appear inconspicuous while wishing to be part of the show.

The one defining characteristic of these gatherings that would be evident only to the knowledgeable eye, and taken for granted by those in attendance, was the social distinction reflected by their members: Ridgers gathered on one side of the gym, Millies on the other.

About midway through the evening, Lincoln was standing alone watching Ashley Armstrong across the floor with her date Montgomery Longworth beside her, the couple whom everyone expected to be named prom king and queen, along with a few friends. A wild idea that had been swirling about in Lincoln's head all day suddenly became more than he could stand. Locating his buddy, he pulled him aside and revealed to him his inspiration.

"Rats, I'm going to do something."

"What's that Kemosabe?"

"I'm going to ask Ashley Armstrong to dance."

Rats nearly choked on the mouthful of punch he had just gulped from his cup.

"You're what?!!"

"I'm going to ask Ashley Armstrong to dance."

"Are you crazy? That dog won't bark. "Have you thought about what might happen?"

"All she can do is say 'yes' or 'no,' and if she says 'no,' I can take rejection."

"Her answer's not what concerns me. It's a Millie asking a Ridger to dance."

Rats continued, "There's all these adults here who are mainly Ridgers and old Billy Ray and his buddies over there have been eyeing us all evening. They're just looking for an excuse to start something because of the other night at Big Al's."

"The Ridgers be damned and Billy Ray, too. I'm going for it," said Lincoln, determined and headed across the dance floor, weaving his way through a sea of hips zigzagging back and forth to the beat of "The Twist."

"Wait a minute Linc," called Rats, "let's talk about this."

But it was too late.

Rats found Bonnie and Amanda and told them to stay close to him. His only response to their question of "Why?" was, "All hell's about to break loose!"

Just as Lincoln reached the petite blonde and her group of associates, the band ceased playing and all was quiet except for the muffled sound of chatter that wafted throughout the assembly. Knowing *who* he was or, at least, *what* he was, the entire group around Ashley ceased their chit chat and looked questioningly at this Milltowner standing before them. To Lincoln, the silence was deafening and the several sets of eyes focused upon him made him feel as conspicuous as graffiti on a brick wall.

After what seemed an eternity, to his relief, the air was suddenly filled with music again as the band resumed playing and, with renewed confidence, he approached his quarry. For Lincoln, it was a moment of truth; a moment he had dreamed about. With extended hand he asked,

"May I have this dance?"

All those gathered around Ashley gasped; shocked at the brazenness of this boy from the other side of the gym, from the other side of town, to subject one of the most popular girls in school to what they considered public embarrassment. At first, Ashley just stared at Lincoln. Then, she turned her head slightly to the left, then the right, judging the reaction of her peers.

Lincoln wondered how long she would take to answer or even if she would answer, and, if she did, what the answer would be. The suspense was nerve racking. He broke out in a cold sweat; his legs felt weak. He suddenly had the urge to run. But, he had crossed the Rubicon; there was no turning back now.

An awareness of the drama was unfolding here and now. It was spreading across the entire gym. The band kept on playing, but no one was dancing. Those who were on the dance floor were just standing, watching, and wondering how this scene was going to play out. No one was more aware of this than Ashley Armstrong.

As Ashley considered her alternatives, there came to mind the memory of an incident that had taken place around the beginning of the school year when, on her way to the ferry, she had taken a wrong turn and wound up lost in the back streets of Milltown along the river. A couple of unsavory young men had stopped her, forced her from her car, and were getting "friendly" with her. Lincoln, who had been fishing along the river, happened upon the scene at a most opportune time. He successfully convinced the two perpetrators of who her father was and that it would be in their best interest to let her be on her way or they would wind up in more shit than a ten-year-old outhouse. As she drove away, she mouthed the words to Lincoln, "I owe you one."

Ashley looked Lincoln in the eye, stepped forward, took his hand, and answered,

"Yes, you may have this dance."

If Ashley's friends had been shocked at Lincoln's forwardness, they were astounded by Ashley's response.

"You...will!" Lincoln, as dumbfounded as anyone in the building, choked the words out. He had rolled the dice and come up a winner. All eyes watched as the Millie boy lead the Ridger girl onto the dance floor. Lincoln couldn't believe he was actually dancing with, holding in his arms, and touching the soft skin of this girl of his dreams attired in an evening gown of white, her long golden tresses falling gracefully across bare shoulders.

The attention of those watching this oddly-matched couple slow dancing together on the half-empty dance floor to the melody of "Moon River" was drawn to a figure approaching them from the sidelines. It was Montgomery Longworth! Again, everyone waited with bated breath to see what the outcome was going to be. When Montgomery reached their side, he hesitated momentarily, then continued on to the other side of the gym where Rats, Bonnie, and Amanda Cross were standing.

Montgomery, extending his hand to Amanda, said something to her to which she initially responded to by shrinking back from him, but after further insistence on his part, reluctantly acquiesced to his gesture. Taking her by the hand, this Ridger boy and Millie girl joined Lincoln and Ashley on the dance floor. The place was now abuzz with a mixed bag of responses from those witness to what was taking place: Ridgers and Millies dancing together.

Most couldn't believe what they were seeing; some were appalled at the sight; a few thought it was humorous; several applauded; a goodly number simply didn't know what to think; and a couple of other "mixed" couples joined them. But, there was one thing that was in the back of all their minds: What was going to happen when the adults became aware of what was in progress? The answer to that question was not long in coming!

Storming across the floor toward their respective offspring squalling like two alley cats with a junkyard dog on their tails were Victoria Armstrong and Cora Sue Longworth. Simultaneously, the school principal was frantically waving his arms at the band and screaming orders at them to stop playing.

Victoria Armstrong grabbed her daughter's arm ripping her out of Lincoln's arms.

"What do you think you'ah doing? Have you lost total control of yo'ah senses?" fumed a flabbergasted Victoria.

"I'm at my senior prom dancing with a friend," replied her daughter politely.

"Don't play coy with me little girl. Yo'ah disgracing yoh self and yo'ah family and dishonoring a generations-old, southern tradition with this shameful public display of social humiliation," lectured her mother whose face was now cardinal red.

"Well perhaps the guardians of your 'generations-old tradition' are just a bunch of bigoted hypocrites whose *traditions* are a social disgrace," retorted Ashley emphatically.

Victoria, gritting her teeth, turned to Lincoln.

"That cheap suit doesn't change you from the white trash you ah. My daughta's from a world you'll neva know anything about, so stay away from her. If you don't, you'll regret it."

Meanwhile, Cora Sue Longworth had confronted her son Montgomery and his dance partner and had exchanged similar words as had Victoria and Ashley, with one exception.

"Amanda, this is my mother, Mrs. Longworth," said Montgomery.

"Mother, this is Amanda Cross…my girlfriend,"

Cora Sue nearly stroked out. She grabbed her chest and began to hyperventilate.

"What do you mean *girlfriend* Montgomery?" she asked after composing herself somewhat.

"Amanda and I have been dating secretly for some time and we will continue to date…now openly."

"How could you get involved with a little Milltown slut like this?" chastised his mother.

"Mother, I'll not tolerate that kind of language directed toward Amanda. She's a very nice young lady."

"Wait until your father hears about this! You'll regret this day!"

By this time, the two family discussions were beginning to become public affairs with other adults and students joining in and taking sides.

As was usual practice, one of the Sheriff's deputies on patrol would stop by the school a time or two on dance nights just to see that there were no problems. They never had any problems to speak of except for the night a few years back when some boys spiked the punch with vodka and most everyone in the place, including faculty, got as drunk as skunks.

That was the night Miss Ellie Mae Thompson, an old maid schoolteacher who had never known a drop of alcohol to have passed her tee totaling lips, got three sheets to the wind. Ellie Mae (who was as graceful as a one-legged ballerina) climbed up on a small table and started strutting and kicking like a Las Vegas showgirl. The table, however, unable to bare the weight of the rather heavy teacher, folded up and left the woman supine on the floor, but on the way down managed to kick the arm of then-Principal Jennings, sending his cigar flying through the air like Hiawatha's arrow.

The cigar happened to land on the stage at the base of the large burgundy-colored curtain that covered the stage opening from floor to ceiling, which immediately went up in flames like a drought-scorched forest struck by lightning. Darn near half the gym burned before the fire department could subdue the blaze. Since then, all alcohol and tobacco products have been banned from all school facilities.

This night, Deputy Clay Cassidy had stopped by a few minutes earlier to check on things and had been there just long enough to size up the situation. From his perch in the balcony, he spied Amanda Cross fleeing out the backdoor of the gym with Montgomery Longworth in hot pursuit and Victoria Armstrong storming out the front with Ashley in tow and Cora Sue Longworth following.

A minute later, he caught sight of Lincoln and Rats standing face to face with Billy Ray Coker and company in the middle of the gym floor. The group was encircled by a throng of chanting students. The deputy recognized that emotions were rising and things were on the verge of getting out of hand. He knew of these particular boys' history and this could get ugly if he didn't stop it quickly.

Bounding down the stairs from the balcony, he told one of the parents to call the Sheriff and huddled for a minute with the school officials in attendance. They all agreed that it was time to end the prom and send everyone home.

Deputy Cassidy waded through the crowd of young people on the gym floor and made his way to the center of the circle where the would-be combatants were trash-talkin and hurling threats and insults back and forth at each other.

"Okay, everyone, it's time to break this up," said Deputy Cassidy, calmly waving his hands in the air.

"Man, you really know how to mess up a prom, don't you Millie," said Billy Ray, pointing a finger at Lincoln.

"Shut up, Ridger, before you get your face messed up like your buddy Edgar," threatened Rats.

"You Millies are going to have to learn the hard way that girls on The Ridge are off limits," sneered Billy Ray as he stepped up close to Lincoln.

"And just what do you think you're going to do about it Billy Boy?" snapped Lincoln, shoving him with two hands in the chest.

Billy Ray tried to respond but the deputy stepped between them.

"All right, that's enough of this," said the deputy forcefully.

"This party's over. Everybody get your things and go home."

"Well, it could have been worse," exclaimed Rats with a sigh of relief as they walked through the parking lot.

"Oh, I thought it went quite well," said Lincoln proudly.

"What came over you?" asked Rats, "I'm the one usually pullin' dumb stunts! You're the quiet one, remember?"

"You can say that again," agreed Amanda, "I could have believed anyone would have done something like *that* before you, Linc. You could have opened a real Pandora's Box."

"Let's just say it was a good thing that Deputy Cassidy was here at the time he was or it might have gotten ugly," stated Rats.

"Speaking of ugly, that Mrs. Armstrong can get *ugly*!" said Amanda.

"Yeah! That bitch could piss off the Pope!" said Lincoln.

"Ashley must take after her father; she's sure not like her mother," added Rats.

"Oh, well! As they say, 'All's well that ends well' and I had my 'fifteen minutes of fame,'" acknowledged Lincoln with satisfaction.

Rats jerked the gearshift on the steering column into first gear, gunned the Chevy, and laid down two black stripes out of the high school parking lot. Lincoln was riding shotgun with Bonnie sandwiched between the two guys; they hadn't been able to find Amanda.

"Now that I think about it, I should have listened to you brother Rats," confessed Lincoln, "I guess I ruined the evening for everyone."

"Well, I suppose it could have been worse," imagined Rats. "Everything considered, it actually didn't turn out too bad."

"Look at it this way. At least you got to dance with Ashley for a minute," said Bonnie.

"Yeah, I guess I did, didn't I?" agreed Lincoln.

"And how about ole Monty!" exclaimed Rats, "Did anybody see that coming?"

"Not in a million years," said Bonnie, shaking her head.

"Not a clue," agreed Lincoln.

"His mama must have peed in her pants at that revelation," laughed Rats.

"He may get exiled from The Ridge," suggested Bonnie.

"Yeah, and Ashley, too," added Lincoln regretfully.

"Well, there's one thing about it," Rats predicted.

"What's that?" asked the other two together.

"The Coldwater High Senior Prom of 1965 is one that will be remembered for a looong time!"

"Man, you got that right!" agreed Lincoln, "and in infamy yet!"

"Certainly not your typical Friday night dance!" said Bonnie.

"Well, let's celebrate the 'infamous' prom," declared Rats, pulling out a couple of six packs of brew from under his legs.

"We might as well toast this prom and really make it one to remember."

"Hear, hear!" chimed Lincoln.

"Where'd you get the brewskies?" asked Bonnie.

"Ole Linc and I made a run over to Central City this afternoon for the guys."

"And Bonnie, you'll never guess who we saw there sneaking in and out of the liquor store," said Lincoln.

"Oh, yeah, babe!" remembered Rats. "You're gonna love this!"

"Okay, so who did you see?"

"Tell her Linc," urged Rats.

"None other than the good reverend Brother Nutter," pronounced Lincoln.

"You're puttin' me on! Not the Right Reverend Clifton Nutter!" she said in exaggerated speech.

"The man himself," swore Rats raising his right hand.

"The man who ran the place told us he comes in about once a month ... purchases the same thing each time," continued Lincoln.

"Yeah, six bottles of Mogen David," chimed in Rats, with emphasis on the brand name, "says he uses it for communion at his church."

"Why that old hypocrite! Sounds like he's been gettin' *into* the spirits as well as *in* the Spirit," mused Bonnie.

"So much for not lettin' that demon rum pass your lips," mocked Rats.

"Or demon wine!" added Lincoln, as they all had good laugh.

A few minutes later, Rats turned into the Little River overlook and pulled into the first parking spot he eyeballed in the rapidly filling lovers' lane which was beginning to look like a drive-in movie theatre. Several vehicles with already steamed-up windows gave evidence that a number of people had abandoned the ill-fated prom early and made a mad dash for the overlook, their primary destination for the evening anyway.

Inside the Chevy, illuminated only by the dim reflection of moonlight shimmering on the water, the sound of popping lids and clinking bottles of amber-colored liquid could be heard, followed by salutes of "to Coldwater High," "to Coldwater High," "to Coldwater High" echoing well into the night.

Chapter 13

Late that night

It was late, how late he didn't know, when Rats and Bonnie dropped him off at his house on MacAnally Flats after the prom. The four fuzzy, distorted hands on his watch made it impossible to make out the correct time, but Lincoln calculated it was most likely well past his time to be in. Even though he was eighteen years old, his father still strictly held him to a midnight curfew. If it was in fact past the witching hour, he surmised that his father would not be in a mood to discuss who would win the American League pennant this year. Stumbling blurry-eyed up the porch steps, he stopped momentarily, held his head with both hands to stop the house from spinning, and then chucked his cookies.

For someone who had never drunk anything stronger than coffee, two, or was it three or four beers (he couldn't remember), can have an acutely disorienting effect on a body not acclimated to the effects of alcohol, not to mention the distress it can wreak on the digestive system.

He took the house being dark as a sign that his parents were asleep and he would be able to slip through the house unnoticed. Once inside his bedroom, he undressed to just shorts and T-shirt and was pulling back the bed covers when suddenly the overhead light lit up the room. Startled, he jumped back against the wall like a fox caught in the hen house. There in the doorway stood his father with that big, black leather belt stretched between his hands and looking as mad as a mule chewing on honeybees. He knew what was coming.

"What are ya doin' tryin' ta sneak in here past one the mornin'?" questioned his father in a nasty tone of voice.

"I didn't want to wake you and mom," answered Lincoln, holding onto the wall.

"No, you didn't want us ta know how late ya got in."

"You must know it's past yer midnight curfew," observed Clovis Crockett as he stepped forward close to Lincoln.

"So, what excuse do ya have fer yourself?"

"I guess I just lost track of time. Hic . . ."

"What's that...lemme smell yer breath! You been a'drankin'!"

Lincoln's eyes rolled over in his head as he weaved a little to one side and caught the headboard of the bed to steady himself.

"Ya ain't just been drankin', you're drunk!" growled his father. Ain't this a fine thang? Out cattin' 'round with that bunch ya run with 'til tha wee hours of the mornin', dancin' like heathens ta that devil music, fillin' yer bellies with tha devil's brew, an truth be know'ed, probly fornicatin' with some little whore, too."

"No, Dad, it wasn't like that...let me explain," he answered, pointing a finger toward his father.

"Explain! Ya can't make up no story that can dress up this kinda sordid behavior to be nothin' more than what it is. Ya wanna add lyin' ta yer lista sins? Ya gotta lot of thangs ta seek redemption fer boy. Tha Bible says, 'spare the rod and spoil the child.' Well, tha rod's not gonna be spared in this here house. Hit's apparently not done much good up'ta now, but long as ya live under this roof, hit's gonna be applied."

The elder Crockett, wielding that black belt like a cat-o'-nine-tails, lit into his son with the religious fervor of a Middle Ages crusader bent on purging the Holy Land of infidels. Again and again, the old man rained lashes of hard leather upon the bare arms and legs of his son. Lincoln doubled up for protection as more bloodletting blows fell upon his back. All the time, Anna Mae was screaming at her husband to stop this inhumane treatment of their son until he at last acquiesced to her pleading.

"Now let this here be a lesson to ya," said his father as Lincoln slumped to the floor in pain and his mother rushed to his side to console him.

Anna Mae, down on her knees, turned toward Clovis as he was leaving the room.

"I hope you burn in hell, you bastard!"

Wincing at the burning pain that coursed through the multiple abrasions left by coarse leather clawing at soft flesh, Lincoln mumbled in a low voice through clenched teeth, "The Bible also says, 'provoke not thy children to wrath.'"

Chapter 14

Too embarrassed to face their neighbors following what they considered a careless display of foolishness by their offspring at the high school prom Friday night, the Armstrongs and Longworths decided to leave their church pews unoccupied this Sunday morning. Foregoing their traditional routine, they opted instead for a light lunch at home followed by a joint family council.

Except for the chatter of a few songbirds darting about among the blossoming trees and the occasional bark of a dog somewhere in the distance, all was quite around town; the streets were vacant. But, that was normal for this time of day on a Sunday. You see, the majority of folks in Coldwater are religious people and the majority of them are filling pews in the town's several churches about this time. Those who aren't religious, and a few of those who are, tend to sleep in on Sunday mornings, and this Sunday will proceed in its usual calm, quiet Sunday manner, that is until noon.

For, if there's one thing that can be said for Coldwater residents, they're creatures of habit if nothing else. That's why you can just about bet the farm that the calm and quiet that has characterized the morning hours will be interrupted by a phenomenon that takes place every Sunday around noon that might be referred to in the vernacular of automobile racing as the "Sunday Lunch 500." This weekly spectacle is triggered by the dismissal of church services at the noon hour (or soon thereafter), with parishioners taking to their automobiles, joined by any late sleepers who will now be rolling out of bed, and all making a mad dash through the heretofore deserted streets with the objective of being first in line at one of their favorite local eating establishments.

Food preparation activities at the few sit-down restaurants and fast food joints around town have been slowly escalating in anticipation of this onslaught of starving saints and sinners beating paths to their doors. Their souls may be filled or empty, but at this point, this drooling herd of diners has two things in common: empty stomachs and a lustful desire to fill them in sinful gluttony.

This is the ritual our two families determined to forego this particular week in favor of a less conspicuous venue. Lunch, instead, was conducted in an atmosphere of silence, interrupted only by the intermittent clinking of tableware and infrequent attempts at meaningless chit-chat. After going through the motions of eating where appetites were in short supply, the Longworths suggested that they and their guests withdraw to the living room and more comfortable seating. Lagging behind the parents were Ashley and Montgomery who exhibited about as much enthusiasm as two convicted felons marching to the gallows.

Cora Sue and Victoria, as somber as mourners at a wake, took seats on a large Victorian couch opposite two matching wingback chairs to which Montgomery and Ashley were directed. Montgomery sat at attention, ready to steadfastly take on whatever came his way while Ashley slouched in her seat like a discarded topcoat. Leland poured two glasses of Jack Daniels, handed one to Emerson, and invited him to speak first. Emerson pulled a side chair up close to the others, took a swallow of whiskey, and began.

"Ashley, Montgomery, we are all distressed over this incident that occurred at the prom the other night and the negative responses it's generating around town. More than that, we're sadly disappointed that you two, our daughter and son, were the main instigators of that incident. For that reason, we decided to talk, both families together, to see if you can explain to us…"

At this point, a red-faced Emerson Armstrong lost his composure, jumped to his feet and shouted, "…what in God's name compelled you to violate such a social taboo?"

"Well, just for the record," spoke up Montgomery, "to be technically correct, it was Lincoln who initiated the incident by asking Ashley to dance."

"Yes! That troublemaking *Millie*," grimaced Victoria. "I hate him. Why did you let that…that…*filth* touch you?" looking at her daughter questioningly. "If you had just ignored him, none of this would have happened."

"So now it's all my fault!" stormed Ashley.

"Yours and that…boy's," fired back her father, "He asked. You accepted. Together, you're responsible."

"I'm glad they both did what they did because it broke the ice and gave me, and others, the courage to do what I did," admitted Montgomery.

"But son, do you see the consequences of your actions; the looks people give us everywhere, the embarrassment it's caused, not only to your family, but to all *our* people?" sobbed Cora Sue, dabbing her teary eyes with a hanky.

"*Our* people, Mother?" questioned Montgomery. "When did it become any of *your* friends' business who *my* friends are?"

"When one is born into class Montgomery," interrupted his father, "it becomes one's duty to maintain the dignity expected of their station and to preserve the conventions of social order."

"And one of those sacred cows you strive to preserve is to keep 'our' people segregated from undesirables such as Millies, blacks, the poor, etc., isn't it?" indicted Ashley, jumping to her feet with arms braced on her hips. Sometimes I'm embarrassed for our riches. All I ever have to choose is which dress to wear or which car to drive while others have to choose whether to buy food or clothes," she continued.

"I'm tired of hearing this northern liberal propaganda y'all are getting indoctrinated with," barked Leland as he emptied his whiskey glass in one gulp.

"But father, what's this we hear at church about all people being equal in God's eyes? Even in our Constitution we declare that all people are created equal? Yet, we build fences around everyone to keep them separated. We talk the talk but don't walk the walk. Don't you see the hypocrisy in that?" asked Montgomery.

"People have always had their own places in society. It's always been that way," said Victoria as if not understanding the issue.

"Okay, okay!" said Emerson, "Enough of the ideology. We'll let the politicians deal with that. Let's deal with the immediate problem in these two families."

Leland walked over to his son and asked, "You referred to this little white trash girl as your girlfriend. Do you intend to continue in this relationship?"

"Yes, sir I do."

"Montgomery! We'd always planned on you marrying some nice girl here on The Ridge," confessed Cora Sue.

"Why, I guess we even dreamed that you and Ashley might even end up being together someday," she added, looking around at Victoria smiling.

"I suppose we've sort of thought that might be a possibility also," admitted Victoria as she returned Cora Sue's smile.

"Montgomery and me…*married*," laughed Ashley, "huh, nothing personal Monty," she said looking at Montgomery.

"None taken," returned Montgomery bowing.

"Marrying Montgomery would be like marrying my brother."

"Agreed, Ash," confirmed Montgomery.

"Then I forbid you to see this girl anymore," said Mr. Longworth looking at Montgomery.

"You can't stop me," answered Montgomery.

"This girl's father works at the furniture mill. It would be a shame for him to lose his job, now wouldn't it?" threatened his father.

"Surely even you wouldn't reach that low!" responded Montgomery, appalled at his father's threat.

"It's your choice: the girl or her father's job."

"And, if it's your decision to choose the girl, your income will also be cut off," he added.

"Damn you!" the words spit out of Montgomery's stiffened body like venom as he stomped out of the room, leaving his father with his mouth hanging open and his mother in tears.

"That's incredibly coldhearted!" lashed out Ashley.

"Do you consider this boy your boyfriend?" asked Ashley's father indignantly.

"Not in the sense you're referring to. We've never dated. He's been a good friend."

"What could you possibly see in a boy like him that would compel you to even want to associate with him?" asked her mother of a scenario that she was personally incapable of fathoming in her own mind.

"You make it sound like he's a leper or a bloodsucking vampire or something. He's not! I like him because he's very intelligent and polite, he works hard, and he's respected by everyone who knows him. He's one of the nicest guys in school…and besides…he's quite good looking," she added with emphasis, rolling her eyes.

"Ohoooo!" exclaimed her mother, clutching her chest as if she had just been struck a mortal blow from some unseen attack upon her person.

"It's obvious that you have some kind of irrational attraction for this…young man, so it's best that this infatuation be nipped in the bud before it has opportunity to blossom into anything more serious," pronounced her father.

"So what sentence has the Armstrong Inquisition determined to pronounce on me for the great sacrilege I've committed?"

"You, too, are to have no contact with this Crockett boy," said her father.

"And, have you concocted some scheme to blackmail me with or will you merely banish me to a convent if I fall from grace?"

"If you 'fall from grace' as you put it, you will forfeit possession of your most prized possession," he answered.

"The T-bird?"

"It's your choice: the boy or the T-bird."

"And, as Leland said, your income will also be forfeited."

Ashley looked about the room at the two sets of parents looking like four lost souls tossed about like boats on troubled waters. They had been born, raised, and still lived in an ordered world that was now in turmoil; a volatile world in which young and old alike were struggling to understand, to make sense of, and to deal with the rapidly changing landscape.

She couldn't resist getting on her soapbox to have the last word.

"You've given Montgomery and me choices, and we'll make those choices, the ones we think are right. But, you're living in the past, in a world that's changing, and that changing world's giving you choices, too. You can make those choices and progress with the rest of the world or you can ignore the choices and be left behind," said Ashley calmly. She turned to walk away.

After a few steps she paused, looked back and added, "And that's your choice."

Chapter 15

Anna Mae and Lincoln said "Amen" to the blessing Clovis prayed over the food laid out on the dining table, then the three of them set into sharing a meal of pinto beans, ham hocks, and cornbread.

"I made you your favorite meal for supper Lincoln, an there's a choc'lit cake, your favorite kind, fer dessert," said Anna Mae proudly.

He looked at the chocolate cake with the number "19" written on it with white icing.

"Thanks, Mom. You went to a lot of trouble."

"Oh, weren't no trouble at all."

After a few bites, Clovis began questioning Lincoln while gnawing on a piece of ham bone.

"Sum'a tha fellers down at tha sawmill been talkin' 'bout a big ruckus over at that school dance tha other night. Seems hit wuz caused by you ana Ridger girl dancin' together."

"There wasn't a big ruckus, more like a misunderstanding," answered Lincoln, swallowing a mouthful of beans.

"Misunderstandin'! That wuz a big mistake! A Millie boy axin' a Ridger girl ta dance."

"It wuz a fool thang ta do," bellowed Clovis, dropping the ham bone and pounding his fist on the table.

"Clovis, please!" pleaded Anna Mae, nervously clutching her napkin to her face.

"Be quiet, woman," scolded her husband.

"Got tha whole town upset. Fellers down at tha mill kiddin' me 'bout it. They doin' tha same to ya mama up at the textile mill."

"Oh, they didn't mean nuthin' by it. They's just funnin'," smiled Anna Mae.

"Well, I didn't see no fun in'it. It wuz embarassin'," scowled Clovis. "Claim we tryin' to marry up inta high society."

"You still ain't answered me boy. Wuz hit you?"

"Yes."

"I hear hit wuz old man Emerson's girl. That right?"

"That's right."

"He know you'n his girl's runnin' around together?"

"We're not running around together. We just danced together. That's all."

"Why you chasin' after a girl like that? Don't ya know The Ridge is as far away from Milltown as tha moon?"

"She's pretty, she's nice, and I like her. Anyway, she's just a girl, what's it matter where she lives?"

"Because she's not one'a us! You gotta remember yor place. When people git outta their place it causes problems," answered Clovis.

"Dad, don't you ever get tired of being told where your place is? Told where you can go and where you can't? Who you can associate with and who you can't? Not having opportunities to do more, have more, be more? And all because of who you are?" asked Lincoln, compassionately looking into his father's eyes.

His father sat for a minute and looked out the window as if lost in thought, and for the first time in his life, Lincoln thought he actually saw his father's eyes tear up a bit.

"Hit don't matter what I thank. I can't change thangs any mor'n I can turn water inta wine."

"But things are changing. There's a new day coming," said Lincoln.

"Not'in this place! I'm a Millie an you're a Millie. We'll always be Millies! Tha sooner ye git that fixed between yer ears, tha better off ye'll be," declared Clovis, jumping to his feet.

"Clovis, please! You're goin' to ruin everthang," pleaded Anna Mae.

"Tha boy's ruinin' things fer hisself puttin' on educated airs, cattin' 'round with a little rich bitch, an rubbin' elbows with them high-falutin' folks down at the Lacy. It's all goin' to his head makin' him fergit where he's frum," fumed Clovis.

"I'm tired of people telling me who I am and who I'm not; where I belong and where I don't; what I can be and what I can't," declared Lincoln, pushing his plate back and standing to face his father.

"I'm an adult now, and I'm going to be who I want to be and I'll not accept a life sentence to prison in Milltown. I'll do whatever it takes to escape this place."

"Even if doin' that shames yer famly?" asks his father indignantly.

"If I wind up in a Vietnam rice paddy with my guts hanging out coming home in a body bag, will you be ashamed of me then, too?" asked Lincoln pointedly.

His mother went scampering toward the bedroom in tears, the possibility and vividness of the scene he described too real in her mind.

Lincoln walked out of the house and slammed the door behind him. He turned down Mill Street toward town leaving his father alone in the dining room.

Clovis walked to the window and watched his son walking away down the street. Turning his head skyward, a tear rolled down his rugged face. Through watery eyes, he gazed as if fixed on some time and place far, far away as the whispered words slipped from quivering lips, "I know son, I know."

Later that evening at the Come-On-In

Lincoln's quarter slid "clink" "clink" "clink" down the slot of the old Wurlitzer juke box. He pushed some buttons on front of the magic box and instantly Hank Snow was on stage vocalizing a rapid-fire list of places he'd been in "I've been everywhere."

He slouched down in the corner booth where Rats was digging into a bowl of piping-hot chili and with his arms crossed, laid his head back against the top of the booth.

"What are you down in the mouth about?" asked Rats.

He proceeded to fill Rats in on what had transpired at the supper table, the gist of the conversation, and how he had stormed out of the house.

"And on my birthday no less!"

"Hey! Today's your birthday? I didn't remember."

"Well, happy birthday partner!"

"Say, did the boss give you anything?"

"They threw me a little party down at the hotel. Just some cake and ice cream."

"Was that all? Just cake and ice cream?"

"Well! There was a fifty-dollar bill."

"Man, ain't you the lucky one."

"What you ordering tonight friend Lincoln…same as your bud?" came a female voice. Mavis came to take his order.

"Nothing for me tonight, Mavis. I'm not hungry," answered Lincoln.

"Man, that's a first!" exclaimed the waitress. "Well, let me know if you change your mind."

"Mavis, if your crowd gets any bigger, you and Joe are going to have to expand the place," said Lincoln.

"Tell me about it," said Mavis wiping her brow, turning to another table.

"Man, ole Hank Snow can really fire off the names of those towns, can't he?" said Rats. "I'd like to see all the places he's been, wouldn't you?" he added, dreaming.

"You think he's really been to all those places?" asked Lincoln.

"Probably not! But he's probably been to a lot of 'em."

"Yeah, probably so."

"I know one place I'd like to have been yesterday," said Rats.

"Where's that?" asked Lincoln

"In Indianapolis, at the Indy 500 race! Wouldn't that have been somethin' to have been there instead of listenin' to it on the radio like we did?"

"Can you imagine goin' a hundred and fifty miles an hour like Jim Clark did winnin' the race?" added Rats swooning.

For a moment, they both savored the thought in a world of imagination.

"I should'a listened to you at a place we *were* at the other night," admitted Lincoln.

"You're not talkin' about the prom, are you?" grinned Rats.

"Yeah," laughed Lincoln, "sorta stirred up a hornet nest didn't I?"

"Well, it wasn't as bad as I imagined it would be. I could just see a riot breaking out."

"Have you by chance seen Ashley since then?" asked Rats.

"Nah."

"You know, the real shocker was the move Montgomery made," noted Rats.

"You said it! That took everyone by surprise. I think it refocused the shock and attention away from Ashley and me and probably defused the whole situation to some extent."

"You may be right."

"I know somewhere I'd liked to have been late that night," said Lincoln gazing solemnly into his bowl.

Rats, detecting a melancholy tone to his buddy's voice and noticing him nonchalantly toying with his food, paused his big spoon full of chili halfway to his mouth and asked: "Where's that?"

"*Anywhere* but at home!" He spit the words out as if he had bitten into a sour pickle.

"Your ole man get mad 'bout us gettin' home late from the prom?"

"You might say that," replied Lincoln sarcastically, "but mostly about the beer."

"He beat you again?"

"The ole bastard beat the hell outta me with that damned belt of his...the worst ever. I've still got red stripes all over where he brought the blood out."

"I'm sorry man. Why don't you call the cops on him?"

"He threatened to do something really bad if either my mom or I ever do."

A sullen Lincoln leaned across the table and looked Rats in the eyes.

"But Rats, one of these days I'm not going to take it anymore," he said in a half whisper through clenched teeth.

Rats got a funny feeling all over. He had never before seen that look in his easygoing old friend's eyes or heard him speak with such eerie authority.

It was just then that a man walked in and looked about for a seat. Glancing at the boys, he nodded a "hello," to which they nodded back, then turned and took a stool at the counter across from their booth. They heard Joe, who appeared to be acquainted with the man, call him Dalton. The boys didn't know him personally but had seen him around, knew that he worked at the furniture company, and that his name was Dalton Jackson. He asked the boys about the chili to which they gave a hearty recommendation.

"Thanks, I'll try it," he said.

Later, they overheard him tell Joe that he was on his way up to the mountains.

They both just stared into space for a minute, sort of lost in the moment, when Elvis broke the mood with his "Good Luck Charm," reminding Lincoln of something.

He snatched his wallet from his hip pocket and extracted a folded piece of paper tucked away in a little side nook. He unfolded the paper and laid it on the table in front of Rats.

"What's this?" asked Rats.

"Maybe a 'good luck charm," winked Lincoln.

"Looks like a telephone number to me," Rats said quizzically.

"It is. A *special* telephone number."

Lincoln went on to explain in detail his encounter with the lady at J.C. Penney's and their flirtation game the day he was buying his prom clothes. At first, Rats thought his buddy was pulling his leg but soon became convinced that he was on the up-and-up. He had heard stories of middle-aged women seducing younger men.

They discussed the pros and cons of making the call. On the "con" side there were two major considerations, both negative: One, if she was married, her ole man could find out—not good! Two, Lincoln's ole man could find out, didn't even want to go there! On the "pro" side, they could only think of a positive, the chance of a lifetime, a boy's dream come true! The decision was made: go for it!

Chapter 16

As it turned out, the brouhaha at the high school prom had consequences above and beyond those for the few students and families directly involved in the incident. That simple act of a boy and girl dancing together at a high school dance, interpreted on both sides of Main Street as a "symbolic" attack upon the local social structure, had stirred up a community-wide caldron of emotions. In light of the national civil rights movement, it was, on The Ridge, considered an assault upon decent society by leftist rabble while, on the south side, it was hailed as a statement against elitist bigots who got their comeuppance.

With passions running high, graduation exercises had been conducted a week after prom under the close scrutiny of school officials and with strictly controlled supervision. In spite of a few murmurings throughout the audience and outbursts by one or two sullen individuals, the program succeeded in running its course without major impediments.

The splash made by the bold action taken by Lincoln Crockett that night and the following tidal wave of social consciousness that lay awash in its wake would remain in the forefront of people's minds and fester for a while. But, just as the cool, temperate days of spring would transition into hot, humid days of summer, so would the passions surrounding those final days of the school year give way to the everyday concerns of day to day life. For life would go on as usual in Coldwater, particularly for those in Milltown, the only observable difference being enduring the temperatures the seasonal change would bring.

Lincoln kept working at the Lacy while he pondered his long-term options. His first objective was to save enough money during the summer to enroll in night school at the community college in the fall. A full schedule of work and classes would also keep him away from home most of the week. His next endeavor was to pursue the favorable reaction he had received from Ashley Armstrong and see what possibilities might exist now that the door had been opened, or at least cracked.

But, little could he have known in those waning days of spring that in the coming months of summer he would learn that dreams can come true, but not always in the manner expected nor without far-reaching consequences, testing the mettle of love, relationships, and longstanding traditions.

Chapter 17

Seven o'clock that Wednesday evening found Lincoln walking along the sidewalk of Fifth Avenue toward the address the J.C. Penney lady had given him. His feelings were a confused mixture of both excitement and nervousness. It had been a couple of weeks since he and Rats had discussed making the call to the woman who had slipped him her phone number. She had seemed somewhat surprised, but delighted, by his call and was looking forward to his visit since she was alone much of the time due to her husband's extensive business travel.

He tried to imagine what was going to take place within the walls of this woman's house in the next few hours. Part of him wanted to turn and run, but the sense of adventure pushed him onward toward house number 321. The sun was beginning to set when he reached a finger for the doorbell.

The door opened and there she stood, just the way he remembered her.

"Come in," she said, smiling sweetly.

"Thank you," answered Lincoln politely.

Seeing the woman again brought back visions of her that day a few weeks ago and streamed vividly back into his mind. That funny, tingling feeling he had felt then once again coursed through his body, only to a greater degree, seeing her there in a long, black negligee.

"I'm Marjorie...Marjorie Henderson, but you may call me Marge," she said holding her hand out to him.

"My name's Lincoln. Nice to meet you," responded Lincoln shaking her hand.

"Like the car?" asked Marge jokingly.

"The car?" said Lincoln, not making the connection.

"The Lincoln car. Your name."

"Oh! Yeah! Lincoln, same as the car."

"I hear Lincoln's are fun to drive," she grinned.

"I wouldn't know."

"Well, we'll have to find out, won't we?" teased Marge.

Marge invited Lincoln to have a seat on a big, plush couch in the dimly lit living room, poured them both a glass of red wine, and sat down beside him.

"I'm not much of a wine connoisseur," admitted Lincoln, "only a little beer now and then."

"Well now, you're in for a treat. This is real good stuff. It'll give you a nice, relaxed, cozy feeling all over."

Lincoln turned up the glass and let a measure of the warm red beverage trickle slowly down his throat. It burned a little all the way down but had a nice fruity flavor and cheery afterglow.

For the next few minutes, they sipped wine and made small talk, getting acquainted swapping tidbits of personal information. He took notice of an unusual-looking coin pendant attached to a small gold chain dangling about her neck and commented on it. She said she knew little about it other than that it was an ancient Roman coin that had been left to her many years ago in the will of a wealthy uncle whom she hardly knew. Upon closer inspection, Lincoln recognized engravings on the coin indicating it as not only being ancient, but quite rare. In 44 B.C., Marcus Brutus had many Denarii struck in commemoration of the assassination of Julius Caesar. The markings on the coin identified it as one of those Denarii, making it a quite valuable treasure.

Just as Lincoln was beginning to feel somewhat relaxed, Marge took the wine glass from his hand and sat it, along with hers, on the coffee table. She cozied up next to him, draped a leg across his, and placed his hand on her thigh; Lincoln felt his face getting warm. Wrapping her arms about his neck, she pulled him close and pressed her mouth to his. He could feel the excitement rising within him. It didn't take him long to get into the act; he was a fast learner.

Suddenly, Marge stood up and reached a hand down to Lincoln.

"Come with me. It's time to take this Lincoln for a drive."

Taking her hand, she led him into the bedroom. After turning the bed covers back, she began to slowly unbutton her young lover's shirt, one button at a time

"The appetizer has been tasty, but the entrée is going to be delicious," promised Marge.

Lincoln felt a bit lightheaded; his breathing became slow and heavy.

In their brain-dazed, erotic interlude they had failed to see the headlights or hear the motor of the car pulling into the driveway. Their first indication that anyone other than the two of them was on the premises was a noise at the front door.

"What's that noise?" asked Lincoln.

Marge ran to the bedroom window and looked out. She saw her husband's car in the driveway and him at the front door fumbling with his keys.

"Oh, my God! It's my husband!" she exclaimed.

"What's he doing here?" asked Lincoln.

"I don't know!"

"I thought you said he was out of town!"

"He's not supposed to be back for two more days."

"Oh, my gosh! He'll see the two wine glasses. How'll I explain *two* wine glasses?" she exclaimed, panicking.

"Wine glasses my ass," chided Lincoln, "how will you explain *me*?"

"Get out the window."

Lincoln tried to open the window but it was stuck.

"It won't open…the damn thing's stuck."

"I've got to get rid of one of those wine glasses. You stay in here. I'll try to get him in the kitchen and let you out the front door. If anyone comes in here, get under the bed."

"What!"

"Just do it!"

Marge dashed out to the living room, grabbed one of the wine glasses, gulped down the remaining beverage, and shoved the glass under the sofa just as her spouse came stumbling through the door with arms full of suitcases and briefcases. At Marge's inquiry as to his unexpected early arrival, he explained that the last client on his itinerary to visit had a death in the family and wasn't going to be available, so he had to cut his trip short.

He, however, had an inquiry of his own. He was curious as to why his wife was in one of her fancy negligees and in full makeup so late at night. Was this a habit of hers when he was away or had she perhaps been entertaining company? She turned on the charm and explained that she had just not gotten around to removing her daily makeup and had been trying on some of her lingerie trying to decide what she wanted to surprise her husband with upon his return.

[79]

Whether he believed her story or not, seeing her in her current state of dress got him into an amorous mood. He refused to take "no" for an answer when proposing that they retire to the bedroom for a session of lovemaking.

Sitting on the side of the bed, Lincoln was thinking about how the fickle finger of fate had turned his good luck charm into the kiss of death when, without warning, the bedroom door opened and he heard the two of them coming into the room.

"Oh, shit," he whispered and scrambled under the bed.

He lay there shaking, knowing that he was going to die there this night in that room at the hands of this woman's jealous husband.

Although he couldn't see what was happening, he heard sounds that night he had never heard before; he heard language spoken in ways he didn't know it could be spoken; he learned things about the sexual relations between a man and a woman that he had never imagined.

The bed under which he could barely fit shook, bounced, and screaked as if possessed by some supernatural force as the two human bodies attacked one another with unbridled animal lust. He could just see the bed breaking and him being crushed under the weight of a mass of springs, mattress, and bodies. At times, male and female moaned and groaned in ecstatic bliss and, at others, screamed as if their very souls were being ripped from their bodies. At one point, he thought they must be killing each other and considered fleeing from the scene. Praises, flattery, swears, and curses alike flowed freely until in one final crescendo of shrieking, all fell silent.

Lincoln lay very still, hardly breathing, listening for some sound, but all he could hear was the drum-like pounding of his own heart. After a few minutes, he decided they both must have had heart attacks and died. He lay there that way for some time fearful of moving. After what seemed an eternity, he heard movement in the bed. Then, he heard Marge whisper.

"Lincoln, come out."

Lincoln crawled out from under the bed and the two of them crept quietly out of the room, taking care not to wake her sleeping husband. As she let him out of the house, Marge apologized to Lincoln for the way things had turned out and asked him to call her again sometime.

As he made his way back down Fifth Avenue, relishing the freedom of the outdoors and fresh air, he stopped and took a deep breath and exhaled slowly trying to calm his insides which were still agitating like a washing machine. His mind raced in replay mode, now under more lucid conditions, the events of the past hour. Sensual feelings of pleasure induced by the warmth of the woman's body, her touch, and her smell, intermingled with cold chills crawling up the back of his neck and visions of what could have happened after the man-of-the-house showed up plagued his thoughts.

His plans for a one-night stand with a mature woman had turned out nothing short of a disaster. All things considered; however, it had been an experience he'd remember for a lifetime. Although he had come "close but no cigar," he had miraculously survived the encounter unscathed. Reaching Main Street, he stopped for a moment and under the floodlit landscape of a bright moon hovering overhead in a cloudless sky, he pulled the folded-up piece of paper next to the Trojan condom from his wallet and tore it up into little pieces.

He decided then and there that a wedding ring on a woman's finger was like a "Beware, Danger" sign, and was intended to warn men that involvement with this type member of the opposite sex could be hazardous to one's health.

When Lincoln crossed Main Street at the Lacy and headed toward the shortcut home, a big grin suddenly broke out across his face. To someone on the outside looking in, the strange set of circumstances that just occurred at 321 Fifth Avenue would appear to be a debacle, a real comedy of errors. Now, he was going to have to decide which version of the story to tell Rats; the one that *was* or the one that *could* have been.

Chapter 18

June, 1965

Dalton Jackson frowned at the taste of the black liquid he slurped from the coffee-stained mug and sat it down with a "clunk" on the windowsill of his office that overlooked the loading docks at the Longworth Furniture Manufacturing Company. He closed the door with a shove of his foot to block out the noise of the docks and dropped heavily into the wooden chair behind his paper-strewn desk.

The chair creaked as he leaned back with hands interlocked behind his head and propped his feet up on the bottom drawer. He stared at Miss June, whose alluring eyes stared back at him from the calendar on the wall. After he had come back to earth from a short-lived flight of imagination with the eight-by-twenty-five-inch centerfold, his thoughts returned to more true-to-life pursuits, like the fishing trip he and some buddies were planning next weekend. Lost in his thoughts, it took Dalton a minute to realize that the far distant sound of bells in his head was actually the telephone ringing, calling him back to the here and now.

"Hello," yawned Dalton, rubbing the drowsiness from his eyes.

"Mr. D, this is Atlanta calling," said a stern voice at the other end of the line.

Dalton jumped to his feet and snapped to attention. He knew the caller.

"Yes Sir, Mr. Logano. How can I be of service?" replied Dalton in his best business voice.

"The Man wants fifty big ones, bulk."

"That's a big order and you know it's out of season. I'll have to check with our supplier about stock and then see when we have wheels going your way."

"The man really wants this. He'll pay big if you can deliver by midmonth. Let us know."

"I'll get back to you as soon as I know if we can work it out," promised Dalton.

Dalton let the receiver drop lightly back onto the cradle and leaned against the side of the desk. He glanced back up at Miss June and smiled thoughtfully.

"Well, June baby, how do you like that? Won't even give a man time to get a second cup 'a coffee in the morning 'til they start callin' wanting something. Oh, well, coffee's not much anyway."

"Better let the boss know and get the ball rollin'," he mumbled to himself.

Dalton Jackson's title at the furniture company was Manager of Transportation and, as such, he was responsible for scheduling the company's fleet of trucks for regular maintenance and seeing that furniture orders were properly loaded for shipment to their various destinations. But this Atlanta order had nothing to do with furniture or his responsibilities at the company; it had nothing to do with Longworth Furniture Company…directly, that is, although some of the company's resources were utilized. It did have to do with a side business Dalton was involved in; a black collar business dealing in the illicit distribution of untaxed goods.

He dialed LW's private number and after three rings got an answer.

"LW, it's Dalton, can we talk?"

"Yes, we can talk."

"We just got a big order from Atlanta."

"Can we satisfy their request this time of the year?" came the question from the other end.

"Don't know if we got the stock. They want fifty big'uns in bulk. I'll hav'ta check with the supplier. They'll pay big if we can deliver by the middle of the month."

"That'll bring a hefty sum. Is it doable?"

"I'll go see our supplier today about the inventory situation. When I have confirmation that we can deliver, I'll bring the other players in."

"Okay, keep me informed."

"Will do, Boss."

Chapter 19

That Afternoon

Leaving the smooth blacktop of State Highway 21 a few miles back for the loose gravel of Notchy Creek Road had been bad enough, but the turn off Notchy Creek amounted to little more than two dusty rain-washed ruts. He'd have to navigate the last leg of his trip into Thunderhead Mountains through more than five miles of backwoods wilderness. Cussing, Dalton Jackson shifted his Toyota pickup into four-wheel drive, slinging dirt and gravel as he did. Besides that, he had never felt comfortable in the mountains; the folks in this neck of the woods were always suspicious of outsiders and would just as soon see none come around.

Due to the particular nature of a special elixir they produced, he could appreciate the supplier's need to live a zillion miles from civilization. Still, he detested having to drive through forty miles of hell to make personal contact with them; but, it was a business necessity. The people in these mountains had never embraced any modern conveniences such as the telephone. They lived very simple lives as they always had and were suspicious of anything new or different.

He guessed it was worth the trouble. After all, Herman Hayworth Culveyhouse III, his wife Elsie, and their son Claudell and daughter Claudene did make the best white lightning in the country. In addition to moonshining, the Culveyhouse's were also in the logging business, cutting trees on Thunderhead Mountain. They had a three-way deal going where Culveyhouse supplied Clifton Ledbetter's sawmill back in Coldwater with timber. Ledbetter, in turn, supplied Longworth Furniture Manufacturing with finished lumber for making furniture. No one knew it, but they had a similar arrangement with selling moonshine. Besides that, it was worth the trip just for the opportunity to lay eyes on Claudene.

It was late afternoon by the time Dalton jolted nosily to a stop in front of the Culveyhouse's two-story log house nestled in a grove of pines, sending chickens and other varmints scattering in all directions. He climbed from the cab and, in moments, appeared like a genie from a magic lantern out of the cloud of dust stirred up by the truck.

"Shut up Bone…be quiet Lady" shouted Claudell at the two blue tick hounds raising a ruckus at Dalton's unannounced appearance. Claudell, a strapping twenty-five-year-old, sat whittling on the front porch steps of the old house, surrounded by clutter and begging for repairs, that had been home to several generations of Culveyhouse's.

"Hello Claudell." said Dalton, "How ya doin' these days?"

"Howdy Mr. Jackson," said Claudell, folding up his pocketknife and laying aside the cedar stick on which he had been whittling.

"Helloooh Daaalton," purred a feminine voice from the other end of the porch.

Dalton turned in the direction of the voice.

There was Claudene, lying in the porch swing, coyly twisting one of two blonde pigtails between her fingers. The girl had more woman packed into her body than its seventeen years could hold. A pair of cutoff jeans covered little of two long legs, one extended across a swing arm, the other draped over the back. A red-checked halter top strained at the seams to keep two ample breasts from escaping its confines.

"He…he…hello, Miss Claudene," stammered Dalton tipping his hat to her. It's funny how a sexy female can reduce any man, no matter how big and tough, to a babbling idiot. Yes, it was worth the trip to see Claudene.

Elsie Culveyhouse came out of the house onto the porch, letting the screen door slam behind her. Standing with hands on hips, she inspected Dalton up and down.

A graying woman in her fifties, Elsie was as country as they came; a woman who, in spite of a face and hands that bore the toll of years of hard work, maintained a pioneer's fortitude. Born and raised in the mountains, the only place she had ever walked on concrete sidewalks was in Coldwater.

"Well, land sakes, if hit ain't Dalton Jackson. Since ye never make social calls, I'm a-guessin' ye got some bis'ness on yore mind."

"Yes ma'am, that's true enough. Is Mr. Cul…"

Before he could finish his question, Herman Hayworth Culveyhouse III came storming around the house toting a 12-gauge shotgun.

"What'n tarnation's goin' on? What's all tha fuss about?"

"Nothing to get alarmed about Mr. Culveyhouse. It's just me," said Dalton.

[85]

"Dalton Jackson! Well, I'll be damned! Whatcha mean ridin' in here like tha damned Marines scarin' tha hell outta man an beast?" protested Herman.

"I'm sorry Sir. I was just in a hurry to git outta that dusty truck," apologized Dalton. "If ya only had a telephone, I wouldn't even hav'ta come all the way out here and bother ya at all."

"Ain't got no need fer them newfangled contraptions. Cost money! Besides, they's a gov'ment conspir'cy ta keep tabs on people. Don't trust 'em," ranted Herman matter-of-factly.

Herman Culveyhouse had lived on this land his entire life, just as his father and grandfather had before him, carrying on the family tradition: making moonshine. Herman was as rough as a corn cob, ornary as a mule, and could be as mean as a sack full of rattlesnakes when he got his feathers ruffled.

Elsie interrupted, "Paw, Dalton's here on bizness matters, but I wuz just gettin' ready to put supper on tha table. Been cookin' up that 'possum Claudell brought in this mornin' an some turnip greens! Claudene, set another place at the table fer Dalton so's he can join us. Tain't often we have comp'ny ta break bread with. After supper, we'll git a jug an talk some bizness."

Dalton wilted at the thought of the 'possum and greens, "Oh, *joy!*" he thought.

At the dinner table, Claudene took a seat next to Dalton. All through the meal she made eyes at him and would occasionally reach down and squeeze his leg. Dalton, with great difficulty, made an effort to ignore her flirtatious gestures and was relieved when the meal was finally over.

When they were all seated comfortably in the living room, Elsie passed around a jug of the clearest, smoothest shine this side of the Smokies. Old Dalton took two or three swigs to try and settle his stomach full of greasy meat and greens that Elsie kept dishing out to him. Between burps, he filled them in on the Atlanta order request.

"Hell, Dalton. You know we can't fill no outta' town order this time'a year," protested Herman.

"By gum, don't them 'air city folks know shine season's in tha fall, September ta November?" added Elsie.

"You have stock, don't you?" asked Dalton.

[86]

"Ya, but that's mostly fer air local folks," said Herman. "It'd 'bout clean us out ta give'em what they want."

"They'll pay big for it," said Dalton, "and we could probly persuade'em to pay double."

"Double?" Elsie's eyes lit up.

"Jus thank, Paw. Fifty George Washingtons a gallon. That'd be a mighty hansome payday."

"Hit'll take a week er so ta rig up a container to transfer the juice an another couple'a days ta deliver hit air usual way," estimated Herman.

"The Atlanta boys will be happy as long as we can get it there within two weeks," said Dalton assuredly.

"Might be cuttin' hit a mite close but we aught ta make hit," said Herman stroking his whiskers.

"Could you speed up the process a little?" pleaded Dalton.

"Hell no!" declared Herman firmly pounding his fist on the table.

"That's why we've had success fer so long. Doin' it right. No shortcuts."

"Besides, I don't cotton ta breakin' the routine, doin' things outta season."

"But it's my ass that's on tha line with Atlanta," said Dalton.

"And hit's our asses on tha line if'n we get caught. If'n hit don't suit ye, find another supplier," offered Herman.

"They's others in the mountains makin' shine," said Elsie.

"Yeah! But, you're the best. I want you," admitted Dalton.

"Okay, let me know when you have the product ready to go. I'll work out things with Atlanta."

"Well, boys an girls, hit's a-gettin' late an time ta hit the hay," said Elsie, looking at the clock on the mantle.

All the Culveyhouse's, especially Claudene, tried to sell Dalton on the wisdom of spending the night and getting an early start back to Coldwater the next morning. At first, he was somewhat apprehensive about staying overnight with this backwoods family. They did seem like good people, as much as he knew about them, but, at the same time, mountain people were a different lot; they had ways and ideas that were strange to people he was used to being around. But, thinking about trying to traverse that cow path of a road back to the main highway in the dark convinced him to accept their invitation.

He didn't, however, quite know what to make of Claudene's gestures when she winked at him and gave him a thumbs-up sign.

Chapter 20

That night

Dalton pulled the sheet over him, laid back on the pillow, and studied the shadows cast about by the bright moonlight that flooded through the open loft bedroom window. He thought about his hosts and their country ways to which he was unaccustomed and about the flirtatious Claudene in the bedroom just below his. He also thought of Herman and his warning about not forgetting whose room was where while he loaded both chambers of his double-barreled shotgun with a sly smile.

Dalton had just gotten settled in and was drifting off to sleep when he suddenly felt a strange presence in the bed. He slowly reached across his back and, at the touch of warm flesh, shivered from head to toe. Without warning, the sheet flew back and the source of that warm flesh was straddling him…it was Claudene!

From the moonlight illuminating the room he could see her clearly. The blond hair, no longer in pigtails, fell in long strands around her bare shoulders.

"Claudene! What are you doing here?" whispered the startled Dalton.

"We'a gonna have some fun!" whispered Claudene back excitedly.

Dalton knew exactly what kind of "fun" the young girl had in mind.

"Claudene, we can't do this!"

"Why not?"

"In the first place, I'm a married man. In the second, you're just a kid."

"Wouldn't ye like ta make love ta me?"

"Well…but that's not the point. The point is we'll be heard and your daddy'll come in here with that 12-gauge and blow my ass to kingdom come."

"Look," said Claudene putting her nose right in Dalton's face, "As you may have noticed, there ain't a big selection of men around here. I gotta get my satisfaction whenever I get a chance to. So, the way I see it, ya have two choices. You can make love to me or I start screaming bloody murder."

"Oh, no, Claudene, don't do that."

"Your choice sweetheart," she purred like a cat with a mouse by the throat.

"Okay, you win. But keep it quiet, please," pleaded Dalton.

Just then they heard the sound of a pair of size twelve clodhoppers trudging up the stairwell. It had to be Herman. Dalton began to sweat. His fears were momentarily confirmed when he heard Herman.

"Claudene! Where are you?"

Dalton grabbed Claudene, dragged her to the window, and pushed her out onto the roof.

"What are you doing?" she protested.

"Getting rid of the thing that's about to get me a ticket to the other side," he said franticly.

"Other side of what?"

"Never mind what...just go!"

Dalton took a flying leap into bed and jerked the covers up just as Herman bolted in with shotgun in hand.

"Seems Claudene is missing. Wouldn't be hidin' out in here would she?"

"Oh! No sir, haven't seen the girl since supper," Dalton lied, hopefully convincingly.

"Okay then," said the man after staring about for a minute or two.

Dalton didn't sleep much the rest of that night. He anticipated the break of dawn when he could make his exodus from these premises.

The next morning

They all engaged in small talk while chowing down on a breakfast of biscuits and gravy that Elsie and Claudene cooked up.

"Did ya sleep well Dalton?" asked Elsie.

"Yes ma'am. I slept just fine." Dalton blushed.

Before he could answer, Herman said, "Thought I hear'd some noise up there once. That's why I come up there an checked on ya."

"Oh, no sir. No problem. Everything was fine."

After finalizing their agreement that the Culveyhouses would have the goods in Coldwater by the middle of the following week and saying their goodbyes, Dalton cranked up his Toyota and began his trek back down the mountain. As he pulled out, he glanced at

Claudene leaning against the porch, her hair back in pigtails, and gave her a quick grin.

In the rearview mirror, he saw her give him a nod of the head and dainty hand wave, and he hoped that he never had to deal with this bunch of crazy mountain people again.

Chapter 21

Gathered in a back room of the Sheriff's office was the most unlikely mix of Christians and sinners, Ridgers and Millies, city boys and hillbillies, politicians and blue collars one could ever imagine. Some restlessly paced the floor, others semi-relaxed on chairs and couches, all sipped glasses of Jim Beam. Sheriff Coker had called an emergency meeting of this unholy alliance consisting of himself, Mayor McKean, Deputy Odom, Dalton Jackson, Clifton Ledbetter, Herman Hayworth Culveyhouse III, and Jonas Franklin to address a recently developed situation; a situation that would have a most adverse effect upon their common business interests, not to mention their personal lives, unless a solution was found.

"Just what's this 'problem' that's so serious and urgent to deal with that you've summoned us here on such short notice," asked Dalton (who was the real brains of the operation) walking around refilling everyone's glasses with a generous portion of whiskey.

The Sheriff swallowed half his glass and grimaced as the alcohol burned a path to his stomach. Standing in the middle of the room, he addressed the group.

"Well, I only chew my cabbage once, so pay attention. There's an individual outside'a this group who knows 'bout our little operation."

"What!" exclaimed half the members as they all sat up straight in their chairs.

"They don't know much, just gotta general idee. An, they don't know 'bout anybody but me an tha mayor being involved."

"Well, sounds ta me like ye an tha Mayer's tha ones got a problim, not us," spoke up Clifton Ledbetter.

"Dammit to hell, Clifton," yelled Buford, throwing his hands up into the air, raining whiskey over half the room, "The mayor and I are not goin' to be fall guys!"

"But I only run tha sawmill," said Clifton innocently.

"*I only run tha sawmill*," parroted the Sheriff in a child-like mocking voice.

"Git this straight, asshole. Y'all are just as much'a part'a this organization as anybody 'round this here table. We all gotta equal part ta play in makin' tha operation work; we all gotta equal responsibility ta do whatever's gotta be done ta protect ourselves; an we all share equally in tha consequences if sumpin' goes wrong."

"Now," continued Buford addressing the whole group, "this person knowing what they know is gonna 'cause big trouble an sumpin's gotta be done about it 'cause if'n I go down, I guarantee you, I won't go down alone."

"Seems ta be a easy 'nuf remedy ta tha problem ta me," offered Herman Culveyhouse, "L'es jes kill the sum'bitch. Ya know they's been people disappear up in them mountains never to be heared of agin," he added, spitting tobacco juice into an empty tin can.

"Or wound up fish bait in Little River," added Jonas Franklin.

"It ain't gonna be that easy, even if we wanted to resort to killin'," responded the Sheriff.

"Look, makin' an sellin' shine's one thang, but I ain't getting' mixed up in murder," protested Clifton, jumping up from his chair.

"By the way, who is this individual that we're talking about?" asked Dalton.

The Sheriff looked at the mayor.

Mayor McKean spoke up, "Her name's Marjorie Henderson...goes by Marge."

"It's a woman?" the whole group sang in unison.

"Who's Marge Henderson?" asked Jonas.

"Some lonely housewife who gets her kicks when her husband's out of town by playing games as one of Miss Jessie's girls," said the mayor.

"And just how did this 'party girl' (Dalton makes air quotes with his fingers) happen to come by this information 'bout you gentlemen and our business venture?" inquired Dalton.

Again, Buford and the mayor looked at each other for a minute before the Sheriff took the initiative to speak.

"Ya see, fellers, me an tha mayor was over at Miss Jessie's one night a while back... with Marge... havin' a little fun together... just tha three of us... ya see... "

"We get the picture!" said Dalton, shaking his head from side to side.

"We didn't know who she was...we'd never met her before," interjected the mayor.

"Anyhow," continued Buford, "when it was over, she got dressed in a hurry an left, or so we thought. The mayor an me took our time getting' dressed an were talkin' over some things while we did."

"So the cat's outta tha bag 'bout air operation 'cause you two damn fools been out bustin' yer balls with this Marge whore with yer tongues waggin' as loose as yer peckers," spoke up an aggravated Herman Culveyhouse.

Mayor McKean interrupted, "But we thought we were talkin' in private. We didn't have any idea she was apparently listening outside tha door. We didn't know until tha next day when she called tha Sheriff an repeated ta him everything we had talked about."

"So, she must be wantin' sumthin. What is it?" asked a nervous Clifton Ledbetter.

"She wants ten thousand dahlas," answered the Sheriff.

"Hit figgurs. Blackmail! She wants ta be paid ta keep quiet 'bout what she knows," deduced Jonas.

"So, whatta we do?" asked Sheriff Buford looking around the room, polling each man with his eyes, beginning with his deputy.

"One thang's fer sure, I ain't goin' to jail because of her," responded Deputy Odom shrugging his shoulders.

"I say we pay her," said Clifton.

"I vote ta remove tha problem," said Herman Culveyhouse, plunking a .45 revolver down on the table matter of factly.

"I second the vote," added Jonas raising his right hand.

Then silence filled the room as all eyes turned to Dalton, waiting in hushed anticipation to see and hear what his reaction to the situation would be.

"What say ye Mr. Jackson, or should I ask what will tha Big Boss'll say?" posed the Sheriff.

Caught up in the concoction of their own personal remedies for the predicament they found themselves facing, they had temporarily failed to remember that there was a "big boss" of this outfit whose only communication with them was through Dalton Jackson and whose identity was known only to Dalton. The Big Boss wasn't originally involved with this motley crew and its clandestine affairs and even after discovering its presence, à la Marjorie Henderson, questioned the wisdom of being associated with such a Black Collar business.

After considering the potential profits that could be made, Big Boss decided instead to take control of the operation, functioning incognito behind the scenes, known only as Big Boss with a trusted colleague acting as the front man. The members of the ring all respected Dalton both for his position at Longworth Furniture and for his position at the righthand of the Big Boss' table. Some members of the ring speculated that the two were one and the same.

"To your first question, it's my own opinion that if you start paying, you'll never stop. A blackmailer will keep comin' back for more and more," answered Dalton.

"As for your second question, since this is the first time I've been informed of the matter, I'll have to take it up with the Big Boss an see what kind of reaction it elicits."

"Now hold on just a minute. You haven't heard the whole story yet. There's more to consider than just whether to pay blackmail money or not, or, God forbid, whether to kill a person or not. It's a bit more complicated than just dealing with Ms. Henderson," warned Mayor McKean.

"Tell them Sheriff."

"Mrs. Henderson claims that she wrote a letter addressed to the District Attorney documentin' everything that she knows, put it in a safety deposit box at tha First National Bank, an gave Mr. Stanley Penrod, the bank president, instructions ta place that letter in tha mail in tha case of her demise," stated the Sherriff.

"I'll be damned!" yelled Jonas, "you two S.O.B.'s shore got us inna plate fulla shit, didn't ye?"

"Tha bitch's got'us by tha balls, ain't she?" lamented Clifton Ledbetter.

"One thang's clear," spoke up Deputy Odom, "regardless of what's done 'bout the woman, we gotta get that letter first."

"Deputy Odom's right," agreed Dalton, "we gotta come up with some plan to get that letter."

"Now jest a doggone minute," interrupted Herman Culveyhouse. "Maybe this here letter or even this here woman's not tha problim. Maybe hit's this here lawman and politician that we needs ta git rid uv. She don't know squat' 'bout tha rest uv us an with these here two horny idiots outta tha way, who cud she accuse?"

Sheriff Coker, red-faced and smoking-mad, charged Herman Culveyhouse like a raging bull and grabbed the shoulder straps of his overalls, one in each hand.

"Ye sorry-assed, backwoods bastard! You're dumb as a bucket of hammers if ya think ya can get rid of the mayor and me ta save some piece of work like yourself?"

Suddenly, in a squall of pain, the Sheriff went staggering backward, his hands wiping furiously at his burning eyes trying to clear them of the acrid tobacco juice shot with blinding accuracy from between Herman's clenched teeth.

With all eyes on Buford, no one saw the .45 revolver in Herman's hand, but the sound of its report resounding through the room sent everyone ducking to the floor, all except Buford. The bullet grazed his head taking a piece of his left ear with it. Deputy Odom's hand grasped the handle of the pistol in his holster but he thought better about drawing it after Herman issued him a warning.

"Don't even giv'it a thought cowboy," warned Herman pointing his weapon right at him.

"I jes give yer boss man a warnin' but I'll blow a hole thru yer gullet ye can stick yer arm through. Ye tell that excuse fer a Sherf if'n' he ever comes up ta my mountin' agin I'll blast that fancy tin star out his ass."

"As fer tha rest uv ye," he said addressing the whole assembly, "do what ye please 'bout tha whore an her letter. Tain't my bis'ness nohow. B'sides, hit's gittin' late in tha day an I need ta be gittin' back up tha mountain. An another thang. We's supposed ta be delivern a order fer Atlanta next week. If ye want it, ye better get this mess settled or I won't be cumin' back down the mountain any time soon."

And with that, Herman Hayworth Culveyhouse III exited the premises.

Buford, with his head hanging over the kitchen sink as he flushed the remaining drops of Red Coon tobacco sputum from his eyes, was as mad as a dog that had had his last bone jerked out from under his nose.

"That crazy hillbilly nearly blinded me an then nearly killed me!" stormed Buford, "I'm…"

Before the Sherriff could continue, Dalton Jackson, the only one in the bunch who had a brain in his head, took charge and got everyone calmed down from the brain cloud they were adrift in and refocused on the original purpose for the meeting. After the preceding that had just taken place, Dalton realized that the chances of this gaggle of misfits reaching an agreement on a sensible and workable solution to the problem at hand was about as likely as Dr. Martin Luther King, Jr. joining the Ku Klux Klan.

It was also his inclination that when push came to shove, none of them, with the possible exception of Herman Hayworth Culveyhouse, had the gumption to take that "pull-the-trigger" step even if it came down to a choice between that or growing old in Blackstone Federal Prison. Dalton convinced the others that he thought he might know of a way to get their mess cleaned up without involving any of them directly. It would probably cost them, but better to pay a one-time service fee to an outside "cleaner" than to remain under the squeeze of an unpredictable blackmailer. They were glad to give Dalton the go-ahead to take care of things anyway he could get them accomplished, as long as they didn't have to dirty their hands.

Dalton didn't waste any time taking care of business. The first thing next morning, in the privacy of his office, Dalton dialed LW's private number and waited for an answer. He wasn't anxious to make this call for he expected the big boss to be as freaked out as the others over this newly developed and potentially explosive situation that could take little to reach critical mass and blow up in all their faces. After several rings, he heard the familiar voice at the other end. He summarized for LW the minutes of the meeting the day before concerning Marge Henderson, who she was, and how she had obtained certain damning information about their enterprise, the letter she had written relative to said information, and the optional solutions that had been identified by which to resolve the problem. His expectations were not unfounded. The big boss was more than a little concerned to say the least, his responses running a gamut of emotions. LW was, however, more frightened than anything, being in a personal position to lose more than anyone else in case things did go south.

"Dalton, it's an ill wind that blows nobody good!" said a worried LW. "I trust you to take care of the problem in whatever way you deem necessary for all our sakes. I don't care how you handle it, and don't want to know. Just handle it."

"Okay. Maybe there's a way to get it done and keep us out of it locally." After gathering his thoughts, he dialed a number in Atlanta.

"This is Dalton Jackson up north. Let me speak to Mr. Logano."

"Mista Jackson," answered a voice laced with a southern drawl.

"Hello, Mr. Logano?" asked Dalton.

"Ya know you're suppose t'call this numba only in case of an emergency," said Louie Logano, better known as "Shooter" to most of his associates.

"Yes sir, I know. But, you might say this is an emergency for both of us. We have a problem that needs, shall we say, some *attention* soon," responded Dalton.

"And just how is it an emergency for both of us?"

Dalton explained in detail the situation in Coldwater to Shooter, just as he had to LW, and emphasized the consequences it could have for his people as well as for them locally if the woman talked or the letter got out. Shooter was outraged! He went off like a Roman Candle at the prospect of the Feds possibly getting a scent on a trail that might lead south to his people. Now their security had been compromised because some ding-dong, hick Sheriff had jabbered like a magpie while humping a whore. He agreed that the situation had to be rectified…and soon!

"Well now Mr. D, correct me if I'm wrong, but it sounds like you ah tellin' me that y'all created this problem, put ow'er bizness in jeopardy, an now y'all are soliciting our assistance ta save yoh hillbilly asses."

"Yes sir. You assume correctly. It's the kind of problem I believe you businessmen in the big city have more experience in dealing with than we little country boys do."

"My bosses are going to find this news most distressin' for they just don't cotton ta screwups that make life difficult. This screwup Sheriff might have ta be called on tha carpet, too, if ya know what I mean," warned Shooter.

"Oh, no," assured Dalton, "that won't be necessary. We'll take care of that on our side."

"Well sur, at any rate, it's gonna cost ya!"

"Understood," answered Dalton, "as they say, there are no free lunches."

Chapter 22

It was a hot, muggy afternoon. Lincoln, wrapped in a blanket of melancholy, trudged heavy-footed along a downtown Coldwater side street. The battleship gray sky matched his mood as he moseyed along, head down, arms pushed deep into pants pockets, aimlessly kicking an empty beer can along in front of him. Thoughts felt like a whirlwind spinning between his ears with more things being randomly tossed about than his mind could keep up with at the moment: the prom, Ashley Armstrong, father's beating, Marge Henderson, his job, and the newly discovered moonshiners. Periods of depression that just seemed to come out of nowhere were becoming more frequent, as were the migraines, punctuated with feelings of doom and gloom. He was having trouble making heads or tails of it all. At times like these, he needed to get away by himself to think; to try and sort out his feelings.

There was one particular place of solitude he liked to go at times like this; it was a place he and Rats went camping from time to time. Speaking of Rats, he had finally broken down and told him the truth about the debacle his "date" with Marge had turned out to be. Rats had thought it was hilarious, as Lincoln knew he would. On another note, he had decided to keep something he had seen and heard at the sawmill a secret, even from Rats, at least for the time being.

Lincoln was so absorbed in his subconscious world that he failed to hear the "honk" of the car horn. His brain did, however, respond to the second "honk" and his sidewalk-focused eyes were redirected to the street and the outline of a car pulling up beside him. Now fully alert and in control of his faculties, the white Thunderbird came clearly into view and his attention was quickly drawn to the driver behind the steering wheel.

Ashley Armstrong was eyeing him with both a frown and look of concern etched into her pretty face. It had been three weeks since the prom and, in that time, he had become resigned to the fact that Ashley Armstrong was to become an old man's memory of a young man's dream, and it showed.

"Are you okay?" asked Ashley.

"Yeah, I'm okay" answered Lincoln with a shrug of the shoulders, trying to force a smile.

"I didn't expect to see you out this way, but I'm glad I ran in to you." observed Ashley.

Lincoln had been so caught up in his thoughts that he had wandered several blocks west of the hotel which, as Ashley had correctly observed, he very seldom ventured into this side of town. There was no particular reason other than he just never had any business on the west side.

"Yes, you're right. I was just wandering…thinking."

Ashley patted the passenger side seat with her hand, "Like to go for a ride?"

"Do you think I…*we*…should?"

"Let's go someplace we can talk undisturbed. Do you know a good place?"

"As a matter of fact, I do. I was just thinking about going there. But, we'll have to cross the river."

Lincoln directed the stylishly dressed blonde along some back streets around town to avoid visibility and had her stop a short distance from the ferry. Determining that there were no other cars waiting to cross the river, they decided that it would be safe to cross on the ferry together. Ashley eased the T-Bird onto the old ferry boat and, at the direction of Obee Franklin, stopped in the center of the boat and turned off the engine.

Jonas Franklin, a cantankerous widower in his sixties, had owned and operated the ferry for many years as his father had before him. He always wore a pair of bib overalls and clodhopper shoes; a worn-out straw hat covered a mop of stringy gray hair hanging down over his ears. When he smiled, his unshaven face exposed what was left of two rows of tobacco-stained teeth.

He was assisted in the ferry's operation by his only child and son Obadiah (whom everyone called Obee), as much help as any person of Obee's mental capacity was capable of helping, that is.

Obee was a thirty-five-year-old man-child; a gapped-out, functional illiterate who, due to an accident when a youngster, never knew what day of the week it was or who was president. When Obee was about ten years old, he took exception to a Billy goat butting him from behind and proceeded to challenge the goat to a butting contest. Well, the goat won and ever since, ole Obee's been dumb as a post.

Jonas cranked up the engine of the little tugboat tethered to the side of the ferry and it began to push the big car carrier across the clear waters of Little River.

"That'll be four bits young lady," said Jonas walking up to Ashley's car.

"Yes, sir. There you are," she replied handing the man two quarters.

Jonas Franklin just stared at the girl for a minute, glanced at Lincoln, then turned and walked over to a small house-like enclosure on the ferry and took a seat.

Obee, dressed in the same attire as his father, began to slowly circle the shiny white sports car with its immaculate red leather interior and look it over like a prospective buyer on a used car lot. When his inspection fell upon the driver, as it frequently did, dressed in tight white slacks and red halter top like one of the car's color-coordinated accessories, his buck teeth would show through a wide grin while his hand made a swipe across his bald head. He never looked at Lincoln.

Ashley sat very uncomfortably in the car and tried to avoid looking in the direction of either of the two men. She and Lincoln made small talk and listened to music on the radio to pass the time, wishing the crossing would go faster. Lincoln had made the ferry crossing many times, but this one seemed to be taking an unusually long time.

"What kind of cattle are those over there?" asked Ashley of Lincoln, pointing to a pasture field on the near side of the river. She was just making conversation.

"I believe those are Black Angus," he answered back.

"That's a big bunch of cows, ain't it?" interrupted Obee.

"Not bunch, herd," said Lincoln.

"Heard what?" asked Obee.

"Herd of cows," answered Lincoln.

"Shore I've heard of cows," said Obee, a bit annoyed.

"No, Obee. A cow herd."

"Well, why shud I care what a cow heard? I got no secrets frum a cow!"

"Oh! Never mind Obee."

"Come over here'n si'down, Obee," called his father.

"I jus a-lookin' at tha purty car, Pa."

"Yeah, I know what yer a-lookin' at!"

"I'd like ta touch it an feel how smooth it is, Pa," grinned Obee.

"Yeah, me too," whispered Jonas under his breath, staring at Ashley like a hungry man eyeballing a juicy steak.

"Now come si'down!"

Chapter 23

"Ever been up on top of the bluff?" Lincoln asked.

"No. I didn't even know you could go up there," she replied.

"There's a level place near the top in front of a cave that has a great view. Not many people know about it. Rats and I come up here and camp sometimes."

With Lincoln leading and Ashley following closely behind, they scaled the hundred yards or so up a narrow footpath through pine trees and shrubs and around and over rocks to the place Lincoln had described. Exhausted from the climb, both of them let out a lung-emptying breath of air. For a couple of minutes, they just stood there, staring across the expanse of country that lay open before them; a view afforded only by this bird's-eye vantage point high upon the bluff.

"Wow," exclaimed Ashley, "it's just like you said, 'a great view.'"

"No, I take that back. It's *awesome!*"

From this lofty perch one could see up and down the length of Little River, across Milltown and the mills, and all along The Ridge. On a clear day, one could see across the Smokies into North Carolina to the east and everything west in the direction of Knoxville.

"It's too bad its overcast today," observed Lincoln.

"On a clear day you can see for miles in every direction."

"Gives you a different perspective on our hometown, doesn't it?" said Ashley thoughtfully.

"Sometimes when I'm up here, I imagine God looking down on us like this and wondering what he thinks about us," pondered Lincoln.

Ashley looked at him thoughtfully.

"That's an interesting point of view."

They sat down in some makeshift "lounge chairs" made out of scrap wood and tree branches that Lincoln and Rats had made during some previous visit and placed near the edge of the bluff.

"Why did you offer me a ride today?" Lincoln asked curiously. "I thought I would be someone to be avoided like the plague."

"You are! I've been ordered to stay away from you and any of your 'kind,' if you catch my drift," answered Ashley rolling her eyes.

"So, what else is new!" he said shrugging his shoulders.

"I've been out driving around some the last few days hoping I'd run into you," said Ashley.

"Why?"

"I wanted to talk with you."

"Sounds like a direct violation of your orders."

"Yes, it does, doesn't it?"

"And what's the penalty for breaking the law?"

"Daddy says he'll take away my car."

Lincoln gapes at Ashley in wonderment.

"Why would you risk losing your T-Bird to talk with me?" he exclaimed in disbelief.

"As I said, I want to talk with you about something."

"What?"

"That night at the prom, why did you ask me to dance?"

Lincoln leaned back, cupped his hands behind his head, and thought carefully about how much to confess to this "girl of his dreams" about his feelings for her. He knew now, and probably always had, that the chances of his dreams of him and Ashley becoming a Prince Charming and Cinderella story were as remote as a man flying to the moon. So, he decided to just spill his guts and let the chips fall where they may with Ashley. What did he have to lose other than be embarrassed beyond belief?

He sat up and leaned forward in his seat, placed his hands in a prayerful pose, and looked straight at Ashley.

"For the past four years I've had a crush on you, thinking that you're the prettiest, nicest girl in school," began Lincoln in a most sincere tone of voice. "I've watched you with guys in your circle of friends and wished I could be as lucky as them. I've imagined what it would be like to have you for a girlfriend. I guess you could say I've loved, if I could use that word, you from afar, in my dreams."

Lincoln stood up and walked to the edge of the bluff, staring across the valley below.

"From this lofty height, Coldwater looks so picturesque, so peaceful and inviting. One could conjure up in one's mind sites along its streets reminiscent of scenes from a Norman Rockwell canvas. But looks can be deceiving—like a façade covering an old building or a cover enclosing the pages of a book. Only with a behind-the-scenes inspection can one know what lies within. Only by living in Coldwater can one know of the invisible walls that divide its inhabitants; only one born and raised here can be aware of the darkness that poisons the town's heart and soul; only one victimized by its engrained traditions can know of the town's true nature; it's a town without pity."

Ashley rose from her place of rest and walked over to the bluff's edge a few feet from where Lincoln stood and surveyed the same scene, waiting silently to see if Lincoln was going to say anything further. Lincoln, staring at the ground and shuffling one foot in some loose gravel, continued.

"We live in the same town, in two different parts of the same town, and therefore, in two very different worlds. And, I know that for a boy like me to have a fantasy like this for a girl like you is just a pipedream, and I'm probably making a total fool of myself telling you all this," confessed Lincoln, turning his bowed head toward Ashley with an apologetic but serious grin.

Ashley, who had also been gazing at the ground as Lincoln spoke, smiled and tilted her head toward Lincoln.

They caught each other's grins out of the corners of their eyes and smiled.

"I'm taking a long time to answer your question aren't I? Anyway, that night at the prom, I realized that there could never be anything between us but I thought that maybe I could at least say that I danced with you one time in my life. So, I took a chance!"

After a minute of silence, Ashley asked, "Are you finished?"

"Yes," answered Lincoln with a deep breath, "I think I've said way too much already!"

"You're *really* in love with me?"

"Crazy, head over heels…I know you must find that pretty ridiculous."

"Not at all, Lincoln. I think it's sweet and I'm flattered." "Back to the prom, did you think about what consequences there might have been in you just asking me to dance?"

"Yes, Rats thought I was crazy. He was afraid there'd be a riot and that we'd get into it with Billy Ray Coker and his buddies. They were just looking for an excuse to start something."

"Billy Ray Coker's a jerk!" interjected Ashley.

"Anyway, I told Rats that I didn't care, and right at that moment I didn't, I was going for it."

[105]

"Now, let me ask you a question," said Lincoln.

"Okay."

"When I asked you to dance, why did you accept? For some reason, you seemed to take a while to make up your mind," he added.

"In the first place, I was shocked. I couldn't believe what you were doing. Then I noticed that everyone had just stopped and was watching to see how I was going to respond. I could have just politely said 'no' and everything would have gone on as usual, but then I saw an opportunity. The situation that exists between social classes and races in Coldwater is no different than what the civil rights movement across the country is all about, just on a smaller scale. I saw a chance to take a stand *against* prejudice and bigotry and *for* equality in our school and community. So, like you, I went for it," affirmed Ashley.

"So, you didn't say 'yes' because you wanted to dance with me. You did it to make a political statement, to take a social stance," said Lincoln.

"I didn't say that...exactly. Although it was, as I said, an opportunity to do that. I wouldn't have said 'yes' if it had been anyone other than you asking me to dance."

"Really?" replied Lincoln suspiciously.

"I didn't say 'yes' just to take advantage of a situation. I said 'yes' to you because I like you, and I wanted to dance with you. I knew it would cause a sensation and get me in big trouble with my parents, and a lot of my friends, but at that moment I didn't really care."

"I guess we did cause a *sensation* didn't we," laughed Lincoln.

"I think that's an understatement," answered Ashley laughing out loud with Lincoln.

"And how about Montgomery! He sure added some fuel to the fire," said Lincoln, reminding Ashley of Montgomery Longworth dancing with Amanda Cross.

"Wow, talk about a shocker out of the blue," answered Ashley.

"She was your date wasn't she?"

"Yes."

"Did you know anything about her and Montgomery's relationship?" asked Ashley.

"No. Amanda and I have known one another for many years and have been friends—not in a girlfriend-boyfriend kinda way—just friends. But, I've never heard her mention Montgomery in any way. How about you? You and he are good friends. Ever hear him mention her in any way?"

"On a few occasions I remember him saying he thought she was a cute girl, but nothing to indicate that they were secretly dating."

"I can imagine that little poisonous pill has been as hard for his parent's southern pride to swallow as it is to still admit today that the south really did lose the war," offered Lincoln.

"You're right about that, and not just his parents!"

Ashley goes into character, striking the pose of an actress on stage with the back of her hand resting delicately against her forehead, head tilted slightly up and to the right, and begins a sarcastic, dramatic soliloquy.

"The good names of generations of Armstrongs and Longworths have been blackened, suffering such a socially disparaging offense from which it may never recover and be able to recapture its rightful and honorable place among the elite of southern gentility."

"Or so said in somewhat the words of Victoria Armstrong," said Ashley as she relaxed and turned to face Lincoln.

"I assume Montgomery has also been ordered to stay away from Amanda," said Lincoln in the way of a question.

"Oh, of course!"

"And if he doesn't?"

"Mr. Longworth says he'll fire Amanda's father from his job at the furniture factory."

"*What!*" shouted Lincoln angrily, "That dirty, lowlife son of a..."

Lincoln caught himself and looked at Ashley apologetically.

"It's time to go," Ashley said quietly and headed toward the path leading down the bluff.

Back in Coldwater

After returning to the town side of the river, Ashley dropped Lincoln off at an inconspicuous spot where there was little chance of them being seen together. The return trip had been spent in relative silence, their only communication being eye contact through the occasional exchange of glimpses at each other.

As Lincoln watched Ashley drive away, he thought about his feelings and tried to piece together just what had occurred in this exchange between him and the Ridger girl. He had just spent an afternoon with Ashley Armstrong, just the two of them! They had learned much about one another and she had even said that she liked him. Their dialog had been positive but had ended so abruptly and on a strange note that he was left confused as to where he stood with the girl.

Although they had agreed to meet again and that Ashley would call him at the hotel when the time was right, what did the future hold? Was there really a future out there where equal opportunity was assured, people were judged on their integrity and not their monetary worth, and everyone respected the rights of others? Lincoln wondered.

Chapter 24

Two weeks after Dalton's trip to Thunder Mountain

Lincoln had worked the second shift at the hotel that night and it was approaching the midnight hour when he clocked out, crossed Main Street, and headed for the shortcut home. It was not often that he had occasion to be out this late at night and when he did, it was his habit to take the lighted route through town. The shortcut could appear a bit spooky at night and, to be honest, was not the safest of places to be wandering around by one's self given its close proximity to Hobo Town just down the tracks. But, tonight he was tired and wanted to get home quickly.

As he was approaching Town Creek Road, he heard the deep-throated rumble from the burned-out exhaust pipes of the old log truck even before he saw it come lumbering around the bend. Concealing himself in the shadows to remain unseen, he waited for it to pass. Faded white letters spelling out "Culveyhouse Logging" were barely visible on the rusted-out door of what had once been a fire-engine red cab. He could make out the figures of three passengers, only one of whom he could identify for sure. That was old man Culveyhouse, riding shotgun with his arm hanging out the window, who turned in Lincoln's direction and launched a spit of tobacco juice into the wind. Lincoln assumed the other two were most likely his son Claudell at the wheel with daughter Claudene sandwiched in between.

Lincoln wasn't personally acquainted with the Culveyhouse clan; he knew them only by sight and reputation. Knowing that they sold timber to the sawmill, he saw their old log truck frequently going to and from the mill, and he had always heard the rumors about them making shine up in the mountains. But, it did seem a bit odd for them to be making a log run at this time of night. He looked at his watch: 11:55 p.m.

After the truck passed, Lincoln stepped out from his place of concealment only to suddenly jump back in at the sight of the emerging headlights of an automobile following a short distance behind the truck; it was Sheriff Coker's police cruiser. When the cruiser was safely past, he darted out into the middle of the road where he could, from that vantage point, see down the road as far as the railroad tracks. The log truck turned off on the road into the sawmill, as he expected it to, and so did the police cruiser. For some reason, this piqued Lincoln's interest.

He wondered why the Sheriff would be following the loggers— and alleged moonshiners—almost casually to the sawmill so late at night. He decided to get closer and see what he could find out. He wished Rats was there.

He slipped down the bank through the willow trees and crossed Town Creek. From there, he scurried across the open field and hid between two tall stacks of fresh-cut lumber a few yards from where the log truck had stopped with the Sheriff's car a short distance behind. Half a dozen or so men were huddled together in front of the truck headlights. With the aid of light from the truck and moon, he could easily identify them by the sounds of their voices.

There was the Sheriff and deputy Lester Odom, Herman Hayworth Culveyhouse, Clifton Ledbetter, who owned the sawmill, Clifton's foreman Charlie Bridger, Dalton Jackson, and "Boone" Bishop, one of Dalton's drivers. He also recognized Claudell Culveyhouse leaning against the fender of the log truck, seemingly uninterested, puffing on a cigarette and his sister Claudene, wandering around looking up at the stars.

Lincoln was able to pick up on pieces of conversation, some of which didn't make much sense to him.

"Well, tha baby's in tha cradle, safe'n sound," said Herman.

"It's a wonder it got here at all on that smoke-belching bucket of bolts an bailing wire that Culveyhouse passes off for something resembling a truck," grumbled the Sheriff.

Herman sent a lip-full of tobacco juice splattering on the dusty ground near the Sheriff's feet.

"Hey, watch the boots, you hillbilly," growled Buford skipping backwards.

"I autta arrest you an confiscate that piece'a junk an run'it in the river."

"Yeah, an how'd ye like me ta take this .45 an take off part of ye other ear, ye tin-badged cowboy?" growled Herman pointing the weapon at the Sheriff threateningly.

Dalton stepped in, "Okay, everyone just cool it!"

"We've got a job to do, so let's get it done."

"Sheriff…Herman, you both did your part. You got the baby here. Now it's our turn."

Dalton continued, "Clifton and Charlie, you get the logs off the truck and then Boone and I can get the baby into the house."

From the dark alleyway between the stacks of lumber that obscured his presence, Lincoln was both fascinated and somewhat shocked by what he was hearing. It was obvious to him that this assemblage of characters was involved in some kind of shady dealings, but what could be the common denominator that would draw such a dissimilar group of individuals together. And, who or what was the "baby?" He watched intently as the drama continued to unfold before his eyes.

After the law officers had left the scene, the big log loader came creeping slowly out of the darkness on its tank-track crawlers with Charlie Bridger at the controls manipulating the machine's single giant arm reminiscent of some pre-historic metal bird and began snaking logs off the truck bed two and three at a gulp as if they were toothpicks. In a matter of minutes, the truck bed, relieved of its burden of harvested trees, revealed a large home-fabricated steel cage bolted to it behind the cab, holding prisoner within it what must be *baby*: a large metal drum. Considering the source of the truck's cargo, it took but a small stretch of the imagination to guess what it contained. It had to be *moonshine*!

Claudell backed the truck up to one end of a loading dock where, unnoticed by Lincoln until now, there was parked at another side of the dock one of the Longworth Furniture Manufacturing trucks used for long hauls. Out of the back of the furniture truck whirled a forklift driven by Boone. He lifted the metal drum, which Dalton and Clifton had by now freed from its confines in the cage and moved it gingerly across the truck bed, over the loading dock, and into the furniture truck. Setting the load down near the front, the three men proceeded to wrap the baby up in a cardboard box of the same fashion as its furniture traveling companions. After branding it with identifying markings, they pushed other boxes around it.

"Well, the shipment's ready for our Atlanta customer," said Dalton.

The men stood around for a few minutes and shared a few laughs, puffed hand-rolled smokes, and passed around a Mason jar that

Clifton had opened. After some time of socializing, Dalton got them back on task.

"Boone, you take the truck on back to the mill and we'll finish loading it in the mornin' with the remainin' orders, then you can be on your way south."

"Okay boss," answered Boone.

In the meantime, Lincoln noticed Claudell and Claudene unloading a few small wooden boxes off the back of the truck that made clinking noises as they carried them inside Clifton Ledbetter's office. Lincoln was familiar with the distinctive clinking that Mason fruit jars make when they rattle against one another from carrying cases of them into their cellar when his mother canned vegetables in the summer, only he was sure these weren't filled with vegetables.

Before the Culveyhouses left the scene, Clifton handed Herman a roll of greenbacks.

"Here's payment fer tha jars," he said.

"Guess these are fer ye cousin as usual?"

"Yep, I'll take 'um to 'em down to the ferry ta'mar."

"Okay, good doin' business with ye. See ye nex time."

All the while, Lincoln had been taking in all the goings-on as bug-eyed as a frog watching a Jimmy Cagney movie at the Palace Theatre. He now understood this group's common denominator, the root of all evil, money! He was also impressed with the ingenuity of their system but could hardly believe this kind of operation was going on right here in Coldwater. Making shine, by the barrel, and shipping it all the way to Atlanta and keeping it concealed was not a small undertaking. And selling it locally at the ferry, wow!

He sat back against the stack of lumber for a minute relishing in this newfound knowledge that, by a mere stroke of luck, had been revealed to him. Now, he knew things that few, if any, in Coldwater, outside the conspirators involved, had any awareness of. It was a funny feeling. Knowledge gives one a sense of pride; a sense of power.

But then it dawned on him, knowledge can be a *dangerous* thing also, especially when it's related to the illegal pursuits of criminals and, more certainly, if it becomes known to those parties involved in such pursuits that one is in possession of such knowledge.

Suddenly, goose bumps of impending death that he had felt with such a sense of stark reality under the bed at Marge's house came crawling across his skin once more. In the course of one eventful evening, the stakes in the game of life for Lincoln Crockett had been, unexpectedly, anted up.

Unbeknown to Lincoln Crockett, it was only a matter of time until the stakes would go even higher.

Chapter 25

Temperatures were rising and July made its debut riding a heat wave, pushing the mercury in thermometers up to the ninety-degree mark. Accounting for the humidity, it seemed even a few sweltering notches above that. Shade, wherever it could be found outdoors, offered little relief from the sun's rays and, those who could, stayed indoors as much as possible where the temperature wasn't much better. But there was another heat wave rolling into town that Lincoln was about to get acquainted with; one with a different kind of heat but just as hot.

Leaning over one end of the check-in counter, Lincoln stood face to face with an old desk fan and tried to soak up as much of its breeze as he could. Lost in the fan's hypnotic humming, he was lost in the memories of the afternoon spent with Ashley on the bluffs that still lingered fresh in his mind.

So absorbed was he in his thoughts that he hadn't noticed the white limo bearing Georgia license plates that had arrived out front. A sudden blast from the driver's horn and the clamor of occupants embarking served to shake him from the doldrums, however, and realizing that he'd been caught unaware of new arrivals, scrambled toward the door to offer assistance.

Before he could reach the doors, two large men the size of Green Bay Packers linemen and dressed in black and white forged through the doors and held them open for the remainder of their party. At the rear of the procession lumbered a sumo wrestler-sized black man dressed in like manner as the first two hulks. All these three grim-faced, tough-looking characters needed were tommy guns hanging under their arms to look like gangsters out of a 1930s Humphrey Bogart movie.

Almost lost among the trees were a man and woman, diminutive in comparison to the stooges surrounding them, the man who was obviously the central figure in the entourage, and the woman, a piece of arm candy, whose role was to provide window dressing.

Louie "Shooter" Logano strutted in as if expecting a brass band to hail the arrival of a dignitary. Dressed in an off-white Pierre Cardin suit with matching fedora, pink silk shirt with a pink rose in the jacket's buttonhole, and brown, saddle oxford leather loafers, Louie (all five feet, four inches of him) marched up to the front desk and demanded to see the manager.

"Mr. Logano, I presume…accordin' to the registration. Welcome to the Lacy. My name's Jessica Wingo, owna an manag'a of the Lacy Hotel," greeted Jessica with her finest southern charm.

"Please accept my sincerest apologies for our failure ta have someone on hand ta greet you on yo'ah arrival at our fine establishment. Our bell boy was, unfortunately, detained… uh… assistin' other guests."

Louie, ready to vehemently protest what he considered rude treatment, was taken aback, not as much by the apology itself, as by the disarming manner in which it was articulated; the way in which the lady's words flowed over her tongue as smoothly and intoxicatingly as a taste of smooth Tennessee sipping whiskey.

"Well, Miss Jessica Wingo," Louie began, wiping perspiration from his brow, "it's truly mah pleasure ta make yo'ah acquaintance. Apology accepted," replied Louie in his slow Georgia drawl, bowing to the hotel proprietor.

While his eyes traced outlines around the body from which the purring voice emanated, Louie proceeded to introduce his entourage.

"By tha way, mah friends call me Shootah, and so may you. This he'ah purty young thang is Dahleen," gesturing to the petite blonde."

Darleen (half the age of the middle-aged Logano) curtsied and smiled. Dressed in a bright yellow, formfitting dress (the hem well above the knee) with a matching bucket-shaped hat that covered a crop of short, platinum-blonde hair, the shy girl clung to the arm of her benefactor tighter than bark on a tree.

"Dahleen's a sing'uh an dance'uh in one of tha clubs in At'lanner."

"Tha two little baw'ez ova tha'uh are Lanny and Julius. As you can see, they aw twins, an tha big one here, gesturing to the behemoth at his side, is called 'Jokah'."

"Is your visit to our fair city one of business or pleasure?" inquired the hostess.

"We're he'ah on a small matta of biz'nes, but hopefully there'll be oppa'tunity to indulge in some time of recreation also," explained Shooter.

"Well, it's nice to have y'all with us. Lincoln will help y'all get settled. If there's anything you need, just let him know. I must excuse myself now; I have otha business to attend to. I hope yo'ah stay with us will be pleasant," said Miss Jessie.

"By the way, the name's Miss Jessie," she added coolly, turning and walking away.

"Oh, I'm su'ah it will. I'm already growin' quite fond of yo'ah hotel," replied Louie, "I'm shu'ah we can become good friends."

Darlene gave him a swift poke in the ribs at which he winced and gave her a sour look.

"You must be Lincoln," said Shooter, turning to the bellman.

"At your service, sir."

"Hey fellas," said Louie, turning to his group, "look, we drove here inna Lincoln an now we gotta Lincoln waitin' on us. How 'bout that?"

"Maybe we could become good friends, too," purred Darlene at the bellman.

This time, Louie gave Darlene a soft pat on the cheek and gave her a sour look.

"Watch it baby."

"Hey, if you can, I can," she countered with a pout.

"Hey, Mr. President," said Louie to Lincoln,

"Get it, Dahleen…President…Lincoln," turning to Darlene.

"Huh?"

"Oh, hell, never mind," growled Louie.

"Mr. President, can ya do anything 'bout this damned heat? I'm burnin' up?" turning back to Lincoln.

"I'm afraid the summer is upon us and it's going to get hotter before it gets cooler."

Lincoln rounded up a couple of bellman's carts from the lobby and rolled them outside to retrieve the party's luggage from the limo with the assistance of two of the men in black, the one called Joker didn't seem inclined to stray far from Shooter's side. Lincoln was awed by the size of Joker. Up until now, Bam Bam was the biggest man he had ever seen, but even he looked small in comparison to this character.

While Lanny and Julius were loading suitcases onto the cart, Lincoln reached into the bottom of the large trunk to drag out the last remaining piece of luggage, a two feet by four feet, flat hard case. He grabbed hold of the case's handle and gave a tug. Being surprised at its weight, the case slipped from his grasp and its latch struck the edge of the trunk causing the lid to pop open. What he saw of the case's contents made his heart jump up in his throat. *Guns!* An assortment of handguns, rifles, and shotguns broken down in pieces.

A shiver went up his spine wondering who these people were and just what kind of "business" they had in Coldwater.

Without warning, a huge hand came down over his shoulder, slammed the case shut, and pushed it back into the trunk.

Lincoln looked up and there looming over him was the face of Lanny. It was like looking in your rearview mirror and seeing nothing but the grill of a Mack truck. He wondered what was coming next.

Lanny grasped Lincoln by the shoulder and held him out to his side with one hand and swung his jacket open with the other revealing a handgun underneath that looked to Lincoln like a small cannon.

"This is ba'tween yous an me, see," scowled the hood.

"Ye…ye…ye…yes sir. It's our secret," stammered Lincoln.

The big man closed his jacket and got hold of Lincoln's collar with both hands.

"Ya didn't see nuttin,' understand?"

"Yes sir, I understand. I'm as blind as a bat!"

After they were settled, Shooter contacted Dalton Jackson to let him know they were in town (as if they didn't stick out like streetwalkers in a convent) and had plans to "stop the singing" and "deliver the mail." Louie warned that that was as much information as anyone locally should know, and that should be limited to Dalton.

Chapter 26

They were the dog days of summer, and that meant time for the annual Independence Day celebration, a day filled with festivities observing the country's birthday. Merriments would begin with a morning parade down Main Street followed by a host of afternoon activities on the courthouse lawn, including picnics, game booths, ball games, speeches, and a beauty contest. The big event of the evening would be an open-air square dance in the town square across from the Lacy Hotel with a day-ending fireworks display.

But, with July 4th falling on Sunday this year and Sunday being traditionally honored in Coldwater as a day reserved for one activity alone and that being the attendance of church services, the Independence Day celebration was postponed until Monday, July 5th.

One new attraction had been added to this year's festivities, the appearance of Colonel Thaddeus P. Browning's World-Famous Show of Shows. As it would turn out, the Colonel's show would be instrumental in making the July 4th celebration of 1965 the most memorable, if not infamous, in the town's history.

Lincoln and Ashley had secretly made plans to meet the morning of July 5th to spend the day together. To their surprise, they, by chance, met up with Rats and Bonnie and decided to make it a foursome. Ashley, appearing incognito, committed, what was to her, a fashion *faux pas* by dressing in a pair of old, loose-fitting jeans and sport shirt, her blond locks pinned up under a billed cap, and sun glasses masking her blue eyes.

"Why Miss Armstrong, I hardly recognized you in your trendy new ensemble," joshed Lincoln. "Is this what all the young ladies will be wearing this season?"

"Oh, of course! Don't you just love this darling little outfit," she replied in an uppity voice as she imitated a fashion model strutting down the runway. Turning with hands on hips, she sternly ordered, "Not a word to anyone!" before breaking into a grin. The four of them chuckled.

From the rooftop of the Lacy Hotel's veranda, to which Lincoln had discovered access through a second-story utility room, they had an unobstructed view of the parade which began promptly at 10:00

a.m. They settled in and watched as dignitaries and beauty queens waved from the back seats of slow-moving antique automobiles, floats decorated in various themes of red, white, and blue streamed by proclaiming freedom, and veterans of the military services marched proudly along in full uniform.

Meanwhile

As Stanley Penrod pulled his '63 Mercedes out of the driveway of his four-bedroom home on The Ridge, he paid little notice to the blue panel truck parked on the opposite side of the street two houses down from his own. It was 9:00 a.m., and he had promised his wife Martha, who had left for town earlier in the morning, that he would meet her at 10:00 a.m. sharp for the beginning of the parade. But he needed to stop by the bank first and make sure everything was shipshape there.

Being preoccupied with thoughts of his wife's and his plans for the remainder of the day, he neither saw the silencer-crowned barrel of a revolver that jutted through the small space of the truck's slightly-open rear door nor heard the muffled pop of its report as he passed. He did, however, hear the "bang" of his front tire exploding from the impact of the piercing, metal projectile and feel his car suddenly yanked into the curb by the pancaked rubber.

The truck started up and sped toward the Mercedes. The big man behind the wheel screeched to a stop beside Penrod's car just as he was climbing out of the driver's side door. The back door of the panel truck flew open and the masked Julius jumped out, grabbing Penrod and shoving him in the back of the truck. On the inside, masked Lanny grasped the abductee's arm and pulled him the rest of the way in. Julius hopped in behind Penrod and slammed the door.

"*Go!*" ordered Julius.

Joker gunned the engine, and in a matter of seconds they were out of sight.

"What's going on here?" protested Penrod. "Who are you people?" Stanley Penrod got no answers to his questions and only one more utterance out of his mouth, "Owooh!"

Lanny thrust a syringe into their reluctant passenger's neck and quickly pressed the plunger. It was only seconds before Stanley's head began to wobble and quickly fell into a deep sleep.

The Lacy Hotel was practically vacant as most of the guests and staff had joined the large crowd assembled up and down Main Street to view the big parade snaking its way along the town's thoroughfare. With all attention around the hotel focused on its Main Street side, no one witnessed the blue panel truck that slipped silently through the alley behind the hotel and backed up to the loading dock at 10:10 a.m.

With Joker leading and making sure the way was clear, Lanny and Julius carried Stanley Penrod—barely able to stumble along in his drug-induced stupor with his arms draped over their shoulders—down the corridor and up the hidden passage to the mezzanine where Shooter and Darlene were awaiting their arrival. They had been unaware of a pair of eyes observing them in the hallway stairwell.

Back on the hotel veranda rooftop

"Is anyone thirsty?" asked Lincoln, as the late morning sun was already making its presence felt from its celestial perch high in the cloudless sky above.

"Absolutely!" answered Rats.

"Yes, something to drink would be nice," agreed the girls.

"Okay. I'll go make a withdrawal from my private stash in the kitchen. I shall return momentarily with drinks in hand," said Lincoln, bowing to his companions. They laughed at his comical gesture.

As Lincoln headed down the last flight of stairs to the lobby floor, he heard what he thought to be familiar voices in the hallway. He took the last few steps slowly and quietly and was able to see into the hallway just in time to catch a glimpse of what appeared to be a group of men pass by. Slipping on down the stairwell and peeking down the hall, he saw from the backside the unmistakable figures of Lanny and Julius half-assisting, half-dragging some fellow along with them.

The scene struck him as unusual. *Who was the man they were carrying? What was wrong with him? Why were they going up to the mezzanine?* he thought to himself. This raised more questions in his mind about who these people were and their business here, especially after what he had seen in the trunk of the limo.

"Well, it took you long enough! Did you get lost or something?" questioned Rats.

"Yeah, or something," said Lincoln passing bottles of Bubble-Up all around.

"Thanks," said each of the girls.

"You're welcome," replied a preoccupied Lincoln.

Inside the hotel

Shooter's henchmen took Mr. Penrod into the Green Door room, which Shooter and Darlene had fashioned into a makeshift photography studio and tossed him unceremoniously onto the bed. Sheriff Coker had arranged with Miss Jessie for Shooter and Darlene to use the room for a short time for what he led her to believe was their own personal enjoyment.

"That paw'rade only lasts about an ow'wah, so we only hav'a shawt time ta git this o'va and outta he'ah," reminded Shooter.

"Baw'ez, y'all take ca'ah the man's clothes."

"Dahlene, honey, y'all know how'ta do tha posin.'"

"An I'll take tha photographs," directed Shooter.

Louie Logano had grown up poor in the Atlanta slums, the only child of uneducated parents who just never seemed to be able to get more than short-lived, menial-labor employment or to break out of the vicious cycle of the welfare system and shantytown life.

Because Louie was small for his size, he was constantly being picked-on by the bigger kids and learned at an early age that if he was going to survive, he was going to have to get tough and fast. In time, he learned that fists and toughness weren't always enough; brass knuckles, a knife, or better yet, a gun would not only level the playing field, but give one a distinct advantage.

Eventually, he found his way into the gang culture where he honed his fighting skills and later into organized crime where, as a soldier, he earned the nickname "shooter" for his willingness to shoot anyone, anytime, anyplace. Now, as a sub-chieftain in the organization, he didn't do much of the dirty work anymore; he had his own soldiers to do it for him.

Shooter's soldiers stripped Stanley Penrod naked and over the next thirty minutes or so, at Darlene's direction, arranged his body, arms, and legs in certain sexually-oriented positions. In each position,

Darlene, naked herself, would position herself on Penrod's body in such a way as to simulate an act of sexual intercourse taking place. Shooter would snap pictures making sure that Stanley's face was clearly visible. Stanley, his head spinning in a whirlwind of blurred objects and flashing lights, could offer little resistance to the manipulation of his being that was taking place.

Back on the hotel veranda rooftop

The two young couples watched the remainder of the parade made up of clowns, fire engines, little baton twirlers, Boy Scouts, and other various and sundry groups that desired to participate. Finally, bringing up the rear of the procession was the high school band decked out in their purple and gold colors and blaring patriotic tunes.

Lincoln hadn't really seen much of the last portion of the parade. He couldn't shake the images of the Atlanta limo's trunk, how out of place these characters looked, and what he had just witnessed inside the hotel. Lincoln had begun gathering up their empty drink bottles when he noticed movement in the alley out of the corner of his eye. It was a man who looked like Julius boarding a blue panel truck and driving away. He thought it peculiar for him to be driving that type of vehicle instead of the white limo. There seemed to be a lot of mystery surrounding the group of visitors from Atlanta.

On one hand, he considered telling someone about what he had witnessed, but who? On the other hand, what had he actually witnessed? He might just stir up trouble for someone, including himself, if it was just his imagination running wild. He decided to keep things to himself for the time being.

Inside the hotel

Shooter and Darlene were returning the Green Door room to its original state as the blue panel truck with the three hoods and Penrod on board was pulling away from the hotel, just as the high school band was passing by. A few minutes later, Shooter's boys had retrieved the keys from Penrod's car, changed the tire, and were backing it into the Penrod's garage. They hauled Stanley, who was beginning to come out of his paralysis, into the living room and plopped him down in a recliner. Lanny stuck another syringe full of drugs into Stanley's arm and he drifted quietly back into La La Land.

"That'll keep'em out for a while," said Lanny.

"Sweet dreams, Stan my man," added Julius.

Chapter 27

That afternoon

To everyone's eager anticipation, Colonel Thadeus P. Browning's World-Famous Show of Shows, with its community of misfits, freaks, and life's dropouts, opened in all its ragtag glory. The midway of this amusement park on wheels was comprised of three areas of entertainment, each offering a distinct form of pastime and pleasure for those from five to a hundred and five.

The Thrill-a-Minute Rides area was a half-acre junkyard of rickety and worn rollercoasters, tilt-a-whirls, bumper cars, and other such carny rides whose better days of service had long since passed. The thrill of riding the swings was more a game of chance to see if one could survive the ride without the chains breaking and being slung-shot into the next county.

In the Games & Food section, the latent gambling instincts of the average person were tempted by simple games of chance to win cheap "made in Japan" stuffed animals and other trifles by popping balloons, tossing rings, and other such tests of skill and dexterity. Food booths, offering a wide variety of ethnic foods along with the traditional cotton candy and candy apples to tantalize the taste buds, were in abundance.

But, it was the Side Show section that proved to hold the greatest mystique and, as it would turn out, the greatest controversy. Here was found the usual lineup of "freaks" associated with such vagabond outfits: The Fat Lady, the Fire Breather, and so on. There was, however, one performance held in this area that would be the source, as aforementioned, of this becoming the most infamous July 4th in Coldwater history.

But, for the time being, under a canopy of dozens of strings of 60-watt light bulbs lighting up the entire midway, with the sight of green and pink cotton candy and red candy apples, the melody of calliope music, and the sounds of barkers hawking their wares all stimulating the senses, Colonel Thadeus P. Browning's World-Famous Show of Shows was a sight to behold.

That evening

Lincoln and Ashley stood on the roof of the Lacy Hotel veranda, where they had watched the parade earlier in the day, staring up at the star-laden sky waiting for the fireworks to begin. They stood side by side holding hands. Before the square dance, Rats and Bonnie had said goodbye and gone off on their own.

"I had a good time today with you and your friends. They're nice," said Ashley.

"Yeah, they are. I had fun with you, too," answered Lincoln.

"Can you believe we must have ridden every ride and played every game at the carnival?" noted Ashley.

"You're right. And some, two or three times," laughed Lincoln.

For the next few minutes they fondly reminisced over the events of the day until their attention was drawn once again skyward by a flash of light and booming sound. The light show was underway. For several minutes, one after another, canopies of streaking color and sound exploded across the heavens, illuminating the earth and eliciting "oohs" and "ahs" from the witnesses below. The light show culminated in a thunderous crescendo of "booms" resembling volleys of cannon fire.

They slowly turned to face each other and something unexpected happened. It was spontaneous; it was magical; it was surreal. It was one of those moments in time when one realizes that his or her destiny is going to be forever altered. Silence surrounded them; words escaped them. They drew closer and closer to each other as if drawn by some irresistible magnetic force until their lips touched. Embracing, their mouths locked in a soft, warm, deep kiss; their eyes closed and they drifted away into a world of their own. When their lips parted, they stood silently, looking deeply into each other's eyes. Oblivious to the noise of the cheering crowd and the smell of smoke drifting on the air around them, they said nothing. There was no need for words; the look reflected in each other's faces and a knowing smile said all that needed to be said. But, in the coming months the mettle of the newfound bond between this poor Millie boy and rich Ridger girl would be severely tested and the fortunes of the lives they touch strained to the limit.

Chapter 28

"Hey, Linc, did ya hear 'bout the show over at the carnival," came the voice of Rats over the phone.

"What show are you talkin' about?"

"The exotic dancers show! That's what show."

"What do you mean the exotic dancers show?"

"It's ole Colonel Browning's Show of Shows and it has these nude women dancing on stage."

"And just how did you hear about this show?" asked an unbelieving Lincoln.

"Willard Garrett was tellin' us all about it down at the service station. He was there…last night…with his uncle. There was two of''em, an older woman an a young girl. Willard said they were even lettin' the men touch 'em."

"C'mon, the city's not going to let them put on a show like that. People will be up in arms," rationalized Lincoln. "Are you sure Willard wasn't just pullin' your leg?"

"Oh, no. He was be'n as truthful as a sinner on his deathbed. I've also heard some others down here saying they've heard the same kind of talk."

"Well, if that's the case, you know what kind of a Sodom and Gomorrah the founding fathers will make out of it and close it down faster than a hot knife through butter."

"I know. That's why we've gotta get over there t'night when the show opens an see it before they do shut it down."

"Nay, I don't think so," said Lincoln.

"Why not?" questioned Rats. "Look, how many chances do you get to see somethin' like this?" he argued.

"I dunno man. Things are different now," said Lincoln heartfelt.

Rats demeanor changed. "I know man. Things have changed for me, too," he answered moodily. "That's why I want you to go with me; one last adventure for old Butch and Sundance before we go our separate ways."

Lincoln listened closely to Rats' words; his voice sounded different. He was no longer listening to the voice of the boy he had known all his life, but the voice of a man; a man looking for one concluding escapade with his best bud to serve as a rite of passage to mark their transition into manhood.

"You know, we could get caught in the middle of some trouble if we're there and ole sheriff Buford shows up," reminded Lincoln with a half chuckle.

"Wouldn't be the first time now, would it?" quipped Rats, reminiscing on their history with the lawman.

"Oh, what the hell, let's go for it!" agreed Lincoln.

"I'll meet you there at 7:30. The show starts at 8:00," stated Rats matter-of-factly.

Lincoln placed the telephone receiver back on its cradle, leaned forward with arms braced on the top of the check-in counter, and thoughtfully shook his head from side to side in humorous fashion. He was forever being amazed and amused at the way his buddy could shanghai him into entanglement in his schemes. As for seeing a naked woman was concerned, he doubted that any woman who would dance in that ragtag carnival, nude or otherwise, couldn't top what his baby browns had focused on in the person of Marge Henderson. Unfortunately, he couldn't let that fact be revealed to Rats even though it would be fun to gloat a bit to his buddy.

That evening

The air was heavy with humidity, and the dust being stirred up by pedestrian traffic sticking to streams of perspiration only added to the misery of traipsing through the carnival grounds. The two sidekicks sidled along, casting eyes in all directions at the side shows in search of their objective. Barkers joked about the heat and enticed customers to their shows while mothers fussed at children for getting their clothes dirty. Since the city had not allowed the carnival to be open on Sunday following the Fourth, tonight was only the second night that the "show" would have been open. Lincoln still wondered if what he had heard about it was true or not.

Then they saw it: a tent that took little imagination to recognize as what must surely be *the* show in this wayfaring show of shows. A large sign across the entrance called out in large, bold, red letters:

EXOTIC DANCERS REVIEW
See Mama June and The Princess
(*must be 18 or older to enter)

Rats grabbed Lincoln by the arm. "Look, there it is!" exclaimed Rats.

Colonel Browning himself was on the tent's front stage and had in his accompaniment The Princess, parading her back and forth across the stage and marketing her as a princess from a Far East kingdom while assuring the audience that one would behold upon the stage a performance from this beguiling beauty more tempting than that of Eve in the garden.

"C'mon, let's get in line. It's almost time to start," Rats said, pulling Lincoln by the arm. The small, forming line was of men who were either holding their heads down trying to look inconspicuous or looking over their shoulders to see if there might be anyone around who recognized them.

"How much?" said Rats to the man in the ticket booth.

"Didja read tha sign? Gotta be a'teen," said the man gruffly.

"Oh, I'm eighteen alright."

"Show me sum ID," ordered the ticket man.

Rats flipped open his wallet and flashed him his driver's license.

"My buddy here and I are both nineteen," he said pointing to Lincoln beside him.

The man nodded to Rats' driver's license and looked suspiciously at Lincoln for a minute.

"Okay, two bucks fer each of ya."

They each handed the man two dollar bills and entered the tent.

Inside, about seven or eight men crowded around a waist-high stage while two or three others hung back at some distance, each to himself. Rats and Lincoln stood at center stage a few steps behind the men lined up there. The tent was void of light except for a series of bright white, red, blue, and green floodlights hanging haphazardly on poles about the stage for its illumination.

Without notice, over a static-filled intercom came a phantom voice that welcomed the audience and gave a flowery introduction to the evening's "world-famous" performers. Then, Mama June, followed by The Princess, came sashaying across the stage bumping and grinding to the strains of "Little Egypt" playing on a scratchy 45-rpm record player.

Rats just stood there as rigid as a Greek statue and unable to speak. Lincoln reacted in much the same manner, staring in disbelief.

"It's…true!" said a surprised Rats.

"I…don't…believe it!" The words fell out of Lincoln's mouth like crumbs of saltine crackers.

There they were, live and in person, the main attraction of Colonel Thaddeus P. Browning's World-Famous Show of Shows, and naked as two jay birds. They didn't even begin wearing some negligible amount of garb to remove with the pretense of revealing more personal and interesting attributes later. One wasn't quite prepared for the shock of suddenly having two bare-assed naked women gyrating like snakes through grass four feet in front of his face.

In contrast to The Princess, Mama June was a woman, 50-ish in age, who had been a Carnie most of her life, the last ten years with Colonel Browning's show. She was not a bad looking woman for her age and her short, bright orange hair matched her gregarious personality and playful sense of humor. She constantly joked and engaged in banter with the men in the audience although few countered her teasing. Standing at the edge of the stage, she encouraged the men to play braille biology on her body, feeling her up and down and all around as they pleased.

The Princess, on the other hand, a young woman in her mid-twenties with long, black hair, was of American Indian heritage, although Colonel Browning promoted her as a Far Eastern princess. He likely thought it sounded more exotic. Unlike Mama June, The Princess never spoke or smiled, went robot-like through her routine, and like Mama June, allowed the men to play the same game on her person.

Rats and Lincoln hadn't been nervously observing the exhibition before them for more than a few minutes before the pulse-pounding beat of the music and the sensuous nature of the scene had pumped their hormones into overdrive and propelled them into an act of participation.

They approached The Princess with some trepidation, extending a hand toward a leg as cautiously as one would reach for a light bulb with fear of being shocked. Lincoln laid the palm of his hand on her calf and slid it slowly up her leg and across her thigh. Her skin was coarser than Marge's had been.

He looked up at her and she was looking down; he couldn't tell if she was looking at or through him. He removed his hand, turned and walked back a few feet. Turning, he faced the stage again. He looked at Mama June. She seemed to be having a grand time as a real trooper. He looked at The Princess. It seemed that she was still looking at him or perhaps she was just staring into space. Still unsmiling, she appeared distracted, uninterested in what was going on around her. He felt sorry for her; he wanted to leave.

Before he could get Rats' attention, there arose a commotion outside the tent's entrance. Even above the din of the pulsating music being spun out of the old 45s, they recognized the voices of Sheriff Coker and Colonel Browning in heated debate against a background of clamoring voices shouting "shut it down," "shut it down," "shut it down!" Suddenly the sheriff and the Colonel burst through the flaps of the tent entrance with deputies Odom and Cassidy and District Attorney Johnny Abraham following closely behind.

"Oh, lord a'mercy! This can't be good," blurted out Rats, who was shielding his face from the intruders.

"Hoooly shit! No it can't. I just knew something like this would happen," agreed Lincoln also trying to assume a lowkey posture.

The two of them sneaked quietly to the rear of the tent in an effort to go unnoticed in the shadows until, at an opportune moment, they would slip under the tent and exit the premises post haste.

All was quiet for a few moments as the representatives of the law surveyed the scene; the quiet seemed eerily strange. The phonograph was silenced from airing its intoxicating drug and what had just moments before seemed so surreal—two forms of seductive female flesh swaying to and fro in a little piece of paradise—was now just a plywood stand with two ordinary naked women standing on it looking ill-at-ease. But, the quiet didn't last long; an argument broke out.

The lawmen and the Colonel argued back and forth in heated debate: the law versus the rights of the individual. The law enforcers contended that the show violated a city ordinance that forbade "the public display of nudity and lewdness" as well as being deficient in socially redeeming qualities. On the other side, the Colonel eloquently maintained that consenting adults of legal age who chose of their own free will to attend an artistic exhibition paying homage to the human form should be allowed to do so. After all, God created people naked in the first place and said it was good.

Before the opposing sides could settle their dispute, storming into the tent like Elliott Ness gunning for John Dillinger, was the Reverend Clifton Nutter with a couple of members of his congregation in tow.

"What the…!" exclaimed Lincoln.

Lincoln and Rats dropped to their hands and knees to be less visible. "I think it's time ta put 'Plan A' inta action an get the hell outta Dodge," advised Rats.

"Right! Wait! What's that?" cautioned Lincoln. While the reverend was shaking both fists in the air, ranting on about the carnival being a den of iniquity inhabited by hell-bound perverts (or something along those lines) and demanding that the sheriff arrest the Colonel and run the rest out of town, there could be heard the sound of horns blowing and the banging of drums surrounding the tent. Then a chorus of voices broke out singing "Joshua Fought the Battle of Jericho."

"You gotta be kiddin' me!" said a bewildered Lincoln, "are these people nuts?"

"Talk about bein' up shit creek without a paddle. Man, we ain't even got a boat," said Rats.

"There's no way outta here without bein' seen," concluded Lincoln like a rabbit trapped in a fox hole.

"Well, we'd best do sumthin' fast 'cause I gotta feelin' the walls of this ole tent are gonna come tumblin' down anytime now," advised Rats.

"Any suggestions?" questioned Lincoln.

"Yep. Just jerk up a piece of this canvas an run like hell. It's better than gettin' caught here."

"Okay, but let's move over here to the side to make our escape and head for that pine thicket down by the railroad. That's the closest cover of any kind from here," suggested Lincoln. On the count of three, they hauled up a section of canvas and bolted underneath, shoulder to shoulder, into the night air. They slammed into the midsection of one of the protestors sending the individual sprawling head over heels to the ground. Without missing a stride, they kangaroo-hopped the unfortunate person and disappeared into the darkness like two scalded dogs with their tails between their legs.

Chapter 29

The attendance at the Saturday morning gathering of the breakfast club at the Lacy Hotel the week following the July fourth festivities was noticeably greater in number than usual, as was the intensity with which the subject of the day was being deliberated. And, in spite of Colonel Browning's carnival less than a week-old memory, that fiasco was, surprisingly, not on the agenda. Perhaps it was the heat, or maybe Tyler Justice's leaving (even though a Millie) was a reminder that the war on the other side of the world had come to Coldwater. Then, maybe it was that reminder combined with a hangover from the weekend display of stars and stripes and patriotism. At any rate, a heated dispute had erupted over some matter and passions were running high.

At the current time in the life of the country, only two subjects could possibly invoke such a demonstrative frenzy of debate in this bastion of the Bible Belt: the war in Vietnam and the civil rights movement. This morning, it was civil rights.

Leading the arguments in favor of civil rights reform were Mayor McKean, Deputy Clay Cassidy, and one city councilman while on the other side was practically everyone else, the most vocal of which was Sheriff Buford Coker; however, there was an additional factor that came into play in today's debate that had been absent from all previous debates: Lincoln Crocket.

Lincoln had always avoided involvement in these weekly bull sessions, choosing instead to remain on the periphery to just listen to the boasting and bragging. He wasn't in a mood for that today, however. Since Rats had told him about leaving for boot camp, he had been down, and this morning he was also feeling the effects of another migraine from the night before. Nevertheless, there was just something about Buford Coker's "know-it-all" haranguing that got under Lincoln's skin and provoked him to join the fracas.

Within a matter of thirty minutes or so, the debate had boiled down to a battle of wits between a worked-up Sheriff Coker and an impassioned Lincoln Crockett. The remainder of the breakfast group, and most everyone else in the restaurant, was transformed into a gallery of spectators observing a back-and-forth sparring match between the old veteran of local politics and the intelligent, young idealist twenty-five years his junior.

"Don't you believe in freedom, Sheriff Coker?" asked Lincoln pointedly.

"Yes, I do. I believe in the Federal Government leavin' us states free ta run our towns the way we want ta run'em," replied Buford, pounding his fist on the table.

"Last year a bunch of godless, Yankee members of Congress got that Civil Rights Act passed tellin' us we gotta innagrate our schools and mix tha races. Now they're tryin' ta pass a votin' rights law. Gonna tell us how ta hold our elections like we don't have sense enough to," ranted Buford.

"You know what you people remind me of?" Lincoln asked rhetorically. "One of those lynch mobs you see in the old Western movies. A gang of rabble, hellbent on silencing any voice that speaks in favor of ways that, in their blind ignorance, they perceive as some uncontrollable force flooding over, through, and around their birthright like the lava of Mount Vesuvius over Pompeii.

"Well, what makes you think you're so smart Mr. Lincoln Crockett?" asked the Sherriff sarcastically, "You're just a kid, and a Millie at that."

There was that word again. It cut Lincoln inside, but he kept his cool and continued.

"A kid you say?" questioned Lincoln.

"Congress is passing a voting rights law that gives eighteen-year-olds the right to vote…that gives *me* the right to vote since I'm nineteen years old. That means eighteen-year-olds are considered adults."

"That's another thing that shows how ridiculous them politicians up North are. Eighteen-year-olds ain't mature enough to understand the issues and vote," charged the Sherriff.

"Oh, I see. We're mature enough to be drafted into the military and sent to fight and die in wars, but we're not mature enough to vote for and elect the leaders that are going to draft us and send us to fight and die in those wars. Is that what you're saying, Sheriff?" challenged Lincoln.

The heads of the onlookers were bouncing back and forth between the combatants' volleys and returns like spectators at a tennis match.

"Well…I…that's the way it's always been," stammered Buford.

"And, therefore, it's written in stone and can't, or shouldn't, be changed?" disputed the young man.

Buford just shrugged his shoulders: "It works!"

"And, are you also intimating that 'Millies,' and I'll include blacks, are by nature less intelligent than Ridgers Sheriff?" dared Lincoln, wrinkling the Sheriff's feathers.

"Well, you're all alike, ain't ye? One's just darker than the other," cracked Buford.

"That's so narrowminded. If I say a cat has a tail, therefore everything with a tail is a cat," postulated Lincoln.

"What does that have to do with anything?" stormed Buford angrily. "We were discussing states' rights. Anyway, how come you've taken over the floor?"

"What's the matter Sheriff? Surely a man of your political prowess could easily best a nineteen-year-old 'kid,' as you so adamantly believe them to be, in debating questions of the legal jurisdiction of the Federal Government versus that of state governments," goaded Lincoln.

The Sheriff, looking around the room at all the eyes focused upon him, realized that everyone watching and listening seemed genuinely fascinated by this *tête-à-tête* between himself and the bellboy and was embarrassed not to continue.

"Okay, boy. Let's hear wha'cha got ta say."

"States having the latitude to follow their own course in certain areas is okay as far as it goes," agreed his young adversary, "but the federal government is obligated to ensure that the rights of citizens as guaranteed by the U.S.A.'s Constitution and Bill of Rights are not abridged by individual states in following those individual courses," he argued.

"*Constitutional rights! Constitutional rights!* Somebody's always hollerin' about their '*constitutional rights*,'" bellowed the Sheriff, prancing about throwing his hands up in the air.

"Don't you believe that every person in the United States should have equal rights? Be treated equally? Have equal opportunity?" asked Lincoln.

"People are not equal, dammit!" shouted Buford. "People are different!"

"You're right, Sheriff. Some people are not equal; some people are looked down on because they're seen as different; some people don't have the freedoms that others have. Through no fault of their own, but because of the ignorance, intolerance, and narrowmindedness of holier-than-thou hypocrites who hold themselves up as the chosen ones due to their color, their social standing, or their birth right and use political power to prop up their status quo.

"It's those very people that you're runnin' down boy, that's built this country up and made it what it is. They deserve ta be on top'a the hill and in charge. You think educated folks can be equals with a bunch'a ignorant lowlife's that don't have no more sense than a mule," jabbed the Sheriff.

"You don't get it, do you?" countered Lincoln.

"I'm talking about God's equality: 'Do unto others as you would have them do unto you,' and 'Love thy neighbor as thyself.'"

"I'm also talking about constitutional equality: equal opportunity for life, liberty, and the pursuit of happiness; equal opportunity for education, jobs, homes, and to elect the government leaders who are responsible for upholding the Constitution," he continued. "They work together!"

Lincoln was on a roll. "Personally, I think it's criminal for a group of prejudicial hate mongers to abuse the power of their elected political positions to hold the Constitution and Bill of Rights hostage by the fabrication of discriminatory laws designed to relegate certain people to second-class citizenship status and deny them the freedoms guaranteed to *all* citizens by those two great documents. In doing so, these morally corrupt bigots make a mockery of all the ideals upon which the founding fathers established such a government. They spit on the graves of those who gave their lives in revolution to make such a country possible and on those who have since fought and died to preserve it for posterity," concluded Lincoln, delivering his discourse as powerfully as any orator who ever stood in any political forum.

A silence filled the room so pronounced that one could hear the "tick-tocking" of a watch. The entire group, including Sheriff Coker, just sat there, mesmerized not only by the words that had proceeded out of the mouth of this poor young man from Milltown, but also by the conviction with which they were spoken. Suddenly, the restaurant erupted in thunderous applause and cheers of "bravo."

Becoming self-conscious of the silence followed by the ovation, Lincoln, embarrassed at the spectacle he felt he had just made of himself, wanted to run but didn't think his legs would hold him up, let alone run. Sheriff Coker took advantage of this brief interlude as an opportunity to make a quiet but hasty retreat from a scene that was becoming increasingly uncomfortable.

Recognizing the distress he was feeling, Miss Jessie took Lincoln by the arm. "Come join me for a cupuh coffee," she said and led him to her table from which she had witnessed the whole affair. It was an invitation which young Crockett readily accepted.

"Besides, it doesn't look like you have anyone left to debate," said the lady. My goodness! You surely have strong feelin's, don't ya? That's quite an oratory ya just gave, an very well spoken, I might add. I surely can't articulate it so eloquently as you have, but just between you and me, I can say that I'm in complete agreement with ya," said Miss Jessie admiringly.

"Thank you. I guess I sort of got carried away," answered Lincoln apologetically.

"Howeva, ya are an employee of tha hotel and ya have ta be careful of getting' into confrontations with hotel guests. But in this case, it was just ole big-mouthed Buford Coker an he's about as sha'p as a mashed potata," cautioned Miss Jessie.

"Yes, ma'am. I'll remember that."

"Anyhow, regardless of how you or I may feel, I don't think those good-ole-boy Suhthen Statesmen in tha'uh are gonna change anythin' sittin' tha'ah foamin' at the mouth, or even by hangin' anyone. Well, let's forget about them foh the time being," suggested Miss Jessie, "an talk about mo'ah personal things. We've both been workin' so hard lately we haven't had much opportunity ta talk," said his boss.

"Okay," answered Lincoln. Yes. The hotel's been quite busy the past few weeks," added Lincoln.

"I wanted ta tell ya how pleased I've been with the good job ya been doin'," she said.

"Well, thank you, ma'am. I really appreciate the opportunity you're giving me here."

"Tell me 'bout yo'ah family. I don't think I know them and I nev'ah hear you talk about them," she inquired.

Lincoln was caught off-guard and taken aback by the lady's question. A wide-eyed expression of surprise momentarily flashed across his face before his countenance dissolved into the stoic blank features of a graven image. His head drooped slowly as he stared at the table in solemn reflection on how to best answer the question that had been posed to him.

Why would she want to know anything about my family? he thought to himself.

He never talked about them or his home life to anyone except Rats. For one, he didn't like to talk about it, and two, if he did, he'd make up something because he was ashamed to tell the truth. He toyed with his cup and saucer and took a sip of the warm java.

"Oh, well, there's not really much to tell. We live in Milltown, as you know. My daddy works at the sawmill and my mama works in the textile mill; that is, when she's able. Her health's not very good. I don't have any brothers or sisters. That's about it."

"Well, I can say one thing for'em. They've raised a very well-mannered, responsible son," said Miss Jessie with an admiring smile, "but, sometimes ya don't seem yourself; like somethin's botherin' you. Is everything okay? Any problems?"

"No. I'm okay. I just get headaches sometimes."

"Okay. Well, you let me know if there's anythin' I can ever help you with."

"Okay, thanks!"

"Would you mind if I asked *you* something," asked Lincoln.

"Sure you may, but I reserve tha right to not ans'a if I consider tha question too pusonal."

"Have you always lived in Coldwater and run the Lacy?"

"Heavens no. I came here about twenty years ago and bought the hotel from tha previous owner who was sellin' out to retire in Florida.

"You come alone?"

Miss Jessie smiled at his question in a question.

"No. Bam Bam accompanied me here."

"Are you really asking if I had a husband an family?" asked Miss Jessie smiling.

Lincoln, blushing at his failed attempt at detective work nodded 'yes.'"

"I was married at one time, but we went our separate ways long ago. No kids either. Well, I think that's enough personal talk for now. We best be gettin' back ta business," said Miss Jessie, finishing off the last drop of coffee in her cup.

It was at that moment that Miss Jessie's attention was drawn to a bevy of young ladies, who had been sharing breakfast at a nearby table, sashaying past her table single file. Each of the girls in turn greeted Miss Jessie as they filed by and the hostess offered in return a polite smile and "Good morning." The last girl to pass, one with long, blonde hair dressed in a black miniskirt and white silk blouse, hesitated briefly, looked over her shoulder at Lincoln, gave him a quick wink, which he returned, and proceeded to catch up with her mates.

Lincoln was unaware that the girls had been present during his and the Sheriff's deliberations on democratic ideology and that Miss Armstrong had been most impressed by his discourse on the subject.

The exchange of "winks" had not eluded Miss Jessie's eyes.

"Sooo," said Miss Jessie slyly, "Looks like what I hud about the prom must be true."

"And, from what I just ubzuved, looks like tha'ah may be mo'ah to it than a dance, huh?"

"Could be," said Lincoln, cocking his head with a grin.

"My, my, when you go fishin' you go fah a big one: *Ashley Ahmstrong.*"

"Yoh'ah playin' with fire, Lincoln," warned Miss Jessie, shaking her head back and forth, "and people who play with fire usually get burned. Be careful."

Chapter 30

As the congregation at the River Street Gospel Tabernacle gathered for worship Sunday morning, they were still riding a spiritual high. Fired up from their victory over Satan the preceding week, they were eager to shout praises of thanksgiving for the eviction of the flesh peddlers who sought to sow seeds of sin in the souls of those in their beloved town who are spiritually weak and morally vulnerable, seeds whose fruit leads unto the paths of unrighteousness and that long road to destruction.

Not only had they been successful in closing to the town's eyes Colonel Browning's Exotic Dancer's Review this Tuesday evening past, but threats of further demonstrations were instrumental in the Colonel's abrupt decision to pack up his entire World-Famous Show of Shows and seek more congenial surroundings elsewhere. The only two things the demonstrators hadn't been able to accomplish were to convince the authorities to sentence the Colonel to life on a chain gang and to burn Mama June and The Princess at the stake.

Soon, the sounds of music, singing, and exultations of joy that reverberated through the rafters of the old church, poured through the open windows and spilled into the streets. Accented with the rhythmic melody of Ms. Lola Albright's piano and the pulsating beat of the band, the choir belted out the strains of that great hymn "Victory in Jesus" with a transcendent fervor, the likes of which they had never before equaled.

The song's exhortations and the hypnotic music kindled a firestorm of exuberant rejoicing that spread through the standing-room-only crowd that soon escalated into a fever pitch before reaching its apex. After this high-spirited ritual had continued for some time, the participants, having exhausted their physical, emotional, and spiritual energies, began settling back into their pews in anticipation of the pastor holding forth on his eagerly awaited sermon for the day: "Lust of the Flesh."

Lincoln, occupying his usual space on the back pew and having gotten his first glance at the sermon title in the church bulletin, recognized that it didn't take much stretch of the imagination to conclude that at the heart of Pastor Nutter's sermon was going to be based on Colonel Browning's Show of Shows.

The aged Reverend Nutter, dressed in his usual signature black suit, marched somberly to the lectern, plopped down his worn Bible upon it, and stared sternly at his flock for a few moments. Then, with the deportment of a godlike courtroom judge pronouncing sentence upon the malefactors of some mortal sin, began to preach.

"God said, 'My people would not harken to my voice… so I gave them up unto their own heart's lust… for if ye live after the flesh, ye shall die'!" He bellowed quotes from the Bible, pounding the lectern with his fist for added emphasis.

Every person in attendance, including Lincoln, stiffened in his or her seat, half out of fear, half out of wonderment, and looked wide-eyed at the pastor. With each pause between affirmations the sanctuary would become as quiet as the wink of an eye.

"The Devil slipped into our beloved town this week adorned in festive attire, concealed behind a mask of cheerful merrymaking," he reminded them. "But underneath that cloak of innocence there lurked an insidious evil whose objective was, as it always has been, and always will be, to lure the innocent and unsuspecting victim into its den of sin and iniquity."

With each passing minute, the fire and passion rose inside the old minister's breast.

"The flesh mongers perpetrated a ruse to debase the moral fabric of men, to pollute their minds with lewd and erotic thoughts, and to lead them astray from the straight and narrow to that wide road that leads to destruction and damnation," he declared with conviction.

The old preacher walked a few paces from the lectern. With his head down and his hands in his pockets, he swiftly turned to his audience members and pointed a finger in their direction.

"But old Lucifer's stay wasn't too long," he said softly. "We put that old boy on the run when the walls of Jericho come'a tumblin' down," he said in an escalating voice as he used gestures of his arms to imitate walls falling.

There followed a round of applause and "amens" from the crowd.

"That godless Colonel and his abominable concubine left town like foxes on the run," he yelled louder, dancing a jig across the stage.

His little caper elicited an even bigger round of applause and shouts from the audience.

"We had a victory in Jesus over the Devil!" the fiery preacher shouted with his arms raised in a victory pose.

At that, a thunderous response rose from the congregation. People jumped, shouted, hugged one another, and cried unashamedly.

Pastor Nutter signaled for quiet as he once again leaned against the bookstand, his countenance portraying feelings of both disappointment and anger as he redirected the focus of his address from one of triumph to one of condemnation.

"But, alas, even in victory there is sorrow. Just as there are casualties in war among men, so there are in spiritual warfare. Not all the lambs in the fold harkened to the voice of the shepherd warning them of the consequences of lusting after the flesh. But, He let them, in their free will, follow the lust of their hearts and the wolf ensnared them and dragged them down into his hellish lair," lamented the preacher pitifully.

All along the rows of pews heads hung low, most offering up some sort of heavenly supplication: those who had not attended the show giving thanks; those who had, pleading for deliverance from this public inquisition. Some petitioned forgiveness on behalf of their unfortunate brethren who had attended, and others who just shook their heads, not caring who did what and who didn't.

Upon close observation of all the goings-on at hand, it struck Lincoln as ironic the number of similarities that existed between Colonel Thaddeus P. Browning and the Reverend Clifton Nutter, that is, in the way they could both work an audience by using charismatic charm, body language, inflection of voice, and emotion to grasp and hold their attention, manipulate their emotional state, and sell them on whatever they were selling. Albeit, they plied their trade in two very different arenas for two very different purposes, but they were two peas in a pod when it came to exercising their skills. They could both sell dance lessons to a one-legged man.

At this point, tension was building all across the congregation. People eyed one another doubtfully and Lincoln felt more and more uncomfortable, wondering just how far down this path the preacher was going to go. He feared that it was going to get worse before it got better. Little did he know at that moment just how much worse!

"It is with great suffering of heart that I implore those among our number, who in a moment of carnal weakness, yielded to sexual temptation and lusted in their minds for the bodies of harlots. I beseech you, come and confess before God and man your sin, and save your soul from damnation."

Aside from Ms. Albright softly playing on the piano, the place was as hushed as a funeral service; the only thing lacking to make it more so would have been a casket with corpse laid out in front of the alter. Women looked suspiciously at their husbands; men returned shrugs of innocence to their wives, but not one man moved in response to the preacher's summons.

Lincoln slouched down in the pew in an effort to become undetectable. Then, the unbelievable (in Lincoln's mind) happened. Reverend Nutter began calling out names; names of men who had been seen at the show. One by one, he read off names and called them to the front of the church to the shock and embarrassment of husband and wife as well as their friends and neighbors. One woman whacked her husband over the head with her purse and stormed out of the church with two kids in tow. Soon there were four married and two single red-faced men lined up looking as if they were about to ascend the final steps to the gallows where awaited the hangman.

Lincoln got a knot in his stomach and began to feel dizzy. *"This can't be happening!"* he thought to himself. His only hope was that he and Rats had gotten away that night without being recognized. But, no such luck!

"There's one more that needs to join our little group of sinners down here," called out Reverend Nutter.

Lincoln didn't move, hoping he meant someone besides him.

"Are you coming Mr. Lincoln Crockett?"

A stunned Clovis and Anna Mae Crockett both rose to their feet and looked to the rear of the building at their son.

"You, too?" barked Lincoln's father.

Lincoln made his way to the end of the pew and stood in the aisle way, looking first at Reverend Nutter standing there indignantly pointing an accusing finger in his direction, and then to his left, at his father's scowling glare with hands on hips. Again, deathly quiet pervaded the room pending the outcome of this confrontation. To his right, he studied his mother's expressionless face for a minute before heading down the aisle to where his father and Pastor Nutter now stood side by side.

Expressionless, he approached the two men until he was practically chest to chest with both of them. In a voice inaudible to anyone but the three of them, he spoke matter-of-factly.

"Pastor Nutter, you have no right to publicly condemn me or anyone else. My relationship with God is personal and He and I will work it out. If you insist on continuing with this pompous display of self-righteous demagoguery, I will address this congregation, and when I speak, I will have something to say. I'm sure this gathering would be quite interested to hear of your monthly excursions to Central City where you purchase certain products at a place of business called Mr. McDougal's that, shall we say, provides for your personal comfort.

The pastor's eye's widened in surprise and his face paled; he wilted like a kid caught with his hands in the cookie jar.

"Likewise, sir," he said, turning his head slightly toward his father, "I'm sure this assembly would also find it of equal interest to see the stripes upon my back and learn how one of their deacons wields a certain object to exercise control over his family members who are disobedient to his will."

Clovis Crockett's body stiffened; red-faced, he trembled and fumed like a steaming pressure cooker ready to blow.

"You wouldn't dare," he grunted between clenched teeth.

"Try me!" he said to both men unflinching.

"I don't think that will be necessary," interjected Reverend Nutter solemnly. "Perhaps there was a case of mistaken identity Brother Clovis."

The Reverend smoothed things over with the congregation while motioning Lincoln on his way.

With that, Lincoln turned and walked slowly toward the front door. Reaching the door, he pushed it open and felt the rush of the July heat upon his face.

"Woe to tha rebellious children…that they add sin ta sin," called out his unforgiving father with arms raised to heaven.

Lincoln looked back.

"Let he who is without sin cast the first stone!" he responded in retaliation, took a deep breath, and stepped out into the noonday sun.

Chapter 31

With celebrations of the Fourth having been concluded and businesses reopening, Louie Logano, an aficionado of style, decked out in the latest of men's fashion, swaggered confidently into the lobby of the First National Bank of Coldwater nodding and tipping his hat to those he encountered, especially the ladies. Oddly, on this particular occasion he didn't have his usual adornment Darlene clinging to his side, and even more unusual, he wasn't parading about in the shadow of Joker, a companion he would never had considered being without in Atlanta.

In Coldwater, he considered his safety to be free from jeopardy and his being there as inconspicuous as any other businessman conducting banking business. But, Louie Logano would be as inconspicuous on the streets of Coldwater as Beau Brummel would be in a nudist colony.

Approaching an open teller's cage, he politely informed the young woman behind the barred enclosure that he wished to speak with the bank president, Mr. Stanley Penrod. The young lady personally escorted Louie to Mr. Penrod's office and announced the visitor's presence to the president.

"Come in, Mr. Logano, and have a seat," invited the bank president, totally unaware that he had had previous contact with the flashy stranger.

"Thank you," replied Louie, surveying the surroundings as he made himself comfortable in a plaid armchair sitting in front of Mr. Penrod's polished maple desk.

"What can I do for you today Mr. Logano?" inquired the bank's man in charge.

"I believe one of yo'ah bank's customuhs, a Ms'us Mahjorie Henduhson, has a safety deeposit box he'ah," stated Louie.

"Yes, that's correct. She rented one from us recently," answered Mr. Penrod looking at Louie questioningly.

"Well, Ms'us Henduhson has placed within the confines of that box a letta and has sent me on huh behalf ta fetch that letta fa huh."

"Why doesn't Mrs. Henderson come get the letter herself?"

"Well, ya see She's a bit unduh tha weatha and unable ta get out. I'm huh cousin up from Atlanta and I'm just doin' huh a favor."

"Well, I'm sorry Mr. Logano. It's the bank's policy that a safety deposit box can be opened by only the owner of the box. Not even bank employees can open one without a court order," explained the banker. He was becoming more and more suspicious of Louie.

"Ms'tah Penrod, I wuz hoping y'all could satisfy this request inna simple an straight forth manna an things wouldn't hav'ta get complicated an messy," said Louie, his demeanor changing from that of the affable Mr. Logano to that of the surly Shooter.

"I'm sorry sir, but I'm not inclined to break bank rules for anyone."

"See if yo'ah still so inclined after ya look at these Ms'tah Penrod!" scolded Shooter, pitching a manila envelope on the desk in front of Stanley.

Shooter leaned forward on folded arms against the edge of the desk as he stared down the man and grinned like the Cheshire Cat.

"What's this?" asked Penrod sitting up straight in his chair.

"Open it. I think y'all will find tha contents...*interestin'*," goaded Shooter.

Stanley Penrod's countenance was blank as he reached for the envelope, cautiously opened it, and peeked inside as if expecting a snake to come slithering out. He glanced back at Shooter, still sitting there grinning at him. He didn't know what kind of game this man was playing, but since he had first walked through his office door, he couldn't help feeling that he knew him from somewhere and that feeling was a bad one.

Penrod held the envelope sideways and out onto his desk came sliding a stack of eight-by-ten glossy photographs. Stanley's face flushed red as he thumbed through the pictures, not believing the images his eyes were seeing.

"This can't be me, I never..."

"Oh, yes ya did."

"When..."

Then something dawned on Stanley. He recalled the strange things he had experienced on Monday, the day of the parade.

"You and some other people did this to me. Monday I was on my way to town when some men stopped me and put me in a van of some kind. They must have drugged me or something and the next thing I remember, I woke up back in my living room. But, in between I remember flashing lights and a voice...your voice."

"That's quite a tale Ms'tah Penrod, and it's also an affront ta mah personal integrity," said Shooter sarcastically.

"You've obviously gone to a lotta trouble to do this for some reason. What's this all about?" asked Penrod.

"Well, pu'haps this he'ah evidence of y'all being 'caught with yo'ah pants down,' so ta speak, will make y'all mo'ah inclined ta conduct a simple business transaction."

"This has something to do with Mrs. Henderson's letter I gather."

"Tha'ut's right. Y'all give me tha letta, and I give y'all the pictures. Simple as tha'ut!"

"I won't do it. It's illegal. I'll report what you did to me and how you're threatening to blackmail me to the District Attorney."

"Come now Mis'tah Penrod. Da ya really think anybody would ev'ah ba'lieve such'a story as that one ya rambled on about a minute ago? People'd think ya wuz outta yo'ah mind."

"It's better than letting you get away with blackmail," threatened Penrod bravely.

"Look Stanley...may I call ya Stanley? I don't balieve yo'ah seein' tha big picture he'ah Stanley, an tha full implications of yo'ah decision," growled Shooter. He was losing patience with the man.

"Thay'uh's a lady tha'ut lives at 4102 Sycamore Street, why I do believe tha'ut's yo'ah address, that I'm shu'ah would find these photographs *most* interestin' And I won'duh what tha mem'buhs of this bank's bo'ad of directors would think about thay'uh bank's president cavortin' about in such a fashion. Then thay'uh's tha school board of which yo'ah a mem'buh. Would tha community tolerate an individual of such puhversion as tha one in these pictures bein' responsible fah tha welfah of thay'uh children? How would tha pastah an membuhs of The Fust Chuch of Tha Trinity, uh, I believe y'all are counted amongst their fellowship are you not, respond ta photographs showin' a promonent membuh of thay'uh congregation in such a compromisin' position?"

"Surely you wouldn't stoop that low, just for some letter," pleaded the astonished Stanley Penrod.

By this time, Shooter was fed up with these cat-and-mouse games and was ready to start playing hardball. He jumped to his feet and pointed a finger at Penrod.

"Listen ta me an listen good ya hick-town, piggybank money changer. Ya got two choices. Either play it my way, or when I get through with ya, ya won't have a marriage, ya career'll be ov'ah, ya'll be excommunicated from tha church, an ya'll be an outcast in yoh community. In short, yer life'll be ov'ah in this backwatta excuse fah a town," fumed Shooter.

"So, git me tha letta dammit! *Now!*"

Chapter 32

Rats finished up the oil change he was working on, pulled a couple of Cokes out of the drink machine, and joined his buddy in the shade of an oak tree beside DeLaney's. Lincoln opened up a sack of chili dogs and fries he had picked up at the Dairy Queen. With both of them working full time, they didn't get to spend as much time together as they used to, so a quick lunch now and then was to be enjoyed. Besides, today Rats had some important news he needed to share.

It was the first time they had seen or talked with each other since they had "escaped" from that tent the night the good people of Coldwater are now referring to as "the day Coldwater sank into a cesspool of depravity." For a few minutes, they relived the experience which they agreed had fallen woefully short of their expectations. Rather than the thrill they had anticipated from the dancers, they actually found themselves feeling sorry for the two women. Rather than the performers having a captive audience, it seemed to be just the reverse; the performers looked more like the captives. They sat in silence for the next few minutes, munching their hot dogs and thinking their own thoughts, until Rats spoke up again.

"You know something?"

"What's that?" asked Lincoln.

"I feel sorry for you. You have such a hard job," ribbed Rats sarcastically.

"Wha'da you mean?" quizzed Lincoln.

"Havin' a job any guy in town would give his right arm for."

"Workin' at the hotel?" asked Lincoln.

"No. Being a lap dog for the sexiest woman in Coldwater!"

"Oh, that!" grinned Lincoln.

"Well, it's tough work, but someone has to do it," said Lincoln, shrugging his shoulders.

"Yeah! Ain't you the lucky one? You know, I'd give my last dollar to be a millionaire," bragged Rats.

"Now, how could you become a millionaire by giving away your last dollar?"

"About as easy I can by *keeping* my last dollar," laughed Rats.

"You're crazy, man!" laughed Lincoln.

"By the way, that was sure a surprise you and Ashley pulled on Bonnie and me Monday, showing up together at the parade. What's going on here?"

"Thanks to the two of you for treating her nice," said Lincoln.

"No problem. She's very nice. We all had a good time together. But, what's going on between you two?"

"Well, here's a news flash! I saw Ashley about three weeks ago," confided Lincoln.

"I was just out walkin' downtown Sunday afternoon when she happens by in her T-Bird and offers me a ride. We went up on the bluff...to the cave."

"What happened?"

"We just talked about the prom...and other things. Mostly, why we each did what we did and how she and Montgomery were ordered by their parents not to see me or Amanda anymore. But, she wants us to see each other again. Man! After the fireworks she laid one heck of a kiss on me."

"You're kiddin' me!"

"I kid you not!" promised Lincoln, raising his arm taking an oath.

"Are you going to tell her about the show at the carnival?"

"Uh, let's just keep any memory of that little escapade between the two of us. Okay?" suggested Lincoln.

"Agreed!"

Then, Rats turned serious.

"Linc, when I asked you to go to that carnival show with me...one more adventure for Butch and Sundance...and all that...you remember?"

"Yeah! I remember."

"I said something had changed for me too and that I'd tell you later."

"Yeah! So!"

"I've got something to tell you," Rats said, in as serious tone of voice as Lincoln had ever heard him speak.

"What's that, my friend," he answered back in the same serious tone.

"I joined the Marines."

Lincoln sat straight up, wide-eyed.

"You what?" he stammered, unbelievingly.

"I've already signed the papers an everything. I'll be leavin' in a few days."

"But, why?

"It's loomin' over all our heads…somethin' we've all gotta face: the draft, the call to military service, the summons to go fight in a war," he answered.

"Why now, anyway?"

"Well, the war's rampin' up. It's gonna get worse before it gets better. The Marines landed back in March. The lottery starts up next month, so they start callin' up everybody by birthday. So, I figure if I'm goin' anyway, I might as well just go ahead an join up," Rats answered again. "Do you know what this crazy war's all about anyway?" Rats asked his friend.

"I'm afraid I've had the ostrich syndrome about it. I've tried to ignore it hoping it would somehow magically go away. Everyone I've talked to or overheard, young and old, seems to know little about it and understand even less. A lot think it's a good chance to die in places they've never heard of, with names they can't pronounce, for people they don't know."

"That is unless you're a member of the privileged class that can get a college deferment like our Ridger *buddies,*" Rats added with a sarcastic tone.

"Yeah, you got that right," agreed Lincoln.

"You won't see any of those hot shots up there gettin' an M-16 strapped to their asses."

"But, you know," said Lincoln thoughtfully, "even if you don't understand everything that goes on, and maybe don't always agree with what's done, I think you have a patriotic duty as a citizen to support the country when you're called on to. What if everybody could just pick and choose their fights? Where would we be then?"

"I tend to agree with you my friend," concurred Rats. "I ain't run from a fight in my life an I don't intend to start now."

Again, they sat in silence, regurgitating in the recesses of their minds the words they had just shared and their possible implications for their futures. They were suddenly jolted out of their trance by the voice of Mr. DeLaney calling to Rats that lunch break was over, which reminded Lincoln also that he was overdue back at the hotel. As they walked back toward the service station, Rats asked Lincoln to do him a favor.

"Linc, when I leave, I want you to take the Indian and keep it for me while I'm gone. Treat it like it's your own and use it all you want. But, I'll be back some day to reclaim it!"

"You bet you'll be back, buddy, and I'll take good care of the Chief for you. Promise!"

Chapter 33

It had been few days since Pastor Nutter had called people on the carpet for attending the Show of Shows when Rats parked the motorcycle next to the sidewalk and walked up to the Crockett house. Anna Mae Crockett was sitting in an old lawn chair on the back porch with needle and thread in hand doing some mending.

"Hello Mrs. Crockett."

"Howdy Tyler," replied Anna Mae (she never did like Rats' nickname).

"How you doin' today?" he asked.

"Just tryin' ta stay cool, but it ain't easy in this heat," she answered, stopping to fan herself.

"How 'bout yourself?"

"Oh! Can't complain," he answered

"Lincoln around?" he inquired.

"Yes, he's inside. He an his father are havin' a 'discussion' about last week's church service.

They been at it quite a while; hope they'll be done soon."

They could hear muffled sounds of the conversation coming from inside the house but not clearly enough to make out what was being said.

"I didn't go to church that day," confessed Rats, "and I'm glad I didn't. Mom told me all about it, and from what I hear, I don't think a lot of people are happy with what took place for one reason or another. Maybe that's dependin' on which side of the aisle you were sittin' on, of course…so to speak."

"Yeah, I guess you're right about that all right," agreed Mrs. Crockett.

"I can imagine that you and your husband weren't exactly overjoyed by your son's summons to appear before the Nutter Inquisition for public ridicule regardless of the circumstances…huh, I'm sorry ma'am, pardon my sarcasm."

Suddenly, their attention was once again drawn to the house by a marked increase in the level of the volume of the goings-on there between father and son.

"Well, I was disappointed in Lincoln to find that he'd gone to that lewd show, but I guess that's part of young men sowin' their wild oats," said Anna Mae.

"Would that be right Mr. Justice?" she asked, peeping up at Tyler with a sly smile.

"I guess that would be right," said Rats, nodding in agreement, "guilty as charged!"

"But," she continued, "I didn't think it was right for the preacher ta call people by name like that. It was embarrassin' for everbody."

"I think my parents feel about the same as you do about it," offered Rats.

"Clovis is more upset than anyone but for different reasons than most. He holds onto ever word that comes out of the mouth of Pastor Nutter like it was a'comin' from the lips of God himself," she said of her husband.

By now, what had started out as a father and son discussion had degenerated into a shouting match to which Mrs. Crockett was becoming more and more embarrassed for both herself and Rats.

"Maybe I should come back…"

But, before Rats could get the words out, they heard scuffling noises coming from the kitchen and the older and younger Crockett engaged in what was now a heated argument. The dialogue and wrangling was now most comprehendible to the two witnesses, especially that of Clovis Crockett whose language was laced with expletives.

Up to this point, they had, for the most part, managed to talk through their issues on a man-to-man basis except for their main bone of contention, one that raised the hackles on Clovis Crockett's back. That was, in Clovis Crockett's view, the blatant disregard for respect his son exhibited toward his spiritual mentors, himself and Pastor Nutter. Lincoln, on the other hand, was of the opinion that to show respect to those undeserving of it would be casting pearls before swine.

It was over this difference of ideals that the outraged Clovis Crockett once again drew the leather strap from the belt loops of his pants like a sword from its scabbard which he judged, from his position of power, wielded greater authority than did the words of oratory to end the conflict. "When diplomacy fails, beat your enemy into submission" was his motto; however, his son's daring sabotaged his intentions when Lincoln unceremoniously disarmed Clovis of his weapon, snatching it from his clutches.

"Damn you! Gimme back that belt you book-nosin' mama's boy," fumed Clovis.

"I told you I'm not a boy anymore and you're not going to whip me with this damned belt again," bristled Lincoln, storming out the kitchen door with his father trailing close behind.

Oblivious to the presence of Anna Mae and Rats only a few feet away, they continued to scrap on the porch like two bad-tempered alley cats that had just gotten on each other's last nerve.

"I said to gimme that belt," said Clovis, gritting his teeth, with his hand extended toward his son.

Lincoln looked down at the big black leather belt he held in his hands; the one he was feeling by hand for the first time; the one he had just seized from the hands of his father; the one he had been flogged with too many times.

"No!" he said emphatically, and flung the belt high into the air, landing far out in the street.

For the first time in his life, Lincoln was, fearfully but courageously, standing up to his father, much to the ole man's ire.

"Well, they's more'an one way ta skin'a cat," declared Clovis shaking his head. Not a boy no more, aye! A big man now! Ta hell with tha belt. You'll just get yer ass whupped like a man then, with fists."

Clovis started toward Lincoln and Lincoln began to back up when the sound of a voice shook them out of their personal little world and back into the larger one.

"Clovis! Don't you dare hit that boy," screamed Anna Mae.

"Anna Mae?" said a startled Clovis.

"Mom? Rats?" echoed Lincoln as if awaking from sleep and then recognizing both his mother and his friend standing nearby.

It was an awkward moment for the four of them. They all just stood there staring at one another for a tongue-tied minute as if they were all naked, each reflecting on the situation and pondering on what to say or do to recover from their current state of embarrassment.

It was Rats who finally broke the silence with a manufactured excuse to make his retreat and to separate the two combatants, if only for a ceasefire.

[154]

"Linc, I just stopped by to see if you'd take one last trip over to town with me before I leave."

"Whatta you mean, 'before you leave' Tyler?" asked Anna Mae curiously.

"Yeah, where ya goin'?" inquired Clovis.

"Oh, I guess Linc hadn't told you," he answered, looking at Lincoln.

Lincoln was shaking his head "no" as he descended the porch steps.

"No, I guess I just hadn't got around to it yet."

"I've enlisted in the Marines. I'm leaving for boot camp in a couple of days," Tyler informed them.

"Well Tyler, I'm disturbed by the news…but ain't surprised," said Mrs. Crockett with a deep breath. "Guess you're the first one from here, but you won't be the last, I'm afraid."

"Yeah, I knew I was probably going to be drafted soon, so I decided to go ahead and join up," explained Rats.

"This is sumthin' that ever boy 'round here has over their heads right now," offered Mr. Crockett, his demeanor having been transformed by the talk of war into one of solemn contemplation as he patted his son on the shoulder in a humble manner as if to be reminded that there are bigger fish to fry in this ocean of life.

"Sure, I'd love to go over in town with you," offered Lincoln.

"Say, while you're over there, would you fella's pick up my prescription at Long's Drug Store?" Anna Mae asked.

"Of course, we'd be glad too," replied Rats.

"How 'bout going down along the creek by the railroad tracks like we used to," Rats suggested.

"Okay, why not?" Lincoln replied.

"Stay clear of the hobos if they's any out down in there," warned Mr. Crockett.

"We'll keep an eye out for'em," said Rats.

"So long, see you later, don't hold supper for me," called Lincoln as they crossed the street and headed through the open field down to Town Creek. They had no thought that the walk down childhood memory lane they were anticipating would turn into an adult nightmare.

Chapter 34

The narrow trail that paralleled the twists and turns of Town Creek was a path on which Lincoln and Rats had, in the days of their youth, laid down thousands of footprints while playing up and down the rural waterway. They soon came upon a huge oak tree draped with monkey vines on which gangs of raucous kids would swing back and forth across the stream. Laughing, they recalled the day when, ironically, Lonnie Vineyard forgot to turn loose of the vine and slammed into the tree breaking his nose.

The more they walked, at every bend, rapid, pool, tree, and rock there could be summoned the memory of some adventure from a by-gone day: snatching crawdads from beneath rocks, victimizing water snakes sunning on low-hanging bushes in a BB-gun war, or sailing stick boats through swirling eddies. They hopscotched across the creek on the ruins of a rock dam built many summers ago, and then there was the big water pipe spanning the creek overhead; the one they had walked like tightrope aerialists in the circus. They marveled at how it didn't look nearly as high now.

As their walk carried them along their old stomping ground of what *used to be* and what *is*, a question occurred to them, "Where are the kids?" It was evident that kids didn't play here anymore. The features and personality of the creek had changed. The grass-choked path was hardly visible; the once open creek banks were now shut off by thickets and waist-high weeds. But, to these two and their friends, this had been an adventure land, a wonderland where one could be anything, do anything, and was limited only by the bounds of one's imagination. Kids seek a different type of entertainment now.

Nearing the end of their trek, a stench in the air served to remind them that all memory lanes aren't yellow brick roads and, unfortunately, some things don't change. Waste materials from the mills continued to be dumped into Town Creek, which then carried the pollution on downstream to Little River. At the mill's dump site, a large cesspool of stagnated water and waste runoff created and propagated by the pollution attracted a population of turtles and carp. Using homemade spears and gigs, they used to spear these swimmers in their habitat of murky goop.

Their stroll down memory lane ended at the edge of "Hobo Town." That's what people called a clearing in the woods next to the railroad tracks at the edge of town where for decades hobos had jumped trains and set up camp. It was still in business, but not on the scale it had been in the old days. Sitting down with their backs against young saplings, they casually tossed small pebbles into the creek.

"I'm sorry you had to hear that back at the house," apologized Lincoln.

"Don't worry 'bout it, Linc. I understand. I'm no stranger to home fights myself," reassured Rats.

"Biggest thing I worry about is how your dad beats you. Looked like he was about to lay one on you and might have if I hadn't been there," said Rats.

"I know. That's the first time he's threatened to hit me with anything other than that belt," said Lincoln.

"He's a damn big dude and could hurt somebody bad with his fists," observed Rats.

"What's happening to you anyway?" asked Rats. "I've never seen you stand up to your Dad before. Stood up to him an ole Preacher Nutter down at the church yesterday and your dad again today. You're becoming a rebel all of a sudden, a real bad-ass," he said laughing.

"I don't know 'bout that, but I'm not going to be beat up anymore. This 'badass' has enough sense not to fight him. I'd get killed, but I'll leave before I get beat up again," swore Lincoln.

"Where would you go?"

"I don't know, but I won't stay there."

They sat silently for a minute, each lost in quiet contemplation.

"It's ironic isn't it?" said Lincoln rhetorically.

"What's that?" questioned Rats.

"Here we've been reminiscing about our days of youth, wishing we could go back to those times, times of carefree fun, times of no responsibility, times of longing to grow up and be out from under the control of parents telling us what to do, how to do, when to do, and be our own men."

"Now, here we are grown up and legally adults. We're free to go our own ways, make our own decisions, live our own lives what, when, how we choose, or so we're led to believe, in the process of becoming adults, but in reality we're no freer as adults than we were as children. The parents have just been replaced by others telling us what we can and can't do with our lives, like the government and society. This whole thing called *your* life is just one big lie. It's a conspiracy to keep people under the control of some type of warden. We are prisoners to be molded into a pattern of conformity designed to serve the whole at the expense of the individual."

"There you go waxing philosophical again. I still say you read too many books. My mind just won't go there today," sighed Rats.

"I know, Kemosabe. I guess I'm just talking to be talking. It doesn't seem real that you're going to be leaving."

"I know. The time's passin' fast," said Rats.

"Say, we'd better get on over to town and pick up your mom's medicine."

"Yeah, I guess you're right. Time waits for no man," said Lincoln.

Chapter 35

"Looky here fellers, we got some comp'ney come ta visit," bragged the man sarcastically to his traveling companions as he pushed Rats and Lincoln out of the trees ahead of him into the large clearing. Rats and Lincoln had literally run headlong into this surly man on the trail, as hairy as a bear and half as big and smelly as one. Garbed in dirty, shabby clothes with tattered, unkempt hair and one bad eye that danced around like the head on a bobble head doll, he did not impress one to be a person of temperament or character as to be mistaken for a Boy Scout leader, especially waving that Bowie knife about as he did.

Then three of the orneriest-looking human beings from the assemblage of society's castaways gathered there in the clearing gravitated toward the hulking man and encircled the two young men, looking them up and down like curiosities. The remainder of the camp's residents either lingered inquisitively at a distance or pretended to have no interest in the proceedings and attended to their own affairs. As for Lincoln and Rats, they just looked at each other and shook their heads. Whether they wanted to be or not, here they found themselves in the middle of Hobo Town. How quickly one's fortunes can change!

"Come join me an my companions at air campfar an share'a cup'a java," said Bad Eye, "and maybe you'can help us with'a problem we got."

"Thanks' for tha invitation, but we're really inna hurry and have to be on our way," said Rats, edging away.

"Uh, that's right," explained Lincoln. "We're just passin' through on our way to town."

"Well now, that ain't bein' very frinly," growled the Bad Eye. "Do ye think so fellers?"

His pals shook their heads in unanimous agreement with the big man who was obviously the boss of this band of ne'er-do-wells.

"C'mon now, we wanna talk to ya," he ordered, cocking his good eye in the boys' direction.

Bad Eye lumbered over to a campsite near the center of the clearing while his trio of cohorts herded the boys along behind him like sheep dogs snipping at their heels. The tramps seated their "guests" on opposite sides of a small campfire and paired themselves off between them.

Rats and Lincoln looked at each other with the same "what do we do now" expression but wore masks of composure disguising the pounding heartbeats of uncertainty that lay beneath their breasts. They had taken notice that Bad Eye had holstered the big hunting knife on his belt, but of greater concern was the demeanor with which the youngest of the group, a skinny, pale-faced lad, kept flipping open and closed a switchblade while watching them unmoving. He was a snake waiting to strike.

Their captors filled tin cans with a dark-colored swill from a pot boiling over the fire and topped them off with the remains of a fifth of Wild Turkey. After offering their visitors a cup, which Lincoln and Rats both refused, they began to enlighten the two victims of happenchance as to the nature of their current situation.

"I'll come right ta tha point," said Bad Eye. "Weez broke an ain't got nuthin'."

"That's right," echoed the others.

"We need money an we gonna git some one way er tha other," said Bad Eye. "Now, you jus give us tha money ye got on ye, an ye can be on yer way."

"But, the only money I have is for my mama's medicine. She's real sick," Lincoln told him.

"Shit, Big Bill," cursed the pale-faced one, "stop foolin' 'round an just take it."

"Shut up, Slim!" Big Bill scowled.

Looking back at the boys with a grin he said patronizingly, "But, it'll jus be like'a loan. We'll pay ye back one uf these days."

"Do you pay interest?" asked Rats.

Everyone's eyes immediately fell upon Rats, none believing the sarcastic remark they had just heard. Rats shrank back pursing his lips. He himself couldn't believe that he had just let such a frivolous remark audibly slip from his mouth at such a dire and inopportune moment.

"Are ye tryin' ta be a smartass?" scowled Bad Eye, jerking the hunting knife from its sheath and stabbing it into the ground in front of him.

The ruffian beside Bad Eye jumped to his feet and pulled Rats up with him. The man frisked Rats up and down and found the wallet in his hip pocket. Unceremoniously ripping it out, he pushed Rats back to the ground and handed the wallet to his superior.

"Twenty bucks!" the man counted out. "Not too shabby."

"Now let's see what ye buddy's got," said Bad Eye.

He pulled the hunting knife out of the ground very deliberately and pushed himself to a standing position in front of Lincoln.

"Gimma yer money pouch!" he commanded, waving the blade back and forth in Lincoln's face.

Lincoln nervously pulled the wallet from his jeans and reached it to the man's outstretched hand. Before reaching the man's hand, however, he let the worn leather case slip from his fingers and fall to the ground. The man was annoyed.

"Don't play games boy, er yer gonna get this pig sticker in yer gut. Now, pick it up!"

Lincoln knelt on his knees clutching the wallet in his left hand while feeling around on the ground with his right. Between the big man's legs he had a clear view of Rats watching him and gave his pal a wink. Rats caught sight of Lincoln wiggle his right hand and the waffle-sized, flat rock in its grasp. Rats nodded that he understood and began to formulate his own plan. It was time to cut and run!

Lincoln looked up at Bad Eye and handed him the wallet. Just as the man took hold of it, Lincoln, with all the strength he could muster, slammed the stone into Bad Eye's genitals. The man bellowed like a bull moose struck by lightning. Both the wallet and knife dropped freely to the ground.

The big hulk grabbed at his groin with both hands as his knees buckled and thighs constricted. The stabbing pain that pierced his abdomen doubled him up like a half sandwich as blood and seminal fluid flowed from ruptured testicles. Stumbling backward a few steps, he toppled like a felled tree on top of the campfire, then rolled to one side into a fetal position. He lay there bug-eyed, feet clawing in the dirt, bawling like a lost calf in a snowstorm.

When Bad Eye had first cried out attracting everyone's attention, Rats rolled to his left and kicked with his right leg striking the vagabond next to him with a well-placed foot to the face sending him head-over-heals backwards. Rolling to his feet, he sprang over his semiconscious victim who was bleeding profusely from a broken nose and took flight toward the railroad tracks faster than the

Israelites fleeing Egypt. Lincoln, as well, had attempted his own getaway at the same point in time, but hadn't met with the same degree of success.

Rats, looking over his back, saw that the little weaselly thug had Lincoln pinned to the ground with that switchblade at his throat. He skidded to a halt; he had to go back and help his friend.

He heard Lincoln yell:

"Run Rats, run!"

The fourth member of the quartet of bad eggs was hot on Rats' tail, swearing and waving the big man's hunting knife. Rats figured the odds were against him, so he decided the best course of action was to do as Lincoln said and go for help. It was at that moment he saw his pursuer suddenly come to a dead stop, drop the knife, and raise his hands into the air. He was puzzled by the man's behavior until he heard a voice behind him. There, just a few feet behind him, stood Deputy Lester Odom with his revolver drawn, pointing straight at his pursuer.

Slim, the switchblade man, upon seeing Deputy Odom, lost his interest in Lincoln, scrambled about grabbing for the two wallets, and sought an escape route in the opposite direction along the creek. His flight for freedom was short-lived, however, when he came face to face with the revolver of Deputy Clay Cassidy who stepped from behind a juniper bush.

With the two knife-wielders handcuffed and seated beside their wounded companions and Lincoln and Rats seated nearby, Sheriff Coker began to question them.

"What happened here?"

The boys described how they happened to be there, how the hobos tried to rob them and how they had taken the two injured ones out of commission in their attempt to escape.

"You're lucky," said Deputy Cassidy, "someone happened to be walkin' the tracks and saw something going on that didn't look right and gave us a call."

"You think you're a couple'a tough guys don't you?" said the Sheriff.

"Seems like everywhere there's something goin' on, you two happen ta be in the middle of it. You think I don't know 'bout that commotion you caused over at the high school that ruined the dance or the fracas down at Big Al's when Edgar McBee got his noggin

[162]

cracked? And, now here you are mixed up in another disturbance. You're like Coldwater's version of Billy the Kid an Jessie James…and you know what happened to them. Now, you go on and get outta here."

As the boys started to leave, the Sheriff got in Lincoln's face.

"I'm keepin' my eye on you. One'a these days you're gonna mess up big time, and I'm gonna put your Millie ass under my jail. I don't coddle Millie trash like Miss Jessie Wingo does," he said spitefully.

Lincoln thought to himself, *Sheriff, wouldn't it be ironic if you found your bootlegging ass locked up in your own jail sometime?*

Chapter 36

The midmorning sun glistened off Lincoln's sweaty, shirtless body as he worked attentively at grooming a section of landscaping at the back of the hotel. The civil, political, and religious upheaval that had had everyone in such a tizzy seemed to have settled down somewhat and things were beginning to get back to business as usual. Around the Lacy, nothing of a noteworthy nature had come to light nor had any personage of a strange or peculiar nature appeared on the scene to break the monotony, but then there was the Logano party still hanging around town for some reason.

Although their group had been keeping a low profile, their behavior seemed somewhat unusual, if not suspicious, to Lincoln at any rate. They had left town for a few days after the July Fourth activities and were just now returning. Consequentially, their departure and return had coincided with Marjorie Henderson and her husband's leaving and return from a two-week vacation. When they were in town, the muscle seldom left the hotel, spending most of their time lounging about the lobby playing cards, chowing down in the restaurant, or holding up in their rooms. Then, from time to time, the trio would disappear for unspecified periods of time.

The only locals Shooter and Darlene fraternized with were Sheriff Coker, Mayor McKean, and Dalton Jackson, and that had only been a time or two. The Atlanta couple had once dined with Miss Jessie. But, to Lincoln, they were like ducks out of water; they just didn't fit in Coldwater and he still couldn't shake the images stuck in the back of his mind of the weapons arsenal he had glimpsed in the trunk of the white limo and the unusual activity at the hotel back on July fifth.

In a conversation with Bam Bam, Lincoln had learned that he, too, had been cognizant of the comings and goings of the visitors from Atlanta and held the same suspicions and concerns about their behaviors and motives. The big man had been unaware, however, of the cache of weaponry they had possession of until Lincoln informed him of the rolling arsenal, which made Bam Bam even more uneasy about the crew's purposes. They agreed to keep a vigilant eye on the group and to keep one another discreetly informed of anything they found out.

Lincoln hadn't noticed that Miss Jessie had taken a seat at a table under one of the large ceiling fans on the veranda where one of the maids had placed a pitcher of fresh lemonade. Miss Jessie had intended to meet with him this morning to discuss some changes in his employment duties, some with additional responsibilities.

Just as she started to call for him to join her, she noticed something that gave her pause; something his tanned skin couldn't hide from very far away. Unaware of her presence, he heard her approach from close behind.

"Lincoln! Where did you get those?" she asked with a concerned sound to her voice and look on her face, referring to the two-inch-wide, red stripes cut into his back.

Startled, Lincoln swirled around.

"What?"

Face to face, she was taken aback at the sight of similar markings across his chest that resembled imprints left by lashes from a belt.

"Oh, my gosh! Who did this to you?" she exclaimed in horror, holding her head in her hands in disbelief.

"I'm sorry," apologized Lincoln, grabbing his shirt and hurriedly putting it on.

"You don't have anything to apologize for," she sympathized. "Did your father do this?"

Lincoln hesitated before answering.

"Yes," he admitted, buttoning his shirt.

"Does he beat your mama too?"

"Not really beats…he hits her sometimes," he answered reluctantly.

"He needs to be reported to the Sheriff," said Miss Jessie.

"No, no, don't do that. That would just make things worst…besides, it won't happen again. Anyhow, ole Buford Coker'd put *me* in jail before he would my ole man," said Lincoln.

"What do you mean?" asked Miss Jessie curiously.

"The old Sheriff and I have had a couple of run-ins and he's just lookin' for an excuse to 'put me under his jail' as he puts it."

"Lincoln, you stay away from Buford Coker. He's bad business."

"You're tellin' me. I know things…"

Lincoln stopped abruptly and thought better of saying anything more.

[165]

"You know what kind of things, Lincoln?" the lady asked sincerely.

"Never mind, it's not important."

"Lincoln, listen to me," she said gravely.

"Do you remember when I told you that messin' with Ashley Armstrong was messin' with fire?"

"Yes ma'am."

"Well, messin' with Buford Coker is messin' with *hellfire*. He's as crooked as a corkscrew and you best stay clear of his path. You hear me?"

"Yes ma'am," he answered, half lost in thought.

"Are you okay?" She looked at him thoughtfully. "You've been awfully quiet the past few days and have not been your usual self."

He went on to explain that he just had a lot of things on his mind, including his friend Tyler joining the Marines and going off to Vietnam, and his own time to be drafted coming soon His boss told him that she had also thought about the possibility of his being drafted. She assured him that, if he was, not to worry about his job, that he would still have a job at the hotel when he returned and, in fact, had come out this morning to talk with him about that very thing, as well as his taking on some additional responsibilities.

While they were taking seats at a table on the veranda, the maid was filling their glasses with lemonade and telling them about the weather bureau predicting severe thunderstorms and heavy rain, with possible flooding in some areas later in the afternoon and evening. Normally, before the months of July and August had become part of the historical record, the sweltering heat of summer would take its toll on gardens and crops, as well as man and beast. The only hope for relief would come in the form of summer rains which were sparse.

"Well, that's welcome news," said Miss Jessie. "Perhaps that will cool things off a bit."

"Yes, and perk things up, since the gardens and lawns and the hotel grounds are drying up," added Lincoln.

Just as they were getting settled down and ready to talk, one of the other bellmen came to the veranda door and called out.

"Excuse me, Miss Jessie. There's a phone call for you, Lincoln. The lady says it's very important that she speak with you," he said teasingly.

"Oh, really!" he answered.

"Best not keep your lady love waiting," advised Miss Jessie, smiling coyly.

"I do declare," said Lincoln jumping up, "that girl's on me like white on rice," he winked at Miss Jessie.

"You sure you aren't fallin' into Johnny Cash's 'Ring of Fire?'" she cautioned.

He just shrugged his shoulders as he looked back at her.

Miss Jessie shook her head back and forth, letting out a deep breath as he disappeared through the veranda door.

"Hello there. What's up?" said Lincoln, answering the telephone with his best Clark Gable impersonation and expecting Ashley Armstrong on the other end of the line.

"Lincoln, this is Marge...Marge Henderson...remember, you came over to my house one night a few weeks ago?"

Lincoln, surprised at hearing a voice he wasn't expecting, felt a bit embarrassed at the manner in which he had answered the phone and it took him a minute to gather himself and depart from the pathway of thought he had anticipated following and refocus them in favor of a new direction...to where he knew not.

"Oh...yes...Marge! I remember." *All too well!* he thought to himself.

"Lincoln, I need for you to come over to my house...today! I must talk to you," she said insistently.

"I don't know if that's a good idea," he said hesitantly.

"Please! I have to talk to someone. It's...it's a matter of life and death. I don't know who else to turn to," she pleaded.

Her petition seemed genuine to Lincoln; he recognized the fear in her voice.

"Okay, I'll come. But, I can't make it 'til later in the day when I get off work. I'll try to be there around 6:00 p.m."

"Thank you. Please don't be late."

Chapter 37

Later that afternoon

The windshield wipers on the '56 Ford were slapping back and forth faster than a fat woman fanning at a hot August Sunday afternoon picnic as they tried to rake the sheets of rainwater off the windshield of the car Lincoln had borrowed from another bellman at the hotel. He squinted through the windshield and tried to make out the lane markings as the car slowly plowed its way through water-glutted lanes and tried to make his way to Marge's house early that evening as he had promised.

When he rapped on the door at 321 5th Avenue, he was about twenty minutes later than he had told her to expect him. Marge responded to the knock almost immediately. Dressed as if going out for the evening, she was attired in a midnight blue skirt and white blouse; a string of white pearls hugged her neck. Welcoming him into dry surroundings, she expressed her appreciation for his willingness to answer her distress call under such inclement weather conditions.

"So, what's this life-or-death situation you have to talk to someone about?" he asked. "Who's life and who's death?"

"Mine! I'm afraid for my life," she answered fretfully, sitting down on the couch.

"Why?" asked Lincoln, sitting down beside her, spooked by what she had said.

"That's not important. I don't want to involve you, or anyone else, in my problems. That's why I'm leaving town."

"Leaving town?" questioned Lincoln.

"Has someone threatened you?"

"Let's just say that I know some things that some bad people don't want me to know," she said, getting up walking about, and wringing her hands nervously.

"What about your husband?" Lincoln asked.

"He doesn't know anything about it. He left a couple of hours ago for Atlanta to attend a week-long conference…won't be back until next Friday. By then I'll be long gone," she added tearfully.

"You're just going to leave him not knowing where you are?" asked Lincoln incredulously, "How could you do that to him?"

"If I tell him the truth, his life will be in danger, too. I have to leave to protect him," she rationalized.

"Yeah, I guess I understand that, but why are you telling me about all this instead of some of your friends? We hardly know each other," Lincoln questioned.

"To be honest, I hardly have any friends. My husband and I just moved here less than a year ago, and with him traveling all the time, we just haven't had much of a social life."

"Why don't you go to the Sheriff and explain all this to him?"

"Huh, I might as well go ahead and shoot myself," she mumbled, looking out the window at the howling wind blowing sheets of rain along the street.

Overhearing Marge's mumbled words, it clicked in Lincoln's brain that he might not be the only one in Coldwater that had uncovered dirt on some of its prominent citizens.

"I think I'm beginning to catch enough of the drift of what you're saying to at least make an educated guess about the source of your concern," speculated Lincoln.

"Well, enough of this," said Marge, changing the subject.

"This is not why I asked you here tonight. I wanted to give you something before I leave."

Marge opened the door of a curio cabinet and took an object off one of the shelves. Walking over to Lincoln, she took his hand, opened it up, and placed the object in it.

"You seemed to admire this so much and know so much about it that I wanted you to have it."

Lincoln looked at the object closely. It was the necklace with the old Roman coin pendant.

"But I can't accept this," he said surprised. "This is a very valuable coin. Besides, it was an inheritance from your uncle. It's a family heirloom."

"Oh, I never really knew the man, and I've never worn it but a time or two. I'd really like for you to have it. You'll appreciate its significance much more than I will," she answered.

"I don't know what to say," said Lincoln, "except, thank you."

"You're very welcome," she replied as she planted a kiss on his check.

"I'm sorry things are going badly for you," sympathized Lincoln.

"It's my own fault. We make decisions and we have to live with the consequences, don't we?" she rationalized.

"What are your plans?" he asked.

"In a few minutes, I'm calling a cab to take me to the bus station. I'm taking the bus over to Knoxville to visit my sister, and from there, who knows?"

On his return trip to the hotel, the rainstorm still raged as peals of thunder resounded through the clouds like the beating of giant bass drums and jagged-edged flashes of electricity pierced the sky like lightning bolts from the hand of Zeus. As he slowly navigated the water-logged streets, he noticed that Town Creek was overflowing its banks and he was going to have a difficult time getting home.

As he drove, he thought of Marge and the day he had first seen her at the J.C. Penny store; the close call they had the night he had gone to her house; tonight, and the story she had told him and the gift of the pendant; and the fact that she would now be just a memory, a person he would remember with fondness in the years to come and always wonder of her fate. Unfortunately for Lincoln, Marjorie Henderson would be back in his life sooner than he expected.

Back at the Lacy Hotel

It was about 7:00 p.m. when Lincoln arrived. He learned from the desk clerk that Miss Jessie had gone out earlier to run an errand.

"In this weather!" exclaimed a much surprised Lincoln.

"Said it was important but would be back in a couple of hours," returned the clerk. "In fact," said the clerk, remembering, "she left just a few minutes after you did."

It was just a short time later that the lady in question came traipsing down the hall from the back entrance and walked up the steps dripping wet. She said not a word to anyone as she headed straight to her quarters.

It was exactly 8:00 p.m. when Shooter Logano, with Darlene prancing along at his side and "Larry," "Curly," and "Moe" trailing behind, poured out of the elevator into the lobby. Shooter and Darlene went immediately to the desk while the muscle retrieved the limo and loaded the several armloads of luggage. Without any prior notice, Mr. Logano claimed that urgent business had arisen back in

Atlanta that required his immediate attention and they must, by necessity, check out and be on their way.

Still, it seemed odd to Lincoln to make such an abrupt exit and embark on a lengthy trip in the midst of such dreadful traveling conditions rather than wait until morning when the tempest had passed.

Looking across the street, he saw Dutch pulling into his cabstand and signaled to him to come over to the hotel and pick him up.

"I need a ride home, Dutch."

"Hop in my friend, it's not fit for men or beasts out tonight," said the cabbie.

"Yeah, I'd probably have to swim half the way, but I don't think I'd get past Town Creek," observed Lincoln.

"You're right about that. It's flooding bad."

Dutch's two-way radio popped and crackled with static.

"Can't get much on tha ole squawk box tonight in this storm," complained Dutch.

"You know a lot about radios, don't you Dutch?" said Lincoln.

"Yeah, quite a bit. Two-way, CB, short-way. Learned 'bout 'em in the military. I talk to the truckers, even people in other countries. Like ta listen in on the emergency band, too…the police an all, ya know."

"Speakin' of calls, I had a strange phone call earlier…t'was around 6:45 p.m." said Dutch as he eased the cab along Main Street.

"How's that?" asked his passenger.

"Had a call from a lady . . . wanted me to pick her up and take her to the bus station."

"Is that right?" said Lincoln, looking at the cabbie and remembering what Marge had said about calling a cab to go to the bus station.

"What's so strange about that?" he asked.

"Well, when I got to her house . . . around 7:00 p.m. must'a been . . . didn't seem to be nobody home. The house was dark."

"I honked the horn a couple of times, but no one come out. So I left and come back to my stand."

"That is strange all right," agreed Lincoln, as the things Marge had told him about being afraid came to mind.

"There was another thing that seemed sort of odd," thought Dutch, scratching his beard.

"What's that?" asked Lincoln.

"Well, it was rainin' so hard I couldn't say fer sure, but when I got close to the house I coulda swore I saw a blue panel truck come tearin' outta that driveway. Durn near run me offa tha road."

Lincoln's eyes lit up. He remembered Julius driving a blue panel truck away from the hotel the day of the parade.

"But, surely there couldn't be any connection," he thought.

"Are you sure you went to the right address?" Lincoln asked Dutch.

"Sure am…wrote it down on that piece of paper right there," answered Dutch pointing to a small piece of brown paper lying on the dashboard.

Lincoln picked up the piece of paper and held it up to the light as they passed under a street lamp so he could read it. His heart sank when he saw the address Dutch had scribbled on the paper: 321 5th Avenue.

Chapter 38

The tires cried, hugging every curve and trying to hold onto the asphalt as the Thunderbird sped down the little winding county road. Ashley gunned the sports car over rises and through dips and roared down straight-ways at sixty…seventy…eighty miles an hour. Lincoln held on to his seat tighter and looked wide-eyed at the driver. He had never seen her drive like this, fully focused but trancelike. He didn't know which the greater risk would be: trying to interfere with her or just riding it out. He decided to just hold on and hope they survived. Shortly thereafter, Ashley steered the T-Bird across the Ridge's Observation Point parking lot and whipped it into a parking space, coming to a screeching halt. She lowered the convertible top, leaned back in her seat and laughed at the wide-eyed Lincoln who gripped the seat.

"What the hell was that all about?" he asked surprised. "You could have killed us both."

"Just felt like doing it!" she exclaimed, throwing her arms up in the air. "Didn't it feel good?"

"Feel good? I thought we were going to die you crazy blonde."

"Yeah, the thought crossed my mind to…" before she could finish.

"Oh! The thought crossed your mind to, but you kept right on going," said Lincoln shaking his head.

She leaned over close and tickled his chin.

"Now admit it. Didn't it really feel good?"

"Well…yeah…but you might give me a little forewarning next time."

The Point, which normally doubled as a lover's lane, was void of vehicles on this particular Sunday evening. Still, Ashley had chosen an inconspicuous spot near the back of the lot to park. It was the first time they had seen each other since the night of the July 4th fireworks.

With heads resting on the back of the red leather seats, they gazed into the clear night sky and searched for the Big Dipper hidden somewhere among the countless stars stretched over the earth like a blanket of twinkling Christmas lights. Out into the far reaches of space, the roman-candle-like burst of light from a shooting star suddenly streaked across the canopy bringing an "ooh" and "ah" from the two amateur astronomers.

"Make a wish," said Ashley.

"I just did," assured Lincoln.

"And you?"

"Ditto!" replied Ashley.

"Isn't it all so magnificently wonderful and mysterious?" she said with amazement.

"What?" he asked.

"The universe, the earth…everything!"

"Yes, it is quite remarkable," he answered.

"Do you ever think about how it all got there?"

"One can make the cosmological argument that all things depend upon something for their existence; therefore, the cosmos must depend upon an independent being, i.e., God. It doesn't take a genius to see that intelligent design is embodied in everything from supernovas to the human eye. The millions of flora and fauna forms of life that exist (including human beings) with the complex internal systems and innate mental capacity they possess could not have come into being by mere chance but must have depended upon the work of a superior, independent being."

Although they had been conversing almost weekly by telephone, this was only the third time they had actually been together since her parents had, so to speak, brought the stone tablet down from The Ridge two months ago with one commandment chiseled on it: "Thou shalt not consort with Millies."

"You seem a little melancholy tonight," observed Ashley.

"Yeah, I guess I am a bit. I just have a lot of things on my mind," answered Lincoln.

"Care to share?"

"Oh, I don't want to burden you with my personal problems or get on my soapbox about what's wrong with the world."

They sat quietly for a minute, gazing at the night sky when Lincoln whispered.

"Listen!"

"To what?"

"The night sounds. Be very quiet and listen to the night sounds."

They sat motionless, almost breathless, eavesdropping on the nocturnal chatter in the stillness of nightfall.

First, there came the cooing of a dove in the distance, then the whoosh of an owl's wings cutting unseen through the air above them, the rustling of chipmunks, and the faint chirping of crickets in the treetops.

"That's amazing," exclaimed Ashley.

"Yes, it is amazing what all there is to hear when we stop and listen," said Lincoln.

"You're sort of amazing yourself," said Ashley.

"You seem to be in tune with so much of the world around you that most people never take notice of, or think about, or even care about."

"On the contrary, my pretty one, I don't feel like I'm in tune with anything. I'm just curious. I wonder about things. I'm continually searching for answers," confessed Lincoln, swinging his head back and forth.

"Answers to what?" asked Ashley.

"The *whys*!"

"The *whys*?

"Yes. *Why* are things the way they are? *Why* is the world so intolerant? *Why* are the religious so pretentious? *Why* is life so unjust? But, mostly, of all God's creation, *why* are human beings the most perplexing?"

"Say! That sounds like me when I get on my soapbox at home. It usually gets me into trouble. Then follow lectures about remembering my place in society, southern traditions, and so on," said Ashley.

Lincoln chuckled.

"To further muddy the water, there's one characteristic all these subjects in question hold in common," continued Lincoln, "and it's a trait that complicates any effort to make sense of them. And that is, that they are all an enigma."

"In what way do you mean an enigma?" asked Ashley.

"In that, on one hand, they may produce good, at least to some degree; yet, on the other hand, they may produce downright evil."

"I see what you mean," agreed Ashley.

Ashley, dressed in heels, skin-tight designer jeans, and a white, off-the-shoulder, gypsy blouse that exposed her midriff, slid sideways in her seat, leaned back against the door, swung her legs across the console, and crossed them on Lincoln's lap. She then redirected the subject of the conversation to what she had originally wanted to discuss with Lincoln.

"By the way, I heard your debate, or at least most of it, with Sheriff Coker last weekend and thought it was wonderful," said Ashley. "I was impressed with your knowledge and understanding of the ideals our government is based on, but most of all with the passion with which you expressed them. I've been anxious to discuss them with you," explained Ashley.

"Uh, I think I forgot where I was and who all was listening and *who* I was debating with and got a little carried away. I'll really be on ole Buford's blacklist now!"

"You sure showed him up, that's for sure. I loved it! Even my girlfriends were impressed and, believe me, it takes a lot to impress them," assured Ashley.

She poked him gently in the ribs with her toe and grinned.

Lincoln grinned.

"Like your T-shirt," she said, poking him again playfully. "It's appropriate for someone who wonders about…even the oddest of things."

On his chest, bold black lettering on a background of white cotton wittily solicited "Who's Pete Sake?"

Assuming a more serious tone, Ashley asked, "Do you really believe in all that you said up there, all that about the Constitution, the Bill of Rights, and freedom and equality for everyone?"

"Absolutely," answered Lincoln, "I think that's what the Founding Fathers believed in and wanted this country to be. They designed a framework in those documents within which a governmental structure could be developed to assure that those objectives could become a reality."

"But, it hasn't quite worked out the way they envisioned it, has it?" reasoned Ashley.

"Uh, you might say that," said Lincoln sarcastically.

"That's what the Civil Rights movement's all about and why I'm so interested in it," said Ashley, "and why I get into so much trouble at home when I mention it. They think I'm being led astray by the rhetoric of socialist radicals," she added.

"Well, people are resistant to things that will bring about change, like the Civil Rights Movement, for example," said Lincoln.

"For the upper classes, part of it is *fear*—fear of endangering their wealth, their social standing, and their traditions. In time, however, those fears can be elevated when they come to understand what equality means in the sense that we, and the Founding Fathers, are talking about. The other part is *prejudice*, and that can be overcome only when people are willing to accept others just as people," preached Lincoln.

"I'm sorry," apologized Lincoln. "Here I am on my soapbox again."

"Oh, no," rebuked Ashley, "I agree."

"It's like this Ridger and Millie business here in our town. It's so ignorant!" she added.

"We have to get legislation passed to ensure civil rights for everyone."

"Well, laws can modify people's behavior but not their attitudes. We can't change prejudice into acceptance any more than we can change stones into bread," rationalized Lincoln.

"You're right of course! But, how do you get people to overcome prejudices that have been engrained in them since day one?" questioned Ashley.

"That, my dear, is one of those enigmas you have to answer the *why* of before you can define a solution," stated Lincoln.

"And," continued Lincoln, "perhaps there are no solutions. Philosophers, scholars, poets, and theologians have contemplated and debated the whys of life for centuries and come up with no definitive conclusions. Perhaps the old country song is right; maybe we are 'rolling downhill like a snowball headed for hell'."

"Enough philosophy for one night," he said. "Come over here, hot rod girl."

Ashley, smiling, climbed over the console and sat in his lap facing him.

"Whatcha got in mind, big boy?" she said coyly.

"This."

He pulled her close to him until their mouths touched and they engaged in a long, slow sensuous kiss.

Ashley Armstrong and Lincoln Crockett are two young people who come from socially conflicting worlds: Ashley's being a world of privilege, Lincoln's being one of deprivation. Yet, these two blue-sky thinking individuals, unfettered by convention, find a common bond in their quest to understand, answer, and perhaps change, at least in their own lives, the *whys* of the world that eat at their souls like a cancer.

Chapter 39

The torrent of water that last weekend's storm had poured out on most of Jackson County and flooded parts of the Milltown river plane had, by now, receded back within the boundaries of the banks of Town Creek. After work, Lincoln decided to try the shortcut home again to see if it was passable. What he found was about what he expected: a mess. All along the creek the flood plain was covered with mud and littered with debris.

The deluge had washed the footbridge free from its moorings on the mill-side bank and pulled it sideways at a cockeyed angle. Walking carefully to the end of the twisted walkway for a closer look, he judged that it would take a giant leap to clear the breach over to the mill side.

Turning to make his way back, he noticed something in the water. It appeared to be an article of clothing next to the bank under the bridge. Upon closer inspection, he recognized something that caused him to freeze in his tracks. Cold chills ran up his arms and the back of his neck. There, was more than just an article of clothing. Lodged beneath the barren roots of a large weeping willow tree was a body, more specifically, the white, puffy, remains of a woman's body.

Instinctively, he looked quickly all around to see if anyone else might be in the vicinity. He saw no one. Even though he could hardly bear to look upon the gory sight, there was something about it that seemed to strike a sense of familiarity somewhere in his memory; some remembrance that compelled him to make a closer inspection.

Although the body was floating face down in dirty water and covered with trash, he could tell it was the body of a woman and she was wearing what appeared to be the remains of a white blouse and a dark blue skirt. Then he remembered. Marge Henderson was dressed in a dark blue skirt and white blouse the last time he had seen her, the night she had given him the pendant.

Could this be her? he thought.

There was one other thing he needed to see to be sure. He climbed down and around on the roots of the willow tree until he found an unobscured vantage point. He leaned down to where he could see her neck. There it was! A string of white pearls clasped tightly to her neck, just like the ones Marge had been wearing. He recalled her talking about fearing for her life, about knowing things some people didn't want her to know, about leaving town.

This must be her, he thought.

He knew he should go back to town and report his discovery to the Sheriff, but after some consideration, thought better of it. He was afraid Sheriff Coker would start asking a lot of questions; questions he wouldn't want to answer (at least truthfully). Besides, the less interaction he had with old Buford the better. He decided to go home and tell his father that he saw something in the creek that looked like it might be a body and maybe he should take a look at it. That way, his father could notify the authorities and tell them he found the body. Besides, that would make him feel like a big man and give him something to brag about. Things worked out just the way Lincoln had hoped they would, but he gained some information from his father that gave him more reason for concern.

"Sheriff said hit'ud take some time ta identify tha person. She dit'en have no identification on her an nobody seems ta know who she is. Couldn't tell much about her anyways in her condition," said his father.

"I guess they don't have any idea how she got there, huh?" asked Lincoln.

"No, but she didn't drown, that's fer shore!" declared Clovis.

"How do you know?" asked Lincoln surprised.

"She been shot. Shot right through tha heart."

"Oh, how awful. Poor dear," said Anna Mae.

Lincoln got those cold chills again. Marge Henderson's words "fear for my life" and "know things people don't want me to know" repeated over and over in his mind like a needle stuck on a phonograph record. Her words set him to thinking about a series of recent events, apparently unrelated, but now might possibly be in some way connected.

First, there were the conversations he had heard while lurking in the shadows that night at the sawmill. Then, there was the arrival of Shooter Logano and his Atlanta hoods, their friendly association with Sheriff Coker, and their abrupt disappearance. And then, Marge Henderson's expression of concern for her life for things she knew and winds up face down in Town Creek with a bullet hole in her. Lincoln concluded that these must be pieces to a puzzle that, if completed, would paint a picture that certain individuals don't want displayed, a picture so damning that they will obviously go to any lengths to keep the puzzle in the box.

Lincoln began to wonder, *Were they the same individuals he knew things about? If so, what if they found out about the things he knows? Were they the same things or, at least, some of the same things Marge Henderson knew about? Did they know about a connection between him and Marge Henderson?*

Things were beginning to get a little dicey. Lincoln knew that from now on he'd have to keep a low profile, avoid the "so called" law as much as possible, and be cautious about what he talked about and to whom. Even with the economic and social differences between Ridgers and Millies, there had never been much crime in Coldwater and what there was of a minor nature. Lincoln could only remember two or three murders in his nineteen years of life.

He didn't know how what he knew about goings-on behind the scenes in Coldwater compared to what Marge Henderson had known, but it was probably enough to paint a bullseye on his back.

Chapter 40

By the end of the following day, news of the woman found in Town Creek, an apparent victim of foul play, had spread across town faster than green grass through a goose. The mysterious circumstances surrounding the death of the "Town Creek Woman" (as she was becoming known) was becoming the number one topic of conversation over backyard fences and street corners and was causing an even greater sensation than had Colonel Thaddeus P. Browning's Show of Shows a month or so earlier.

Rumor mills were in no short supply as people speculated as to the cause of her grizzly fate while stories abounded as to the identity of the perpetrator of the foul deed, despite the fact that the woman's identity had not yet been established, nor a determination made as to what had actually precipitated her demise.

Much to the chagrin of Sheriff Coker, he was compelled to turn the body over to Doc Campbell, who was also the County Coroner, to perform an autopsy. He was fully aware of the conclusions the good doctor would draw from the results of this procedure. The Sheriff also knew that he himself would have little, if any, difficulty in identifying the corpse since he had been ninety-nine percent sure of who she was upon first seeing the body.

It was around noon, and over at the Lacy Hotel, Jessica Wingo was just arriving at work, excusing her tardiness with a headache. As was her usual practice, she made her first stop at the check-in counter to pick up mail and perhaps engage in light-hearted conversation with employees and guests in the lobby.

Today, Jessica was not in her usual jovial mood and remained only within listening distance of those about her; close enough to overhear the conversations, which were, for the most part, about the woman in Town Creek, but far enough removed from not to require engaging in. She immediately turned her attention to hotel business: "Lincoln, I'd like to see you for a minute. I need you to contact this new office products supplier I met this morning as soon as…?"

She suddenly came to an abrupt halt in midsentence at the sight of something that caught her attention. A pall cast over her countenance and she shuddered as if having seen a ghost from the past. Lincoln wondered if the woman had been, without warning, stricken with some strange affliction. The penetrating stare from her eyes felt like daggers piercing his chest and gave him pause for alarm. Regaining some composure, in a voice barely above a whisper with words cold and deliberate, she continued.

"On second thought, I'd like to talk with you in private. Could you come to my quarters, at say 8:00 p.m. this evening?"

"Uh…yes…I guess so." stammered Lincoln surprised.

"Good! I'll see you then."

Lincoln looked puzzled. He didn't know what to make of the lady's change in demeanor.

Later that evening

Lincoln found himself at 8:00 p.m. promptly sitting, not in his boss's office as he might have expected, but ill-at-ease on a large white sofa in Jessica Wingo's living quarters. His and Jessica Wingo's relationship was one that might be described as friendly yet detached (as hers was with most everyone) and he was always intimidated by the air of elegance and sophistication that seemed to fill the room with the redheaded beauty's presence, especially in private.

Contrary to her usual demeanor, Jessica nervously pulled a chair up beside the couch and began to talk to Lincoln in a quiet but serious tone, which was somewhat out of character for the usually unflappable Jessica Wingo.

"Lincoln, I don't usually poke inta oth'a people's affairs; their business is their own. But, I saw somethin' earlier, and still do that causes me a great deal of concern."

"Did I do or say something that offended a guest?" he asked alarmed.

"No, no! You'ah doin' a great job. This has nothin' ta do with yo'ah work."

"It's th'at pendant around yo'ah neck. Where did ya get it?"

"Oh, this?" he asked, reaching for the old Roman coin pendant and rubbing it between his fingers.

"A friend gave it to me," he said, nonchalantly shrugging it off.

Jessica began to question him coyly.

"Ya know, I know someone who has a coin pendant exactly like th'at."

"Really? Lincoln began to feel very uncomfortable.

"I wonda if we might have tha same friend?" she asked.

"That'd be quite a coincidence wouldn't it?" bluffed Lincoln.

A cold chill ran over him; he had a bad feeling about where this was headed.

"Lincoln, I want ya to tell me where ya got that pendant. It's important." said Miss Jessie.

"Marjorie Henderson gave it to me." Then her demeanor changed into one of matter-of-fact interrogation.

"Okay, Lincoln. Let's stop beatin' 'round tha bush and get down to serious business. You may be in big-time trouble and not know it. Now, how did ya come to know Mah'ge?"

"I met her shopping at a store one day and helped her with some packages," he said, (lying about the packages), "and she invited me over to her house one evening."

"Yes, and I can imagine what fo'ah," deduced Miss Jessie, folding her arms and tapping one foot on the floor. "How often have ya visited Mah'ge," inquired Miss Jessie.

"Only that one time," he replied (lying again).

"Why did she give you the pendant?"

"Well, she was wearing the pendant which I commented on, and since I knew so much about its history and admired it so much, she gave it to me as a gift."

"You only saw huh one time and she gave you a gift of a valuable pendant?"

"Yes ma'am," he answered (lying again), avoiding eye contact with the lady asking the questions. He didn't want anyone to know that he'd also seen her on the night she was murdered.

"Well, you must have been good!" she grinned.

"Good! Wait...what do you mean...oh! I catch your drift. No, nothing like that happened."

"By the way, when was this rendezvous you had with Mah'ge?"

"Oh, it was a couple of months ago."

"I've not seen her in a while myself. I was beginning to wonda if she had *disappeared* or something," declared Miss Jessie lightheartedly. "Do ya know where she got the pendant?"

"She told me that she inherited it from an uncle of hers who had died."

"I see."

Lincoln was as nervous as a cat in a dog pound. He squirmed on the couch in discomfort. Jessica got up from the chair, walked slowly over to the couch and sat down beside Lincoln.

"I know you take a shortcut home sometimes ov'ah a footbridge on tha creek right where tha body was found. I think you took th'at shortcut last Tuesday and found tha body in tha creek instead of yo'ah father didn't you?"

Lincoln nodded "yes."

"And you recognized tha body as being that of Ma'jorie Hen'dason didn't you?"

Again, Lincoln nodded "yes."

"And ya got yo'ah father to go down and 'find' tha body so nobody would connect you with her."

"That's about it in a nutshell," confessed Lincoln.

"Well, that was smart," admitted Miss Jessie.

"However, I've got a feeling you 'ah not coming completely clean with me, and if yoh'ah not, yoh could be in a boatload of trouble. Now, there's a couple uh things ya need to do."

Jessica advised Lincoln to put the pendant somewhere out of sight, to keep quiet about knowing anything about or having any contact with Marjorie Henderson, and to let her know if anyone, especially Sheriff Coker, asked him anything about the woman in the creek. Then Jessica's demeanor changed completely again. Dressed in a long white silk robe trimmed in white fur at the collar, cuffs, and hem, she stood up and faced Lincoln. "Have you ever *had* a woman?" she asked seriously.

"Wha...? Well.... No." he confessed.

Never taking her eyes off his, Jessica slowly unbuttoned the buttons down the front of her robe then pulled back the folds revealing her completely nude body. Lincoln's jaw dropped. He sat there, mesmerized by the sight of the female form posed before him. He had always thought Jessica Wingo was one of the most beautiful women he had ever seen, and that was when she was dressed; but, this was her in the flesh, and she was like one of those Greek sculptures in a museum. He recalled Marge Henderson, who was quite attractive, but nothing to compare to this woman. The closest he had seen was Miss August in this month's issue of Playboy, but she was just a picture on a magazine page; Miss Jessie was alive and in person.

"Follow me," she said, taking him by the hand.

Under the spell of feminine allure (to which men throughout the pages of history have fallen victim), and fueled by the urge of hormones running amuck, Lincoln, wrapped in the folds of red satin sheets, was ushered through a sexual fantasy land that evening that most young men can only conjure up in their wildest dreams.

His guide on this trip was obviously a connoisseur of the erotic delights to be shared between members of the opposite sex. It wasn't like the crude groping he had experienced with Marge Henderson or the animalistic mating he had overheard between her and her husband. Led by his lover on a sensual exploration of both male and female forms, they sampled pleasures from Aphrodite's smorgasbord of carnal pleasures. Tutored in the art of giving and receiving pleasure, he realized that true lovemaking involves not just the physical person, but it's unification with the emotional and spiritual person.

It was an unbelievable, dreamlike journey, like nothing he'd ever experienced. But, if the trip was unbelievable, the end was indescribable; that moment the French call "the little death."

Lying in bed listening to the water running in Miss Jessie's shower, he pinched himself. "Ow!"

No, he wasn't dreaming; this night had really happened. Thinking back over the past hour, he couldn't get over how incredible her body was, but what was most amazing was that he had just had sex with the woman any man in town would give his right arm to have. But, no one would ever know; Miss Jessie had sworn him to secrecy. As he opened the door to leave, he took one last look around the apartment. Although he'd never forget it, he'd probably never see it again.

"It had been an unbelievable night, one he would never forget," he thought to himself, closing the door behind him.

But, suddenly a feeling of gloom came over him. He thought of Ashley. What had he done? Momentarily caught up in a swirling vortex of carnal desire, his brain intoxicated by the sensuous allure of a captivating woman, he had yielded to the temptation of temptations and betrayed his true love. The experience he had just had suddenly lost all its luster, all its meaning, all its enjoyment. In fact, it felt just the opposite; it felt dirty. But, what was done was done and nothing could change it. He would have to live with it but he knew he could never let Ashley, or anyone else for that matter, know about it.

Yes, this was a night Lincoln Crockett would never forget, in more ways than he could imagine.

Upon leaving Miss Jessie's abode, he wandered outside and strolled through the hotel grounds, contemplating the revelations of the past few days. Marge Henderson knew things that, in all likelihood, had bought her a one-way ticket to the Promised Land. Sometimes you can know too much; things you don't have to know, don't need to know, don't want to know, wish you didn't know. Right now, he wished he'd never seen Culveyhouse's damned old log truck that night at the sawmill, had never seen the arsenal in the trunk of Shooter Logano's limo, and had never met Marjorie Henderson that day at J.C. Penney's. But, like they say, hindsight is twenty-twenty.

Back in her apartment, Jessica Wingo stared at a faded five-by-seven photograph she held in her trembling hands; a photograph of a man and a woman, two ghosts from the past.

Chapter 41

"Are ye shor hit wuz this here Henderson woman that wuz found in tha creek?" inquired a sullen Herman Culveyhouse, who had reluctantly agreed to grace another meeting of the brotherhood of moonshiners with his presence after unceremoniously storming out of the last one.

"Yeah, it's her all right," disgustedly answered the Sheriff, pacing back and forth.

"Well now, which Albert Einstein's idea wuz it ta throw'er in tha damn creek where she'd be found easy enough?" demanded Jonas Franklin.

"An who wuz it decided ta kill'er in the fust place?" blurted out Clifton Ledbetter, "I wudn't fer havin' no part in'a killin'."

"Well, whoever it was that done what, shore got it messed up didn't they?" surmised Deputy Odom.

"I shoud'a knowed it," exclaimed Herman. "If'n you city fellers' brains all put together wuz dynamite, ya wouldn't have enough ta blow the snot out'uv a knat's nose!"

"And who'er you ta talk, you dumb hillbilly?" yelled the Sheriff, pointing a finger at Herman. "You couldn't find yer ass with'a flashlight in both hands!"

"Looky here ya…"

And that's how the meeting of the brotherhood got underway that afternoon just off an old logging road a short distance outside of town. It had been two days since the woman's body had been found in Town Creek, and the Sheriff had gathered the brothers to discuss this latest development in the continuing Marge Henderson saga.

But, before long, the discussing had digressed into a mostly cussing match, with verbal abuses being served up faster than balls from four-armed tennis players. It was then that Mayor McKeen took charge and managed to restore a reasonable degree of order to the proceedings before the participants came to blows.

"Now as I recall," said the Mayor, "at the last meeting, we couldn't settle on a course of action, so we agreed to leave it up to Dalton, after consulting with the Big Boss, to take care of the problem in whatever manner he deemed most expeditious and we'd back him up. All eyes turned toward Dalton; he now had the floor.

Dalton began by telling them about the Atlanta "professionals" that he had contracted with who were experienced in providing solutions to problems of this nature. He went on to say that the Sheriff and mayor had met the leader of the group, but only in a social setting. Without going into any details of the operation, he explained that the contractors had successfully "persuaded" the bank president to turn over the letter that Ms. Henderson had on deposit in his bank. After that, the plan was that Ms. Henderson would be taken for a ride, making it look like she just left town and disappeared.

"Ha, they weren't too professional on that last part, were they?" sniggered Deputy Odom, who continued, "floatin' in Town Creek in tha middle of town ain't exactly a Houdini trick."

"Huh! Professionals my ass. Even this here hick Sheriff's got more sense'n to shoot somebody'n throw their carcass in'tha creek," said Herman, grinning and spitting a lip full of tobacco juice on the ground in the general direction of Buford.

"Alright, watch yer mouth ye backwoods, two-legged tobacco worm," growled Buford.

"If'n they hadn't shot'er…just drown'd her…we wouldn't hav'a prob'lim," reasoned Jonas.

"Yep, but tha problem is, she's gotta slug in'er chest," said the Sheriff, "and Doc Simpson's post mortum'll show that she died from the gunshot wound and not from drownin'."

Deputy Odom said, "In plain an simple terms it'll say she was murdered."

"Damnation!" stormed Clifton fearfully."That means there'll be a murder investigation."

"Yeah, but the Sheriff and me will be doin' the investigation ya dope," reminded the deputy.

"Yes we will," said the Sheriff, hitching up his pants and smiling confidently.

"We need'a fall guy," he continued, looking around the circle of malcontents.

"Hey, don't go gittin' any idees 'bout tryin' ta pin this on any of us," warned Herman, squinting his eyes as he raised his double-barrel waist high.

"No, no," assured Buford, patting the air in front of him with his hands.

"When a wife's murdered, who's the first suspect?" he asked.

"The husband," answered the deputy.

"Right ya are deputy," answered his boss, "and I've got an idea."

"The rest of y'all go on home. Lester an me'll take care of this."

On the highway

The police cruiser stopped at the end of the logging road to wait for a motorcycle to pass before pulling out onto the highway.

"Looks like that Justice boy on that old Indian motorcycle," growled the Sheriff.

"Can't be him," said Deputy Odom, "'cause he's in the army now. Probably goin' to Nam soon."

"That right!" answered Buford.

"When we get back to town," said Buford, "we'll see if we can't come up with a plan to implicate Mr. Henderson in his own wife's murder."

Lincoln gave a quick look at the two cops sitting there on the logging road in the police cruiser as he sped past. But, his thoughts were otherwise occupied as he instinctively guided the motorcycle through the curves of the country road where the asphalt was hot enough to fry an egg.

Back in town, he had felt trapped in a world of confusion, imprisoned behind walls that closed in and suffocated him, but on the bike, leaning through snakelike turns and speeding by fields and meadows with only the "whoosh" of the passing wind and the drumming of the engine to be heard, he felt free, as free as a bird in flight. Rats leaving the Indian in his care had provided a great escape.

Over the past few weeks, the periods of depression that had, for a long time, been sporadic in their frequency were now becoming more recurrent, as were the headaches. Since the prom, it seemed that there had been an endless string of incidences, one leading to another like falling dominos that plagued his thoughts day in and day out. The more he tried to sort them out, the more jumbled they got, like a deck of cards carelessly spilled on the floor.

But today, astraddle the two-wheeled metal horse speeding down the highway, all those worries and cares seemed a thousand miles away, somewhere in another world, another life. Today, he was free, free to go as far as the Indian and his windswept mind could carry him.

He flicked the shifter into fourth gear with his toe and gave the throttle a twist. The engine responded with a roar and the Indian leaped forward with an exhilarating rush of power that flowed through both machine and rider. The speed was invigorating as trees and fence posts flew by. He wished he could just keep the throttle open, follow his nose, and never look back.

Chapter 42

It was around 6:00 p.m. on Friday evening when a gray sedan pulled into the driveway at 321 5th Avenue and a man fitting Donald Henderson's description emerged from the vehicle and entered the house. Within minutes, a police car, driven by deputy Odom who had been keeping an eye on the house, pulled into the driveway behind the gray sedan, followed by the Sheriff's cruiser.

Sheriff Coker had learned from Jessica Wingo that Marjorie Henderson's husband was a traveling salesman who was normally on the road most weekdays and home on the weekends. The officers had first reached the address obtained from Jessica shortly after noon but found the premises vacant.

After identifying themselves and gaining admittance to the house, the officers divulged to Mr. Henderson the unhappy news of his wife's demise, having drowned in the flood of the weekend past. They purposely omitted the small detail of her having also been shot.

The Sheriff reached into his back pocket and withdrew a .38 caliber revolver that had been wiped clean with one round discharged from the cylinder. Holding it by the barrel he handed it to Mr. Henderson and asked him to take it.

Although puzzled by the strange request, the man, distraught over the news of his wife's death, complied, unwittingly falling into Buford Coker's trap.

"Donald Henderson, yoh ah un'da arrest for the murder of yo'ah wife Marjorie Henderson," stated the Sheriff.

"What! What do you mean murder?"

"Don't play innocent Mr. Henderson," replied Buford proudly. "We know you shot yoh wife. We found this gun in your bedroom, which I'm sure will prove to be the murder weapon."

"Deputy, cuff'im and stuff'im."

And with that, a bewildered Donald Henderson was unceremoniously led away in handcuffs to the Coldwater jail, labeled a spouse-killer.

Chapter 43

Following Donald Henderson's arrest, stories carried by the *Coldwater News* over the next few days confirmed that the Town Creek Woman was, in fact, Marjorie Henderson, that she was the victim of foul play, and that her husband, Donald Henderson, had been arrested and charged as the perpetrator of the foul deed. Between the news media and the tongue-waggers, the rumor mills were being supplied with enough fodder to choke a hay bailing machine and the telephone lines were so hot with gossip they were practically melting on the poles.

Doc Simpson's autopsy of the corpse also verified that a gunshot wound to the chest from a .38 caliber bullet was the *coup de grâce* and had been dispensed prior to the body being consigned to the murky waters of Town Creek. Coincidentally, the Sheriff announced that his investigation had uncovered "evidence" that would prove it to be an open-and-shut case, having recovered the murder weapon in the possession of the accused.

The only hitch in the Sheriff's scheme was one Johnny Abraham, the newly elected district attorney. He would have to convince the young, idealistic DA of the prisoner's guilt being a foregone conclusion and steer him away from sniffing around like a bloodhound for superfluous details.

Even with the trial date set a month away in mid-August, people would be waiting with bated breath for the day to arrive, no less than if the Ringling Brothers circus was coming to town. The courtroom was sure to be packed to overflowing with curiosity seekers. This would be the biggest trial to hit Coldwater since Sherman McAdo caught his wife Sadie and neighbor farmer Luke Lawson together in the hayloft of Sherman's barn back in '52.

It seems that Sadie and Luke were going at it like two dogs in heat and were so caught up in an animalistic frenzy that they didn't hear Sherman come up behind them. Neither did they see the pitchfork before it drove through their sweat-soaked bodies. The raging Sherman took no pity, raining blow after blow of steel spikes punctuated with a slew of profanity onto them until their bloodied bodies were riddled from head to toe with more holes than a block of Swiss cheese. Sherman's trial caused a sensation for miles around, and his hanging in the town square drew a larger crowd than the Founder's Day celebration.

With excitement over the current events growing to a fever pitch, most everyone was being drawn into the happenings in one form or another, be it soaking up every word off the printing presses, following the parade of curiosity seekers past the Henderson home, or making a morbid pilgrimage to the death scene. Saturday morning shoppers congregated on street corners along Main Street were so engaged in their chin-wagging that the young man and woman who entered the Palace Theatre did so unnoticed.

At the movie theatre

After paying the ticket booth attendant $2.50 for two tickets, Lincoln and Ashley climbed the stairs to the balcony and took seats on the back row of the half-lit theatre. Two hours before movie time, they had come early in order to have some time alone.

"By the way, what movie's playing anyway?" asked Ashley.

"The ad on the marquee said *Cat Ballou* staring Lee Marvin," answered Lincoln.

Ashley turned in her seat to face Lincoln.

"I have some news to tell you," she said.

"Sounds serious from the look on your face."

"Montgomery's joining the Air Force," she disclosed, her head drooping.

"Why? He can get a college deferment?"

"I know. But he says he wants to go. So, he saw a recruiter and signed up."

"So, Monty's going to be a flyboy," said Lincoln in wonderment.

"I hate to see him go. He's always been a good friend," said Ashley, a tear trickling out the corner of her eye.

"I know," whispered Lincoln, reaching and holding her hand.

"What did his parents have to say about his signing up?" asked Lincoln.

"He said they went absolutely bonkers. But there's nothing they can do about it. What's done is done."

"Yeah! What's done is done," he repeated, looking down at the floor, his mind at another time and place.

[194]

"Say, are you okay? You seem a little nervous and distant," observed Ashley, concerned.

"Oh, no," he replied quickly. "Everything's fine," he said, forcing a smile. He couldn't let the girl know the guilt he was feeling.

"By the way, Montgomery asked me to ask you if you would do him a favor," said Ashley.

"Sure! Do anything I can."

"He wants you to check on Amanda now and then to see how she's doing and let him know."

"Sure, I'd be glad to."

Ashley smiled.

"You're a good friend to…to Montgomery…and me, too."

She leaned over and kissed him softly on the lips.

"Luv ya," she whispered in his ear.

A broad smile broke across Lincoln's face. She smiled back at him. That was the first time she had actually said "the word."

"Say, what do you think about all this business with the murdered woman?" Ashley asked.

Lincoln went about playing dumb as he summarized for her his own version of what took place. That is, how his father found the body and reported it to the police; how he only got a glimpse of it when it was removed from the water, and what a dreadful site it was.

"I can only imagine," said Ashley with a shiver.

"According to the newspaper, her husband did it and has been arrested. It usually is the husband, don't you think?" she asked.

"Not necessarily," he hedged, knowing the truth.

He knew that Donald Henderson couldn't have committed the crime because he was at the Henderson home with Marge after Mr. Henderson had already left on his trip. It also seemed obvious to Lincoln that Donald Henderson was being set up by someone to take the fall for the murder.

Lincoln was between a rock and a hard place. By failing to come forward and reveal the facts he knew, an innocent man, wrongly accused, was going to be convicted of murder. But, in being forthcoming with the truth, the resulting repercussions would prove to have serious implications for himself: becoming a murder suspect; a target of the real killer; a person of interest to those setting up Mr. Henderson; facing the ire of his father; the object of gossip; and the unknown effect on his and Ashley's relationship.

[195]

But, deep down in his heart of hearts, Lincoln knew there was only one right thing to do regardless of the personal consequences. Before taking that step, however, he needed to talk with someone about it. But, who could he trust to confide in? From what he had discovered to date, who knew how many individuals where connected in this web of deceit. He had to proceed with caution.

Chapter 44

August, 1965

The hot days of summer, hot enough to peel the paint off a house, dragged on. The weather and the murder mystery were about the only topics of conversation on people's minds. The gossip network continued to try and wring more truths, half-truths, judgments, and opinions out of the Henderson murder affair than blood could be wrung out of a turnip. But, that horse was about dead for the time being. When the trial did get under way, that nag would be resurrected to more glorified tongue-wagging than Lazarus' emergence from the tomb. In the meantime, they could complain about the sweltering ninety-degree heat and the effect it was having on crops.

News media from all over had descended upon the little town like buzzards on roadkill to cover the sensational story of the Town Creek Woman and, as a result, had brought to this backwater burg a minor degree of national attention. But, with this lull had come the withdrawal of said media and a corresponding decrease in business at the hotel that had before strained the town's capacity to provide lodging.

Taking advantage of the hiatus, Lincoln headed for the river and his favorite fishing hole. He parked the Indian in the shade of a grove of sycamore trees a few yards downstream from Franklin's Ferry. Unstrapping a fishing rod and tackle box from the bike, he walked down to the water's edge next to the ferry boat.

"How you doin' today, Mr. Franklin," he called out, waving to the ferry boat operator.

Ole man Franklin just waved and nodded his head without saying anything.

"Howdy there Mista Lincoln," shouted Obee, waving.

Obee always called men "mista" in conjunction with their first name. He did the same with ladies using "Mis."

"Hello Obee," answered Lincoln.

"Goin' feeshin'?"

"Yeah," Lincoln replied, "see you later."

"Wher's ya purty white car?"

"Oh! That's wasn't my car Obee. See you later."

Lincoln walked down the railroad tracks that ran parallel to the river as far as where Town Creek emptied into Little River. At the mouth of the creek, a stand of willow trees cast their shade over several large rocks that jutted out from the bank, making an ideal spot to sit and fish in comfort. Approaching the site, he saw that his friend Zeke was there, leaning comfortably against a tree puffing on a corncob pipe.

"Hiya Zeke," called out Lincoln cheerfully, "long time, no see."

"Mista Lincoln, how ya doin' man," returned Zeke, with a big smile.

Lincoln had known the old man for a long time although he didn't know much about him personally.

He was a black man, slight of body and frail. Lincoln didn't know how old he was; Zeke himself probably didn't know exactly. He wore faded overalls and an old flop hat covering nappy, gray hair. In wrinkled, calloused hands and deep, carved features of a face that framed hollow, distant eyes, there lay a novel etched in time. Through the pain and woe of hardship and a world that had told him lies, he was a survivor of life's storms; a flesh and bone manifestation of that old song, "The Wayfaring Stranger." Lincoln somehow felt a strange connection with this man some fifty years his senior.

"Hiya 'Trouble'," said Lincoln, patting Zeke's black and gray coon dog on the head who looked about as old as Zeke.

"How's the fishing today, Zeke?"

"'Bout as sorry as a two-dollar watch. Have ketched a couple'a small saugers though."

"Well, that'll make supper," said Lincoln.

"Yep! I'll fry'em up ta'nite; one fer me an one fer Trouble."

"Zeke, you need a wife to take care of you," suggested Lincoln, with a smile. You need to find you a good-looking gal over there in Johnnytown and marry her."

"Oh, no. That's all I need's is sum woman trouble," answered Zeke, shaking his head back and forth.

Since Zeke's wife had passed on a few years back and his children were only memories, it had just been Zeke and Trouble keeping each other company in their little one-room shack on the outskirts of Johnnytown.

Johnnytown was a community of approximately one hundred black folks a bit farther downstream, located between the river and the swamps. It was established years ago by Dr. Johnny Jericho, an herbalist of some renown and purveyor of home remedies, hence, the town's namesake.

While they waited in the stillness of the moment, quietly watching the bobbers on their lines glide up and down over ripples in the water, Zeke began to play the air guitar and vocalize the words to some old down-and-out Blues song.

"Yoh like's tha Blues Mista Lincoln?"

"Sure do. When I get to feeling down, I like to listen to some Blues music."

"That's what tha Blues are. Tha 'bout feelin's, 'bout 'speriences…tha 'bout life. Sumtimes I jus likes ta fergit 'bout evathang an have me a Blue Ribbon day a listenin' ta John Lee's Memphis Sound all day, all night long."

"I know what you mean, Zeke, I know what you mean!" said Lincoln, staring at the ground, scratching in the dirt with a stick.

"Look like yoh lost in them Blues now young'n," observed the old man.

"Somewhat," admitted the young man, "got a lot on my mind."

"Big uproar ova there 'bout that dead woman in tha creek," stated Zeke,

"Find it right near where yoh live, that right?" he questioned.

"Yeah, that's right," confirmed Lincoln, looking up.

"Got any idees 'bout tha whole affair?" asked Zeke.

"Between you and me and the Devil, I know more than I'd like to know," he said looking straight at this old man he trusted.

"Well, they probly blame it on some Johnnie down here," guessed Zeke.

"I don't think so, Zeke. There's something rotten going on in Coldwater."

"They's been sump'n rotten 'round here fer a long time. It's name's Buford Coker," whispered Zeke as if someone might hear.

"I'm beginning to find that out. And where there's one rat, there's usually a nest of'em," answered Lincoln.

"Lincoln, you needs ta come on down ta Johnnytown one night'n goes ta Annie McCool's place with me."

"I've heard of Annie McCool's. What's it like?"

"Oh, son!" declared the old man, "Yoh ain't lived 'til ya been ta Annie's on a Satadee night."

Now, Sweet Annie McCool's is a noisy place where cheap beer and wine is served up to the sound of loud music and lively dancing, especially on the weekends. More specifically, the kind of place most folks refer to as a "honkytonk." But what separates Sweet Annie's from other honkytonks is the food. She can cook up the most tantalizing specialties to please the palate of Soul Food lovers.

"They's always a bunch'a musicians gather 'round an jam ta the sound'a them sweet Memphis Blues," explained Zeke. "Soon, that rhythm git the ladies mojo goin' an they goes slip-slidin' out onta the dance floor, tantalizin' all tha men folk with their gyratin' Hoochy Koochy dance."

"Bowls fulla the best steamin' hot collard greens, ham hocks'un johnnycakes on the river, topped off with that sweet Muscat and Blue Ribbon, with cool music an hot dancin' mixed in, and yoh gotcha self one helluva night in store," he continued.

"Sounds like quite an experience. The Friday night dances at the Memorial Building over in Coldwater definitely pale in comparison," affirmed Lincoln.

"Why don't'cha come over an go with me one night?

"I don't think I'd fit in very well. I'd stand out like a steering wheel on a mule," reckoned Lincoln.

Zeke laughed. "That's a good'un."

"Don't let that stop ye though. Nobody'll care."

"You know, I might just do that sometime," promised Lincoln.

"But, if'n ya do come ova this'a way, a word'a warnin', don't go near tha old conjure woman out in tha swamps," warned Zeke.

"Who's she?"

"Some calls her a witch. I dunno what she is. I does know she got bad juju…dabbles in black magic…carries a Ouija board 'round with her," said Zeke, looking about cautious like.

"Sounds like a spooky old gal alright," said Lincoln.

"They sez she put's spells on people with that Voodoo Hoodoo stuff. I stay's clear uf'her myself," added Zeke matter of factly.

After an hour or so with no bites in sight, the two fishermen agreed to call it a day. Zeke decided he'd accompany Lincoln back down to the ferry to pick up something he needed for his "miseries" as he called them.

The August sun was bearing down hot as they began their trek down the Southern Railway tracks to Franklin's Ferry.

"Zeke, you need to see a doctor about your 'miseries,'" said Lincoln

"Don't cotton to them'ar doctors an their fancy ways. 'Sides, can't afford'em anyways."

"But, you know, Congress passed that new Social Security bill this year that provides health care insurance for retired people over sixty-five. You should check up on that."

"Nope! I don't wants nuthin' frum the gov'ment. I ain't never paid them no Social Security an I don't wants nuthin' back."

"Really! You've never paid Social Security?"

"That's right. They don't owe me nuthin' an I don't owe them nuthin'."

The oddly matched pair continued on down the tracks, the younger one listening intently to the soulful tune the older one was blowing on his mouth organ.

After a few minutes, Zeke suddenly paused and spoke up:

"Retired! What's ya mean *retired*?"

He stared into space reflectively.

"I'z been a dirt farmer all my life...an that's all I'll eva be...guess I'll jes..." (his voice trailed off) "...die in tha harness."

Lincoln liked talking with the old man. He seemed to have a second sight, or maybe it was just a down-to-earth, common-sense way of looking at things that was honest and sincere that he found lacking in so many people.

When they were within sight of the ferry, Lincoln remembered something Zeke had said earlier.

"By the way Zeke, you said you were coming to the ferry to get something for your miseries. What could you get at the ferry for the miseries? All the Franklin's do is ferry cars; I only know of one thing that they sell."

"An jes what would that be?"

"A clear liquid made from corn squeezing's...comes in a Mason jar...goes by different names...some call it Shine!" Lincoln led the old man on.

"Well, I wouldn't know 'bout all that," said Zeke, shaking his head, "I jus gits some misery medicine."

The two looked at each other serious-like for a minute then broke out into a leg-slapping laugh.

All was quiet as they wandered onto the boat, which appeared to be unattended, and there were no vehicles waiting to cross the river in either direction. They called out a few times before Obee appeared from some nearby bushes where he had been napping. He explained that his father had gone into town, but he was in charge. Now ole Obee was about two sandwiches short of a picnic, but he could operate the ferry boat if push came to shove.

"Obee, I need's a pint'a 'medicine' fer my miseries," said Zeke.

"Oh! I can't sell no medicine. Jus my paw can sell medicine," said Obee seriously.

It took some talking, but the old man finally convinced the half-witted Obee that he needed to get back home and needed the medicine real bad.

"Okay," agreed Obee, "but don't tell Paw."

They followed the ferry operator across the deck next to the pilot house where he moved the two straight-backed chairs he and his daddy sat in all the time. Throwing back the piece of old carpet the chairs had been sitting on, he revealed a large trap door in the floor. There in a compartment in the belly of the ferry lay wooden boxes containing pint and quart Mason jars filled with nearly a hundred gallons of clear liquid.

Lincoln thought to himself, *So that's where they store it!*

"How much ya want Mr. Zeke?" asked Obee.

"One pint."

"How's 'bout you Mister Lincoln?"

"Huh, no thanks, Obee."

While Obee returned things in the pilot house to their original condition, Zeke tested the taste of the "medicine."

"Here Mista Lincoln, try a taste," offered Zeke.

Zeke talked the reluctant uninitiated into indulging his taste buds in one of nature's finer concoctions. Lincoln took a big mouthful and swallowed it down. At first, it wasn't bad. But, a minute later, his eyes bugged out and he clinched at his throat as the fire burned a path all the way to his stomach.

Zeke laughed.

"Ya 'posed ta let it trickle down."

"Now you tell me," moaned Lincoln, speaking at a whisper. "I guess it takes an acquired taste."

It would have been easier to make a pint of moonshine than to try and pay Obee for the pint.

"Tha price five dollars, 25 cent," Obee told the man

Zeke explained to Obee, "Yoh daddy promised me a dollar off'a my nex purchase fer sum work I dun fer him."

Obee, without question, agreed to the price of four dollars and twenty-five cents.

Zeke then handed young Franklin a five-dollar bill. That proved to be the undoing of the whole transaction.

"If'n y'all gimme seventy-five cents change, we'll be even," Zeke instructed the less than astute man child.

Obee couldn't have been more stupefied at the sight of the five-dollar bill and Zeke's directions if he had been hit between the eyes with a baseball bat. The concept of making change was as foreign to Obee's simple mind as doing algebra was to a three-year-old. For the better part of the next thirty minutes, Zeke and Lincoln tried every way they could think of to get Obee to see that five dollars minus four dollars and twenty-five cents is seventy-five cents and that's what he owed Zeke.

"No! Obee *take* money; Obee not *give* money," he said, red in the face.

For what few sales transactions Obee had conducted, he had never given back money; he had always taken money, the exact amount of money.

The more they tried, the worse it got. By now, ole Obee was so confused he didn't know whether to scratch his watch or wind his ass.

Bowing up like an old Tom cat with its fur bristling, he bawled at his customers: "Keep you damned ole five dollars, I keep my damned ole shine," and stalked off to the pilot house in a huff.

Lincoln and Zeke just stood there looking at each other, shrugging their shoulders when they heard someone coming. Turning around, they saw Jonas Franklin boarding the ferry.

"What's all tha commotion?" asked Jonas.

Zeke and Lincoln filled Jonas in on all that had taken place, just laughing off the whole affair to keep Jonas from taking any retribution against Obee. Jonas completed the sales transaction with

Zeke and everyone left satisfied. By tomorrow, Obee will have forgotten about the whole thing, and so will everyone else.

That is, with the exception of Lincoln Crockett. For him, another piece of the puzzle had just fallen into place.

Chapter 45

Lincoln stroked the fur of Amanda Cross' calico cat who was lying in his lap as he and the feline's owner swung gently back and forth in the Cross' front porch swing.

"I understand Montgomery's joined the air force," said Lincoln.

"That's right," answered the somewhat shy, dark-haired girl.

"He's only been gone a week, but I miss him already," she said in her soft-spoken way.

"Do you know why he went? He could have gotten a college deferment."

"Oh! You know Monty (her face perked up). Always talking about duty and honor and things like that, and how to save..." suddenly hesitating, her face lost all expression.

"Your daddy's job?" Lincoln questioned as he finished her sentence.

She looked inquisitively at Lincoln.

"It's alright, Amanda. I know all about it."

"Ashley?"

"Yes, she told me. Seems she and Monty got similar sentences."

"Are y'all still seein' each other?"

"Every chance we get."

"Monty thought it would be better if he got away for a while, even farther away than college," she explained.

"He asked me to check in on you from time to time...see how you're doing," he informed her.

"Thoughtful of him," she said, smiling.

She then drew closer to Lincoln.

"Lincoln, I'm going to tell you something, but you have to keep it a secret. Monty said to tell no one except you and Ashley. Okay?" she said as she swore him to secrecy with her hands in a prayer-like pose.

"Sure! What's the big secret?"

"Montgomery and I got married before he left," she whispered in his ear.

Lincoln's eyes widened, his chin dropped, and his mouth opened like a large mouth bass. For a minute, he couldn't speak. When Amanda's announcement had time to register in his brain and he had recovered from the initial shock, he was finally able to get his mouth into gear.

"Ho-lee shit! I don't want to be around when that bomb falls," he said with that bug-eyed look still on his face. Then he broke out in a big smile. "Or maybe I do!" he said gleefully.

Following some chitchat about the details, the two lifelong friends hugged each other and said goodbye. Straddling the Indian motorcycle, Lincoln looked back at Amanda, took his index finger and wiped it across his pursed lips. Just then he heard someone calling his name.

"Lincoln! Lincoln!"

He looked up and saw Tommy John Ponder, Amanda's sixteen-year-old, next-door neighbor, flying off his porch and across the yard straight for him. The agile youngster cleared the low fence between their yards in a single bound and in a moment's notice was in Lincoln's face.

"Please, Lincoln, gimmee a ride down'ta Flatwood Street. I'm inna hurry," begged the boy, wiping perspiration from his face.

"Hey! What's the hurry? Is there a fire or something down on Flatwood?" Lincoln asked.

"Huh … yeah … huh … somethin'," stammered Tommy John.

"Well, must be something big," joked Lincoln.

"Yeah. I don't wanna be late. It's only a few blocks. Please?" the boy pleaded, with a pitiful look.

"Okay. Hop on."

It was getting dusky dark when "T.J.," as Tommy John was known to most people, directed Lincoln into an alley midway down Flatwood Street, signaling him to a stop a short distance from the street.

"C'mon! I wanna show ye sumthin'," motioned T.J. to Lincoln.

"I really need to be on my way, T.J.," answered Lincoln.

"Oh, c'mon. Ye won't believe this," teased T.J., flicking his index finger at Lincoln as if coaxing a dog.

"Okay, okay, I'll come," agreed Lincoln to appease his young friend.

Following young Ponder's lead, they sneaked quickly across backyards while ducking clotheslines and tripping over children's playthings until they reached the third house from the alley on Flatwood. Circling the back porch, they came to a small, ground-level window that afforded an unobstructed view into the house's basement. Crouching close to the window, they heard the rhythmic beat of rock-an-roll music being spun across the airwaves by a disc jockey identified to his radio audience as Clifford "The Cat" Streeter.

Kneeling down on all fours, T.J. whispered excitedly,

"Look at this Mr. Lincoln Crockett!"

Following T.J.'s lead, Lincoln knelt down in like manner and peered into the basement.

The scene that unfolded before Lincoln's eyes in that room left him thunderstruck...if not completely dumbfounded.

"Ain't that sumpin' ta behold!" marveled T.J..

Lincoln looked at T.J., speechless; then looked back through the window.

There, in the middle of the room, cavorting and pirouetting about to the drumming of the music was a slightly overweight, middle-aged woman, both arms raised high overhead, a can of Budweiser in one hand, a half burned-out Camel cigarette in the other, blowing smoke rings with the last draw off the fag. And, she was performing this boogie ballet in the buff, as buck-naked as a newborn baby. But this alone was not the bombshell that had left Lincoln shell-shocked; this was a mere firecracker in comparison.

Dancing around the woman was a ring of six or eight teenaged boys, indulging in a game of braille biology with the woman's body the game board. 'Round and 'round they skipped and joked, feeling up the woman from head to toe as she giddily urged them on. Lincoln didn't know who the woman was or the boys or how such a thing ever got started.

Lincoln slumped back against the side of the house and just sat there for a minute shaking his head. He thought to himself, *Man! All the things that go on in this town that I don't know about...never have known about! I must be either blind or dumb...or maybe both!*

"Come on T.J., I'm taking you back home!"

Chapter 46

It was early afternoon when Southern Railway's *Southerner* chugged to a stop at the Coldwater station dragging four parlor cars and eight coaches behind it with a red caboose hanging on the end. Deftly hopping from the steps of the last coach car onto the end of the platform next to the parking lot was a no-nonsense looking man of average height and weight, wearing black-rimmed glasses and sporting a thick five o'clock shadow. He was dressed in a gray Sears & Roebuck suit with a matching tie that hung loose at the collar and a black hat that sat cocked to one side with the brim pulled down low in front.

He straightened up and flexed a He-Man pose to stretch the kinks out of his tired, stiff body, then relaxed and surveyed his surroundings for a few studious minutes. Reaching into his shirt pocket for a cigarette to feed his nicotine hunger, he frowned at the sight of the empty Lucky Strike pack in his hand and crushed it between his fingers. Disgusted, he started to flip the crumpled debris aside, but then thought better of it. "Crap!" he muttered as he jammed the mangled pack back into the shirt pocket. After getting his bearings, he picked up with one hand an old, tan-colored valise that lay next to him and a new, black leather briefcase with the other. He stepped off the platform into the loose gravels of the parking lot.

"Ride, mister?"

The man looked about and saw that the question had come from a short, scruffy fellow of some age who reminded him of Gabby Hayes of Hollywood western movie fame. The fellow leaned against a faded yellow taxicab that looked about as scruffy as its owner.

"Could be, if you know where a man can find a hotel room in your town?"

"Oh! I know where to find 'em. Depends on whether you prefer chandeliers in the lobby or flashing neon signs outside your window. Now, I noticed you're traveling coach, so . . ."

"Very observant," interrupted the train passenger, "but don't make any assumptions based on that. Where my mode of travel is concerned, I like to economize, but when it comes to my lodgings, I prefer a bit of luxury."

The cabbie, pushing his billed cap back on his head, responded with a wink, "Then it'll be the Lacy Hotel for you, finest hotel in these parts. And, it's only a block away," he added motioning up the street with his thumb in the manner of hitching a ride.

The man, who had spotted the hotel in his earlier survey of the surrounding area, and could have easily walked the short distance, decided to hire this quaint character's yellow taxi service and engage him in some further conversation.

"Then lead on, driver," said the man.

"Yes Sir, Captain," replied the cab's owner with a salute.

The man from the train leaned over and set his valise on the ground but held on to the briefcase. In doing so, his jacket fell open just enough to allow the old man a glimpse of the .38 caliber Smith and Wesson revolver concealed from view in a brown shoulder holster. The cabbie's demeanor changed. He gulped and in a more serious tone than before introduced himself.

"Name's Patrick McNally, but everybody 'round these parts just calls me 'Dutch'."

"What'd you say yer name wuz, mister?"

"I didn't," replied his passenger.

"Oh! Yeah," said the driver quietly, picking up the valise, "thought I just missed it."

He tossed the man's valise into the trunk of the cab.

"Uh, what business wuz'it ye said you'uz in?" quizzed the driver cautiously.

"I didn't," replied the man again.

"Oh! Yeah, guess ye didn't, did ye?" said the driver in an apologetic tone as he tried not to stare at the man.

The stranger crawled into the back seat of the cab while the driver slid under the steering wheel, fired up the engine, and pulled out of the Southern Railway parking lot.

"Next stop, the Lacy Hotel," barked the cabbie. "Baltimore!"

"I beg your pardon" said the man in the backseat.

"Baltimore! It wuz Baltimore ye said ye wuz from," said the driver shaking his head in a "yes" motion as if trying to persuade his passenger to agree with his statement.

"No, I didn't say where I'm from."

"Oh!" replied the cabbie with a frown.

A slightly humorous grin spread across the man's face at the cabbie's attempt to pump him for information, which ironically was exactly his intentions for getting friendly with the cabbie. It would be good to make an acquaintance with someone like Dutch who probably had sort of a finger on the pulse of the town. He could prove to be a valuable resource later.

The passenger enjoyed a bit of banter with the old fellow as they circled the block and pulled up directly in front of the hotel lobby. All the time, Dutch watched his passenger suspiciously through the rearview mirror, offering only short answers to the man's few questions about the hotel and town.

"Good evening, sir. Welcome to the Lacy Hotel," greeted Lincoln to the man exiting the taxi.

"Thank you."

"Evenin' Dutch," said Lincoln to the cabbie.

"Howdy Lincoln," returned Dutch.

At the back of the car, Dutch retrieved the valise from the trunk, handed it to Lincoln, and whispered, "Lincoln, keep'a eye on this feller. I gotta funny feeling 'bout him."

"What do you mean *a funny feeling*?"

"I don't know exactly, but he ain't the typical visitor we get 'round here."

"What do you mean not *typical*?"

"He's packin,'" whispered Dutch.

"*Packin'*?" said Lincoln quizzically.

"You know. He's armed," replied Dutch still whispering while fashioning the figure of a gun with his hand.

"Okay, Dutch. I'll keep an eye on him," nodded Lincoln.

"It was nice meeting you, Dutch," smiled his passenger slipping Dutch a few folded bills via their handshake.

Dutch glanced at the bills in his hand; his eyes brightened; he looked back at the stranger. "Yeah, same here!" he answered enthusiastically.

"See you around," said the man turning to follow the bellman.

"Anytime," answered Dutch, scratching his ragged gray beard.

"Say, that's a right smart-looking ring ye got on yer finger there," admired Dutch.

"Oh, you like that?" asked the stranger, holding his hand up with fingers spread apart to display a rectangular gold ring with the letters

"ATF" set in relief diagonally between two corners and two small diamonds set in the opposing corners.

"Must'a set ye back a pretty penny," probed Dutch.

"Everything has its price, Dutch, everything has its price."

Lincoln got the new arrival registered and settled in his room. He seemed an okay enough chap to Lincoln and Lincoln didn't see any reason for misgivings about him as Dutch appeared to have. It wasn't all that unusual to see individuals around Coldwater, especially traveling businessmen, in possession of a firearm although carrying one in a shoulder holster was a rarity. Old Dutch could get some strange ideas sometimes, but, he'd file it away just for future reference.

In fact, that's how Patrick McNally came to get his nickname "Dutch," getting into Dutch over an incident at the Presbyterian church years ago before Lincoln was even born. It seems that Patrick's seat in the choir was directly behind Miss Bertha Burton's, a woman of some considerable size.

One hot August night at choir practice, the back of Miss Bertha's dress, which from the rear looked like two pigs in a shopping bag fighting to get out, was caught up in her crack. Patrick, being a gentleman, politely leaned forward and gently withdrew the trapped material from the trench within which it had become rooted, thus, relieving Miss Bertha of the embarrassment she would have endured if this most unfortunate circumstance had not been rectified before it was publicly exposed.

But, Miss Bertha, not having all the facts and being ignorant of Pat's good intentions and purposes, took issue with his hand being placed in too familiar places on her person, turned and in one fell swoop caught Patrick across the side of the head with her hymnal.

"Well! I never! And right in church, too," she said, indignantly and red-faced.

Ole Pat's eyes rolled around like the wheels in a slot machine for a couple of minutes before he could read the words on the page again.

Well, Patrick thought he must have been wrong and that she must have wanted the dress that way. So, he decided that he should make amends by undoing what he had done and put things back the way they were. He politely leaned forward again and, with a flattened hand, gently tucked her dress back into the crevice between her cheeks from which he had moments ago extracted it. He leaned back smiling and continued singing knowing he had done a good deed.

Miss Bertha's eyes opened wide at the feel of something once again crawling up her posterior. She turned with the rage of a snorting bull and clenched fists. With all her three hundred pounds behind it, she hammered ole Pat with a right cross that knocked him as goofy as a cross-eyed mule.

"If there's anything you need Mister, just call the front desk or let me know if you see me around," Lincoln informed the new guest.

"Thank you ... *Lincoln* ... I believe it is. I'll do that. My name's Christian...Wallace Christian," the man said, introducing himself.

"Nice to meet you sir," smiled the bellman as the two shook hands.

"How long have you lived in Coldwater, Lincoln?"

"All my life, sir."

"I suppose you must know a lot of people in town and what goes on around here?"

"I don't know everyone, but I know quite a few. And it's a small town so it's hard to do much without people knowing about it."

"Maybe one day while I'm here you could tell me about the people in your town."

"What would anybody want to know about people in Coldwater? Nobody special here."

"Oh, you'd be surprised what you can learn about a place from the people who live there, Lincoln. Maybe you could point out some individuals who know what goes on 'behind the scenes' if you know what I mean?" he said, rubbing the thumb and fingers of one hand together indicating that compensation could be forthcoming.

"I think I catch your drift," said Lincoln with a smile. "Yeah, I could probably do that."

"But right now I've got to finish my shift and then meet my friend Rats over at Big Al's like I promised him I would."

"*Rats* and *Big Al*. Interesting sounding names," said Mr. Christian rubbing his chin thoughtfully.

"Rats is my buddy and Big Al runs Big Al's Pool Hall. We're going to shoot a few games of pool. I'll see you later."

"Yes, you can count on it," said the stranger under his breath.

Chapter 47

There was an air of excitement in town today! The big day that everyone had been awaiting with eager anticipation had finally arrived, August 16th, trial day! Today, Donald Henderson, charged a few weeks back with fatally shooting his wife Marjorie and disposing of her body in Town Creek, would go on trial. Lincoln had finally decided to reveal to Dr. Jonas Simpson, a longtime friend and man he held in high regard, that he was personal witness to evidence in the Henderson case; evidence that would prove Donald Henderson to be innocent of the crime with which he had been charged. The doctor had been empathetic toward Lincoln's catch-22 situation, but, in the days leading up to the trial, had persuaded him to reveal this evidence to his old friend, Henry Buckles, who was also Donald Henderson's defense attorney.

After Judge DeWitt Hastings, District Attorney Johnny Abraham, and Defense Attorney Henry Buckles had seated twelve acceptable individuals of the defendant's peers in the jury box, the remainder of the morning was taken up by the prosecution presenting its case.

As District Attorney, Abraham rose from his seat, he felt the weight of the world on his shoulders. His first case to prosecute as an elected official had to be the biggest legal action to be argued within the walls of the old court of law in many years. He felt ill-prepared as he began calling his only three witnesses. The first witness, Dr. Jonas Simpson, verified that the cause of death was from a gunshot wound caused by a bullet of the .38 caliber variety taken from the victim's chest and that she was thrown into the waters of Town Creek after she was dead. The second witness, Sheriff Buford Coker (lying), verified that a .38 caliber pistol showed to him by the DA was the gun that fired the bullet taken from the victim, that the weapon was found in Mr. Henderson's possession, and that Mr. Henderson's fingerprints were on it.

Up to that point the atmosphere in the courtroom had been rather somber, but it became suddenly abuzz like the droning of a beehive at the call of the third witness to the witness stand, Miss Jessica Wingo.

Tap, tap, tap, sounded Judge Hastings' gavel on his bench. "Order!" he barked.

"Miss Wingo, tell the court about a conversation you had with Marjorie Henderson a few days before her demise," said the district attorney.

A stone-faced Jessica Wingo stared coldly at Sheriff Coker, then at Mayor McKean. After a minute of silence, the judge prompted the witness: "Miss Wingo, please respond to the prosecutor's request."

In Miss Jessie's testimony, she (lying) gave an account of how Marjorie Henderson had told her that her husband Donald had accused her of being unfaithful to him, of having become one of Miss Jessie's "girls," and had threatened her over it. Defense attorney Buckles passed on cross-examination of each of the prosecution's witnesses at the time they were called but reserved the right to recall them at a later time.

The prosecution believed the damning evidence they had presented amounted to nothing less than an open-and-shut case. They anticipated that the defense, in rebuttal, had little chance of mounting more than a half-hearted attempt to refute the proof submitted and its corroboration, leaving the jury no recourse except to return an iron-clad indictment against the defendant. It is understandable that the prosecution was somewhat taken aback by what seemed an unusual line of questioning embarked upon by Defense Attorney Buckles when court resumed following the lunch recess.

That afternoon

When the judge opened the trial's afternoon session, attorney Buckles called his first witness by recalling Sheriff Coker.

"Sheriff Coker," began Mr. Buckles, "you've already given testimony about the murder and murder weapon, but I'd like to ask you a couple of questions related to the weather that night. Sheriff, have you ever made trips between Coldwater and Atlanta, Georgia?"

"Yes, it's been mah pleasure ta visit th'at fair city on several occasions."

"Based on the distance between these two cities and the established speed limits and also on your personal experience of having made this trip, how long would you estimate, on average, it takes to drive from Coldwater to Atlanta?" queried the attorney.

"A good three an'a half 'owurs," answered the Sheriff without hesitation.

"How much more time would one need to add if it was during a time of heavy rain and wind?"

"Oh! At least another half 'owur," the lawman affirmed.

"So, you're saying it would take at least four hours to drive from Coldwater to Atlanta on a night like that of Friday, July 30. Is that correct?"

The Sheriff hesitated.

"Is that correct Sheriff?" prompted the attorney.

"Yes ... that's correct," replied the Sheriff slowly, suddenly feeling he somehow wasn't sure what he was answering to.

"That's all the questions I have for this witness Your Honor," indicated Mr. Buckles to Judge Hastings.

The prosecution chose to forego any questions.

The defense then recalled Doctor Jonas Simpson.

"Doctor Simpson, I have three questions for you," said Attorney Buckles to the new witness. "First, did you perform an autopsy on the deceased?"

"Yes sir, I did," answered the doctor.

"Second, was the cause of death the gunshot wound to the chest or drowning?"

"The gunshot wound. She was shot and killed first and then put in the water."

"Third, about what time can you best establish as the time of death?"

"The best I was able to estimate from the autopsy was between 6:00 p.m. and 8:00 p.m."

"Thank you, Doctor Simpson," said the defense attorney.

Again, the prosecution chose to forego any questions.

"The defense calls Mr. Lincoln Crockett to the witness stand," called out the defense attorney.

When Lincoln heard the bailiff's announcement of his name, it resounded throughout the courtroom like the clanging of church bells echoing around and about the cavernous halls of a great cathedral. He had agonized through the morning session, fidgeting in his seat, wringing hands, nibbling at fingernails. The growing knot in his stomach that had stifled any desire for groceries during the lunch break now felt like a brick.

Again, a buzz filled the courtroom. The eyes of a gallery full of spectators wearing puzzled looks fell upon Lincoln. All wondered what could be the connection of this young man with the case at hand? The walk down the aisle was like a death march to the gallows. Lincoln tried desperately to ignore the crowd but couldn't resist a quick glance to the right at his parents staring in disbelief, and up to the balcony, where on the edge of her seat, hands grasping the handrail, sat a wide-eyed Ashley Armstrong.

"Mr. Crockett, would you tell the court your whereabouts on the evening of Friday, July 30…the night of the murder…around 6:00 p.m.?" asked the defense attorney.

Lincoln gulped and said, "I was at the home of Mrs. Marjorie Henderson at 321 5th Avenue."

Oooh's and *aaah's* emanated from the audience; Sheriff Coker and friends sat up and swapped concerned looks.

"How did you come to know Mrs. Henderson?"

"I was only slightly acquainted with her. I ran into her one day a few months ago at the J.C. Penny store and helped her with some packages," answered Lincoln (fudging the truth a bit about the packages).

"Go on!" prompted Mr. Buckles.

"Your Honor!" protested the district attorney, "I fail to see what this line of questioning from this young man has to do with the case."

"If Your Honor will just bear with me," pleaded Mr. Buckles, "I'm developing a timeline of events that will exonerate my client of any wrongdoing."

"Okay," ruled the Judge, "but make some progress."

Lincoln's hands and brow were sweaty. He took a deep breath. "Well, on that Friday afternoon, I received a call from her at the Lacy Hotel. I must have said something to her about working there. She seemed very upset and asked me to come over, that she wanted to talk to me. I didn't really want to since I hardly knew her, but she sounded desperate … said it was a matter of life and death. So, I told her I would, but that I couldn't until after work … around 6:00 p.m.

"What was Mrs. Henderson like when you got there?"

"She acted nervous, upset, scared … she kept pacing about, looking out the windows."

"What did she want to talk to you about?"

"She wanted to give me a gift. A pendant made from an old coin on a chain," answered Lincoln.

"This one?" asked Mr. Buckles, holding up a pendant and chain for him to identify.

"Yes sir."

Lincoln had turned the pendant over to Mr. Buckles earlier which the attorney now entered into evidence in court.

"Why did she want to give you this pendant?"

"When I had seen her earlier, she was wearing the pendant and I recognized the coin as being an old Roman coin of historical significance. I told her about the time and circumstances under which the coin had been struck and she seemed impressed. That night at her house she told me that the coin had never really meant that much to her and since I knew so much about it, she thought that I would have greater appreciation for it than she, and she wanted me to have it."

"Your Honor," protested DA Abraham again, "what does this have to do with the case?"

"Mr. Buckles, I fail to see any progress with this line of questioning," cautioned Judge Hastings, head down, peering over the top of his black-rimmed glasses.

"Just a couple of more questions and I'll be finished with this witness Your Honor, and things will become much clearer," assured the attorney.

"For your sake it had better, counselor," said the Judge sternly.

"That's surely not the reason she was so agitated. Did she tell you why she appeared to be so troubled?" continued the defense attorney.

Lincoln felt weak all over; he swallowed hard. "She said that she was leaving town never to return because she feared for her life. That's why she wanted to give me the pendant before she left."

"Did she say *why* she feared for her life?"

"She said that she knew things about people that they didn't want her to know."

"Did she say if her husband was one of these people she feared?"

"On the contrary! She was going to leave and not even tell him where she was in order to protect him from any harm from these people."

"And what time did you leave the Henderson residence?"

"Around 6:30 p.m."

"So, when you left her house at 6:30 p.m. Mrs. Marjorie Henderson was alive and well. Is that correct, Mr. Crockett?" asked Mr. Buckles.

"That is correct!" stated Mr. Crockett.

"Thank you very much Mr. Crockett. No more questions."

"Your witness," Mr. Prosecutor.

"Mr. Crockett, just out of curiosity, just what is the historical significance of the Roman coin in this pendant?" asked the D.A. holding it up for close inspection.

"It's one of many Denarii Marcus Brutus struck in 44 B.C. in commemoration of the assassination of Julius Caesar."

DA Abraham continued, "Interesting! But, more to the point, did Mrs. Henderson reveal what *kinds* of things she supposedly knew that would be so incriminating as to cause her to fear for her life?"

"No sir."

"Did she identify any of the *people* that she supposedly knew things about or what could be so incriminating to them that they may threaten her life?"

"No sir."

"Did she give any indication as to where she might be going when she left?"

"I think she said something about going to a sister's house ... over in Knoxville, I believe."

"No more questions," said the District Attorney.

Weak-kneed and dripping with perspiration, Lincoln made for the exit, running a gauntlet of six pairs of suspicious men's eyes in the gallery that weren't exactly overjoyed at the revelations brought to light by Sheriff Coker's antagonist from Milltown. Of equal concern, was that a departing peek to the balcony revealed that Miss Armstrong had also taken leave of the premises; at what point in time; however, he could not know. By midafternoon it was getting hot in the old courthouse, and everyone was getting a bit restless and edgy, so the judge ordered the trial be continued the next morning.

Chapter 48

The next morning

While the breakfast crowd streamed into the Piano Room for the early buffet, Miss Jessie and Lincoln shared work plans and thoughts on the trial. Suddenly, their conversation was interrupted by a commotion in the lobby. It turned out to be Mr. Christian, the "suspicious" gentleman Dutch had warned Lincoln about. Christian bound down the stairway and held his left hand wrapped in a towel. Looking about, he spotted Lincoln and Miss Jessie in the restaurant discussing work plans over coffee and headed in their direction. Seeing the man hurriedly approaching and sensing that something was wrong, Lincoln rose to meet him. Being a familiar face, Christian addressed Lincoln first.

"Pardon me Lincoln ... I believe it is, Madam, he said as he turned his head toward Miss Jessie. You told me if I needed anything to call on you. Well, I've cut my hand, quiet badly I'm afraid. Is there a doctor nearby?"

"Miss Jessie, this is Mr. ...Christian. He came in yesterday afternoon on the Southerner," explained Lincoln.

"This is Miss Jessica Wingo, the owner of the Lacy," said Lincoln, introducing his boss to Mr. Christian.

"Madam," he nodded.

"Don't worry sir, we'll have you taken care of," assured Miss Wingo, rising from her chair to meet the new hotel guest.

"Lincoln," said Jessica, "get my car and take Mr. Christian down to the clinic."

"Yes, ma'am!"

"I'll call Maggie and let them know you're coming."

"Come with me Mr. Christian," directed Lincoln.

At the Coldwater Clinic

Maggie Simpson ushered the wounded patient into a treatment room where Dr. Simpson was waiting for him. Dr. Jonas Simpson, a lifelong resident of Coldwater, had graduated from Harvard Medical School but turned down a position at a prestigious, big-city hospital up east to return to his hometown where he had now been in practice for some thirty years. He and his wife, Maggie, a registered nurse, with the assistance of a receptionist and a couple of nurse's aides, operated the clinic.

The clinic, a four-bed facility containing three examining rooms, an X-ray and diagnostics space, a small laboratory, and a surgical area, provided them with the means to provide general health care services and run-of-the-mill surgeries for the local community. Most of the residents of Coldwater had also been ushered into the world by the Simpsons.

"I am in your debt, sir, to see to my needs on such a short notice, Dr. Simpson, being from out of town and all," said Wallace Christian.

"Oh, no problem…Mr….*Christian*, is that correct?

"Yes, that's correct."

"Folks must be pretty healthy in Coldwater today for we've only seen two patients. That's good I guess," added Jonas.

"How'd you cut this hand?"

"Shaving!"

"I know. How can one cut one's hand while shaving his face? Well, I was trying to use an old-fashioned straight razor when I clumsily dropped it and, just out of reaction, made an attempt to apprehend the thing in midair, which, in retrospect, was not an advisable course of action," explained Christian.

"I was, however, successful in the ill-advised attempt. Unfortunately, I caught the razor by the blade instead of the handle. This is one time I would have been better off to have been a failure," he added with a chuckle,

Dr. Simpson laughed, nodding his head in agreement.

"Well, it's going to take a few stitches to close the wound, but it's not as serious as it looks. If you'll slide that ring off your finger, I'll clean the blood off of it when I clean up your hand."

Mr. Christian removed the gold ring from his finger and placed it on the table. While the doctor went about his business, Wallace Christian struck up a conversation.

"The young gentleman who accompanied me here, Lincoln, I believe his name is, seems like a quite likeable fellow," observed Wallace.

"I also found him to be a rather astute conversationalist."

"Yes, he is. Exceptional young fella, especially considering his environment.

"At the risk of being too personal, may I ask what you mean by his *environment*?""

"Oh! It's just the way things are here in Coldwater, not just for him, but for all those living in Milltown."

"Ah, yes," began Christian with a quizzical tone to his voice, "I overheard people making reference to "Milltown," "Millies," and "Ridgers" spoken of with varying degrees of animosity while I was strolling about last evening. Perhaps you could enlighten me on the subject."

"Well, Mr. Christian, Coldwater is a town divided, a town divided geographically and socially. Has been for as long as I can remember, and, ironically, the geographical division is a reflection of the social division and symbolizes the unstated but understood social structure, if not caste system, that exists here."

"Main Street is the line of demarcation between two distinct geographical areas, a ridge and a plain. The ridge is a white-collar, well-to-do, residential area; hence, 'The 'Ridge' and 'Ridgers.' The plain is a blue-collar, industrial 'slash' lower-class, residential area; hence, 'Milltown' and 'Millies.' Milltown is what in most towns would be referred to as the 'other side of the tracks.' People from both areas shop in the same stores, do business together, kids go to the same schools, and so on, but they don't date, marry, or socialize together in any way."

"I see," said Mr. Christian, who had been listening intently to Dr. Simpson's explanation. "That certainly makes the conversations I've been privy to more comprehensible. Tell me, how did this prejudice and labeling develop?"

"Well, in my own socioeconomic analysis, I would venture to say that over time, with the success of the mills' development, the community evolved from a farming community into an industrial one, and out of that grew, from necessity, two levels of workers, managers and laborers. The disparity in wages between these groups created two distinct economic levels and the associated frictions that can exist between "haves" and "have not's," postulated Dr. Simpson.

"I would not be inclined to disagree with your examination of the subject doctor. It's the age-old case of the rich getting richer and the

[221]

poor getting poorer. And, it doesn't matter what rung of the ladder of success one is on, people must have someone to feel superior to, someone to look down on."

"There, all finished," said Dr. Simpson, wiping his hands and handing Christian his ring. "It should be healed up in a week or so, but you're probably going to be 'one-handed' for a few days."

"It'll be a bit inconvenient, but I'll manage. Fortunately, it's not my right hand," winced Christian gingerly flexing his hand.

"Here on business or pleasure?" asked Doc.

"Just thought I'd take a little trip south . . . get a feel for life in Dixie."

"Sounds like you must be from somewhere up north?"

"That's right, a big city."

"Well, I hope you'll find our little town to your liking. Going to be in town long?"

"Not sure, a few days at least."

"Well, come by and let me check that hand in a couple of days."

"I'll make it a point. Thank you again for your kind consideration, Doctor!"

Just then, Maggie stuck her head in the examining room door.

"Sorry to interrupt, Doc. Just thought I'd let you know that Sam Cheatum's here again complaining of the same ole problem."

"Okay, we're about finished up here. Tell Sam I'll be with him shortly," said the doctor, shaking his head and pitifully pursing his lips.

Mr. Christian, noticing the concern on the doctor's face, inquired, "From the look on your face, must be a difficult patient."

"Yeah," replied the doctor sadly, "he's killing himself with that rotgut shine. Not much I can do for 'im at this point. Been trying to get him to quit drinking for years but to no avail, like some others around here. I wish we could get rid of that stuff."

Wallace Christian's ears perked up at what Doctor Simpson was saying. He hesitated and turned back toward the doctor. "Dr. Simpson, I wonder if we might have dinner together one evening. You've lived here a long time and know the people. I bet you could help a big-city boy learn a lot about living in a small town."

"I don't see why not. In fact, why don't you come over to the house and have a homecooked meal with Maggie and me?"

"That sounds delightful! I'd like that."

As Wallace opened the door to leave, Doc Simpson called out, "If I'm not being too personal, may I inquire as to the type of business you're in Mr. Christian?"

"Please, call me Wallace, and I'm a writer, of sorts."

"Oh! What do you write about?" asked Doc.

"Crime." Wallace answered matter-of-factly, looking the doc straight in the eye.

"Fiction or true?"

"Sometimes it's hard to tell where one ends and the other begins," he answered grimly.

"And, what *manner* of writer are you?"

"One who seeks the truth," he answered, slipping the gold ring back onto his finger.

"And how do you know when you've found it?" Doc asked.

"Those who know…know; those who don't know, don't care to know," he answered.

"For the truth will make you free," he added with emphasis, tipping his hat and smiling as he closed the door.

Chapter 49

Before the morning court session resumed, Wallace Christian decided to take advantage of the Sheriff's office's close proximity to the courthouse and stop in for a visit with the local law enforcement officers. He found the office located in the rear of the building and entered unannounced. In the center of the room Sheriff Coker was laid back in his office chair, legs crossed atop the desk, eyes closed. To the Sheriff's right at a desk in the back, Deputy Lester Odom was busy cleaning a revolver, and to his left was Deputy Clay Cassidy, leaning against a wooden banister that separates the officers from the public, slurping a cup of java while thumbing through a manual of some sort.

His entrance caught the officers off guard and all three turned simultaneously toward the stranger at the door. He wore the same loose-fitting suit, tie, and hat that he had been wearing when he arrived on the train.

"Good morning officers," greeted Wallace tipping his hat.

Buford asked, "What can we do you fer mister?"

Wallace Christian introduced himself and explained that his purpose for visiting Coldwater was to do some research on southern small-town life for a proposed literary project. He said he had been talking with a variety of residents around town to get a cross-section of perspectives on life in Coldwater and would like to interview one of the town's police officers to get a perspective on crime from a law enforcement point of view.

Deputy Cassidy stood nearby, arms crossed, listening intently and nodding his head as if in agreement. Deputy Odom, who was cleaning his revolver, however, glared suspiciously at the stranger while glancing back and forth between his gun and the stranger. The Sheriff, now leaning on the banister with one leg and the other on the floor, naturally didn't want anyone poking around in police business, especially a stranger and one he guessed to be a Yankee at that.

"Say, ya look an sound ta me like a Yankee," said the Sheriff, "Where ya hail from mister?"

"From up north, so, I guess you might call me a Yankee."

"Sounds like yoh'ah might be one'a them civil rights agitators come down he'ah ta stir up things," said the Sheriff standing up and looking straight at Wallace Christian.

"Oh, no, no! I'm not one of them," replied Wallace defensively, "I'm just what I said I am and I'm here for no other reason."

"Looks like yoh'ah already got yoh self inta a mite of trouble," observed the Sheriff looking at Wallace's bandaged hand.

"Oh, yeah," said Wallace, holding up his hand, "cut it…shaving," he answered with a grin.

All three officers just stopped and looked at each other right funny like and decided it wasn't worth asking.

Buford returned to his desk and did not show much interest in satisfying the man's request until he popped a question that nearly knocked both the Sheriff and Deputy Odom out of their shoes.

"By the way, do you happen to know any moonshiners?"

Lester jumped like he'd been snake-bitten.

Buford, his eyes wide open, nearly peed in his pants.

Good ole innocent Clay just laughed.

"Wha'da yoh mean, 'Do we know any moonshiners,?'" roared Buford.

"Well, I guess you don't or you'd have them in one of those cells over there, wouldn't you? I guess what I really mean is, do you know how I could meet a moonshiner?"

"Why'da you wanna meet a moonshiner?" asked Deputy Odom.

"I'd like to talk to him. Interview him. Write about him."

"What makes ya think there's any moonshiners 'round here?" asked Deputy Cassidy.

"I've heard stories about moonshiners and bootleggers in the south, especially around the mountains, for years. I assumed there might just as well be some around this area as anywhere else."

The Sheriff chimed in, "Mr. Uh . . . "

"Christian," said Wallace, "Wallace Christian."

"Mr. Christian," the Sheriff continued, "in tha fust place, I don't know of any moonshiners or bootleggers 'round he'ah. In tha second place, just foh tha sake'a argument, let's say that there was one. Do'ya think he'd let yoh know who he is? Tell ya all about himself? Let yoh write 'bout'im inna book?"

"No, I don't suppose he would care for that kind of publicity would he?"

[225]

"These ain't the kind'a people yoh have tea with. They'a dangerous people whose jealous'a their privacy an guard it with their lives. They'a not hesitant ta deal with strangers and trespassers inna extremely ruthless manna," lectured Buford in very strong language.

"But, you said there are none of those kind of people around here so, we don't have to worry about any of that. Right?" said Mr. Christian with a hint of sarcasm in his voice.

"Uh…yeah…right!" answered Buford trying to relax his stiffened body into a calmer demeanor.

"Well, I don't want to keep you gentlemen from your jobs of keeping your citizens safe from the bad guys, so I'll be on my way. Thanks for your time. It's been a most enlightening conversation," said Wallace Christian turning to leave. "Have a good day now," he said as he reached for the door.

"Oh, Mr. Christian. I was just beginning to make my morning rounds," said Deputy Cassidy, picking up his hat. "Be glad to have you ride along and see some of the town—that is if the Sheriff don't mind," he offered, looking toward Buford.

"Yeah, why not?" answered Buford with a wave of his hand.

"Yes, that would be great. Thank you," answered Mr. Christian.

"Lesta, keep'a eye on that guy," said Buford,

"I wanna know everwhere he goes, everbody he talks to."

"He's just tha kind'a root hog that could go nosing inta places he don't need ta be an get his nose stuck or maybe cut off."

Chapter 50

Defense Attorney Buckles opened the morning session by calling cab driver Patrick McNally to the witness stand.

"Mr. McNally, you operate a taxicab stand across the street from the Lacy Hotel, do you not?" questioned the lawyer.

"That's right! Been doin' business there for more'n twenty-five years," answered Patrick.

"Tell the court about an unusual call you received on the evening of Friday, July 30, the night Mrs. Henderson was murdered," instructed the attorney.

"I got a call at 6:45 p.m. from a lady wanting me to come to 321 5th Avenue. Wanted to go to the bus station. Said she was in a hurry."

"You're sure of the time?" quizzed Mr. Buckles.

"Yep! I log all my calls in a logbook," Patrick answered proudly.

"But, what was unusual about the call?"

"Well, when I got there, there was nobody home. The place was dark with no lights on. I honked the horn a few times, but nobody came out. So, I left."

"What time was that?" asked the attorney.

"Exactly 7:00 p.m."

"Mr. McNally," asked Mr. Buckles, "did anything happen there that struck you as peculiar?"

"Well," he added with a troubled look on his face, "there was one sort of strange thing."

"And what was that?"

"Just as I was approachin' the house in my cab, a panel truck with no headlights on com'a tearin' across the street. It nearly hit me. I coud'a swore it come outta the driveway of house 321, but I can't be for sure."

"Thank you, Mr. McNally. No more questions."

"Your witness," Mr. Prosecutor.

"Only one question at this time," responded the Prosecutor.

"Mr. McNally, could you identify this panel truck again if you saw it?"

"I doubt it, sir. It was dark and rainin' so, I could barely make out it was a panel truck."

"Thank you, Mr. McNally. No more questions."

Young Johnny Abraham had, at first, been surprised at the lack of any attempt on the part of the opposition to repudiate any of the means and motive evidence presented by the prosecution. His wily old adversary had instead chosen to adopt a strategy of proving lack of opportunity on the part of the defendant, the most critical of the three components—his alibis. Inside, Johnny smiled at the acuteness of the veteran attorney and grimaced at his own level of professional effort invested in this legal proceeding.

In spite of his better judgment, he had allowed himself to be overly influenced by the Sheriff and mayor, both of whom had shown an unusual interest in the prosecution of this particular case. He would not allow that to happen again!

"The defense calls Donald Henderson, your Honor," said Attorney Buckles.

Again, the courtroom was abuzz with the humming of dozens of wagging tongues whispering their own opinions, speculations, and pronouncements of judgment on the tall, slender man, who looked somewhat shell-shocked as he made his way to the witness stand.

"Mr. Henderson," the defense began, "tell the court of your schedule on the evening and night of Friday, July 30."

"I left my home at 321 5th Avenue around 5:00 p.m. and drove to Atlanta, Georgia, to attend a week-long conference for sales representatives of the Life Long Life Insurance Company. The conference was held at the Sanderson Arms Hotel, where I arrived and checked in at approximately 9:00 p.m."

The defense attorney then submitted into evidence receipts from the hotel verifying the defendant's claim and turned the witness over to the prosecution, having asked only the one question.

When pressed under cross-examination by the prosecutor to explain the alleged murder weapon being found in his office desk at home, the defendant steadfastly affirmed having no knowledge of said weapon. Under further questioning to explain how his fingerprints came to be on the firearm, an agitated Donald Henderson pointed at Buford Coker in the gallery and vehemently insisted that the first time he ever saw the gun was when the Sheriff shoved it into his hand at the time of his arrest. He also denied jealousy of his wife as a motive for wanting to kill her, claiming he had no knowledge of anyone called "Miss Jessie's girls" or of any infidelity on his spouse's part.

Upon reexamination, Defense Attorney Buckles recalled the Sheriff to serve as his final witness.

"Sheriff Coker, from the testimony of Mr. Lincoln Crockett, we've established the fact that Marjorie Henderson was alive at 6:30 p.m. that evening because he was at her house at that time engaged in conversation with her. And, from the testimony of Mr. Patrick McNally, we've established the fact that Marjorie Henderson was alive at 6:45 p.m. that evening because he received a telephone call from her at that time soliciting transportation to the bus station. And, from written evidence and eyewitness accounts, we've established that Mr. Donald Henderson checked into the Sanderson Arms Hotel in Atlanta at 9:00 p.m. that evening."

"Now Sheriff, if you recall, in your earlier testimony you stated that in your 'expert' opinion that given the weather conditions of Friday, July 30, it would take at least four hours to drive from Coldwater to Atlanta. Is that correct, sir?"

"Ye'ah, th'aht's what I said as I recall," answered the Sheriff.

"Well Sheriff, from the evidence submitted, if Mr. Henderson had killed his wife, he couldn't have committed the foul deed until at least 6:45 p.m. right?"

"It'd seem so," admitted Buford reluctantly.

"Now Sheriff, I'll admit I'm no great mathematician, but it don't take a rocket scientist to figure out that from 6:45 p.m. to 9:00 p.m. is two hours and fifteen minutes."

"Sheriff, is it possible for anyone to get from Coldwater to Atlanta in two hours and fifteen minutes, other than by plane?"

"Not that I know of."

"One last question Sheriff."

"If Donald Henderson was in Atlanta at 9:00 p.m., is there any way possible that he could have been in Coldwater at 6:45 p.m. to kill his wife?"

One could almost see the black smoke pouring from the Sheriff's ears. Ole Buford found himself behind the eight ball, realizing that he'd been duped into being a pawn for the defense to sabotage his own case.

It took less than an hour for the jury to return a verdict of *not guilty*, much to the relief of one Donald Henderson and much to the disappointment of the six members of the brotherhood of moonshiners. And, judging from the reactions of the throng in attendance, there was undoubtedly a degree of disappointment with the outcome of the legal proceedings on the part of some of the curiosity-seeking onlookers.

With the pronouncement of a *guilty* verdict and a resulting "hanging," the bloodthirsty lynch party would have been afforded an opportunity to follow the poor condemned soul all the way to the gallows. With an acquittal, it just ends.

That is, for everyone except Lincoln Crockett; his troubles had just begun!

Chapter 51

It was getting dusky dark when Dalton Jackson wheeled his pickup truck into a small clearing off an old logging road just outside of town, their usual meeting place. He noticed that the rest of his gang of boy scouts were already there and waiting impatiently for his arrival. They shielded their eyes from his approaching headlights and cursed under their breaths.

"Well, Mr. Jackson. We'ah so glad you could take tha time ta grace us with yoh company!" said the Sheriff sarcastically.

"Keep your badge on. I got held up at the mill," answered an irritated Dalton.

"What's tha purpus uf this durn fool meetin' anyhow?" complained Herman Culveyhouse as usual.

"Don't ye know we're workin' the corn crops gittin' ready fer tha season.' Corn's gonna be commin' in pretty soon now an we'ez gonna be busy'er makin' an runnin' product than a cat tryin' ta cover up crap onna marble floor."

"This is the third time we've met," said a nervous Clifton Ledbetter. "Ever time we've met it's been ta make a new plan cause the last'un didn't work. I gotta bad feelin' there's another problem."

"It seems yore plan ta hang that Henderson woman's killin' on her old man didn't exactly turn out tha way ye planned now did it Mr. Jackson?" said Jonas Franklin with a hint of sarcasm in his voice.

Herman chimed in again, "Well, what's hit matter anyhow? Even if they did mess up disposin' uf tha body, that bunch frum Atlanta did do tha shootin'."

Dalton looked around the group and said, "I want to know something."

"Who in this group owns a .38 caliber handgun?"

"Why? Do you think one of us done it?" asked the mayor?

"Just answer the question," demanded Dalton.

Everyone shook their heads indicating that none of them had such a piece in their arsenal.

"Listen!" said Dalton, holding up his hands signaling for quiet.

"I just had a call from my contractor for the job saying they didn't do the job. He says that when his boys got to the Henderson house, they saw Marge Henderson through the window lying on the floor dead and could hear somebody ransacking the place. So, they cut and run and headed for the state line."

"But, if they didn't kill her, an none of us did, an her old man didn't, then who did?" pondered Sheriff Coker, scratching his head.

"How about that Crockett boy?" asked Jonas Franklin. "He was there?"

"Yeah! I'd like ta hang it on that Millie," chimed in the Sheriff.

"Naw! If the Atlanta boys heard someone in the house, it wasn't Crockett. He would have been back at the Lacy by then," reasoned Dalton.

"Then I repeat," said Buford, "who did?"

"That's the question Sheriff," said Dalton, scratching his head, "who did kill Marjorie Henderson…and why?"

Chapter 52

"Well, where'n hell have you been?" stormed Clovis Crockett, leaping from his recliner at his son coming through the kitchen door.

"I've been up at the bluffs," answered Lincoln.

"We been worried sick 'bout ya son," called out his mother, quickly emerging from the bedroom and embracing him. We didn't know where ya wuz."

"I'm sorry I worried you, Mom. After that trial, I just had to get away from everybody fo ra while, ," he apologized.

"Fine thang! Been gone three days. Nobody in town knowed where ya'z at since at trial. Thought maybe sump'n happin' to ya. Then ya jus show up here late at night like Laz'rus reser'rected frum tha grave!" ranted Clovis.

"I said I'm sorry."

"You's sorry all right, a sorry excuse fer a son," his father lashed out.

"*Clovis*!" chastised Anna Mae. "That's a terrible thang ta say ta yer son."

"Come si'down, Lincoln. Ya must be tired'n hungry. I'll gitcha some supper," invited his mother.

"Yeah, there ya go pettin' an pamperin' him after all he's done ta embarrass us," said Clovis, pointing an accusing finger at both of them. "First, he causes a hullabaloo at tha school dance, then gits caught at tha girly show, shames us before tha church, gits mixed up with a married woman in a public trial, an then jus disappears fer three days without tha curtisy ta even tell his mama where he's at," sounded off Clovis as he listed his son's transgressions.

"Oh, Clovis, ya make it sound worse than it is," chided Anna Mae.

"Up at the bluffs my ass. Probly been shacked up with another one of Jessica Wingo's middle-aged whores," accused Clovis, kicking a dining room chair over.

"Okay! I was wrong to go off and worry you and Mom like that. I said I'm sorry," confessed Lincoln, "but, what gives you the right to judge anyone?" and walked away.

Anna Mae got in her husband's face.

"Now just shut up Clovis. I ain't gonna listen ta any more'a that kind'a talk about our son's behavior."

"Don't tell me'ta shut up, woman," retorted Clovis, slapping his wife across the face.

"*Stop it*! Don't hit her again," yelled Lincoln at his father, jumping up from his seat.

"An just what will ya do 'bout it boy?" scowled his father back at him. "Lemma tell ya sump'n else. Ya can either straighten up, er ya can move out."

Lincoln just stood there gritting his teeth.

"Anna Mae, put that knife down."

"*Knife*?" Lincoln thought, "What *knife*?"

He looked around and there was his mother standing in the dining room, both hands wrapped around the handle of a carving knife, waving it at his father.

"If anybody's gonna straighten up er get out, it'll be you," snipped Anna Mae back at her husband. The married couple stood there for a minute or two exchanging salvos of abrasive words and other weepings, wailings, and gnashing of teeth.

In an attempt to disarm his wife, Clovis lunged at her and grabbed her forearms, but in the process, a quick swipe of the blade by Anna Mae caught Clovis across the wrist.

"Damn you bitch! You cut me!" shrieked Clovis.

Wrenching her arms apart, the frail woman moaned in pain as the wooden-handled knife fell to the floor. With a swift kick from a number twelve work boot, Clovis sent it skittering across the floor, coming to a stop against the kitchen door. The big man slung Anna Mae around and with one hand grasping her throat, pinned her against the wall and bellowed, "I told ya what ya'd get if ya ever hit me again!" and drew back his right arm with a doubled-up fist.

With that site before his eyes, Lincoln's greatest nightmare was becoming a reality, a reality that he had always feared might come, a time when his mother and he would die at the hands of his father.

It seemed as if time suddenly staggered into slow motion. Lincoln endeavored to lodge a word of protest, but his voice sounded remote, like that of one crying in the wilderness. The big man's fist was reaching closer, ever closer, to the helpless woman's face. He struggled to intervene in the impending collision between fist and face, but his body moved with the weight of a thousand pounds, straining against the exaggerated force of gravity.

The inescapable impact between the brute Clovis' powerful fist and the defenseless Anna Mae's face came with a sickening "thud" as her head popped like a melon and snapped her neck like a matchstick. Backing away, he watched her slight-of-frame body slide slowly down to the dining room floor into a crumpled, motionless heap.

Trembling at the site, a sickening wave of nausea coursed over Lincoln's body. In his nightmares, it was at this point he envisioned himself running. But, now that reality was at hand, for some reason, he didn't run.

Somewhere deep down inside, something snapped inside Lincoln Crockett that night. The seething pressure cooker of pent-up anger that had boiled inside him for so long, held at bay by fear of the unknown, suddenly blew its top. He was no longer sick, no longer trembling, no longer scared; he was mad, just plain damn mad! With a newfound courage, he charged his father and slammed into him like a linebacker.

"You've killed her, you murdering bastard, you've killed her!"

Clovis Crockett wrestled his son loose and, with a hand to the face, shoved him back against the dining table.

"Well, what's this? Mama's boy ta tha rescue? Well I'll jus teach ya a lesson, too."

As his father stepped toward him, Lincoln could see his face clearly. He didn't see the face of a man, but that of an animal. His heaving, hairy chest labored to suck in oxygen; glassy, bloodshot eyes set in a face flushed red with blood stared unfocused into space while drool dripped from the corners of his mouth like a rabid dog, and clenched teeth glared through snarled lips. Lincoln thought he had seen rage in his father before, but nothing like this. Looking upon this face was chilling, like gazing into the face of the Devil himself.

Without warning Clovis lunged forward catching his son around the shoulders with both arms like a lineman sacking a quarterback. His momentum carried both of them on top of the dining table pinning Lincoln down with his father's right forearm across his neck. His throat ached from the vice-grip hold on it; his lungs burned for the want of air. Squirming around, Lincoln finally got one leg free enough to ram a knee into the man's groin.

Clovis rolled off the table. He bent at the waist on buckled knees, grimacing in pain while vomiting a slew of Sunday school words from his mouth. Lincoln slid off the other side of the table, stumbled toward the kitchen, and coughed and gasped trying to clear the cobwebs from his head while clutching his aching ribs.

"You son of a bitch, I'll kill you fer that!" stormed the older Crockett attacking the younger one. Lincoln turned just in time to see the right cross coming directly at him and managed to dodge just enough to avoid the full impact of the blow. It did, however, send him reeling headlong into the kitchen counter. Pots, pans, dishes, and silverware stacked there crashed to the floor with him as he landed on his back in the middle of the clutter next to the door. Before he could recover from the fall and regain his footing his father was astraddle his stomach with his hands around his throat in another death grip.

"Kick me in the nuts will you?" scowled his father.

With arms and legs floundering helplessly about, he was in a completely defenseless position. Panic flooded Lincoln's mind for he knew he was going to suffocate if he didn't free himself from the pressure being exerted by the massive hands crushing his larynx and shutting off the air to his lungs and brain. But he couldn't move the big man; the light in his eyes began to grow dim. This time he was surely going to die.

His hands thrashed about on the debris-strewn floor in search of something to employ as a weapon. Finally, his right hand grasped what felt like the handle of some object which he grasped and swung wildly at the hulk on top of him.

"*Aarrgg*," came a cry of pain from his father accompanied by a loosening of the grip on Lincoln's throat.

Lincoln's body was beginning to tingle; his strength was draining away like the last drops of juice squeezed from an orange; a mirage of spots swirled before his eyes. With all the strength he could muster, he swung the object in his hand a second time.

"*Aarrgg*." Another moan of pain rolled off the tongue of his father and the fingers that had imprisoned Lincoln's neck went limp. Sensing deliverance to be at hand, Lincoln gripped the object as tight as he could manage and swung again, and again, and, the big man rolled over onto the floor beside him. As the world faded into darkness, the last thing he heard was a gruesome bubbling sound that echoed from somewhere in the far distance.

Unknown to him, he had heard the "death rattle," the gurgling sound in the throat of a dying Clovis Crockett.

A few minutes later

Piercing waves of acrid vapor penetrated his nostrils and jolted Lincoln to consciousness. Startled as wide-eyed as an owl at midnight, his brain tried to make connection with his surroundings, a foggy world of blurry objects, hazy lights, and muffled sounds.

"Whaaat? Wheeer?" he tried to speak, but the words got stuck in the back of his throat.

"Just lie still for a minute," he heard the sound of a familiar sounding voice say.

After a few deep breaths of oxygen had filtered through his lungs and effects of the pungent odor of smelling salts had dissipated, Lincoln recovered to an almost full state of awareness. Kneeling beside him on one side, he could now clearly see a visibly shaken Dr. Simpson, wearing the look of a man carrying a heavy heart. On his other side knelt a grim Deputy Clay Cassidy, his patrolman's hat pushed back on his head, trying to mask the concern evident in his face by wearing an artificial smile.

The battered and bruised Lincoln tried to sit up but couldn't.

"You stay right where you're at," cautioned the doctor. "You've had a close call, and that throat needs some attention. So, for right now, you just stay put. I'll be back in a minute."

"Hey man, how you feeling?" asked Deputy Cassidy.

Lincoln found that he could talk if he whispered. "Like I've been in a train wreck. Oooo! I hurt all over," he groaned, trying to move.

"What tha hell happened he'ah boy?" barked a gruff voice above them.

Looking up, he and the deputy saw the broad frame of Sheriff Buford Coker looming over them, hands on his hips, with a half-smoked stogie hanging from his mouth.

"Well," Lincoln began, but his whisper trailed off abruptly for two reasons—one, because he couldn't talk for long even at a whisper, and two, because all at once, memory of his father's assault on him and his mother came flooding fearfully back into his mind. Raising up on an elbow to get a clear view into the living room, he saw Dr. Simpson and two ambulance attendants placing a body covered with a white sheet on a stretcher.

He felt the touch of Deputy Cassidy's hand on his shoulder.

"Your mother's dead, Lincoln and so is..."

"Ya'ah, looks like yo'ah maw an paw have both bought tha farm," blurted out Sheriff Coker coldly, interrupting the deputy. "Yo'ah old lady's gotta busted head an neck an yo'ah old man's been cut open with *this*!" he said, holding up a bloody butcher knife.

"For goodness sakes Sheriff, have some consideration," appealed Deputy Cassidy.

"Look Deputy, yoh deal with these people yo'ah way, I'll deal with 'em mine."

"Know where we found this blade?" taunted the Sherriff, "In yo'ah right hand!"

Lincoln held his right hand up in front of his face, studied the dark red substance caked on it, but said not a word.

Lincoln directed his attention through the Sheriff's legs and, for the first time, saw the lifeless, bloody body of his father, then trained his eyes on the bloodstained butcher knife dangling from the lawman's fingers. The entirety of that nightmarish evening came racing back, detail by detail, through Lincoln's thoughts, from the snap of his mother's neck, to the demonic look on his father's face, to the vicelike choke hold on his throat, to the sensation of drowning in an airless vacuum, to the frantic flailing at his father with some object. That is, every detail with the exception of one. He couldn't recall a butcher knife, only some mysterious *object* that turned out to be his savior.

"Appears like when there's any kind'a trouble goin' on, yoh seem ta' be right in'tha middle of it, don't ya Millie?" accused the Sheriff. "Well, sho looks like yoh got yoh'ah self right in'tha middle of a shitload'a misfortune don't it? First, this he'ah Henderson woman shows up dead, an you tha last one ta see her alive. Now, yo'ah ole man's a'layin he'ah stuck lika pig, an you holdin' the pig sticker. Sure looks like you're guilty for shore in one an a suspect in tha other. Stuff 'em an cuff 'em, deputy," he ordered Deputy Cassidy.

"Not so fast Buford," intervened an irritated Doc Simpson. "Lincoln has throat and neck injuries from being nearly choked to death. He's going to the clinic, and he'll stay there until I say he's ready to leave," Doc added matter-of-factly.

Buford wasn't pleased with the doctor's pronouncement but had to abide by the doctor's orders.

"Okay, Doc, whateva ya say," said the Sheriff pacing about puffing his cigar. Deputy Cassidy, when tha good doctor here releases tha suspect, yoh place him unda arrest an book him at the jail," ordered the Sheriff.

"What?" exclaimed the surprised deputy. "On what charge?"

"We'll hold him fa questionin' until tha investigation is complete."

"The investigation?" questioned the deputy, "Investigation of what? It's clear what happened here!"

"No! That's why we'll conduct an investigation…ta see just what *did* happen here," said Buford smartly. An then we'll question him as a suspect in tha Henderson case."

Buford walked over to where Lincoln was still laid out on the floor, knelt down at his side, and said, "I knew it was just a matta of time 'til I got you in my jail Millie." With that, he blew a smoke ring in the direction of Lincoln's face and grinned like a possum eating persimmons.

Chapter 53

It was early morning; the Piano Room was empty except for two solemn-faced individuals who occupied a table in the very back. They sipped coffee and spoke quietly.

"First of all, Lincoln, I'm so, so, sorry for this horrible thing that you've experienced with your family. I can't imagine what you must be going through. If there's anything I can do, please let me know. Second, we've been avoiding one another for a couple of weeks and we both know why," she said.

Lincoln nodded in agreement.

"If we're going to continue to work together, and I hope we can, we're going to have to face what happened and come to some understanding about it. Do you agree?" she asked.

"Yes, mam. To be honest, I'd welcome the opportunity to resolve the conflict it's causing me in the context of relationships," he answered.

"Good. I want you to know that I take full responsibility for what took place at my apartment the other night. First of all, I, a mature adult, took advantage of an innocent and sexually inexperienced young man, although I'm not convinced that you're being completely honest about your encounter with Marge. Still, it was wrong for me to seduce you as I did. Second, to offer some degree of excuse in my defense, I had just returned from a business meeting in Central City where, in a social setting following the meeting, I had consumed a few alcoholic drinks and was feeling a bit giddy and conducted myself in a manner contrary to my normal demeanor. In short, I lost control of my good senses. I assure you that I don't throw myself at men in this manner. So, I hope you can forgive me for that intrusion upon your being."

"Well, one person can't bear all the blame." said Lincoln. "It takes two to tango. I had a choice. I could have walked away, although the pressure against that choice was extremely high. Nothing against you personally, but hindsight being what it is, I wish now I had made the other choice, given my relationship with Ashley."

"Lincoln, I propose that we both try to put that night out of our minds and pretend it never happened. We'll resume our relationship the way it has always been: employer and employee. Can we do that?"

"I think that was just a dream I had, Boss."

The Simpsons had invited Lincoln to spend some time with them rather than be alone in the house where the images of death still remained so vivid. So, he had whiled away the past few days doing some reading from Dr. Simpson's vast library while determining what his options were for the immediate future.

Much to his disappointment, Lincoln had been unable to arrange a *tête-à-tête* with Ashley as he had desperately longed to. He learned from the Armstrong's maid that the family had set out for parts unknown for a weekend getaway and weren't expected to return until sometime the following week. So, he would have to bide his time until he could attempt making contact with the blonde-haired Ashley.

He wasn't even sure if she would see him or what the status of their relationship was at this point. He hadn't had any contact with her since the trial so he had no way to gauge what effect, if any, the revelations at the Henderson trial had made on their involvement. Neither had she contacted him concerning the deaths of his parents. He didn't interpret her lack of sympathy (usually her long suit) during either of these events to be a particularly encouraging sign.

Even though the Simpson's house was quite spacious, he was beginning to get a bit stir crazy and claustrophobic and was not looking forward to his parents' funerals tomorrow. It was getting to be late afternoon, and he needed to get out-of-doors for a while and enjoy some fresh air. So, he straddled the Indian, roared out of MacAnally Flats, and headed toward the river. He remembered Zeke talking about Sweet Annie McCool's and his invitation to join him there sometime. Annie's sounded just like the kind of place that might shake him out of his doldrums.

Sweet Annie McCool's place could be heard long before it was seen. The haunting beat of blues and rhythmic melodies of jazz riding on the night air drifted through the willows, echoed across the swamps, and wafted along the riverbanks as sweetly as the fragrance of honeysuckles in spring. The little Johnnytown honkytonk was an old, large, one-room, board building with a tin roof and a front porch framed with strings of yellow electric lights and a flashing neon sign overhead that bid everyone welcome.

Lincoln approached the front door with some misgivings, but with the assurance of his mentor that there was nothing to fear but fear itself, stepped inside, stopping momentarily to observe the sights and sounds.

Inside, the sound of hypnotic music that reverberated against the four walls, the free-flowing intoxicating spirits, the sight of revelers in party mode, and the aroma of an assortment of mouthwatering foods being served up was just like Zeke had described it.

After meeting up with Zeke, the oddly-paired fishing buddies found themselves anchored at a table right in the middle of a sea of blaring music, funky musicians, gyrating dancers, and lighthearted shenanigans where (Lincoln believed) Zeke had intentionally gotten them seated. Lincoln's plan had been to seek out a table in the back in order to remain as inconspicuous as possible, but, regardless of their seating, he would still have stood out like a full moon on a cloudless night. He was the only white person in the joint.

Over the next few hours, Zeke introduced his young friend to the delights of soul food, some items of which his protégé didn't find pleasing to his palette, especially hog jowls and pig's feet. Not being a "drinker" either, he did not find the beverages to his particular liking, especially the Muscat.

"Wait right here. I'll be back inna minute," said Zeke, leaving the table.

"Where you goin'?"

"Jus waits right here. I'll be back."

They were both beginning to feel the effects of what little wine and beer they had drunk. Zeke was gone for about fifteen minutes before returning with a half-gallon Mason jar in hand. He plunked it down on the table. It was filled with a pink liquid.

"Looks like pink lemonade," observed Lincoln.

"Oh, this's better'n pink lemonade," promised Zeke, proceeding to pour two small glasses full.

He pushed one of the glasses over in front of Lincoln. "Try this. Take'a mouthful 'n let it go down slow'n easy," instructed Zeke.

Lincoln did as he was instructed.

After the pink liquid had hit his stomach, Lincoln closed his eyes and took a deep breath. Then, as he exhaled, his eyes widened like two Moon Pies.

"Whoa! That was good!" he exclaimed.

"Hee, hee, hee," laughed Zeke.

"What is that stuff?" Lincoln wanted to know.

"Son, that's a medicine when you's sick, a tonic fer tha spirit when you's down, an a magic potion ta cure all ills. Lincoln, my boy, that's *watermelon wine*."

"I don't know about all that you said, but it sure makes you feel warm all over," said Lincoln.

"That's a fact!" agreed Zeke.

Over the next hour, they emptied that jug of watermelon wine in between verses of old crying-in-your-beer blues songs. Lincoln emptied his soul, as well, as old Zeke just sat and let him babble on, nodding his head in agreement and interjecting some of his own sorrows along life's road. At times, their singing got louder than the lady on stage. That was bad enough, but sometimes they would be singing a different song.

"My man, thas a heavy burden fer a young man ta bear," sympathized Zeke, referring to Lincoln's killing his father.

It was a strange sight to see, an old black man and a young white man, staggering arm-in-arm at midnight, three sheets to the wind, ambling down the road leading out of Johnnytown and singing "You Are My Sunshine" at the top of their voices.

Chapter 54

The next day

It was not the best of days to have to be out and about. The misty drizzle that fell from dark overcast skies had transformed Potter's Field into a bed of soft mud pockmarked with pools of water. The foul weather accentuated the somber mood that cast a shadow over the group of mourners who followed two hearses into the cemetery that afternoon. Friends and neighbors braved the elements to pay final respects to Anna Mae and Clovis Crockett, the victims of tragic deaths.

Dr. and Mrs. Simpson sat with Lincoln between them while Reverend Nutter waxed eloquently over the dearly departed (especially Deacon Clovis), extolling their virtuous lives as he ferried them off to the great beyond and the heavenly rewards awaiting them. When the preacher had concluded his remarks, the Simpsons, like stalwart bookends, supported Lincoln as he stood wavering and watched, seemingly unemotional and unattached, as the bodies of his departed mother and father were laid to rest in their final earthly abode under six feet of clay. Everyone noticed but discounted Lincoln's strange behavior and disheveled appearance to the extraordinary circumstances surrounding his parents' passing. No one knew about the extraordinary evening he had spent at Sweet Annie McCool's the night before.

He reflected on his mother. He thought of the hard life she had lived, the things she had needed and wanted but was denied, and the poor health she had endured. He also remembered things she had taught him, especially how she had supported and stood up for him against his father. She was a good person; she had been an important part of his life, and he had been lucky to have her.

A few minutes later, waiting beside the cemetery gate for the Simpsons to pick him up for the ride home, he stuffed his hands into his trouser pockets and watched tiny water droplets fall gently from his face into a puddle at his feet. He pondered the *whys* of life and death.

Since that night when he was aroused from his trip to never-never land to the sight of his parents' lifeless bodies, being told of their deaths, and seeing the bloody knife they said was found in his hand, Lincoln had been lost in a state of shock and depression. He wondered at the way in which the final chapter in their lives had ended in almost the exact way he had conjured up in his imagination. That is, with the exception of his father's death coming at his hand; he couldn't have imagined that in a thousand years. To consider what repercussions from this life-altering event would be manifest in his life was, at this point, unfathomable. Against his wishes, the Simpson's had persuaded him to stay at their house until he felt better or, at least, until after the funerals.

In another development preceding the funerals, the results of the district attorney's investigation concluded that Anna Mae Crockett had died from a blow to the head administered by her husband, Clovis Crockett, and that he, in turn, had died from stab wounds received from his son in defense of his life. The DA had then ordered Sheriff Coker to drop all charges against Lincoln. The Sheriff did so, much to his consternation at being denied the opportunity to "keep that Millie in his jail."

For some reason, Lincoln's attention was suddenly drawn to the street, making him aware of two women who had become, and would become more so, important in his life. He watched attentively as the black sedan rolled slowly by with Bam Bam at the wheel, knowing that concealed behind those dark windows sat Jessica Wingo. He was somewhat surprised that she had come out on this occasion.

Not far behind followed a white T-Bird. Lincoln cracked a slight smile. The car stopped. The blonde behind the wheel stared expressionless at him for a minute. She didn't smile, blow him a kiss, or make any of her other usual gestures. Lincoln hadn't seen Ashley since the day of the trial when he caught sight of her in the balcony, and he hadn't talked with her since three weeks ago when they had met at the movie theatre. A car horn honked. He turned his head to see the Simpsons waving to him. He looked back to the street. The T-Bird was gone.

Lincoln was suddenly gripped with fear; fear of what, he couldn't say, but something from which he felt a strong urge to flee. Without provocation, he took flight as if trying to escape a swarm of yellow jackets and broke into a full-sprint down the rain-puddled street. The light rain peppered his face and blurred his vision. After running for some amount of time and distance, neither of which he was able to ascertain, his lungs began to burn. He came to an abrupt halt and doubled over with his hands on his knees gasping for breath. His chest felt like it was caught in the grasp of the big arms of Bam Bam.

Lincoln had fallen into the clutches of a force he had never before experienced, at least not to its fullest extent, even on the family circle battleground. That is, being wrapped in the blinding, debilitating tentacles of overpowering uncontrollable *panic*!

Chapter 55

"Good morning Miss Wingo. Good morning Mr. Crockett," came the call across the lobby.

Miss Jessie and Lincoln both turned and saw Wallace Christian rushing toward them.

"Good mornin' to you, too, Mr. Christian," answered Miss Jessie.

"I'm glad I caught the two of you, although, Lincoln, I didn't expect to see you back at work so soon."

"Well, I was just getting restless and needed to come back to work and get busy to get my mind off things," he replied.

"If I may detain you, I would like to speak with both of you for just a minute," said the gentleman.

"By all means! Would you join us for some breakfast? We were just on our way to the restaurant," said Miss Jessie.

"That sounds very inviting, but I really don't have the time."

"Okay. Let's just take a sit here in the lobby. What's on yoh mind Mista Christian?" asked Jessica, signaling the waiter to bring coffee to the table.

"First of all, let me say to Lincoln that I am so sorry for the most unfortunate and tragic events that have occurred in your and your family's lives. I offer you both condolences for your loss and best wishes in dealing with the future. Second, I'm catching the Friday train tomorrow morning and going back up north for the Labor Day weekend, but, before I leave, I wanted to thank both of you for the hospitality you've shown and for the assistance Lincoln has given me in finding my way around town."

"It's been a pleasure havin' ya as a guest and if ya ev'a find yoh'self down this way again, we hope you'll come see us again," said Miss Jessie.

Christian went on to explain that his trip had been worthwhile, that he had learned a great deal about southern small-town life in the month he had spent there, and that he had met some noteworthy personalities. Most notably, he had been intrigued with the suspicious acting law officers, particularly the deputy dog that had trailing him around like a bloodhound sniffing out a trail.

"I don't like those two or the Sheriff's son," admitted Lincoln. "I try to avoid them as much as possible."

"Looks like you've sized up some folks 'round here pretty well," noted Miss Jessie.

"But, ya didn't say how you've sized up the present company, Mr. Christian," she added with a slow, teasing southern accent.

"Well ma'am, anyone can see that you size up quite well...uh...that is...to say, that anyone can tell that you're obviously a real southern lady," stammered the half-embarrassed man.

"Ya know, Mr. Christian, ya can't always judge a book by its cover,'" Miss Jessie nodded with a mischievous smile.

The visitor stood up, thanked them for the time and conversation, and turned to go. Hesitating, he turned back to the table as if remembering something he'd forgotten.

"You know," he said, "there is one strange characteristic that I've noticed about everyone I talked to here in Coldwater. Everyone's been very friendly until I mention the word *moonshine*; then they get this funny look and clam up like they've been struck with a sudden case of lockjaw.

Lincoln stiffened as he had a flashback to what he had recently witnessed at the sawmill.

Miss Jessie just sat there with no change in her expression or demeanor.

"Sort of like the two of you right now," said the professor with a slight smile forming across his mouth.

"The only one that didn't," he continued, "was Doc Simpson. I had supper with him and his wife at their home the other night; had a very interesting conversation on the subject. Still wonder what that stuff tastes like. I guess I'm just not going to get to see on this trip . . . .maybe next time!"

"Oh, "yes, there is one more person I have yet to chat with before I can be on my way."

"Who's that?" asked Lincoln.

"That would be a Mr. Jonathan Abraham," answered Mr. Christian.

"Johnny Abraham, the District Attorney!" exclaimed Jessica perking up.

"Yes, he's been out of town some, and I haven't been able to catch him."

"Why would you want to talk to him?" inquired Jessica.

"Oh, as the one responsible for prosecuting law breakers, he should be able to give me some idea about the range and variety of criminal activities that are prevalent in the community."

"Well, we don't have any crime to speak of, any major crime that is, here in Coldwater," pointed out Miss Jessie.

"That would seem to be the case alright, Miss Wingo, but, as you say, you can't always judge a book, or a town, by its cover."

Mr. Christian nodded, and with a tip of his hat, made his exit.

Chapter 56

September, 1965

A week had passed before Lincoln and Ashley had been able to arrange a rendezvous. Vestiges of fall were in the air signaling that the hot, muggy days of summer were numbered. A slight chill rode on the breeze and small stains of color were beginning to bleed into the leaves, telltale signs that autumn was near at hand. The young man smiled at the way the breeze that drifted along the banks of the river ever so gently stirred the young lady's golden-blonde mane the same way it did the long stringy limbs of the willow trees making them undulate like the tentacles of a jellyfish. The young couple looked thoughtfully at one another as they nibbled at a picnic lunch of chicken and fries.

"How was your weekend trip?" Lincoln asked.

"Oh, it was wonderful! If you enjoy sitting around listening to a group of old relatives reminisce about their glory days," answered Ashley.

They both smiled at the hint of sarcasm in her voice as they stretched out on the picnic blanket and admired the billowy, cloud-filled, noonday sky.

Ashley rolled over and propped her head up on one elbow.

"Say, that's not a bad looking car you're driving there," Ashley said, looking at the '52 Plymouth parked in the shade of a tree near them.

"Yeah! It's old but it's in real good shape. It belonged to my dad. Guess I sort of inherited it," said Lincoln.

"Well, I'm glad you have some good transportation now."

"Listen, you said you wanted to see me today because you needed to 'explain' some things. So, what 'things' do you feel a need to enlighten me on?" said Ashley.

Lincoln raised up and sat cross-legged.

"I've missed you," he said, heartfelt, staring at the ground.

"Rats and you are the only two people I've ever been able to talk to, and with him gone, and you . . ." (His voice trailed off.)

"Not around?" interjected Ashley. "I know. I'm sorry. I've missed you, too. But let me explain. Linc, I know you've been going through a rough time these past few weeks and I wanted to be there to be your friend and support you. But, there's been all this publicity and rumors bandied about portraying you as involved in an adulterous affair with a married woman, a suspect in her murder, and, some say, murderer of your father. Well, my parents took all this to heart and laid down the law. They've threatened to ship me off to an all-girls school in Switzerland if I'm caught 'fraternizing' with you again. So, I'm taking a real chance being here today."

"I'm sorry Ashley. You should have told me that your *sentence* had been increased and I wouldn't have asked you to come and put yourself in greater jeopardy," said Lincoln apologetically.

"It's alright. I chose to come. I wanted to come," she said sympathetically.

"Ashley, sometimes I think I'm going crazy!" he cried out, shaking and burying his face in his hands.

Ashley moved over beside her troubled friend and held him until he stopped shaking and composed himself. "No wonder you feel that way, Linc. You've been through a lot in a short period of time, more than anyone deserves to endure. And, in order to save an innocent man from going to prison, you told things about yourself in that trial that you knew would cause people to question your character. That took a lot of courage. And then the horrible tragedy of your parents' deaths and the circumstances under which they occurred, followed by their funerals? That's too much for any mortal to bear."

"Ashley, what I said about knowing Marge Henderson is true. Nothing happened between us."

"To be honest, that did bother me and make me wonder. I guess I was jealous," said Ashley, "but, I believe you. If you're anything, you're honest."

"And, I almost didn't testify at that trial. It took a lot of soul searching," admitted Lincoln.

"Well, I'm glad you did. You're a hero for doing that."

"Yeah? Well, I may have saved Mr. Henderson's rear end, but it put me on Sheriff Coker's suspect list. You know he also wanted to charge me with murder in my father's death but the district attorney wouldn't buy it. But, he'll keep trying; I know things."

"You *know* things?" said a surprised Ashley, jumping to her feet.

"About Sheriff Coker? What kind of things?" she continued with concern in her voice.

"I can't tell you. I've said too much already," answered Lincoln.

"Are you implying that you know something that could implicate Sheriff Coker in that Henderson woman's death?"

Lincoln stood up and walked down to the bank of the river.

Ashley followed.

"To say more would place you in danger," he said, looking into the deep water. "But, it goes even deeper than that, 'bout as deep as old Little River here," he said pensively.

Chapter 57

A repeated "knock," "knock," "knock" roused Lincoln from a groggy slumber. At first, he couldn't decide if the knocking was coming from the front door or inside his head. Through blurry eyes he squinted at his watch. It was late afternoon! He looked about at familiar surroundings. Then he remembered. He had decided to take the afternoon off and return to his parents' house to get things in order. He had to first dispose of their belongings and then determine what to do about providing for a roof over his own head. He must have fallen asleep on the couch. The "knock," "knock," "knock" came again, followed by someone calling his name. Dragging himself off the couch, he staggered half-awake in the direction of the door, and with some effort, managed to open it to a man that he had been expecting sooner or later.

"Lincoln Crockett! I believe you must be the man of the house these days," said Ike Butler.

"I'm…" he started to continue, extending his hand, but Lincoln interrupted him. "I don't know what you're selling, but come on in."

For the people who lived in the Milltown mill houses, there was one day of the month when answering the knock at the front door was not a day to be looked forward to with great anticipation. First of all, it meant that it was time to pony up the month's rent, but worse, it meant having to deal face-to-face with the surly Ike Butler. Armstrong Textiles and Longworth Furniture Company had contracted with Ike Butler to serve as landlord over the row houses to collect rent, fill vacancies, and maintain the properties.

Ike Butler was a bottom feeder, a real lowlife. A thirty-year-old who looked fifty, he was small in stature, stoop shouldered, always dirty and shabbily dressed in long shaggy, unkempt hair hanging over his ears. When he grinned (which he did a lot) a mouth full of tobacco-stained teeth stood out like the dirty grill of a '49 Ford, for he was a weaseling, little, nicotine fiend who continuously sucked on coffin nails like babies suck on nipples.

The renters all hated Butler. He was ill-mannered, disrespectful, and insisted that they address him as "Mr. Butler," which they did with a degree of sarcasm. Behind his back, they referred to him as "Little Ikey."

Although he was the landlord, Ike had no real authority in his own right. The only clout he held was through his association with Messrs. Armstrong and Longworth. Being a jack-of-all-trades and master of none, he had the prerogative to contract out any major work necessary, with the approval of either Mr. Armstrong or Mr. Longworth.

He had also learned that he could demand the renters' respect through that same association. But, even if he didn't garner their respect, he could at least repulse any attempt on their part to squabble or dispute with him in any way for fear of retribution in the form of eviction. One word from him to the owners and tenants could be out on the street. This management-by-fear tactic had worked well for him for the most part, except for one incident about two years ago that almost proved disastrous for Mr. Butler and resulted in a softening in his approach to personal interactions with his tenants.

On that particular occasion Ikey had gone into a home to collect the first month's rent from a couple who were new to Coldwater, to Milltown, and to who was whom and what was what. Ikey, in his usual style and manner, got a little too friendly with the lady of the house and made some off-color remarks concerning the pleasantness of her physical appearance, to which her husband took exception. It was then that a fist from the man's right hand sent Ikey sprawling into the street, and from there, via ambulance, to a three-week hospital stay where he damn near died from a concussion.

"Now then, Crockett, I assume you know the purpose for my visit," said Ike.

"Hell, I don't even know where I'm at or who you are."

Lincoln's brain had not yet fully recovered from several nights of insomnia.

"I'm Ike Butler, your *landlord*," the man said with emphasis.

"Oh, yeah! Things are beginning to come back now," said Lincoln, shaking his head.

"Well, in any case, I doubt that it's to offer your condolences," answered Lincoln, sarcastically.

"*Condolences*? Oh, yes…your parents. Tragic situation. Please do accept my sympathies for these most distressing and untimely misfortunes that have befallen your family," interjected the insensitive Ike as an afterthought. "But, my main concern," he continued, "is with one particular situation."

"And that would be the thing nearest and dearest to your heart...collecting rent," surmised Lincoln, again sarcastically.

"Well now, I have but a conscientious dedication to the responsibility to which my employer has entrusted me to collect his dues in a timely and efficient manner; however, in this particular situation, I'm afraid the matter goes beyond a simple matter of collecting rent," said Ike.

"How's that?" quizzed Lincoln.

"You see, the mill houses are to be rented only to employees of one of the mills," Ike informed Lincoln, "and you're not a mill employee, are you?"

"No, I'm not," stated Lincoln.

"No, you're not," affirmed Ike.

"Normally, I would require you to vacate the premises by the weekend, but given the untimely circumstances that have befallen you, I'll give you until Monday the sixth."

"That's not very much time to get everything taken care of and besides, it's a holiday, Labor Day" argued Lincoln.

"Just another to labor. Out by Monday," Ike said firmly, pointing his finger at Lincoln, "or I'll have to have Sheriff Coker to come with an eviction notice, and the Sheriff said he'd love to come help you move," Ike chuckled.

Oh, I just bet he would, thought Lincoln.

When Lincoln walked away from that little white house on MacAnally Flats for the last time, he stopped, looked back, and studied it for a minute. He thought it ironic that such an inanimate object, the picture of innocence sitting there in its emptiness, could appear as a sentient persona, inciting within the heart feelings of fear and hate. How many times had he wished to be free and never see that house or its inhabitants again? But, now that his wish had been realized, where could he go from here? He was free—physically, anyway—but so many drastic changes had occurred in his life in such a short period of time that it felt like his world had been turned upside down. Rather than feeling free, he felt more like a man in a cage than ever.

So, having been evicted from the mill house due to his parents' deaths, Lincoln had nowhere to go or anyone to turn to, other than the possible exception of a couple of little-known, out-of-state relatives who were virtual strangers. His mother had a younger sister down in Florida (who had been unable to attend the funeral due to a family illness) that he had seen only once when he was very young.

Likewise, his father had a brother over in North Carolina whose family Lincoln had heard about but had never actually met until they showed up for the funeral service. After sizing up that limb on the flesh and blood family tree, he figured it must have been grafted in from some other variety somewhere along the way.

That little band of "Tobacco Road" refugees appeared like they hadn't been out of the hills in twenty years. Their little family circle consisted of the father, Silas Crockett, the mother, Hattie, and two big raw-boned, twenty-year-old twin girls named Bessie and Gert. Those twins were downright scary looking, especially when they got close and puffed smoke in your face from their homemade cigars. It would take no small stretch of one's imagination to envision these lasses in makeup and frilly dresses sashaying off to the prom.

In the first place it'd wear out a weed eater shaving their hairy legs that a mule would be proud of. It would be a pretty sure bet they'd never make the cover of *Glamour* magazine, and it wouldn't take a gambling man to bet dollars to doughnuts that they could take any tag team on the men's wrestling circuit. Fortunately, Lincoln didn't have to consider the option of living with out-of-town relatives or remaining homeless.

Miss Jessie reached out to Lincoln with a helping hand by offering him room and board at the hotel. With the help of some of the hotel staff, he was able to fashion some quite comfortable living quarters out of a storage room in the basement that was large enough to hold several pieces of furniture from the mill house. Since he was working fulltime at the hotel, staying there fulltime worked out quite well. Yet, in spite of his assets and all he had going in his favor, he still had a lot on his plate with more problems and worries to sort out and deal with than any nineteen-year-old on his own should have to bear the weight of on his young shoulders. Despite all appearances, Lincoln Crockett was troubled in both mind and soul.

Chapter 58

They sat side by side on a large rock that jutted out from the rim of the bluff, legs dangling over the edge, gazing with mixed emotions into the valley below. With her recent high school graduation Ashley had reached that milestone on her road of life that ritually defines that time of transition into adulthood and self-dependency, that long-awaited time to pursue a future filled with hopes and dreams of one's own making and design. This was the same time Lincoln had passed into just one year earlier which ended so tragically.

Events had taken place during this summer of discontent that had infused into each of them feelings and insights which they had never before felt or experienced, feelings that clouded the future with doubt and confusion, which they now faced with uncertainty. Could there really be a future where the idealism of the civil rights movement was realized in the country? Could there really be a future for a town known simply as Coldwater without references to "Ridgers" and "Millies?" Could there be a future for a Ridger girl and a Millie boy?

"Sorry to hear you're getting kicked out of your house," sympathized Ashley.

"Oh, well, I knew that was just a matter of time coming," said Lincoln. "But, the good news is, Miss Jessie's letting me fix up some living quarters in a large storage room there in the hotel that isn't being used for anything. So, I think it will work out okay."

"Say, that's mighty nice of her."

"Yeah. Some of the guys at the hotel are going to help me with it this week."

"Let me know how that goes. My folks are going to be driving me up to State University on Labor Day for the beginning of fall semester," said Ashley wistfully. "You can call me up there."

"Thanks again for continuing to take chances to meet me. I really wanted to see you one more time before you left," said Lincoln, turning toward her. "I'm sorry I've caused you so many problems with your parents and friends," he added apologetically, holding her hands and looking longingly into her face.

"I guess I should never have asked you to dance at that prom," he said.

"Well, I didn't have to accept, did I? "she asked.

"No."

"And, I haven't exactly discouraged you," she said.

"That's true. By the way, why haven't you?"

"Different reasons, I guess," she said smiling.

"In the beginning, it was partly being rebellious. You know, popular Ridger girl with Millie boy. Partly for the adventure and the intrigue. But, I genuinely got to liking you. I've always thought you were a nice guy, but I found that we have a lot of things in common. We're more alike than different."

They got up and she took him by the hand as they walked along the bluff.

"The last time we were here, you told me that you loved me," reminded Ashley.

"I guess I did, didn't I!"

"Do you still feel that way?" she asked, half playfully, half seriously.

"Yes...yes I do," answered Lincoln, firmly. "Would you like for me to say it again?" he asked.

Ashley stopped, faced Lincoln, and put her arms around his neck.

"If you like."

He placed his hands on the sides of her waist.

"Ashley Armstrong, I love you," he repeated with all seriousness.

They slowly embraced. Their eyes, locked on each other's, guided their lips closer together until they were engaged in a slow, passionate kiss.

"Lincoln, I'm falling more in love with you every day," whispered Ashley, as they just stood for a minute and hugged, listening to the rustling leaves among the trees.

"What are we going to do?" she asked.

"You're going to State and get your degree just like you've always planned," stated Lincoln matter-of-factly, shaking a finger in her face. "I'm going to keep working at the Lacy and see what happens with the draft. In the meantime, I'm going to take courses at the community college as much as I can. That'll give us time to figure *us* out."

"Sounds like a plan," agreed Ashley.

[258]

"That is…if you're sure you want there to be an *us*?" asked Lincoln, holding his breath.

"Yes, Lincoln, I'm sure. I do want there to be an *us*," she answered with a serious look.

"It won't be easy trying to have a secret relationship, and the time will come when we'll have to face your family with it. I hate to think what it will be like," he said, exhaling a big breath.

"I know!" grimaced Ashley, "There'll be the devil to pay. We'll have to stick together through whatever comes."

And when one deals with the devil, the price is usually high.

Chapter 59

"*No! Stop! Don't!*" cried out Lincoln as he tossed and turned somewhere beneath the surface of a restless slumber. Thrashing like a fish out of water, he became more and more entangled in the bed clothes. With a scream of terror, he sat straight up in bed, abruptly jolted awake from a nightmare-afflicted sleep.

Heart racing like a rabbit being chased by a pack of dogs, he looked around cautiously, confused by the unfamiliar surroundings that were coming gradually into focus. Hyperventilating, he hugged himself tightly trying to calm the pounding in his chest. Soaked from head to toe with perspiration, the pajamas he had worn to bed were plastered to his body like a second layer of skin.

After regaining control of his faculties, it became clear that the terrifying incident he had just experienced had not occurred within the space of three-dimensional reality, but within the unfathomable depths of the subconscious dream state, making it no less existent to the dreamer. It was just one more in the increasing number of nightmares plaguing his sleep, with one exception.

Since his parents' deaths, the nightmares had taken on a new twist. Reruns of the family show *Father Knows Best* starring Clovis Crockett, which had previously filled this time slot, had been replaced by the drama *The Fugitive* starring Lincoln Crockett. The latest of these sleep-shrouded visions had him on the run, fleeing from his father who hounds him through street and dell trying to kill him. Just as his father is about to strike the death blow, Lincoln awakens.

Lincoln fell back onto his pillow, limp and exhausted. He looked at the clock on the nightstand. It wasn't there. He saw one across the room on a chest of drawers. It said 3:00 a.m. He remembered now. He was in his new room at the hotel, not his old house. That's why things looked unfamiliar.

Good grief, he thought, *what a relief.*

But, another night without sleep! He was afraid to sleep; afraid those awful nightmares would come back. He went to the window and opened the curtains. Some light filtered in from a streetlight, offering enough for Lincoln to see his way around the room. He paced back and forth mumbling to himself, practicing some self-psychoanalysis.

"I feel like a caged animal. Sometimes, it feels like the walls are closing in on me . . . can't breathe . . . can't think! At times, I want to run, but there's no place to run. What kind of madness is this? In all of heaven or hell, is there some law I've broken? Have I provoked God's wrath? Is this my penance for sin, or is it just one of life's cruel jokes?"

He opened the window, sat on the sill, and looked at the sky for several minutes.

"I have to talk to someone," he decided, "I have to talk to *Ashley*!"

Chapter 60

Dr. Jonas Simpson stood on the front porch of his home, surveying the swirling gray and black clouds that tumbled overhead like billows on the ocean before a gale. He pulled the collar of his smoking jacket tighter about his neck for protection against the gusty wind that whistled around the corners of the old, two-story, frame house that had been in his family for three generations. Rather than endure the weather outdoors on this Sunday afternoon, he decided to wait inside in more hospitable surroundings for his patient and friend who had called asking to see him.

Dr. Simpson had known Lincoln Crockett all of Lincoln's life. In fact, he had delivered Lincoln just as he had a great many of the young people in Coldwater. There had been complications associated with Lincoln's birth, and Jonas had always wondered if he had done the right thing in resolving them.

At any rate, Lincoln had always been special to Jonas or maybe he just felt sorry for him. Lincoln appeared to have his share of problems. What others construed in Lincoln as being moody and withdrawn, the doctor saw as a reserved and serious young man whose concerns with life lay on a higher plane than the average young person's, or even adult's, for that matter, so whenever Lincoln needed to, Jonas would sit down with him in private and just "talk about things."

Lincoln, having forgotten last night that Ashley had left for college last week, had turned to his old ally when he needed a confidant he could trust. Funny, he was beginning to feel that way about Ashley.

"So, how have you been feeling since our last talk?" asked Doc Simpson.

"Okay, I guess," answered Lincoln, "I'm still not sleeping very well. The nightmares still come most nights, but with a new twist. Now, my father is chasing me and trying to kill me!"

The doctor settled back into his favorite wingback chair.

They discussed this change in the imagery of his dreams while Lincoln wandered restlessly about doc's library, peaking at titles on the book-laden shelves.

"How about the frequency and duration of the headaches? Any change?" inquired the doctor.

"About the same at a couple of times a week. Doc, sometimes it feels like my head will explode, and I have to lie on the bed for hours and not move."

"I wish there was more I could do. Come by my office tomorrow and we'll try some stronger pain medicine. I'll also give you a few sleeping pills to see if that will help you get some more sleep. How's it working out living at the hotel?" Doc asked.

"Oh, it's working out quite well. Everyone there's being very nice and helping me a lot. It's been much more, peaceful, you know."

"I understand. I'm glad your living conditions have changed, in that respect."

"Yeah. But, I miss mom."

"Yes, I'm sure you do! It will take time, but time is a great healer in coping with death and the loss of a loved one," encouraged Doc.

Lincoln slouched in a big leather chair close to Doc's as the doctor poured them a cup of coffee from the silver service his wife, Maggie, had placed on the coffee table.

"I got a letter from Rats this week," said Lincoln.

"That's nice. How's Tyler doing at boot camp?"

"Says he's taking right to military life! You know Rats. Always the John Wayne type."

"That's right! If anybody can make a marine, Tyler can," said Doc.

"He's getting ready to ship out to Nam," Lincoln added.

"Well, we'll pray that he makes it and gets back home soon," said Doc, quietly.

"I really miss that guy. Since he's gone, there's only two people around I can talk to.

"Oh, now who would they be?" asked Doc curiously.

"One of them is you, of course," said Lincoln.

"Oh, of course," Doc answered sarcastically. "And, the other one wouldn't just happen to be a pretty little blonde now, would it," he continued, with a sly smile on his face.

Lincoln grinned, "Yeah! But she's off at college now."

Doc leaned forward in his seat. "How far do you and this girl plan on trying to take this relationship?"

"To the limit. We've decided that we want to have a life together."

"My boy, even if this is a match made in heaven, it'll be like trying to mix oil and water because there are opposing forces that won't allow it to mix," Doc warned.

"We're well aware of the obstacles and know it won't be easy, but, that's what we're committed to."

"In that case, I wish you the best," said Doc, standing and offering his hand to his young friend.

"Thank you, Doctor Simpson," replied Lincoln, standing and shaking hands with Doc. "Doc, is there any rhyme or reason to why things work the way they do?"

"In other words, still searching for answers to life?" inferred Doc.

"There seem to be no real answers, none that satisfy all the questions anyway." concluded Lincoln.

"For example," said Doc.

"Well, is God in charge? Some people say He has a master plan for people's lives; a purpose, a destiny they are equipped to fulfill. If that be so, then why are some peoples' roads of life so difficult, filled with hills and valleys, while other peoples' are smooth, flat, and straight? If God's in charge, why are there so many mean people and so much suffering? We can also ask if Satan is a player in this game of life. Does the Devil and his demon playmates roam about sowing seeds of mischief whenever and wherever they find it convenient, thus upsetting the goodly order of things? It might certainly appear so!

"On the other hand, is man in charge? Is man's gift of free will a blessing or a curse, a double-edged sword of choice that breeds consequences of wickedness as well as goodness? Did God leave man in charge as an experiment to see how he would fare managing his own environment, or are we but human pawns on an earthly chess board to amuse the whims of spiritual lords?

"Lastly, is it Lady Luck? When someone has good fortune, we say they were in the right place at the right time. When they experience misfortune, it's because they were in the wrong place at the wrong time. Is life just a roll of the dice, fate, or just dumb luck?"

"You've raised some interesting hypotheses, Mr. Crockett," said Doctor Simpson, tapping his finger on his lips and shaking his head.

"So, Doctor Simpson, do you think one of these in charge, or some combination of them, or perhaps all of them, come to the table and play a hand of their own?

"Well, Crockett, I can see that you've certainly put a lot of thought into the subject. Personally, I'd have to give your ideas more serious thought before making any comments, but I'll certainly give them some consideration and respond the next time we talk. Are you leaning toward any particular conclusion yourself or is that still up in the air?"

"I've decided one thing for sure." said Lincoln. "The world is a hard and demanding place, and to make sense of it is beyond our understanding. In the final analysis, you'll find the fact that life has no truth is life's truth realized."

Lincoln's demeanor suddenly changed from cheeriness to one of moodiness. He began to pace about the room in silence, head down, hands stuffed into his pants pockets, lost in his own private world. Doctor Simpson recognized it immediately; he had seen it happen more than once before when, without warning, young Crockett would suddenly slip into the throes of deep depression. He got his patient seated comfortably and began to talk with him quietly.

"How are you feeling Lincoln?"

"Very tired," he answered.

"I sense that there's something bothering you beyond the answers to life, the loss of your parents, and the future with Ashley Armstrong," voiced Doc.

"Are my senses in fact reality or simply imagination?" he asked. "There has been something playing on my mind, especially since the Henderson trial, that I can't decide how to deal with or if I even need to deal with it."

"What does the Henderson trial have to do with it?" inquired Doc.

"Marjorie Henderson was killed for what she knew about something or someone in this town," answered Lincoln.

"And?" questioned Doc.

"You might say that I'm, unfortunately, in the same boat that Marjorie Henderson was in."

"Are you saying that you are privy to the same information that she was?" called out Doc, rising from his seat.

"No. I don't know what she knew, but I do know things, and certain parties would not be happy if they knew that I knew."

"I assume this concerns prominent people," says Doc.

Lincoln nodded.

"Just how damning is this intelligence?"

"You remember when Sampson pulled down the pillars and the whole temple came crashing down?" said Lincoln.

"Of course!"

"Well, you get the picture," said Lincoln.

"Good Lord!" said Doc. "That big, huh?" shaking his head.

"The only problem is I don't have proof of anything; nothing that would stand up in court. It would just be my word against theirs. So, I'm the one in jeopardy. I can't tell anyone and possibly put them in a position of risk also."

"Okay. But can you tell me what it generally involves, like prostitution, gambling, etc.?" asked Doc.

"Alright, but I'm not saying anymore. *Bootlegging*," whispered Lincoln.

"Bootlegging!" blurted out Doc Simpson.

The doctor paced the floor for a minute, envisioning possibilities in his mind. "You know, I know a man who would be very interested in talking to you."

Chapter 61

Lieutenant Cordell McPherson leaned back in his chair and began to conscientiously peruse the file of test results. For the next few minutes, he studied the pages with care, occasionally pausing to cast an eye over the top of a pair of black-rim glasses that hung perilously close to the end of his nose, toward the young draftee seated on the other side of his government-gray desk. It was Lieutenant McPherson, as resident psychologist at the Army Recruitment Center in Central City, whose duty it was to make the final determination as to one's acceptance or rejection for service in the United States Army. Suddenly, he sat up straight and rested his arms on the desk with fingers intertwined.

"Mr. Crockett," he began, "the results of the tests that have been administered to you here today indicate that you are quite healthy and fit, physically speaking that is, with one exception. These migraine headaches are a problem, but, of greater concern, however, is your psychological profile," he added, removing his glasses from a face wrinkled with worry, and placing them on the desk.

"Oh," said Lincoln. "Are you saying I'm not normal, a little wacked out?"

"No, no, don't get excited. On the one hand, your test scores indicate that you are an extremely intelligent young man. But, on the other hand, I see any number of aberrations in your answers to certain types of questions that deviate from the norm. And, for me, that raises a red flag. You brought with you a large envelope from a Dr. Jonas Simpson. Did you ask Dr. Simpson to provide you with this information to bring here today?"

"No sir. When I left home, Doc gave me that envelope and told me to give it to someone in charge. I have no idea what's in it."

"Well, Mr. Crockett, this Dr. Simpson apparently cares a lot for you."

The lieutenant went on to say that in the letter the good doctor explained much about his young friend's life situation and experiences and included copies of medical records documenting Lincoln's chronic health issues with migraine headaches and depression.

"The psychological evaluation that I conducted of you today is consistent with Dr. Simpson's findings. I believe that both your physical and emotional problems that manifest themselves in the form of headaches and depression are due to unresolved, deep-seated psychological issues. I'm sure Dr. Simpson is doing his best to help you, but he's a medical doctor. You need the benefit of professional counseling and I encourage you to find a way to get it. At any rate, I don't think we can use you in this man's army."

With a "plunk" Lieutenant McPherson stamped REJECTED on the front of Lincoln's file and stood up.

"Good luck to you Mr. Crockett," said the Lieutenant.

"Thank you, sir."

"Next!" He heard the Lieutenant call out as he exited the recruitment center, strangely, with mixed emotions.

Chapter 62

He looked like a riverboat gambler. The man in the white suit and fedora accented with a black bolo tie, who strolled confidently across the Lacy Hotel lobby that day in mid-September, leaned up against the check-in counter, and ordered the receptionist to summon the manager directly.

The lady, taken aback by such abrasiveness, looked up and down at the slender, well-tanned man sporting a black, pencil mustache with thin lips that held a half-smoked cigarillo. He had dull, black eyes that seemed to look nowhere. A mischievous smile stretched across a not-so-handsome face, the result of having been served his share of knuckle sandwiches.

Annoyed that she and her staff were being ordered about in a rude manner by such a pompous individual, Miss Jessie deliberately took her leisure in acquiescing to his demands. Upon her appearance, she found him still leaning on the counter, his back toward her. She approached to within a few steps and stopped.

"You asked for tha manaja, he'ah she is. So, what's so important?" stated Miss Jessie with a bit of indignation.

The man turned slowly to face the lady, tipped his hat, and with that menacing smile said,

"Hello, Dixie, longtime no see. Oh! Pardon me, I believe it's *Miss Jessie* these days."

At the sight of the scarred face, the color drained from Jessica Wingo's face; at the sight of the mischievous smile, weakness flooded her body; at the sight of those cold, dark eyes, she gasped and for a moment couldn't speak. At the sight of this man she hadn't seen in twenty years, she felt like she'd just been sucker punched in the stomach. She reached for the edge of the counter to steady herself.

"*Yancy*," she forced the name out as if it choked her to speak it. It was difficult to tell if it was a statement or a question.

He looked at her with a wicked smile.

"Yeah! Never thought you'd see ole Yancy again did you, after you ran out on me down there in New Orleans so many years ago? But, like they say, 'you can run but you can't hide'' especially from the 'Sugarman.'"

Yancy "Sugarman" DuPree was not exactly one of your more likely candidates for outstanding citizen of the year award. Gambler, thief, conman, drug dealer, and pimp, "Sugar" (as he was known to his closest confidants) was into any business he could parlay into a quick and easy buck and was not above wielding a Saturday night special to ensure success. In fact, one would have to search long and hard (and low) through the back streets of the Big Easy to find a much sleazier character than this mother's son lost on a one-way road to perdition.

"How did..." Jessica started to speak but cut herself short when she noticed the receptionist behind the counter, along with Lincoln who had since joined her, staring at her and the stranger. After composing herself, she invited the stranger to join her in her office to continue their conversation in private and gave those at the check-in counter orders that they were not to be disturbed.

"So, Dixie, you've come a long way from The Black Garter Club in Nawlins to managing a fancy hotel, even if it is up here in 'the sticks, '" said Yancy, giving the hotel a onceover.

"I *own* the hotel," corrected Jessica proudly.

"Oh! A businesswoman! My, my, you have come a long way," noted Yancy.

"So how did ya find out where I was livin' after twenty ye'ahs? I'm sure ya didn't just decide to come to Coldwater, Tennessee, on'a vacation."

"I'll have to admit I'd probably never have found you if it hadn't been for a stroke of luck having a common denominator in both our lives...that being one Marjorie Henderson."

"Mah'jorie Hen'dason!" said a surprised Jessica, "What does she hav'ta do with us?"

"She was working for me at the Black Garter and a year or so ago, and she stole some valuables of mine, including a Roman coin pendant, and headed for parts unknown. We were finally able to locate her by tracking down her husband's employer's local office. That's how where knew where she and Mr. Henderson had relocated."

"Did you see Maj?" she questioned.

"Yeah! But, by the time I got to her she was laid low. Guess somebody else wanted something she had, too." He didn't tell her the whole story.

"How did that lead you to me?" she asked.

"Marge and her ole man got a lot of publicity. You got your share also," Yancy reminded her, "with all that talk about Marge and 'Jessie's Girls' got another little business going on the side, huh? ld habits die hard," the man sneered. "Besides, you were both former employees of the Black Garter."

Jessica turned away without answering.

"Anyway, looks like I killed two birds with one stone. I found out where you are and I found out that this 'Lincoln Crockett' guy has my pendant and he works, even lives, right here at your hotel."

"A real Mike Hammer aren't you?" said Jessica, sarcastically.

"I inquired about Mr. Crockett down at the service station when I was getting gas. The attendant told me all about your act of Christian charity when his family suffered such a tragic event."

Again, Jessica didn't respond. She just looked at him wide-eyed surprise.

"Now, ain't that nice? Everything I need to right wrongs of the past all wrapped up in a neat little package right here in your hotel."

"Yancy, don't go makin' trouble for people he'ah. They don't need any of the kind'a bother that follows you around," warned Jessica.

"Now, don't concern yourself Dixie girl. You know Yancy. I'm just a happy-go-lucky guy. There's not going to be any trouble as long as I get what I want, and the first thing I want is for you to put me up in one of your best rooms," said Yancy.

"Go stay someplace else; I don't have any rooms," she answered.

(His mood changes to Sugarman.)

"Oh, you can make room to take in some stray off the street but you don't have a room for your *husband*," snapped Yancy like a snarling dog, cleaning off half the top of Jessica's desk with one swipe of his arm.

"I told you we don't have any rooms. It's the weekend. We're all booked up!" screamed Jessica.

"Bang," "bang," "bang" came a pounding on the office door.

"Miss Jessie, you okay?" inquired the concerned sound of a voice from outside the office.

"Yes, I'm okay Bam Bam," she answered.

"So, you still got that big ox hanging around, huh? Figures!"

Jessica, regaining some of her "Miss Jessie" swagger, faced up to Yancy.

"Listen lowlife. We are, unfortunately, still *legally* married," admitted Jessica, "but that's as fah as it goes. I'd soon'ah be married to a lep'ah than the likes of you, and if you go gittin' any otha ideas, I'll sick that 'big ox,' as you call him, on you and he'll finish the job on that ugly mug. Now befo'ah you go throwin' too much weight around, Mr. DuPree, just remem'ba you're not in Nawlins now, and you're not badass *Sugarman* up he'ah. I'm among friends he'ah, some of whom can play just as rough as you, and with a word from me about who killed Mah'jorie Hen'dason, your sorry ass could wind up face down in Town Creek like hers did."

"And you remember, bitch," scolded Yancy, "there's a Louisiana Sheriff that would love to drag your and your big friend's asses across a few hundred miles of hard road and lock you up in his jail before you answer charges before the judge."

"But 'Nawlins' is a long way off and I can rat you out to the Sheriff right he'ah," she reminded him. "So, if you want to play that game, let's see who winds up lookin' through bars from the inside out first," the lady challenged the gambler.

Chapter 63

"Come in Lincoln," said the dark-haired Amanda, opening the door with a smile. "It's nice to see you again."

"Thanks, it's good to see you again, too," replied Lincoln.

"You're just in time for supper."

"Thanks, but I can't stay long. There's something I have to do."

"You look tired," she said.

"I'm beat. It's been a mad house at the hotel the last few weeks."

As well as making his weekly visit with Amanda, Lincoln was anxious to hear news of Montgomery. As they engaged in so much small talk, Amanda noticed her visitor looking at her rather curiously from time to time, but hesitant to make any comment. Finally, she addressed his observations.

"As you may have noticed, I've gained a few pounds."

"Well...I..." he stammered.

"It's okay. To be honest, I haven't told you everything about Montgomery and me."

"Oh."

"Lincoln, Montgomery and I not only got married because we love each other, but I'm also pregnant."

Just as he had been the day she told him they were married, he was once again dumbstruck.

"Ho-lee shit! And I thought his parents finding out you two are married was going to be a bombshell. This is going to be a nuclear blast!"

"Yeah, probably," she answered with teary eyes.

"What's going on, Amanda?"

"Oh, Lincoln, everything's such a mess!" she cried.

"What's happened? Tell me."

"Everything. I'm pregnant, Montgomery's gone, his folks are going to try to break us up when they find out—I know they will—,and Mr. Longworth fired my father from his job down at the mill yesterday."

"Why? For what reason?" growled Lincoln.

"He said for stealing company property."

"What is it that he is supposed to have stolen?"

"Dad picked up a few pieces of scrap wood that had been tossed on the burn pile and brought them home to build a cradle for the baby when it comes because we couldn't afford to buy a new one. Dad's foreman told Mr. Longworth about it, and he accused Dad of stealing it. Dad tried to tell him it was throw-away stuff and offered to pay him for it anyway, but Mr. Longworth wouldn't hear of it and fired him."

"That sorry son of a . . ." fumed Lincoln.

"Does Montgomery know?"

"I wrote him when I found out."

"Looks like I'm going to have to have a little come-to-Jesus meeting with one Leland Longworth," said Lincoln emphatically, pounding a fist into his open hand.

"Oh, please don't Lincoln. You'll get in trouble and it'll just make things worse," she pleaded. "Promise me!"

"Okay, but some time, some place, this man will pay for his sin."

The prophecy rolled off the tongue of Lincoln Crockett with a macabre smile.

Later That Night

It seemed an eternity before someone finally answered the endlessly ringing telephone in the girls' dormitory at State University.

"Hello."

"I'd like to speak with Ashley Armstrong please."

"Just a minute please."

"Hello darlin,'" came the sound of a soft, put-on sexy voice into Lincoln's ear.

"Ashley?" questioned Lincoln with a puzzled expression.

"Who else answers your calls that way?" teased Ashley.

"How did you know it was me? Do you always answer the phone like that?"

"Oh, I knew it was you."

"How?"

"Julie answered the phone and said the caller sounded like a cute fellow."

"Huh, how does someone *sound* cute? Oh, never mind, I probably wouldn't understand it anyway. I have some news to tell you," said Lincoln.

"Good or bad?"

"Guess it depends on your point of view."

"Sounds like another one of those enigmas."

"Yeah, I guess so. I went to the Army Induction Center Friday."

"You didn't tell me you had been called," she chided him.

"I didn't want to tell you until after I had been."

"So, how did it go?" she asked.

"I guess I missed the Big Dance; they turned me down."

"Well, that's good!" she answered, excitedly, "I'm sorry for those who have to go to Vietnam, like Rats and Monty, but I'm glad you don't have to go. From my point of view, that would be the good news. Now, what's the bad news?"

"They said I'm crazy," stated Lincoln.

"They said what?"

"Well, not exactly in those terms. I failed the psychological exam and because of my history of migraines and depression, they said that I would be a liability to other soldiers in combat. They also said that I need professional counseling. If you're too messed up to be in the military, you must be pretty messed up, huh?"

Ashley could feel how down the young man she cared for so much was at this moment, not so much about being turned down for military service as by what he had learned about his emotional health. He had always been concerned about the debilitating headaches and especially the bouts of depression. What was their source? What did they mean? Where would they lead? He had, in the past, tried to pass them off as nothing of consequence, but to have them validated by a professional source gave them an added sense of reality.

Ashley tried to mitigate his fears by appealing to his powers of reason and logic. She reminded him that he had experienced a great deal of trauma and tragedy and been under a great deal of stress, reasoning that emotional ills are no different than physical ones in that they can both be treated and healed. She also reminded him that he had a great friend and ally in Dr. Simpson and promised that she would be there to support him to the extent possible.

After sharing more details about his trip to the induction center and listening to Ashley talk about her continuing acclamation to campus life, Lincoln steered the conversation to his second big news item of the day.

"Ash, I stopped by Amanda's house this afternoon."

"Yeah, how's she doing?"

"She's pregnant, three months' worth." There was silence at the other end of the telephone line.

"Ash, you there?" whispered Lincoln.

"Linc, did you say what I think you said?"

"You heard right. She said that's another reason she and Monty got married before he left."

"Married and pregnant! Ole Leland and Miss Cora Sue will absolutely stroke out when they get this double-barreled news flash," announced Ashley.

"Well, the Crosses have already felt the wrath of the Longworth vengeance."

"What do you mean, Linc?"

"Ole Leland fired Mr. Cross on a trumped up charge of stealing company property which was more accurately a few pieces of scrap wood he was going to build a cradle with for the new baby."

"You've got to be kidding me," stormed Ashley.

"Nope! That's what Amanda told me."

"Damn him!" stormed Ashley.

"I've never met the man, but I know that around midday, every day, he takes a little constitutional around the company grounds. Well, one day at high noon, I'm going to meet up with the man and introduce myself to him. And, then, we're going to get very personally acquainted."

"No, no, Linc, don't do that. You'll only get in trouble with ole Buford. Besides, this is on my side of Main Street. Let's let this ride for the time being. I'll be coming home soon for a few days and I'm sure I'll have the opportunity when the time's right to address the issue with them. And, believe me, I *will* address the issue."

"Okay, if you insist."

"I do." Ashley let out a big sigh. "I say darlin' you're full of more news than Huntley and Brinkley."

Chapter 64

Sunday morning found Lincoln wandering along the empty, tree-lined streets of Coldwater with no particular direction or destination in mind. With the streets void of vehicular and pedestrian traffic, the only discernable movement to speak of was the trees swaying gently back and forth in the balmy breeze blowing down from the mountains. With the exception of the occasional bark of a dog somewhere in the distance, the only thing to break the quiet of the morning was that of the wind rustling through the leaves. Lincoln paid little attention to either.

Lincoln was lost in his thoughts, as he usually is on these solitary walks, as the familiar refrain of a hymn began to echo softly in the back of his mind. Unconsciously, he began to hum along with the chorus inside his head. Growing louder, he stopped suddenly, realizing that what he was hearing was not just in his head, but was live and nearby. Looking about, he discovered that the music and singing were coming from the First Church of The Trinity, in front of which he happened to be standing. He wondered if Ashley was inside, but he didn't dare go in to see.

He had not been in church since his parents' funerals. Frankly, he missed it. He enjoyed the music, the singing, the fellowship with the people at the River Street Gospel Tabernacle. After all, they were his neighbors. He liked the general idea of worship. But, he would not go back there; he didn't trust Reverend Nutter, and the First Church of The Trinity was not an option.

Returning to the hotel, he stopped by Dutch's taxi stand to chat a minute. "How you doin' today, Dutch?" he greeted his old friend with a smile.

"Oh, I'm jus fine-an-dandy. How 'bout ya' self?" returned the cabbie.

"Can't complain! Well, I guess I could, but nobody'd listen. So, might as well just smile and go on my way," said Lincoln.

"My sentiments exactly," agreed Dutch.

"Say," said Dutch, turning serious, "ya remember that Christian feller frum up north that wuz here back in June?"

"Well Dutch, I imagine there's been any number of Christian men from up north here recently," answered Lincoln, playing with the old man.

"Dag nabbit," fussed Dutch, "I don't mean 'Christian' Christian, I mean *named* Christian. He claimed ta be a writer or something."

"Yes, I remember him. Why?"

"Well, he's back. Jus checked into the hotel, an he's still a'packin.'"

"Is that right? He said he might come back for another visit, but I didn't think about it being this soon," said a half-surprised Lincoln.

"I still don't think that guy's what he claims ta be," warned Dutch, climbing into his cab. "You know where he's frum?" asked Dutch.

"Somewhere up north's all I know. What's with all the questions, Dutch?" asked Lincoln curiously.

"No particular reason, just curious," mumbled Dutch. "Keep an eye on'im. Ya know, we've had our share uv strange characters 'round here lately an strange hapnins."

"I'll make a note of it."

"Think I'll walk over to the bus station and grab a cup," said Dutch. "Watch my stand for a few minutes?"

"Sure." answered Lincoln. "By the way, you got an adjustable wrench I could borrow? Need one to work on the motorcycle with."

"I think there's one in the cab there somewhere. You're welcome to it if it's there."

A search of the cab's interior failed to turn up the tool in question, so he decided to see if the trunk was unlocked, which it was. He found the wrench he was looking for in an old toolbox next to the spare tire. But, in moving the toolbox, he bumped it against a cardboard box covered by a blanket. The bump caused a familiar clinking sound. His curiosity aroused, he threw the cover off the box and what he saw caused him some alarm.

To his surprise, inside the box packed with newspapers, were two-quart Mason jars full of crystal-clear liquid. He wondered why Dutch would have shine hidden in the trunk of his cab; he'd never known Dutch to drink the stuff himself. Oh, well! He decided that was Dutch's business and covered up the contraband.

Back at the hotel lobby, Lincoln found a call from Doc Simpson waiting for him.

"Hi Doc, what's up with you today?"

"Lincoln, you remember I told you that I knew a man that would be interested in talking with you?"

"Yes, I remember."

"Well, he's in town and I'd like for you to meet him. Could you come to a meeting at Johnny Abraham's office sometime tomorrow?"

"Johnny Abraham's office?" exclaimed a surprised Lincoln. "Why?"

"Oh, nothing to get concerned about," assured Doc. "I think you'll find this man to be a quite interesting fellow."

"Okay, if you say so. I get off work at six every night this week."

"Good! I'll set the meeting up for around six tomorrow. See you then," said Doc as he hung up.

Chapter 65

In the three weeks that he'd been in town, Yancy DuPree had made his gregarious presence seen and felt by both hotel staff and guests in his uniquely overly demanding style. Most people, however, found his self-centered flamboyance obnoxious and attempted to steer clear of him as much as possible. In Yancy's case, such was an intelligent decision, for, just behind the façade of the carefree Yancy was always lurking the irascible thug Sugarman, whose fiery temper could, on a whim, be triggered faster than Quickdraw McGraw.

It had become obvious to everyone that Mr. DuPree and Miss Jessie, who each passed off the other as being an old acquaintance, had been spending a great deal of time in each other's company. Miss Jessie had made a bargain with Yancy: She would acquire the pendant and return it to him on the condition that he not cause any problems in Coldwater for anyone, would pretend to just be passing through, and would leave town as soon as he had the pendant in his possession. To this, Yancy agreed. That is, if you can to take the word of a man who's as amoral as a fungus.

One afternoon in the privacy of her office, she took a small brown box from her purse and slid it across her office desk in Yancy's direction. He quickly trapped it with his hand like a cat snatching a mouse with its paw just before it went over the edge of the desk.

He smiled a sly smile of satisfaction.

Miss Jessie remained expressionless.

"I believe tha'uts what ya came fah," she said.

Yancy opened the box and looked inside, then looked back at Jessica and smiled again. "You are a woman of your word, Dixie," said Yancy, pulling the pendant slowly from the box.

Miss Jessie had told Lincoln the truth about the pendant. She explained how Marjorie Henderson had stolen it from Mr. DuPree in New Orleans, how she got here, and how Mr. DuPree located her and came here to reclaim his property. She had paid Lincoln (on behalf of Mr. DuPree) a handsome "finder's fee" for his trouble.

"Now that you have yo'ah property there's no reason fah you to remain he'ah any longer," said Miss Jessie, walking around the desk to face him. "Besides, we had a bah'gan. I kept my end, and now you keep yo'ahs and be on yo'ah way."

"I been thinkin' Dixie," said Yancy in a crafty manner, as he held the pendant up and let the chain curl snakelike back down into the brown box, "This is a nice setup you got here. Lotta possibilities. You and me as a husband and wife team could make out good here."

"In a pig's eye," she said, hands on her hips. "I wouldn't go inta business with you sellin' peanuts ta monkeys. I got you outta my life once an now I want you outta my life again...fah good!"

"Damn you bitch," raged Yancy, "ya think you're so high and mighty 'cause you runnin' a fancy hotel up here in tha sticks. Well, you and me know what ya really are, just a two-bit whore from Bourbon Street that I took in and made something of. Then you left with a customer of yours that musclebound Bam Bam had beat senseless in my place and left me holding a one-way ticket for a nine-month stretch in the slammer for assault. Now, as I see it, you owe me, so, I'm going to bring some of the boys up here and set up some new operations, whether you like it or not!" boasted Yancy.

"I told ya, Yancy, I don't want ta see anything of you but yo'ah backside leavin' town."

"Dixie darlin' you got two choices," barked Yancey, pointing two fingers at her. "Either you go into business with me, or I go down and have a chat with the editor of the *Coldwater News* and give him the background story on the owner of the Lacy Hotel. What editor wouldn't love to have a juicy story like that? What would that kind of publicity do for your business?"

Jessica fumed, "Damn you ta hell, Yancy! I neva realized just how much I hated ya until this minute. I'm tired of being blackmailed. Now get out before I kill ya here and now!" she ordered.

Yancy was startled at the sight of the .38 caliber pistol in Jessica's hand pointing at him. He took one step toward her.

"Well, let me tell you, nobody runs out on the Sugarman or points a gun at him without paying a price," he snarled, suddenly grabbing the pistol with one hand and whipping out a stiletto with the other and holding the thin blade up to her throat.

A heartbeat later Sugarman squalled from the searing pain of bones splintering in his right arm from the karate chop administered by Bam Bam. A following elbow to the chest drained the air from his lungs and put him flat on his back. In spite of the pain and a disabled right appendage, with his left hand Sugarman managed to retrieve his gun from the shoulder holster under his jacket.

[281]

Waving the snub-nosed .22 awkwardly in the direction of the charging Bam Bam, he fired just as Jessica kicked at his hand. The shot went wild. Bam Bam jerked the moaning Sugarman to his feet, raised him over his head, and tossed him against the wall like a sack of potatoes.

"Bam Bam, take Mr. DuPree here down to tha station an put him onna train with a one-way ticket to Nawlins."

Yancy, too bruised, beaten, and in pain to argue, didn't resist.

"You better use that pea shooter now Dixie, while you have the chance. 'Cause, I'll be back, and I won't be alone. You owe the Sugarman and the Sugarman collects his debts."

Chapter 66

It was 6:00 p.m. on the dot when Lincoln entered the office of District Attorney Johnny Abraham and was ushered by his secretary into the conference room where he found Dr. Simpson waiting for him, along with the District Attorney and Wallace Christian, whom he assumed was the "interesting fellow" the doctor had wanted him to meet.

"Ahh, right on time," observed Dr. Simpson looking at the clock on the wall.

"Come in Lincoln, let me introduce you," said the doctor.

"I believe you know the DA, Mr. Abraham."

"Yes sir. We've met," acknowledged Lincoln, reaching out to take the man's hand.

"Good to see you again, Mr. Crockett, under better circumstances," replied the DA shaking hands with him.

"And, Lincoln, this is Mr. Wallace Christian," he said next.

"Yes, I know. The writer from up north that was here this summer," said Lincoln.

"Hello, Lincoln. Good to see you again," smiled Mr. Christian, standing and greeting Lincoln.

"Likewise," nodded Lincoln. "How's the hand?"

"Oh! It's healed up just fine. The doctor here did a good job on it."

"You're partially correct Lincoln," said the doctor, "Wallace was here all right, but only pretending to be a writer gathering fodder for a book."

"Yes," continued Wallace Christian, "I'm afraid I was a bit deceitful with everyone and moving about under false pretenses. But, my intentions were honorable. In reality, I'm a federal agent with the Alcohol, Tobacco, and Firearms Division."

"A federal agent!" exclaimed a surprised Lincoln.

"That's right, Mr. Crockett," said the agent, as all three of the men grinned at Lincoln's reaction. "I must advise you that everything you hear in this meeting is to be held in strict confidence," said the agent. "Agreed?"

"Agreed." answered Lincoln.

"For some time, my agents and I have been trying to locate and break a bootlegging operation that we're for sure is based somewhere in this vicinity and whose operations reach from upper Virginia to Atlanta. To date, we've not been able to pinpoint where they make the stuff and how they transport it."

"That's why we in local law enforcement," added Johnny Abraham, "are going to form a local task force to work closely with Agent Christian and his people to identify these people and put them out of business and rid ourselves of this blight on our community. The good doctor here believes you may just be the break we've been looking for in this case and that you may have knowledge of some individuals who may be engaged in activities related to bootlegging. He also said you are also concerned that having this knowledge could be hazardous to your health if these people knew what you know. Is that about the size of the situation?"

"Marge Henderson wound up face down in the water for knowing 'things' didn't she?" he pointed out.

"You believe she was murdered by this bunch?"

"I don't know exactly who killed her or exactly what she knew. But, I believe it was what she knew that got her killed."

"If we promise to protect our source, namely you, will you tell us what you know, that is names, places, activities, etc.?"

Lincoln looked at Doc Simpson.

Doc nodded, "It's the right thing to do."

"Okay, count me in. Names, huh? Well, the Culveyhouse's make the stuff. There may be others in the mountains who contribute as well. I don't know."

The other three men nodded in agreement.

"We knew they were, but just haven't been able to catch them at it," said Agent Christian.

"There's the Ledbetters and Charlie Bridger at the sawmill," continued Lincoln, "and Dalton Jackson and his truck driver Boone at the furniture company, and the Franklins at the ferry."

The three men raised eyebrows in surprise.

"That many different people involved? How?" asked the Fed.

"I'll get to that in a minute, but there's more rats in the pack," said Lincoln. "Now, you might want to rethink that local law enforcement task force. One of the ring leaders appears to be Sheriff Buford Coker with Deputy Lester Odom along for the ride."

The other three men sat up wide-eyed but not entirely in disbelief at the revelation.

"Well, that explains a lot of things that haven't seemed quite right to me since I've been here," exclaimed the District Attorney.

"Doesn't surprise me one iota," snorted Doc Simpson, pounding his fist on the table.

"And, I wouldn't look past the mayor either. He and ole Buford are big buddies," said Lincoln.

Lincoln went on to describe to them how he had accidently stumbled onto their operation that night back in June and explained how the Sheriff provided escort service and how they hid the big container of shine under the logs on the log truck, transferred it to the Longworth Furniture truck, and packaged it in furniture boxes. He also told about the cases of Mason fruit jars that were moved to the ferry for local sale and how Obee showed him where they stored it on the boat.

Agent Christian exhaled, "Well, I'll have to give them credit. This is a pretty slick operation. Lincoln, I don't know if we'd ever have broken them without this kind of information. But now we'll be able to do it for sure."

"You know," said Doc Simpson, squinting and rubbing his chin, "I've known this bunch of characters for a long time, and while they might not be Sunday school teachers, I can see them involved in runnin' shine, but I can't really see any of them committing murder."

"Desperate men can do desperate things when they feel they have a lot to lose," reminded Agent Christian.

"And maybe they had some outside assistance, like maybe from Atlanta," said Lincoln, almost whispering.

"Do you mean there might be an Atlanta connection?" exclaimed Agent Christian.

Lincoln went on to tell them about Shooter Logano and company, the guns in the white limo, their mysterious movements around town, and their frequent social meetings with Sheriff Coker and Mayor McKean. This news was of particular interest to Agent Christian who contacted the ATF Atlanta office to follow up.

"This Atlanta group seems a more likely source of your murder suspect," surmised the Fed.

"Oh, there's one last thing I just thought of," Lincoln said.

What's that?" asked Agent Christian.

"You might just have a man on the inside over at the Sheriff's office...Deputy Cassidy."

"Why do you say that?" asked the district attorney.

"Because he's a real nice guy and appears to be on the up-and-up, and old Buford and Lester seem to cut him out of everything. They don't include him in the 'good-ole-boy' circle."

"Say, now that you mention it," observed Doc Simpson, "you're right about that."

"Mr. Crockett," said Agent Christian, "you seem to be the man in the know around here. We'll check out Deputy Cassidy. He may be our ace in the hole."

"Yeah, but sometimes you can know too much," joked Lincoln.

They all chuckled.

All the ingredients for a moonshine war in Jackson County were in the pot and beginning to boil.

Chapter 67

Delbert Justice invited Lincoln to take a seat next to him on the couch while his wife Eunice solemnly seated herself in a side chair next to them. He readily detected tearstained eyes in the faces of Tyler Justice's parents, eyes that betrayed some inward agony rending their souls.

From the time he had received the phone call from Mr. Justice asking him to come see them as soon as possible, and hearing the sound of the man's shaky voice, Lincoln had feared something grave had come to pass. Upon his arrival at their home, his fears were confirmed. Of the many times he had been a guest in the Justice's home, he had never before experienced so somber an atmosphere as it was at that moment.

Without speaking, Mr. Justice, trembling, handed a folded sheet of paper to Lincoln. It was a letter on United States Marine Corps letterhead. The words immediately jumped out at Lincoln like a newspaper headline. It read, ". . . your son Tyler was killed in combat." That's all he could or needed to read. As he handed the paper back to Rats' father, he looked back into two blank faces staring back at him, faces that seemed to be looking to him to answer their *whys*.

Why did their son have to die so young?

Why did their son have to die in a war on the other side of the world?

Why did their son have to die for something most people don't seem to understand or care about?

He felt sick inside, numb and empty. He remembered the day just two months ago when his buddy had told him that he was joining the Marines and to take care of things here for him until he returned. He didn't have the answers his friend's parents were looking for. None of them seemed to have words to speak. For the longest time they just sat there and wept together. After spending some time trying to console his best friend's mom and dad, he took his leave, promising to return.

Inside the house he was suffocating; the walls were closing in on him. He was grateful to get out into the open air. He stood against the backdrop of billowy white clouds that measured the depth of a deep blue sky. He was surrounded by the glories of the fall colors that normally exhilarated the senses. The bright colors made the pall that swallowed up that little house he had just left seem unreal. The contrast was staggering! *Which is the real world? They both are*, he determined. Blue skies and dark clouds; sun and rain; good times and bad times; peace and war; living and dying; all are just human events patchworked together in no particular order to be dealt with in no particular order, a non-order that we call life. He picked up a leaf from the ground and studied it. It occurred to him ironic that we appreciate the leaves most when they are dying. *Rats was like this leaf,* he thought, *here for a season, then gone, ashes to ashes, dust to dust.*

It was hard to imagine that he would never see his buddy again. He crumbled up the leaf in his hand, and let the bits fall to the ground. The word of Tyler "Rats" Justice's death spread through town mostly by word of mouth. Although he had been the first casualty of the Vietnam war from Coldwater, the death's significance had been lost in the simple writeup it had received at the bottom of page one of the local newspaper and a brief mention in the local radio's noon newscast. After all, he was only a Millie.

Chapter 68

Agent Wallace Christian had wasted no time in assembling an armed strike force and formulating a plan of attack to smash the Jackson County bootlegging ring, and at the same time, rid the county of some unscrupulous public servants. He had brought a dozen of his colleagues down from Washington and armed them with shotguns and .45 caliber Thompson machine guns. Assistance had also been secured in the form of a team of FBI agents to accompany them in the operation.

As it turned out, Deputy Clay Cassidy was more aware of Sheriff Buford and company's clandestine operations than his fellow officers realized, but his hands were tied. He could do nothing about it. As a result, the deputy was more than willing to join the ATF team and serve as an inside informant.

Doctor Simpson and Lincoln had been enlisted to keep their eyes and ears open and provide the team with any information that came their way. As private citizens, however, they were not to participate in any police actions on "D-Day" when the assault plan was executed. Agent Christian hoped to take the culprits by surprise and minimize collateral damage.

Agent Christian had it confirmed from the Atlanta office that Louie "Shooter" Logano had strong ties to the Mob in Atlanta. He concluded that Logano was probably not the Coldwater group's primary Atlanta customer but some muscle acting as their go-between. The agent's primary concern, however, was with cleaning out the rat nest in Jackson County. He planned to leave the Logano gang for their associates in Georgia to deal with on their side.

The team had determined that the Longworth Furniture Company made a weekly run to Atlanta every Friday to one of their customers. What the team didn't know was whether or not they hauled a load of shine on every weekly run. The key would be the delivery of a load of logs to the sawmill, probably on a Thursday night.

It was far from an ideal situation. So, they would have to be vigilant and watch for this scenario to develop on a Thursday and be ready to scramble.

When the time came, the ATF agents would rally on the street above Town Creek, descend the tree-camouflaged bank along the creek, then fan out and charge across the open plane to the cover of the log stacks facing the office. If everything went well to that point, at the sound of the team leader's whistle, they would converge on the sawmill. Meanwhile, several of the FBI agents would descend upon the ferry. Seemed like a workable plan.

But, seldom do plans go according to plan. It seems there's invariably a fly in the ointment that shows its ugly face and fouls up the works. So would there be this time!

Chapter 69

A week after Tyler Justice's parents had received the news that their son had been killed in combat, he was laid to rest with standard military honors. The River Street Gospel Tabernacle was filled to overflowing that afternoon with mourners attending the Tyler Justice memorial service. Many of Milltown's residents, those who were personally acquainted with the young man fondly known as "Rats" and others who weren't, came out to pay homage to one of their own; for he was community. He represented them: the poor, the disenfranchised, those among their number who were yet to follow in his footsteps.

It was an emotionally charged service. What else would it be, given the times and circumstances? At the podium Pastor Nutter shared his eulogy to the deceased, extolling Rats' virtues of patriotism, honor, and goodness. Nutter then proceeded to lay blame for the untimely demise of this fine Christian American son at the feet of godless politicians while heaping condemnation upon the wickedness of man in general.

He lamented, " . . . .men covet all they see; they desire to rule and seek their own will and lie in sinners' beds. Their hearts become cold and hardened until there's no room left for the love of God. It is then that men die on the field, the helpless are displaced, and the innocent are killed." By the time he finished, half of those in attendance were sobbing uncontrollably for the dead young soldier, and the other half were ready to march on Washington.

Pallbearers bore the American flag-draped coffin by hand, leading the bereaved down the one-mile distance walk from the church to the cemetery. Along the way, people who didn't join the procession stood silently in front of their homes as the marchers, who sang "Peace In The Valley," passed by.

Later in the day when the graveside services had ended, the last vestiges of light from the sun that hovered just above the horizon, filtered through a layer of thin stringy clouds and radiated an eerie golden glow across the sky. In the long, deep shadows cast across the now-silent cemetery, there stood, at a distance, a young man and woman, arm in arm, heads bowed, quietly reflecting upon the freshly decorated grave.

After several minutes, they approached the grave. The woman, wearing a hooded jacket, stepped forward, laid a single red rose next to the head stone, then stepped back and took the man's arm. Momentarily, the man knelt at the foot of the grave and pushed a wooden sign into the ground which bore the following epitaph:

Farewell!
For in that word—that fatal word—howe'er
We promise—hope—believe—there breathes despair.
-- Lord Byron

"Aw Rats!"

Lincoln had lingered in the shadows throughout the proceedings surrounding Rats' funeral; he hadn't been able emotionally to get too closely involved. He was having a difficult time saying goodbye to his lifelong friend, lying there in the cold ground not far from where his parents lay.

"I'm so sorry. I know you must miss him terribly."

"Thank you, Ash," answered Linc.

"I don't know how I would have gotten through this without you."

"You're welcome, Love," smiled Ashley. "It's going to be hard for a while."

He suddenly no longer felt young; he felt old, very old. It seemed as if he'd already lived a lifetime filled with fear and suffering, marked by death, in which he had felt the weight of the world on his shoulders. Now, standing there with the two best friends he'd ever known, one untouchable, the other, even though physically beside him, by some conventions almost as far removed, he wondered what new woe the dawning of another day would bring.

As he considered the possibilities, a portion of a verse that he had come across somewhere, sometime in some of his readings encroached upon his thoughts. He said aloud, "I cry out to my God as Job of olden years, but yet to no avail, my ear no answer hears."

The sun slipped below the mountains leaving them surrounded by darkness. The close of another day was at hand, as was the close of another chapter in the life of Lincoln Crockett.

Chapter 70

On the home front, even in times of social unrest, the national trends continued to filter their way down to the local level and Jackson County was no exception. Even in Coldwater women's skirts were getting shorter while men's hair was getting longer. The Rolling Stones' "Get Off My Cloud" was Number One, and Dr. Martin Luther King, Jr.'s civil rights marches in Alabama were in the news. To date, however, with the exception of Montgomery Longworth's volunteering and now Tyler Justice's death, the war in Southeast Asia had had little impact on Coldwater. But, that was beginning to change.

President Lyndon Johnson was rapidly escalating U.S. involvement, increasing the numbers of U.S. ground troops, and ramping up the totals of draftees. Three more had just received their notices (two Ridgers and one Millie). Plus, Billy Ray Coker had enlisted in the Marines followed by his two buddies Edgar McBee and Sammie Stoner. Coldwater was quickly becoming known as a military town, and the month of October was not being a good one for them with so many of their sons gone. Then, on the heels of the Tyler Justice tragedy, there came another announcement that shook the community again,

"I need to see you, ASAP!" Lincoln couldn't get the words out of his mind. They were just simple words scribbled on a piece of paper, but he could sense the emotion, the urgency they conveyed. He had a bad feeling about the message Amanda Cross had left for him. A sick, sinking feeling in the pit of his stomach was growing as he sped down Main Street in the '52 Plymouth toward Milltown.

At Amanda's home, he unfolded the letter she handed him. It was on United States Air Force letterhead, much like the one Rats' father had shown him only a few days earlier. Worrisome words leapt from the page like trout from a stream . . . "your husband Montgomery" . . . "missing in action." Montgomery's B-52 had been shot down and crashed somewhere over Thailand while returning from a bombing run over North Vietnam. The fate of the crew was unknown.

"What am I going to do, Lincoln?" sobbed Amanda.

"All we can do is hope and pray that he and his buddies are alive, that they haven't been captured, and that they get rescued."

"There's another thing. His parents have to be told," she said. "I can't face them Lincoln," she cringed, " because I know they hate me."

"Okay, okay! Don't worry about that," he assured her.

Later that evening

He dialed the number of the telephone in the girls' dorm at State University and, while waiting for an answer, he tried to collect his thoughts. Coming on the heels of Rats' death, this was too much. It seemed as if the whole world was closing in on him and there was no place to hide. Finally, he heard a familiar voice answer.

"Hello, Ashley speaking."

"Hello Ash. It's Linc," he said rather glumly.

"Hey, my hero! Say, what's up? It's been a couple of weeks since…the funeral. I haven't called and since you haven't, I thought you probably needed the space. You still sound as though you might."

"Yeah, well, something else has come up. Ash, I have some more bad news."

Chapter 71

1965 had thus far been an atypical year for life in Coldwater. In contrast to its traditional nothing-ever-changes, life-on-a-treadmill persona, this small southern community had been turned topsy-turvy with issues the like of which it had never been forced to deal with on either number or scale. Matters of crime, death, war, and social unrest had become monthly and even weekly events; many had difficulty coming to grips with how to respond to what was happening in their community. That said, since the hot, muggy days of summer had faded into the pages of history, and the fall season was now in full force with the colors of October at their peak, there seemed to have been a somewhat short respite in unpleasant happenings. Main Street, looking forward to the holidays, was carrying on with business-as-usual routineness. The ATF team had been waiting…waiting…waiting, wondering if they had overlooked something or if the moonshiners were on to them. They were hoping for a break shortly for the moonshine season would soon be drawing to a close.

It had only been a week or so since Tyler Justice's funeral and Lincoln sat slumped over the counter at Long's Drug Store soda fountain, slowly swirling the ice in a glass of cherry coke. Dutch McNally occupied a stool beside him, bending his ear on various subjects.

"By the way, I see your Dodgers made it to the World Series," said Lincoln.

"That's right! Starts this week. Gonna play the Minnesota Twins. Gonna beat 'em,' too," bragged Dutch.

"I don't know," questioned Lincoln, "the Twins have some big hitters."

"Yeah, but tha Dodgers got Koufax and Drysdale on tha mound. They'll shut 'em down," bragged Dutch confidently.

Deputy Cassidy happened in about that time and took the stool on the other side of Lincoln.

"Good morning, Linc…Dutch," greeted the Deputy.

"Mornin', Clay," Lincoln mumbled.

"Say, you sound…and look…pretty down in the dumps."

"Yeah, I guess I am."

"Been try'n to cheer him up," said Dutch.

"Haven't seen you since the funeral. Sorry 'bout your buddy Rats." said Clay.

"Thanks. Aren't you just touched by the outpouring of sympathy from the local community?" said Lincoln, sarcastically.

"I understand your feelings, Linc," said the young officer, patting Linc on the shoulder. "It's a rotten shame things are the way they are."

"So, how's your morning going, Lone Ranger?" asked Lincoln.

"Yeah," sniggered Clay, "now I know how he felt. Actually, I've felt that way for a long time. But, the Lone Ranger did have a sidekick to keep him company."

"Well, if you get in a tight spot and need a Tonto, give me a shout," offered Lincoln.

"Thanks! I'll keep that in mind. Anyway, not much going on. It's been pretty quiet so far. Did ticket some out-of-towners for speeding!"

"All right!" said Lincoln. "Can't let those lawbreakers go speeding through our town."

"Was out of the ordinary though," said the officer, with a puzzled look.

"What do you mean 'out of the ordinary'?" asked Lincoln.

"It was a big white limo."

Lincoln came to attention and straightened into an upright position.

"Didn't by chance have Georgia plates, did it?"

"As a matter of fact it did! How did you..."

Lincoln turned to face Clay and cut him off short.

Dutch's ears perked up, too.

"Clay, I just remembered something I need to do over at the hotel. Give me a ride?"

"Sure. Let's go," the deputy answered looking puzzled.

"Talk to you later, Dutch," said Lincoln.

In the cruiser, Lincoln explained to Clay about what he found in the trunk of Dutch's cab and said he just didn't want to talk in front of him about "things," just to be cautious.

"Now, where were we at in our conversation?"

"Was there a fancy dressed fellow and a blonde gal in the car?"

"Don't know. I couldn't see everyone in the car."

"What did the driver look like?" he asked excitedly.

"Big dude. Looked like a wrestler. Driver's license gave his name as Julius Nikolas."

Lincoln knew it had to be Shooter Logano and his bunch back in town. But why? He knew something must be up.

"Hey, that squares with a bug ole Dutch put in my ear yesterday. He told me there's been rumblings underground about something big about to happen."

"C'mon Clay, we have to see the man."

Unknown to Deputy Cassidy, while he had been writing out the speeding ticket for Julius, a black panel truck that had been trailing about a quarter mile behind the limo passed to which Julius tipped his hat. Behind the wheel of the van was his twin brother Lanny. The panel truck was marked "Smith Brothers Florist." Lanny Nikolas was on his way to a funeral, but he wasn't delivering flowers.

Chapter 72

Ashley strolled leisurely through the Longworth home, as she had on many occasions, admiring the rich wood decor and handsome furnishings, but this time it seemed different. A feeling of melancholy followed her from room to room. She expected at any moment to see Montgomery come bounding down the big staircase to greet her as he had on so many occasions. But this wouldn't be one of those times. Things were different now; things were changing; things would never be the same again.

"Ashley, it seems like you've been gone for months instead of weeks," observed Cora Sue.

"It certainly does," remarked her father. "The house seems so empty without her around."

"Yes, I agree. But, I'm most curious about this drop-in visit out of the blue and your pressing need to talk with both of us," said Victoria, inquisitively.

"Are you finding things to your liking up at State?" inquired Leland.

"Oh, yes, very much so."

"I'm glad you're happy there my dear," said Cora Sue, smiling. "I'm sure you'll do well in your studies. By the way, when have you heard from Montgomery?" asked Victoria to no one specifically.

"We receive a correspondence from him almost every week," answered Cora Sue. "I also send him one in return. He says it means so much to hear from home."

"Oh, I'm sure it does," replied Victoria.

"But, we haven't received one for several weeks now. It concerns me that something has happened," added Cora Sue nervously.

"Oh, I'm sure they stay quite busy and don't have a lot of time to think about us over here," offered Emerson, trying to dispel the Longworths' fears.

"By the way, how's he dealing with the situation?" inquired Emerson.

"The boy seems to be holding up well," reported Leland, "…says his bomber crew makes bombing runs out of Thailand into North Vietnam almost every day."

"It's oh, so depressing," sniffled Cora Sue. "I still don't understand why he wanted to go when he didn't have to."

"Neither do I," agreed Leland, "but at least it got him away from that little white trash Millie girl he was getting mixed up with."

Ashley gritted her teeth.

"Well, we just hope and pray that he gets back home safely from that awful war," sympathized Victoria.

"Amen to that!" offered Emerson.

"You know what?" said Cora Sue, whispering as if anyone other than those around the table could hear, "speaking of that little Millie girl, Leland was told by her father's supervisor that she's *pregnant*," shaking her hands as if the word might stick to her just by speaking it.

"Well, I'm not surprised," said Victoria disgustedly.

Ashley was fuming inside.

"And, on top of that, I had to fire her father the other day," said Leland.

"What for?" asked Emerson curiously.

"Stealing company property, lumber, to be exact. He was taking it without anyone's knowledge, until he got caught. A thief is a thief. You can't have employees stealing from the company."

Ashley finally spoke up, "But how can you do that? What's that family going to do? How are they going to live?"

"Ashley, this is not any of our business dear," reminded Victoria.

"But, Amanda's going to need medical care for her and the baby," Ashley reasoned.

"Listen, the little skag'n her bastard kid are not my problem," fumed Leland, shrugging his shoulders as he rose from the table.

"Would you feel the same way and be calling them names if the baby were your grandchild?" challenged Ashley, jumping to her feet.

"Now that's about enough young lady!" demanded her father. "You apologize to our hosts this instant."

"Oh, thank God that's not the case," swooned Cora Sue, feigning passing out, "what an unimaginable tragedy that would be."

Ashley realized that she was about to reveal some things that would result in unpredictable consequences, but she could just not stand silently by while these self-righteous bigots slandered decent people. "But it is the case, Mrs. Longworth. Amanda Cross is pregnant with Montgomery's child."

Needless to say, that made them wake up and smell the coffee. Cora Sue just sat there trembling like a drunk with the shakes. Leland, wide-eyed as a trapped opossum, pounded on the table three times with his fists cussing "damn," "damn," "damn." Ashley's parents just stared, first at each other, then at their daughter.

Ashley had gone this far, she decided she might as well go for broke. "And that's not all. They're also married!" That was the *coup de grâce*. Cora Sue collapsed into a heap of tears, babbling incoherent sentences.

The shock waves from the first announcement had hardly subsided when Leland began beating the table again yelling "dammit," "dammit," "dammit."

An astonished Emerson Armstrong exclaimed, "Great Scott!"

"And how do you know so much about this Amanda's and Montgomery's relationship?" asked her mother, staring darts at her.

"I just know," she said.

Ashley glanced at her father. He was looking straight at her shaking his head, looking disgusted by the whole affair.

After a few minutes when everyone had had time to settle down and compose themselves, Ashley attempted to speak again although a tenseness hung pervasively in the air.

"If you'd allow me, I'd like to say something else," she said politely.

"Young lady, I think you've said quite enough for one evening," warned her father sternly.

"Look, I know what you heard has been a shock to all of you and I'm sorry. I lost my temper because of the bad things you were saying about Amanda and her family."

"But, please Mr. and Mrs. Longworth, let me tell you something about Montgomery and Amanda."

"Okay my dear, it can't be any worse than what we heard so far," said Cora Sue feebly, wiping red, mascara streaked eyes.

"No. I've heard all I want to hear. Just wait 'til I get my hands on that son of mine," said a red-faced Leland.

"But, Mr. Longworth," she pleaded, "regardless of what you think about her, she's a good person and she loves your son and he loves

[300]

her. If you love your son, you should at least accept the one he chooses to love."

"If he loved us he'd respect our wishes…our position," he retorted.

"But…," she tried to respond.

"That's enough Ashley!" yelled her father, grabbing her by the arm.

"We're leaving now," he said.

"No!" she said, jerking away.

"I have one more thing to say and I'm going to say it," she shouted, tears streaming down her cheeks."

"That little baby Amanda's carrying inside her is not only Montgomery's child, it's your grandchild and nothing in this world is going to change that. If you have any feelings at all for your own flesh and blood, you'll help your future daughter-in-law and grandchild have what they need until Montgomery gets home to take care of them himself."

"You make a complicated mess seem so simple and easy, don't you Ashley?" asked a frustrated Leland Longworth. "It's not that cut and dried."

"Why not, Mr. Longworth? It's not complicated to just care about people," she replied.

"Ashley, *Shut Up!*" stormed her mother, slapping her across the face. Ashley Armstrong's face turned blood red as she stepped within inches of her mother's face. Her body stiffened.

Looking straight into Victoria's eyes with her clenched fists, she warned, "Don't you *ever* do that again!" She started to storm out of the house but then stopped and turned. "You got me so flustered I forgot to tell you some other really important news on Amanda's behalf. She wanted to tell you herself but she was afraid to face you."

Ashley went on to explain to them about the letter Amanda had received from the Air Force informing her that her *husband's* plane had been shot down and that he and the crew were missing in action.

She added, "This would be an excellent opportunity for you to reach out to your daughter-in-law and coming grandchild." They all just stood there staring at her in stone-cold silence.

Chapter 73

Culveyhouse's old log truck was weighed down with a load of freshly cut logs. It weaved, swayed, and bounced its way through the rut-scarred gravel tracks of Sawmill Road and, just short of the sawmill's two-story office building, it belched a loud backfire from its guts and sputtered to a stop.

Two men climbed from the truck and entered the building. It was a surprise to those waiting inside, for the two men were strangers. The truck drivers got a surprise of their own when they walked into a room full of firearms pointed in their direction.

"Who the hell are you?" demanded Clifton Ledbetter.

"I...I...I'm Jed Culveyhouse an this here's my boy Malcolm," said the older of the two men, both of them wide-eyed with their hands in the air.

"We'uz expectin' Herman," said one of the men bearing arms.

"Uh, he coud'n come taday cause it's Herman's birthday, an the famly's havin' a big shindig. So, he ax'd me—I'm his cousin—if I'd make this here run fer 'im."

"Well! I'll be damned!" cussed Sheriff Coker. "He was supposed to bring some more guns."

"We gotta couple'a .22's in tha truck," spoke up Malcolm.

Everyone just looked at him sort of dumb-like.

"Well, thank you, Billy Sunday," said the Sheriff blankly.

Word was leaked that a move against a moonshine ring up in Tennessee was being planned. So, Shooter Logano and his cohorts in Coldwater leaked news of an upcoming shipment in order to plan a surprise party for the Feds when they showed up. Shooter had come with his regular crew plus a half-dozen soldiers he had pulled off the streets; all well-armed and experienced in street warfare. They had also been counting on the Culveyhouse clan for additional support.

Their undercover informant in Coldwater had fingered Wallace Christian as the likely federal agent, operating under the guise of an author doing research, along with several newly-arrived faces in town with whom he had had regular contact. The stoolie had also dropped a bug in the ears of a certain individual with a date and time for a big shine run.

Meanwhile, from the opposite side of the creek bottom, the ATF team had slipped through the waist-high weeds and made their way to the stacks of logs that lined the road parallel to the office. Having caught sight of their approach, Dalton Jackson had everyone take up battle positions in and around the office building.

The hometown boys (Dalton, his drivers Boone and Willis, Deputy Odom, Clifton Ledbetter, and Charlie Bridger) took up positions in the upstairs windows, while Shooter, Joker, and three of his triggermen covered the first floor with one watching the rear of the building. The two delegates of Culveyhouse clan crawled under the log truck and Shooter's street soldiers dispersed among the lumber stacks adjacent to where the ATF team was positioned in order to set up a crossfire.

Meanwhile, Lincoln had established an observation post at a point on Town Creek Road near the west entrance to Sawmill Road that provided an unobstructed view of the action.

He looked at his watch.

"It's 3:00 p.m.," he whispered to himself.

He tugged at his coat collar and pulled it tighter against the gusty October winds that swirled about on the chilly, overcast afternoon.

Scanning the surroundings with binoculars, he caught sight of something near a shed behind the office. It gave him a start.

"Oh, crap!" he said out loud.

Next to the shed was parked a police cruiser, a white limo, and a big black van.

He could make out figures he didn't recognize filing from the back of the office building and sneaking across the road into the lumber stacks.

"It looks like Logano must have brought some reinforcements!" he whispered to himself.

"Christian's boys are about to find themselves between a knot and a hard place. I've got to get their attention."

Lincoln had to assume that Agent Christian was not only unaware that his plan for a surprise attack had been compromised but also that he was unaware that they were outflanked and outnumbered. If so, when they attacked the office building, it would be like Custer's Last Stand. He jumped on the Indian and went tearing up the road toward the sawmill. Revving up the engine, he held on to the motorcycle like a bucking bronco squalling like a Tasmanian devil as it fishtailed through the ruts and crevices. It was all Lincoln could do to hang on, but he held the throttle wide open.

Back up the road, both armies waiting to do battle were, for the present, frozen in place trying to figure out what in the name of heaven was coming at them like a demon with a case of the screaming memees.

Before reaching the office, Lincoln swerved off the road, made a bee line for the shed where the cars were parked, and slid to a stop. He looked in the police cruiser. The keys were in it. He jumped in and just started to turn the ignition key.

"Get out of the car Lincoln."

"What?" he said as he rolled down the window.

"I said to get out of the car."

"Dutch! What are you doing? You can't…"

He stopped in midsentence. Lincoln had been looking Dutch in the face. He had just noticed the gun in Dutch's hand.

"Now some things are beginning to make sense," Lincoln said sadly. "Why, Dutch?"

"Man's gotta make a living."

"But, Dutch…"

"Just get outta the car Lincoln," he interrupted.

Lincoln opened the door. He swung one leg out of the car and with the other leg slammed the door back against Dutch, knocking him down and disarming him. It didn't take much effort for him to subdue the old cabbie. To keep him from alarming the others, the quickest thing he could think to do with him was to stuff him in the trunk of the cruiser. After fiddling with some switches, he got the siren and red lights flashing. Speeding past the office, he brought the cruiser to a screeching halt in the road where the headlights were focused on the lumber stacks, then scrambled away.

Now, those Atlanta street hoodlums hiding out in the lumber stacks didn't know what to think. The only time they had ever been looking down the headlights of a police car with lights flashing and siren wailing was when they had been caught with their pants down on a job gone wrong. So, they responded in the way they had become accustomed to in this particular type of situation.

They all cut loose on the cruiser with automatic weapons and shotguns and riddled it with more holes than a tennis racket, all in deference to Deputy Odom's ordering them to cease fire. The profusion of profanities he hurled at them was hard to make out above all the gunfire. Lincoln made out some things about questioning the legitimacy of their births and damning somebody to hell. When the gas tank blew engulfing the vehicle in a flaming fireball the deputy knew the Sheriff's brand new cruiser was condemned to a smoking pile of junk and ole Buford would be as mad as a hornet.

Lincoln's ruse had worked. The villains inside the building had revealed their numbers when they had poked their heads out of the windows to watch the police car going up in flames, and the gunmen in the lumber stacks had exposed their positions and armament.

At first, Agent Christian had been angered by the crazy antics of the unidentified motorcycle rider who, he believed, was going to muddle up their plans to attack the moonshiners; and he did. But now, he was glad. If they had followed their original plan, they would have walked into a buzz saw and been cut to pieces. He owed that guy one. He didn't know who he was, but he had a sneaking suspicion.

While the Atlanta bad boys were taking out the black-and-white, the ATF agents had been able to relocate their positions in the lumber stacks by the muzzle fire discharging from their weapons. Agent Christian repositioned his men strategically around the stacks of logs to fight on two fronts and dug in. It was going to be a tougher fight now, but at least they were on even ground with their adversaries. It was time to go to Plan B.

Chapter 74

During the brief interlude that followed, it appeared to the Culveyhouse boys that this was developing into something they hadn't bargained for. They weren't inclined to get involved in a fight they didn't have a dog in. Besides, they didn't know any of the folks on either side of the road and they could take up whatever grievance they had with cousin Herman himself. So, they decided to cut and run.

The silence that had pervaded this soon-to-be combat zone following the cessation of gunfire was suddenly broken by the grinding of the old log truck's motor cranking up. Jed gunned it and the old metal beast of burden slowly moaned and groaned its way around the burned out, smoking shell of Buford's cruiser. With Jed grinding the gears trying to gain some momentum, the Feds opened fire to prevent their getaway.

A hail of bullets showered the truck, peppering the weathered cab and windows until it looked like a block of Swiss cheese.

"Great Godamighty, Daddy! We're gonna die! We're gonna die!" yelled Malcolm, slumping down into the floorboard.

Jed, who had ducked under the steering wheel, looked up just in time to see the white T-Bird coming down the east side of Sawmill Road, where it had been re-graveled, skidding to a stop. He jerked the steering wheel hard left to avoid it.

Lincoln had been watching the fireworks from cover of the vehicles where he had commandeered the police cruiser. Upon seeing the T-Bird, he jumped from his hiding place.

"Ashley! What the hell is she doing here?" he exclaimed out loud.

He started to run to her but halted when he saw Dalton Jackson running from the building in her direction. He decided to wait and see what unfolded.

Dalton raced down to the car, pulled Ashley from it, and dragged her, against her most pronounced protests, into the office building. He had a sudden notion that, if push came to shove, she would make a valuable bargaining tool in negotiating certain demands for their side. Lincoln would have to bide his time until he could determine her location in the building.

A second volley of ATF fire blew out a front tire on the escaping truck, causing the vehicle to pull hard to the left. The wheels slipped over the edge of a three-foot embankment next to the lumber stacks, ground to a stop, and teetered there on the edge. Jed and Malcolm scrambled out of the truck before it toppled ever so slowly over onto its side like a huge beast lying down to sleep.

The weight of the logs was too much, however, for the straining log chains to contain and snapped like two-pound fishing line against a twenty-pound bass. Tons of large logs went bounding wildly into the stacks of lumber like cigar-shaped bowling balls, toppling the neatly-arranged stacks and scattering boards in all directions.

The truck followed the logs, cartwheeling across piles of splintered lumber spewing gasoline from one of its ruptured fuel tanks before one last flip landed it belly up. A spark from the ruptured gas tank ignited the gasoline and in minutes the bone-dry lumber erupted into a raging bonfire. It took little time for the truck to become engulfed in flames with the heat cooking up the pressure in the other twin, twenty-gallon fuel tank. When it blew, it was like a dozen flame throwers had been activated as they spewed flaming petrol for yards in all directions. Shooter's contingent was in dire straits; they were caught in the middle of the firestorm.

There was a bigger one yet to come. There was that fifty-gallon drum of shine underneath the truck and bolted to the bed. As the fire raged hotter and hotter on the truck, the pressure in that drum rose higher and higher until it reached critical mass. And, then, it went off like a bomb.

The ground shook and windows rattled for blocks as a fireball shot fifty feet into the air. Shock waves blew out windows in the sawmill office and fragments of burning lumber rained down on the immediate area like fire and brimstone on Sodom and Gomorrah.

What few of the Atlanta gangsters weren't crushed under the falling stacks of lumber, flattened by steamrolling logs, annihilated by the explosion, or consumed by the blazes, escaped into the open, choosing to take their chances against machine guns. Their chances were little to none as they were summarily dispatched by a contingent of the ATF team which had divided their force. The other half of the team took the initiative to storm the office building before its shell-shocked occupants could fully recover from the effect this most unlikely set of bizarre events had had in turning the tide in their favor.

The roof of the office building was, by this time, in flames from the burning, falling debris. Lincoln had to do something quickly to get Ashley out of there. By the time he had reached the back window of the office, the gunfire had diminished to sporadic shots here and there, and much shouting could be heard being exchanged among the combatants. Some had laid down their arms in surrender, some were dead, and some were wounded.

Suddenly, two individuals burst through the back door into the open like their pants were on fire and disappeared into the darkness. It was Shooter and Dalton. Apparently, both had decided to depart the sinking ship *post haste* and leave their cohorts to fend for themselves.

A quick look through the window showed Ashley sitting in a corner with the Joker hulking over her pointing a gun at her head. To take on the big man was to dice with death, but he had to or Ashley was going to die. Lincoln grabbed a short-handled shovel leaning against the building and charged into the room shouting Joker's name. The big man whirled around just as Lincoln swung the shovel, catching Joker across the forearm leaving an ugly gash. The hulk screamed in pain as the handgun went flying across the room.

Before Lincoln could cock his arms for a second swing at the villain, Joker charged, grabbed Lincoln by the shoulders, and slung him across the office into the wall. Lincoln, half-dazed and on all fours, tried to get to his feet, but Joker's big hands caught him by the throat before he could.

Déjà vu! Those feelings of suffocating panic and impending death that had held his brain hostage that night his father's hands had clutched his neck in a death grip came flooding back into Lincoln's head. Once again, fate came to his rescue. On the floor between his legs, Lincoln felt a long, thin, nail-like piece of metal set into a circular-shaped piece of wood; it was the receipt holder.

Now that's about as handy as a pocket in a shirt, he thought to himself.

Joker leaned down almost face to face with his victim and grinned. The insolent Lincoln raised one hand and gave the big man the finger. Infuriated, the big fellow spit in Lincoln's face and tightened the hold on his throat. Lincoln slammed the receipt holder into Joker's lower mouth behind his chin. The steel spike pierced Joker's tongue and drove upward through the roof of his mouth into an eye socket, hit the edge of his left eye socket, and bent outward.

Joker released the death grip on his prey and staggered backward grabbing at his face. He tried to scream but couldn't. He couldn't speak, swallow, or breathe; his mouth, tongue, and throat were all locked together. He clutched at the wooden base of the contraption and began pulling, twisting, and turning, trying to remove the death device from his head. But, that only served to swivel the spike 'round and 'round, slicing up his eyeball like a boiled egg in a food processor. He wobbled about for a few moments, choking on a swollen tongue, drowning in his own blood. Shortly, the big man toppled to the floor, jerked a few times like a fish out of water, then lay still like a baby at slumber.

With the building now engulfed in flames, Lincoln raced to lead his lady from the fiery furnace. They crawled along the floor underneath the choking smoke and made their way out the back door to deep breaths of fresh, cool air. They found Agent Christian taking stock of a situation that looked like a scene from a World War II movie. It did appear that the hostilities had ceased and order had been restored. Emergency personnel had been summoned and were on the scene.

"Well! That was the screwiest operation I've ever been a part of," Christian declared, shaking his head in wonderment, "God does move in mysterious ways!"

Assessing the damages, he took a head count of the quick and the dead. Clifton Ledbetter, Charlie Bridger, Deputy Odom, and Lanny Nikolas had all been taken into custody along with Jed and Malcom Culveyhouse. The two ringleaders Dalton Jackson and the Shooter Logano had escaped.

Counted among the casualties were the Joker and Julius Nikolas, along with Shooter's Atlanta soldiers who had either been gunned down or perished in the blazing inferno. One of the ATF agents was also added to this list.

"Don't forget about ole Dutch McNally," added Lincoln rather somberly.

"The old cabby?" asked Agent Christian. "What's he have to do with anything?"

"He was their informant," said Lincoln, "and, he made house calls delivering shine."

"Well, I'll be damned," said Agent Christian, shaking his head, hands perched on his hips. "Where is he now?"

"Over there in the trunk of that police car," replied Lincoln, nodding toward the burned-out carcass of Sheriff Coker's police cruiser.

"No shit!" said the agent.

"Yeah, I was just trying to expose those guys hiding in lumber stacks. I didn't think about them shooting the thing all to hell and setting it on fire when I put him in the trunk."

"Oh, well, the turncoat got his just desserts," reasoned Agent Christian. "By the way, Mr. Crockett, that was some fast thinking on your part, coming like the cavalry to save our asses the way you did. Thanks!"

"Glad to be of service, sir."

"Well, that leaves us with two unfinished tasks," said Agent Christian addressing the whole team. "One, we have to track down the two fugitives: Dalton Jackson and Shooter Logano. And two, we have to go up in those mountains and make a call on the Culveyhouse's. But right now, wonder if we could find a hot dinner around here anywhere?"

Lincoln then turned to Ashley who was still shaking from her ordeal.

"My lady, I want to have a talk with you. Just what in the name of heaven were you doing down here? You could have gotten killed!"

"I heard all the noise and wanted to see what was going on," she explained. And, anyway, what were *you* doing down here? So, you could have gotten killed also, dummy," she exclaimed tearfully, pounding him in the chest with both fists.

Meanwhile, down the road, FBI agents had moved against Franklin's Ferry.

Chapter 75

One patrol boat struggled to make headway against the river's swift current as it plowed its way slowly upriver from behind the ferry boat. The two FBI agents on board, attempting to reach the ferry from downstream, questioned if the Sheriff Department's old boat was going to be up to the task. Two agents in a second boat, attempting an approach from upstream, were having difficulty keeping their boat from being swept downriver and overshooting the target. From the shoreline, additional agents observed this maneuvering through binoculars and communicated with their comrades via radio. It appeared that Jonas Franklin's tactics had caused the difficulties he had counted on.

Jonas had guided the ferry boat out into the middle of the river to make it more difficult for the lawmen to reach them. Little River was normally a slow-running, lazy river of clear water, but runoff from rains high in the mountains had filled its banks with a deluge of storm water. It was a risky move on Jonas' part to stop the ferry in midstream, placing ferry, tugboat, and cables in positions of greater stress against the rushing water than it would normally withstand secured to its moorings at the landing.

Jonas manned the tugboat while Obee ran around the ferryboat waving a shotgun, laughing, and yelling unintelligible jargon like he was commanding a battleship. The FBI agents' plan was for the downstream boat to draw near to the tugboat with the intent of reasoning with Mr. Franklin to abandon his foolhardy undertaking while the agents on the upriver side made an attempt to board the ferry.

The first part of the plan was doomed to failure from the beginning due to the agents' inability to communicate with their adversary over the din of the droning boat motors and churning waters. They were, in fact, fortunate that neither of them was killed by Jonas' shotgun blast that ripped the windshield off the police boat.

The team on the upstream side had no better luck in boarding the ferry. Now, ole Obee may have had only one oar in the water, but he wasn't as dumb as a post either. And, he was a fair shot with a rifle and shotgun. Obee had lined the perimeter of the ferry with quart jars of shine and every time the agents' boat would come up to the edge and an agent would try to board, Obee would cut loose on one of those jars with his 12-gauge and scatter wood splinters, moonshine, and broken glass all over the agents, causing them to back off.

After several attempts by the troops on the water had failed to produce any tangible results, agents on shore decided to have a go at it from their vantage point and take a more drastic course of action. A sharpshooter tried to level the sights of a high-powered rifle on the shadowy figure of a man inside the tugboat cabin as the tugboat pitched and rolled in the swelling waters. He squeezed the trigger just as the boat rolled away from him. The bullet penetrated the cabin wall, slammed into the engine, shattering the oil pump, and sent oil spewing in every direction. Within minutes, deprived of its vital cooling lubricant, the overheated engine started smoking, screeching, and shaking like it was somehow possessed. It suddenly ground to a halt, dead as roadkill.

In the meantime, the hot engine had ignited the shower of oil and both the engine room and cabin were now in flames. The burning liquid leap-frogged to the ferry and was leaking through the deck. It would soon be lapping its fiery tongue at the compartment where a large store of flammable, hundred-proof moonshine lay in its path.

Jonas clambered out of the tug onto the deck. Without the tugboat, they were at the mercy of the raging river. The only thing holding them was the overhead guide cable anchored to the trunks of two large trees on each side of the river. But, it was doubtful that the cable could hold them against the force of the rushing water for very long. Within minutes the rusting two-inch steel cable, stretched to its limit, snapped somewhere along its length and whiplashed across the deck of the ferry boat with a wicked "pop." Obee, unfortunately, was standing in just the right place to catch the deadly backlash and it took his head off as clean as a double-edged sword.

With her moorings gone and no means of controlling it, the old vehicle hauler and Jonas were now at the mercy of the river. Rising and falling up and down like a giant fishing bobber, the rig would be swept down the watercourse inescapably into the rocky shoals at Sutter's Bend which would spell death for the ferry and her captain. With the storm waters driving it across the rocks of the bend, the tugboat would be ground up like peppercorns in a pepper mill, and the remains deposited into the deep waters that followed.

The boat didn't have to wait for the river! When the buildup of heat from the fire reached critical mass inside the hull of that old boat, that shine went off like Fourth-of-July fireworks. It blew that old ferry to kingdom come. The old river got to chew up only the leftover scraps.

No remains of the Franklins were ever found. Within the course of one hour, all signs that a Franklin family and business had ever existed there had been swallowed up by Little River. All their lives the river had been their home; in the end, it became their tombs.

Chapter 76

Back in his office at Longworth Manufacturing, Dalton Jackson nervously paced back and forth. He was beside himself. The whole operation had fallen apart. He needed to talk with the big boss. There came a knock at the door. He jumped! Holding the knob, he called softly. "Who is it?"

"It's *me*! Open the door."

"Come in LW," he said, opening the door slowly.

"It looks, and *sounds* like your operation isn't going as planned, doesn't it?" observed LW

"Oh, cut the sarcasm. This is your operation as much as mine. You're in this thing as deep as I am. The thing is, what are we going to do now?" asked Dalton.

"No, Mr. Jackson, you're wrong. I'm not in this as deep as you, or anyone else for that matter. You forget, sir, the only person who knows of my connection to this operation is you. And, if you're not around to point a finger, no one will know anything about me."

"And, what do you mean if I'm not around?"

"I mean...not around."

The last thing Dalton Jackson saw was the puff of smoke from the small pearl-handled derringer in LW's hand. The last thing he felt was a searing pain in his chest. The last words he tried to speak fell short, "You...."

Meanwhile at the sawmill

Emerson Armstrong arrived on the scene to determine the cause of all the commotion and discovered Ashley and Lincoln, dirty, disheveled, and wrapped in each other's arms. Concerned, he raced toward his daughter but was intercepted by Doctor Simpson before he reached them.

"Emerson," holding Ashley's father by the arms, "Ashley's had a life-threatening experience on two counts," cautioned the doctor.

"What happened?" Armstrong growled. "It's probably that boy's fault!"

"You're wrong Emerson, you're wrong, Lincoln saved her," pleaded the doctor.

Just then, Agent Christian walked up and introduced himself. "Is that your daughter, sir?" he asked Mr. Armstrong as he pointed to Ashley.

Emerson answered that she was.

"Then you owe that young man a debt of gratitude. He saved her life. He rescued her from a thug and pulled her out of that burning building."

Ashley rushed to her father and threw herself into his arms.

"Oh, Daddy, it was awful! I'd be dead right now if it weren't for Lincoln," she sobbed.

She motioned for Lincoln to join them.

"Daddy, this is Lincoln Crockett. Lincoln, this is my father, Mr. Armstrong," she said, introducing the two of them.

Emerson Armstrong reluctantly took Lincoln's outreached hand and shook it.

"Well! It appears that I owe you my daughter's life. Thank you," he said in a gentlemanly manner.

"You're welcome, sir. It was my pleasure," answered Lincoln smiling.

Before they could continue, Leland Longworth walked up to join them.

"Hello, Leland," said Emerson, "didn't know you were down here."

"Yeah, funny. Got an anonymous call to come down and check on things at the plant. Didn't find anything unusual. Man, this place is a mess."

Suddenly, storming into their midst like Teddy Roosevelt charging up San Juan Hill was Sheriff Coker in a cop car, screeching to a stop, siren wailing and lights flashing. Buford emerged from the black and white and innocently demanded, "What's goin' on here?"

"Well, as if you didn't know," answered a sarcastic Agent Christian, who went on to describe to him just what had gone on there. Buford claimed that he'd been trying to break that moonshine ring for a long time and offered to take custody of the prisoners.

"I don't think so," said Agent Christian, "this is my party, but you're invited."

"Cowboy to Leader One, come in," crackled the voice of Deputy Cassidy on Christian's walkie talkie.

"This is Leader One. Go ahead, Cowboy."

"I got a call from a plant security guard at the Longworth plant. Found Dalton Jackson in his office over there…dead. Shot with small caliber pistol. Been trying to locate Mr. Longworth. Found something real interesting. The deceased had a letter in his coat pocket addressed to the DA signed by one Marjorie Henderson. It lists names of people involved in an illegal moonshine operation here in Coldwater. Over."

"Copy that Cowboy."

"Now I guess we know why that woman was killed, but *who* pulled the trigger and *why*?"

"Leader One over and out."

"Cowboy out."

"Sheriff Buford Coker, you're under arrest!"

Meanwhile, Ashley, her father, Mr. Longworth, Lincoln, and Dr. Simpson congregated next to Emerson Armstrong's automobile and reviewed the details of Ashley's abduction and rescue by Lincoln when Ashley's mother came rushing up, grabbed her daughter, and hugged her.

"I just heard what happened to you! Are you all right my dear?" she asked franticly.

"Yes, mother, I'm fine, thanks to Lincoln."

"Is Cora Sue not with you?" asked Leland.

"No. She left in a hurry right after you did. Said she had some business to attend to," said Victoria.

"Huh! Wonder what urgent business she had that couldn't wait," pondered Leland.

Ashley tried to introduce Lincoln to her mother.

Taking Lincoln by the hand and leading him toward Mrs. Armstrong, she said, "Mother, you've never really met Lincoln, this is…"

"I know as much about who he is as I care to know," she pronounced. "I know that wherever there's trouble, he seems to be in the middle of it and has my daughter in it with him, and I know that I want my daughter to stay away from him and him to stay away from her." She spit out the words like a mouthful of rancid meat.

"Victoria!" Emerson spoke up harshly, "The young man just saved your daughter's life. If you love your daughter, you could at least show some gratitude for what he's done."

"Well, that's no more than any good citizen would have done," she retorted.

"Mother! I don't believe you," screamed Ashley, incredulously, "I could be dead right now except for Lincoln, and you can't even say a simple 'Thank you' to the man!"

"Mrs. Emerson," asked Lincoln, "why do you hate me so?"

"You were born," she said expressionless, and turned and walked away.

The others just watched her, dumbfounded, as she made her way to her car, climbed in, and drove away.

Unaware of what was actually going on with all the explosions, gunfire, rising columns of smoke, and wailing sirens, many residents imagined that the town was under attack by the Russians, some believed the Rapture was underway, others that they were in the wake of some natural disaster, as well as any number of other curses being cast upon their settlement, all to the result that things were in utter chaos.

In the aftermath of the upheaval, which proved to be a mixture of calamity, tragedy, comedy, and plain bad luck, and which in time would become known simply as "The Battle of the Sawmill," conversation continued about it either by way of discourse, debate, or criticism for the immediate future. Cleanup operations took some time to complete, and when, or if, a means of river crossing could be reestablished was anyone's guess.

Marge Henderson's letter proved to be the *coup de grâce* that broke the moonshine ring once and for all and led to the arrest of Sheriff Coker and Mayor McKean. It also answered the question as to why she was murdered but gave no clue as to who murdered her. Gang members confessed to authorities that Dalton Jackson had contracted with someone in Atlanta to do the job. They also informed the Feds that Dalton was the ringleader but had a confidant he called the "Big Boss," whom he always consulted on matters. He was once overheard referring to this person as "LW"

Deputy Cassidy was appointed acting Sheriff and charged first with re-staffing the office with trustworthy individuals. His second assignment was to be the investigation of the Marjorie Henderson and Dalton Jackson murders. Before Agent Christian and his associates returned north, an assault conducted on the Culveyhouse property proved unproductive, finding the premises were completely vacated. It appeared that the clan had retreated deeper into the mountains and what few neighbors could be contacted denied having any knowledge of their whereabouts.

On a more personal note, as a result of his several heroic acts, Mr. Lincoln Crockett had received much deserved accolades, in particular for saving the life of the daughter of one of Coldwater's leading citizens. This was also the point in time when Ashley wanted to be open with everyone about her and Lincoln's feelings for each other, regardless of the consequences. Lincoln cautioned against it, advising Ashley to wait for a suitable occasion.

Although it would take their acceptance of a paradigm shift in social conventions, the Armstrongs could no longer threaten their daughter with punishments for they knew she would leave home and go with Crockett. In time, Victoria would come around to accepting, if not Crockett himself, the fact he was owed a debt that could never be paid for the life of their one and only child.

A few days following the battle with the bootleggers, the new Sheriff offered Lincoln a job as deputy on his new staff. The rookie Sheriff had been impressed with the cool-headedness and bravery the young Crockett had exhibited under fire. At first, Lincoln could not imagine himself in the role of lawman but, after some deliberation, decided to accept the opportunity to improve his station in life. Suddenly, with this one stroke of luck or fate, his life had gained a greater degree of stability, both in social recognition and financial gain, than he had known in his entire life

Chapter 77

Halloween took on a little different flavor that year in Coldwater. Oh, there was the usual throng of young trick-or-treaters, sneaking about incognito in scary costumes extorting candy (the price for avoiding trickery) from their neighbors. The sporadic pop and crackle of firecrackers echoed through the streets and the occasional trail of a bottle rocket could be seen streaking across the dusky evening sky. And as was always predictable, there were the mischievous few boys who found amusement in victimizing jack-o-lanterns and mailboxes with cherry bombs. But, Halloween of 1965 will be remembered, not for the customary celebration and shenanigans surrounding the holiday, but for an event that took place at the Southern Railway Station.

It was precisely 6:00 p.m. when the Tennessean pulled into the depot. A large crowd, made up mostly of Ridgers, was on hand to meet the train for the homecoming of a war hero. A large sign above their heads spelled out the words "Welcome Home Montgomery" in bold red letters. The ovation that went up for Montgomery Longworth when he first appeared in the open doorway of the passenger car suddenly trailed off into near silence as the crowd's attention, one by one, was drawn to the two wooden crutches supporting him, made necessary due to a missing right leg. Having been uninformed about the extent of his injuries, the crowd stared in awkward disbelief, but after collecting themselves, a chorus of cheers went up as his friends rushed forward to greet him.

The real heartstopper came when the Longworths and Armstrongs caught sight of those wooden props. Stunned at the sight of their one-legged son, Cora Sue went into hysterics and passed out. While Leland tried to attend to his wife, assisted by the Armstrongs, Montgomery and Amanda embraced and kissed with Ashley by their side. The two girls helped Montgomery make his way through the crowd to his family.

By this time, Cora Sue had recovered sufficiently from the initial shock so that she and Leland could embrace their son and welcome him home. When Montgomery tried to introduce Amanda to them as his wife, they passed him off without a chance and told him they would deal with "things" later. Montgomery frowned.

"Why weren't we told about your condition?" cried Cora Sue.

"I guess your 'wife' didn't think it was important enough for us to know," said Leland, sarcastically.

"Mom, Dad, I told Amanda not to tell you. I didn't want you to worry."

"Right now, I just want to go home with my family and friends and get to talk with everyone."

"Well, let's just keep it to family right now son, you, me, Dad, and the Armstrongs," suggested Cora Sue.

"Look, there's something I want everyone to understand right now," said Montgomery firmly and straight-faced, "Amanda and I are husband and wife. That child inside her is ours and we're going to be a family. We want you to be part of our family, too, and us yours, but you have to take us all. That's the way it is! So, make up your minds."

"And that goes for my friend Lincoln also!" Ashley smiled.

As they headed toward their vehicles, the Longworths and Emersons just looked at one another blankly and shook their heads. Ashley, lagging behind the group, looked across her left shoulder and blew a kiss toward a shadowy figure lurking beneath an overhead light dangling from the eaves of the train station.

After the two families had departed the train station, Lincoln began his walking patrol of the downtown streets, checking buildings to make sure they were secure, and watching the trick-or-treaters to see that they were safe and not getting into any mischief. Reaching the Lacy, he stepped inside the lobby where Miss Jessie was giving out candy to young goblins.

"You here to trick or to treat, lawman?" asked Miss Jessie, dressed out in an authentic black witch getup.

"Never fear, Madam Witch," he answered, waving his arms, "I'm just here to keep the peace."

"Say, you look sharp in that cowboy outfit," she laughed, "and it's going to take some getting used to seeing you as a real policeman. I would never have thought it!"

"I'm going to do my best."

"I know you will," she said seriously.

"But, you know, you left me with a lot of work around here. You were doing a whole lot more than I had realized. You're going to be hard to replace! Say, that was a bad scene down at the station, " said Miss Jessie, jerking her head toward the train station.

"Yeah," said Lincoln, "I feel bad about Montgomery. He's a good guy."

"First, there was your buddy Rats, now this Longworth boy, and I'm afraid there will be others on the list before all is said and done," said Miss Jessie. "I'm glad you missed that mess," she added.

"Ain't I the lucky one." he answered, thoughtfully.

Chapter 78

November, 1965

The holidays are just around the corner and the spirit of the coming season will soon be filling the air. Thanksgiving is less than a month away and then, before you can say Ebenezer Scrooge, Christmas bells will be ringing. Given the alienations dividing the Longworths' and their son's family, and the hostility of Victoria Emerson for Lincoln serving as a wall between them and their daughter, Lincoln can, with feelings of great consternation, envision dreadful holiday celebrations forthcoming in view of the season's traditional emphasis on "family."

He carefully studied the two-toned colored capsule that he rolled over and over in his fingers. He wondered how it worked; what the narcotic inside the little plastic tube did to the nerves and blood vessels inside his brain to stop the jabbing pain in his eye, to take away the flashing colored lights, to stem the flood of nausea that welled up in his stomach. He didn't really care; he just knew it worked.

He popped the pill, washed it down with a swallow of water, and leaned back against the pillow propped up against the headboard of his bed. Lying there in his room as quiet as a tomb, he stared into the darkness. He thought of Ashley. Even the love of his darling Ashley couldn't drive away the pain or the demons of depression, but the drugs could, at least temporarily.

His thoughts of trying to make sense of recent events and what to him was irrational behavior on the part of seemingly intelligent people got to be a mixture of himself and the downers talking. The bootleg gang, for example, chose to set up an illegal operation to produce and distribute a product to people that could possibly kill them, support it with violence, and willingly defend it with risk of life and limb, all to the detriment of society. Why not invest their knowledge, expertise, and energy in constructive enterprises?

And, then there were the Longworths and Armstrongs. Why could they not see that their obstinacy in not accepting their children's choices of mates was devastating their families? Were their generations-old social traditions really that important that they were willing to risk losing family rather than to make some concessions and simply accept people as people? Finally, Lincoln wrestled with the idea that perhaps it's not logical to try to figure out whether humans are logical or not. The drugs finally won out and Lincoln tripped off to La La Land.

A few hours later, he was awakened by someone shaking him into a state of semi-consciousness and the sound of a voice that seemed somewhat distant and unearthly.

"Man, you're really zonked out this morning," said Ashley, kissing him on the head.

"Yeah! I guess I am," he replied, shaking the cobwebs from his head.

"You have another headache?" she asked, eyeing the bottle of pills on the nightstand.

"Yeah. It's gone, but you're right. I'm really zoned out now," he answered, rubbing his eyes.

"What are you doing here?" he asked.

"I wanted to talk with you about something."

"If it's about your mother, I think we've talked that horse to death."

"You're right about that and nothing's going to change, at least for a long time," agreed Ashley.

"Any brilliant ideas about how we proceed from here?" he asked.

They sat in the middle of Lincoln's bed Indian-style, nose-to-nose, with legs wrapped around one another.

"Do you *really* love me as you've said you do?" she softly asked.

"More than anything in the world," he whispered. "Do you *really* love me?" he asked in return.

"More than anything in the world," she whispered.

"Then let's do it," Ashley said firmly.

"Are you sure?" Lincoln asked

"You won't have to handcuff me, Deputy Crockett!"

"Then let's do it," affirmed Lincoln.

They locked lips in a long, slow kiss.

Chapter 79

For a town that had historically lacked for excitement like the Sahara Desert lacks for rain, with the Colonel Browning carnival fiasco, the Crockett family tragedy, the Battle of the Sawmill, and three murders, 1965 was sure to be a banner year for Coldwater. The feelings of exhilaration that had surrounded these events were beginning to lose some of their gratification, however repercussions from the fallout of these unfortunate incidents were not only taking the luster off them but were also slowly transforming the general mood of the community into one of uneasiness and concern. Seeds of worry were budding that something dark and sinister might be taking hold in their beloved peaceful community, and their concerns were not altogether unfounded. That was especially true for two particular families; for them, the worst was yet to come.

In spite of his son's debilitating war wounds and his choice of an unpedigreed girl with whom to frolic in connubial bliss, Leland Longworth had a skip in his step and a spark in his spirit as he entered the house in midafternoon. After all, it was the day before Thanksgiving, one of his favorite holidays, and tomorrow he and the family would share a big thanksgiving lunch with friends and watch some football on TV. He was also of good cheer for another reason. He had finished his Christmas shopping ahead of time and had made it a point to arrive home in advance of the rest of the family to allow him sufficient time to seek out a hiding place for the gifts he clutched underarm, and he knew just the place.

He rummaged through the storage room above the garage to find a suitable spot for he knew Cora Sue never came up there, or so he thought. Rearranging some junk and unstacking a few boxes to make room, he was surprised when he uncovered an old trunk, which to his recollection, he had never seen before. His curiosity piqued, he tried to open the chest only to find it locked. Noticing a key hanging on a nearby nail, he decided to give it a try; it worked.

Unlocking the trunk and opening the lid, what to his wondering eyes did appear but stacks of neatly bound one-hundred-dollar bills arranged in rows. Each stack was bound and labeled "LW"

Who is LW? he wondered.

In the back of the box under a stack of bills lay a pearl-handled derringer that, upon close inspection, appeared to have been recently fired. Leland was dumbstruck.

"Holy Cow!" he exclaimed.

He thought, *Where the hell did this come from?*

He didn't put it there, so it must have been Cora Sue. But, where did she get it? And what about the gun? He did have a gun like that registered to him, but he hadn't seen it in years. Where did she get it? Too many questions!

Thoughts of the moonshine ring, Dalton Jackson killed, shot with a small gun, suddenly crossed his mind. He got a bad feeling in his stomach. She had been spending a lot of money on clothes and jewelry in recent months, and that new car! But, no! That was too ludicrous to even consider. Surely even a dumb broad like Cora Sue was smarter than to get involved in something like that and most assuredly incapable of killing someone. No, there had to be some reasonable explanation.

Chapter 80

In the Longworth's dining room the table was laid out with Cora Sue's finest dinner service and spread with all the food stuffs of a traditional Thanksgiving meal. Decorations, resplendent in fall colors, adorned the house and holiday music played in the background, enhancing the festive atmosphere the Armstrongs and Longworths so customarily experienced at their annual shared Thanksgiving lunch; however, this year it would take a bit more than decorations, music, and a turkey on the table to relieve the tension that hung like a shroud over the occasion due to the occupant of one new seat at the dinner table: the Millie and very pregnant wife of Montgomery.

The Emersons and Longworths, along with Montgomery and Amanda, took their places around the table. Leland stood and offered the blessing and began carving the turkey while Cora Sue filled everyone's wine glass. The atmosphere was tense but polite, not the relaxed, lighthearted bantering and holiday talk that normally filled the room.

"Where's Ashley?" asked Montgomery, "I thought she was going to be joining us today."

"She's late as usual," answered her father.

"She left earlier, said she had something to do. She promised that she would be back by lunch time."

"As you can see she isn't here," said Victoria, "so we'll just start without her."

"I'm sure she's gone to see 'that boy,'" she continued, "I wish Emerson would take her car away so she would have to stay home."

"Well, he has transportation himself now," replied Emerson.

"That may be true, but we could forbid his coming to the house," she retorted.

Just then the sound of the front door opening was heard followed by a small commotion in the foyer. Momentarily, Ashley entered the dining room with Lincoln in tow, making excuses for their tardiness and asking for another place to be set for Lincoln beside her at the table. Everyone was surprised at Lincoln's presence and Ashley's boldness.

Victoria was outraged at her daughter's brashness but attempted to remain civil.

"My dear, we weren't expecting to have or prepared for guests today," she seethed through clenched teeth. "This was only to be a family get-together." Her face turned as red as the wine in the carafe she held in her trembling hands.

"Oh, that's just fine then mother because Lincoln is family now," glowed Ashley.

A pin dropping on the carpet could have been heard as silence flooded the room. Everyone froze as all eyes fixed upon Lincoln, who looked as if he was looking down the barrel of a gun.

"What do you mean 'he's family?'" asked her father, breaking the quiet.

"Oh! Lincoln and I are married. Actually for a few weeks now, by a justice of the peace over in Central City," pronounced Ashley.

The only sound to be heard was the breaking of glass when the wine carafe Victoria had been holding hit the floor. She was as white as if all the blood had drained out of her body and had to grab hold of her husband's chair to maintain her balance.

"Married!" exclaimed her father.

"Now, why did you go and do a fool thing like that?" he stormed.

"This is your fault," fumed Victoria, shaking her finger at Lincoln, "and, well, we'll just have it annulled."

"'Fraid not Mom. I'm eighteen and can legally do whatever I choose."

"Mr. and Mrs. Emerson," said Lincoln, "let me assure you that Ashley is going to continue with college and get her degree just as she…and you…have always planned."

"But dear, you didn't have the wedding we always planned," said her mother, tearfully.

"Mother, would I be anymore married?"

While Montgomery and Amanda congratulated the newlyweds, the two pairs of parents just sat there shaking their heads in wonderment. They just couldn't understand what was happening to their families in what appeared to them to be a helter-skelter world.

"Now, now, Mother. Everything's going to be okay. Besides, you wouldn't want your grandchild to be a bastard child would you? No father and all that."

"What do you mean my *grandchild*?"

"Because you and daddy will be grandparents when I get pregnant!"

"Pregnant!" exclaimed her father again.

"Now how's that going to happen?" he stormed.

"Oh! The regular way Daddy. It won't be a virgin birth. Oh! By the way," added Ashley, taking Lincoln by the arm, "you may address me now by my husband's name, Mrs. Crockett."

"Now really everyone, don't you just think that my husband looks quite official in his police uniform?" she bragged.

Victoria's eyes widened in disbelief. Every muscle in her body stiffened and shook as if struck by the palsy. Her face glowed blood red.

From the perspective of the young couples, the 1960s are both a time of uncertainty and challenges, as well as a time fostering unprecedented change, resulting in the opening of doors of opportunity that, heretofore, never existed. From the perspective of their parents, however, the changing landscape is viewed as rebellion against the status quo and an attack on the traditions and social fabric that has defined American society for three-hundred years. One sees their world rising; the other sees their world crumbling.

Later that afternoon the dinner table still lay as it had before noon, laden with nature's bounty untouched by human hands. The Armstrongs had departed the scene in a huff with Victoria distraught and in tears and Emerson mumbling something about wishing the entire Crockett clan had been killed at the Alamo. The two young couples retreated to the sunroom where Ashley scrunched up on a love seat next to Lincoln, whose mind, hijacked by a bout of depression, watched blankly through the window as a paper cup bounced topsy-turvy across the lawn by gusts of wind. Amanda and Montgomery sat side by side, she in a side chair and Montgomery in his wheelchair. They relaxed, sharing stories and getting up to date on each other's situations. It was the first time they had been alone to mull over old times and talk about the future since Montgomery's return from Nam. They couldn't hear the confrontation that was going on the far side of the house the library.

"My money! Why are you accusing me of squirreling away money in a trunk in the garage?" chided an irritated Cora Sue. I should be asking you. You're the big businessman!"

"Cora Sue, you know as well as I that it's not mine. I guess I know now how you've been paying for all the expensive clothes and jewelry you've been wearing recently, and that new car in the garage. But, where did it come from? How did you get it?" responded Leland.

Cora Sue's demeanor changed. She turned toward her husband with an indignant look on her face and waltzed toward him with hands on hips, stopping a step short of him.

"In the first place, husband dear, let's just say I've become affiliated with a group of, you might say, entrepreneurs, in a sort of business venture that has been quite profitable," she said coyly. In the second place, it's really none of your business," she said smartly. "In the third place," she said with a devilish grin, "you wouldn't give a damn anyway, would ya darlin'?" as she stroked him under the chin and turned away.

"For heaven's sake woman, tell me you haven't been messed up with Dalton Jackson and that bunch."

"Ya know, that Dalton was a man who really knew how to satisfy a woman," she teased, licking her lips, "but, that's something you wouldn't know about anymore, would ya dear husband," she taunted.

"Damn you, bitch, I ought to...."

"You ought to *what*?" Cora Sue screamed. "You don't have the balls to do anything."

"Did you kill Dalton," asked Leland, "with this?" He pulled the derringer from his pocket and showed it to her.

"Why, Leland, do you think I could do such a dreadful thing?"

She admitted that Dalton was her only connection to the bootlegging gang and with him out of the way, her secret was safe. But now, Leland had become another loophole that would have to be closed.

"Now you wouldn't want your children's mother to go to jail and disgrace the family name would you? If not, you best join me in safeguarding the secret. Hmmm."

"Cora Sue, how could you!" shouted an angry Leland, shoving the gun in her face. "I could shoot you."

Cora Sue immediately backed up against the wall and began screaming.

The two young couples, hearing Cora Sue's screams from the sunroom, came rushing into the room.

"What's going on? What's wrong?" asked Lincoln.

"Montgomery, Montgomery, your father's threatening to shoot me...to kill me," sobbed his mother.

"No, I'm not," he pleaded, trying to hide the gun in his hand (which everyone was staring at).

"Yes, he just admitted to me that he killed Dalton Jackson and has been a member of that awful moonshine gang that was broken up. He's got a big stash of money stored in a trunk in the garage and everything," she said in phony tears.

"But that's not the way it was. She's turning it all around to make it sound like it was me," pleaded Leland.

"Give me the gun Mr. Longworth," said Lincoln, reaching his hand out to Leland.

Leland looked down, almost absent-mindedly at the small pistol in his hand and then surrendered it to Lincoln.

"Mr. Longworth, I'm going to have to place you under arrest for suspicion of murder and take you down to the station."

Leland said nothing as Deputy Crockett handcuffed him and led him out of the house.

The others just watched in disbelief.

"I'll drive you since we came in my car," offered Ashley.

"Thanks. I'll call the Sheriff and ask him to meet us there."

"I'm sorry, Montgomery," said Lincoln, "we'll get this all sorted out later.

As he passed, Cora Sue turned her head toward her husband and blew him a kiss through pursed lips which melted into a wicked smile.

Chapter 81

The disdain that Victoria Armstrong held for Millies, in general, and for Lincoln Crockett, specifically, could not allow her to entertain the thought of a Millie even crossing the threshold to her home, let alone having one take up residency within walls where the elite of society had rubbed shoulders. Even more repugnant were the thoughts of that Millie wallowing in sexual lust with her daughter a matter of only a few feet down the hallway from her own bedroom.

So, finding themselves denied occupancy in the Big House, the "mixed" couple found themselves relegated to Lincoln's small one-room "apartment" (if it could be called that) at the Lacy Hotel. Her parents had also repossessed Ashley's car, which only served to drive the wedge of division in their relationships even deeper. Miss Jessie had maintained her support for Lincoln through all his ups and downs and continued that support now for Ashley and him as a couple.

It was getting late, and the only light in the hotel lobby was moonlight spilling through the windows illuminating here and casting shadows there throughout the yuletide-decorated room. The room was vacant except for Lincoln and Ashley engaged in conversation when they heard a commotion at the front door. It was Miss Jessie returning from a short holiday trip, fumbling with keys and suitcases and trying to get in. She was a bit startled when they appeared at her side to offer assistance.

"Well, if it's not Coldwater's own Bonnie and Clyde. You two have certainly become the brunt of rumors," stated Miss Jessie, matter-of-factly.

They looked a bit puzzled.

"Oh! Bam Bam brought me up to date on all the local goings on during the ride over here from the train station."

They smiled knowingly.

"That is a fact! But, if people weren't so dogmatic in their opinions things wouldn't have to be this way," Lincoln said, shaking his head.

"You're not going to overnight change a way of thinking that's been drilled into people's heads for generations," deduced Miss Jessie.

"Given that announcing a couple of weeks ago that we were married caused enough anxiety attacks, the next bombshell will probably result in weeping and wailing, etc.," said Ashley.

"I bet I can just about guess what that bombshell is," said Miss Jessie.

Nodding their heads in the affirmative, Lincoln said, "Ashley's pregnant."

"We didn't mean to get pregnant now," frowned Ashley,

"It's my fault," she said shrugging her shoulders. I missed a couple of pills."

"Well, Christmas will be coming up in a little more than a month. Maybe they'll have had time to get used to the idea by then," said Miss Jessie.

"If we receive an invitation to Christmas dinner or any other activity related to the day, it will probably come at the insistence of Daddy. So, we'll wait and see. If not, we'll just have our own little Christmas celebration," answered Ashley. "Right?" she said, looking at Lincoln.

"Right!" he answered.

Suddenly, their *tête-à-tête* was interrupted by a noise in the back of the hotel and then, without warning, the shock of the lobby lights bursting into full illumination jolted them to their feet.

Yancy Dupree stood with his hands on his hips and smiled as he surveyed the place.

Lincoln went to check out the commotion in the back.

"Yancy, I told you to never show your face around here again," Miss Jessie spit out,

"And I told you that the Sugarman collects his debts, and you owe me little lady!" he fired back.

"You see, I got plans for this place."

Lincoln came rushing back into the room returning from his investigation in the back of the hotel.

"Miss Jessie, do you know what's going on back there?

"Obviously not!"

"Well now. Who's this boy scout?" asked Yancy, sarcastically.

"I'm Sheriff Cassidy's new deputy," answered Lincoln turning to face Yancy.

Turning back toward Miss Jessie he continued, "They're unloading a van filled with slot machines and other gambling paraphernalia and moving it upstairs."

"They're what!" she screamed, almost bursting an artery.

"Oh, it's just some of my, or should I say our, business equipment," said Yancy.

"*Business equipment*," mocked Miss Jessie.

"That's right. We're going to renovate those three rooms upstairs and put them to a much more productive use. Just imagine it. A mini Las Vegas casino," bragged Yancy, like an expectant father over a new child.

"Like hell you say. Over my dead body, you sewer rat," defied Miss Jessie.

"Well, that can be arranged if need be," snarled Yancy.

At that threat, stepping out of the shadows and making a move toward the villain was the ever-present Bam Bam.

"Call off your dog Dixie before he gets hurt," warned Yancy, motioning back over his shoulder with a flick of his thumb.

There stood one of his goons holding one side of his jacket open displaying a handgun that looked more like a toy cannon.

"But, hey, let's not go there. Let's make this a cozy little family venture.

"I won't let you get away with it Sugar. I'll have the law on you. Gambling's illegal here."

"Now who you gonna call, Dixie? All your old cronies are either dead or in jail. And what's this Boy Scout here and that green-behind-the-ears new Sheriff, gonna do against my boys who are packing some serious fire power" said Yancy, looking at Miss Jessie with a taunting smile. All along, Lincoln and Ashley had been standing to the side observing this exchange between the two rivals. Lincoln moved to Jessica's side as her body stiffened, trembling with anger. He thought if she had a gun, she'd shoot him right then and there. But, Yancy held all the cards, a full house, and Miss Jessica was out of aces unless she had one hidden up her sleeve somewhere. Lincoln knew that even with a larger police force than Sheriff Cassidy's it was going to be a formidable task dislodging this nest of hoods from town.

Chapter 82

December, 1965

In a town the size of Coldwater, trying to keep something secret is like trying to hide a bonfire in the forest at midnight. It's just a matter of time until it's seen, and when it gets out of control, it spreads like wildfire, and one was ablaze in Coldwater.

Most folks had hardly finished their pumpkin pie before the chatter bugs were once again busier than bees on caffeine spreading the latest news, rumors, and hearsay concerning the two biggest bombshells to be dropped since Hiroshima and Nagasaki. On the trials and tribulations of the Armstrongs and Longworths, most people (in Milltown) seemed to care less if the scuttlebutt being bandied about was fact or fiction; it was about Ridgers! Scandal was rocking the elite on the north side of the tracks. Folks on the south side were loving it.

During the month between Thanksgiving and Christmas, Leland Longworth had first been charged with the murder of Dalton Jackson, freed on bail, and awaited trial sometime after the holidays. His family and friends were, as was the public in general, less stunned by the temperament of the long-time community leader to commit murder than they were by his apparent willingness to unite with a loathsome pack of social inferiors in such a vile enterprise as the manufacture of illegal spirits. If others were stunned, Leland was dumbfounded! Distraught, he wandered about trying to figure out how he had from one day to the next fallen from business man to felon and perplexed as to why the person he'd been married to for umpteen years could have evolved into a gun moll and framed him for the death of a man that she coldly shot to cover her own ass in said enterprise. Well, Leland figured, she at least let him off easier than she did old Dalton!

As for Cora Sue, she had kept quiet, neither denying nor admitting anything. admitting nothing. She simply went about refusing to acknowledge the whole affair, probably on the advice of her attorney. She and Leland had agreed to remain together and continue life as usual and do so with proper decorum even though in private the two of them hardly spoke.

As it would turn out, the Black Widow's trap was sabotaged by her own little fingers. The fingerprints of both her and Dalton Jackson would be identified on the paper strips labeled "LW" that bound the stacks of ill-gained money in the trunk she had stored away at home. This evidence, in conjunction with said fingerprints, also identified on the murder weapon proved to be the lady's damnation and her spouse's salvation. In addition, payoff records found in Dalton Jackson's possession contained entries referring to LW as *Longworth* and Longworth as *she,* would prove more than sufficient evidence for a jury to send Mrs. Longworth to the slammer for a long time.

At the Longworth residence

Jonas Simpson and Leland Longworth rested in soft leather chairs in Leland's den, alternating between conversing and watching the crackling fire in the fireplace. The conversing primarily consisted of Leland baring his soul and Doc attentively listening.

"Doc, I've heard it said…don't know by who…that you should always be prepared, for you never know how life will turn out," said Leland, a little slow and deliberate. The alcohol from the fifth of Jack Daniels whiskey he had been sipping was beginning to make contact with his brain.

"Yes, I suppose that's true. We never know what tomorrow holds," replied Doc Simpson, sitting in a leather chair watching the crackling fire in the fireplace.

"You know, Doc, I've worked all my life to have a successful business, to raise my family, have a good retirement, leave a good legacy, and pass on to my reward in peace."
Leland stands, takes another swig of whiskey, and walks about waving his arms.

"But look how it's turned out! My son can't take over the family business because he's a cripple. He's married to a Millie. My wife's an adulteress, a criminal, and a murderess who will probably spend the rest of her life in prison…or worse! My retirement's ruined and our family name has been disgraced, an here just two weeks or so before Crismus…what kinda Crismus is that? Doctor Simpson, hic, how can anybody be per…per…PERpared for all that?" he said leaning down nearly in Doc's face.

"Yes, Leland, one could say that you've had a pretty bad run of luck lately, but, you're not going to find any answers in that bottle you're holding," cautioned Doc.

"Yeah! You're are smart man. That's why I pre-sha-nate...ugh...appreciate you coming over here tonight and talking to me...an...an giving me some advice, hic," wept Leland as he collapsed into a chair adjacent to the doctor.

"Well, Leland, I don't know that there's much advice I can give you about your family's current predicaments, but first of all, let's get rid of the booze."

Doc took the bottle from Leland, poured out the remaining contents, and trashed the bottle.

"You know, Leland, I would have thought you would have been seeking advice from Emerson Armstrong. After all, he seems to be your best friend."

"You're right, and I have. Emerson and I have had a very close relationship through the years. He paid my bail you know!"

"No, I didn't know."

"We've shared many personal things with one another. Some things we later maybe wished we hadn't...especially old Emerson."

"Is that right?" smiled Doc.

"Right! I can't really bother Emerson with my problems; he's got plenty of his own right now. You know his girl married that Millie boy and to complicate things, she's pregnant, and that's causing his family a world of worry just like mine."

"Yes. It seems that morals are not the same as they used to be with the younger generation," commented Doc.

"Well, you can't say much more for some older folks either," said Leland.

"Like Emerson, he's got secrets, and a big one, too," added Leland shaking his head.

"I guess most everyone has some skeletons hidden in his closet," said Doc.

"You could be right, Doc, but Emerson's got one that would shake this town."

"That so?"

Leland moved up close to Doc as if there was someone around that might hear him.

"There was something happened about nineteen years ago that only he and one other person know about. That is, until one night about five or so years ago when he and I were playing cards late and both had a little too much to drink and he got a little loose-lipped and told me about it. I'm sure you remember back at that time when Miss Jessie got pregnant and said it was some old boyfriend who done the deed, then rode off into the sunset leaving her holding the bag as it were."

"Yes, something like that," nodded Doc.

"Well, old Emerson confessed to me that the story Miss Jessie told wasn't true. He said that he and Miss Jessie had a one-night stand and that she got pregnant as a result. According to him, he is the father of Miss Jessie's child and she made up that story to protect him and not cause a scandal."

"Leland," Doc grabbed him by the shoulders and looked him in the eye, "was Emerson just bragging or was he telling the truth?"

"Oh, yes, he was telling the truth all right. When he realized what he had said he got very upset and swore me to secrecy. Told me if I ever told anyone he'd kill me…oh Lord, I just told you. Please Doc, don't tell him I told you, please."   "Don't worry, Leland. Your secret's safe with me. Leland, I've got to go. Something very important has just come up."

"But Doc!"

"I'm sorry to leave so abruptly, but I have to go.

On his way home from Leland's, the tale that Leland Longworth had told haunted Doctor Simpson as he played the words over and over in his mind. Was the tale just the manifestation of an alcoholic fantasy or the revelation of a dirty weekend under the influence of intoxicating spirits? The thought of it being true sent a wave of chills coursing through his body, the thought that he might have made a terrible mistake sometime in the past.

If you are right Mr. Longworth, this old town hasn't seen anything yet! Doc thought to himself.

Chapter 83

It was a picturesque setting on the outskirts of town where Jonas and Maggie Simpson lived in an old, white two-story frame house. That particular Sunday afternoon, just days before Christmas, was a beautiful but blustery one. Gusty winds, charged with a chill, stirred leaves shed by the now barren trees about in swirls of small wind devils beneath a bright blue sky dotted with puffy, white cumulus clouds. Inside the old farmhouse that had been in his family for four generations, Dr. Simpson stared nervously out the living room window. He hoped she would come as she had promised she would. The other four guests they had invited had already arrived and were being served tea in the parlor by Maggie and making small talk. Jonas decided to join them.

He had not been looking forward to this "meeting" he had called today with this group of individuals. On the contrary, he was facing it with a great deal of trepidation. The invitees were under the assumption they were simply attending a social function called by the Simpsons. It was just a week until Christmas, and the doctor had considered waiting until after the holidays since their lives had already been turned topsy-turvy, and what he was going to reveal to them today was going to have even greater dire consequences in their lives. He decided it was best to get it over with. Then, there came a knock at the door.

Dr. Simpson greeted Jessica Wingo at the front door and stowed her fur wrap in the hall closet, while Maggie led her into the parlor to a somewhat shocked group of guests. Maggie proceeded to introduce Miss Jessie to the others, all of whom were acquainted with one another, at least by name or reputation, if not personally. Besides Miss Jessie there were Lincoln and Ashley Crockett and Ashley's parents, Emerson and Victoria Armstrong, the latter couple seemingly annoyed at Miss Jessie's presence. After inviting everyone to be seated, Maggie addressed their visitors.

"By the looks on your faces, I'm sure you're all wondering why the doctor and I have invited you here today. Due to some recent events that have taken place, we…well…we feel there are some things you need to know…some important information that you need to have. With that, I'm going to let Doc take over."

Everyone sat up alertly in their chairs, staring questioningly, first at Maggie, then at Doc, then at one another.

Dr. Simpson began, "There are some things that happened many years ago in the lives of two people in this room that have been held innocently in confidence all this time by Maggie and me; however, due to a recent development involving two individuals in this room, plus a piece of information from the past that was unintentionally disclosed to me, we believe that it would be in the best interest of all parties concerned to have all this information revealed at this time. This is due to the possibility that a serious situation could develop for certain ones in the near future. Doing so will have untold consequences on personal relationships within the family."

The group looked more puzzled than ever.

"Doctor Simpson," said Emerson, "you're sounding very mysterious. I can't imagine what you could be getting at that could involve all of us."

"Just be patient with me Mr. Armstrong. You'll see in just a few minutes. I'm trying to take this slow and easy." He continued, "However, in bringing these facts to light will require of me the breaking of a promise I made to someone, the confession of an action I took and have held in confidence for many years, and the disclosure of information which, by its very nature, will, as I said, forever change the lives and relationships of all of you. How your lives *are* affected by what you hear today will depend upon how you receive and respond to the information you are about to receive."

The old doctor added with heartfelt sincerity, "Maggie and I have discussed at length whether or not to follow through with these revelations and I've done much soul-searching concerning the matter. We've decided that, in the long run, the truth is the best course of action even at the risk of causing disharmony. So, may you and God forgive me."

"First, I want to transport you back several years in time and describe to you an incident that occurred, whether by coincidence or by fate, when the lives of two women, two babies, a doctor and a nurse intersected one cold winter night in December, 1945. I'm going to spare you the details and just give you the main points. I remember the night well; it was the year we were socked in for a week by the big snowstorm. Maggie and I were in bed when the phone woke us from a sound sleep in the middle of the night. Two women called about the same time, both in labor."

"The first woman got to the clinic about the same time we did and the second a few minutes later. The first woman was giving her baby up for adoption, and we were going to take care of it that night and call the adoptive parents the next day. Her delivery went fine and she had a healthy baby boy. The second woman was a different story, however."

"She had not been a healthy lady and had had a difficult pregnancy. She did not look good when she came into the clinic, had a difficult time, and her baby was stillborn. Maggie and I felt so sorry for them; they had wanted a baby so badly. Well, for right or wrong, good or bad, we made a decision. We gave the baby that woman Number One had delivered to Woman Number Two and told the adoptive couple that the baby they were going to get was the stillborn baby."

A gasp followed by the shattering of china echoed through the room, interrupting the serene ambiance created by Dr. Simpson's mesmerizing narrative. The noise jolted everyone to attention. A startled Miss Jessie had lost her grasp of the delicate teacup and saucer which had shattered on the shiny hardwood floor.

After apologizing for the broken cup and saucer, Miss Jessie looked straight at the doctor.

"Doctor Simpson, how far do you intend on going with this story?" she asked, sensing something personal. "Are you going to reveal the identities of these women?" she continued, looking Dr. Simpson squarely in the eye, speaking in a controlled but slightly shaky voice.

"Yes, that's the objective, Ms. Wingo," answered the doctor squinting at her over the eyeglasses drooping down at the end of his nose, "If I could have your permission to continue?" he said with a pleading tone to his voice.

"Well, that's all fine and good I suppose," interrupted Victoria "and I admit it is an interesting little tale of local lore that you're imparting here Doctor Simpson, but I can't imagine that any seedy affair of this nature could involve anyone in our family."

"I assure you madam, if you'll just endure for a few more minutes everything will be made clear to one and all," promised the doctor. "You shall know the truth and the truth shall make you free, *if* you let it," he added. "Yes, as Ms. Wingo anticipated, I will now reveal the identities of the actual players in this 'affair,' as Mrs. Armstrong refers to it, along with rest of the story. First, Patient Number One was Miss Jessica Wingo."

Every head in the room immediately whirled in Miss Jessie's direction. Every eye examined her like a germ under a microscope, and the looks on their faces exhibiting everything from surprise, to shock, to alarm.

"Well, I could have guessed!" offered Victoria in her haughty, indignant way with eyebrows vaulted like the golden arches at McDonald's.

"Listen! You self-righteous..." lashed out a fuming Miss Jessie, stopping in midsentence while jumping to her feet and staring daggers at Victoria. "Your family may not be as immune from dirt as you think they are, Miss High and Mighty." Miss Jessie pointed her finger at Dr. Simpson and said, "Doc, you better make sure you know where you're going with this," then turned to everyone in the room and stated, "What's said in this room today had better stay in this room."

"Okay, Jessica, this is going to turn out okay, you'll see," assured Doc. "Now, let me continue. Patient Number Two was Mrs. Ina Crockett."

"My mother!" spoke up Lincoln, wondering how his mother could be the one in Doc's tale.

The others had the same questioning look on their faces.

Doc continued, "Mrs. Crockett never knew that the baby boy she came home with from the clinic was not her natural born son, who she raised as Lincoln Crockett, but was the baby boy born to Ms. Jessica Wingo."

Everyone just sat stunned and speechless in their chairs as if suddenly having been turned into pillars of salt. The silence was deafening.

Finally, Miss Jessie broke the silence, "You're telling me that Lincoln Crockett is my...my SON!" whispered Miss Jessie.

"That's correct," affirmed Dr. Simpson.

"And you're telling *me*," inquired Lincoln, "that Miss Jessie is *my* MOTHER!"

"Correct again," nodded the doctor.

Everyone was too dumbfounded to speak.

Miss Jessie and Lincoln just looked at each other for a long moment when suddenly Miss Jessie uttered an, "Oh!" and placed the fingers of her right hand over her mouth as her eyes widened. Her reaction held a double meaning, the second of which no one there could have imagined. That is, with one exception. Lincoln, having no difficulty cluing into her reaction, sensed a feeling of nausea welling up inside him. There was that night on the occasion of his nineteenth birthday when they had shared Miss Jessie's bed, unknown to them at the time, in an incestuous relationship.

After an awkward minute or two had passed, Victoria spoke up. "Well Dr. Simpson, this is all very touching and all. You've reunited a long-lost mother and son and found solace for your soul for something you feel was a regrettable mistake on your part many years ago. But, I don't see how this involves our family, so I suppose all's well that ends well."

"Yes, Dr. Simpson, I don't see that revealing what you have has served any purpose but to embarrass Lincoln and Miss Wingo. Just think, if you hadn't done what you did, Lincoln would have grown up some place else, we would never have met and wouldn't be together today," said Ashley.

"That's right!" remembered Victoria.

"Doctor, it's your fault that that boy is here."

"Hey! That's right Doc!" fumed Lincoln, "Why did you condemn me to a life in Milltown? To be a 'Millie' when I could have been with this other couple and lived someplace else and had a better life. Where did they live?"

"But Linc," reminded Ashley, "if you had, we would never have met. We wouldn't be together today," reasoned Ashley.

"See Doctor Simpson, everything would be fine in our home if you would have left well enough alone," said Victoria, pointing a finger his way.

"But everyone just wait a minute. There's something else…something important," said Doc.

"You're right about one thing, Ashley. There are two primary reasons I've called you all here today. One is because you and Lincoln *are* together. The second is because of Lincoln's father. He's the key player in this little drama."

"Well, who is my father anyway?" asked Lincoln.

"There are two people here…besides Maggie and me…who know. Should I reveal the name or would someone like to volunteer?"

"Oh, hell, Emerson, there's only two men here and it wasn't Dr. Simpson. You might as well face the music," spoke up Miss Jessie turning to Emerson Armstrong.

Emerson Armstrong had seen the writing on the wall; there was no way out.

"Emerson, what's she talking about?" said Victoria quizzically.

"It's true," confessed Emerson reluctantly, "we had a short affair many years ago and…." Emerson threw his hands up into the air in a gesture of helplessness.

"*Emerson*! You bastard! How could you? With this whore?" shouted Victoria.

Dr. Simpson called for calmness. "Several issues have been raised," he said, "but, do you all see the bigger problem now?"

It suddenly became clear to Lincoln as he looked at Emerson Armstrong and then Ashley.

"Yes," blurted out Lincoln, "Ashley and I have the same father. We're brother and sister."

Ashley's mouth fell open and her eyes opened wide in disbelief.

So, did everyone else's.

"You're actually *half* brother and sister," corrected Dr. Simpson, "and Ashley is pregnant."

"Oh, my G…" was all that came out of Victoria Armstrong's mouth as she collapsed into a crumpled heap on the floor.

Chapter 84

He parked the Plymouth at Delaney's service station, walked to the corner, and turned down Mill Street. He wanted to duplicate the walk home from school that he had followed so many times as a kid. A block after turning right on MacAnally it came into view: that little white house. That house, the very sight of which used to strike terror in his heart now seemed, somehow, sort of sad looking. That house that could appear as a living, breathing monster that could devour and consume, now appeared a benign pile of bricks, boards, and nails embodying a humble abode.

Lincoln hadn't seen his parents' old house since he'd been evicted, and apparently, Ike Butler hadn't been able to rent it, yet, for it sat empty. In fact, for whatever reason, it was closed up. He approached cautiously, perhaps more from feelings of past experience than for any current concerns of retribution from this harmless old place. He walked slowly and deliberately around the house surveying the yard and remembering games he used to play there.

Venturing up the steps, he hesitated in front of the back door and stared at that door: that door that he had stood by so many nights while his parents fought, that door whose doorknob he had clutched in a death grip like a life preserver night after night when he thought he might die, that door that had provided him with his only means of escape from the screaming, cursing, fighting, and fear that permeated this dwelling. He asked himself, *Do I dare enter and face my demons, or do I turn and flee?*

He decided that he must finish what he had begun if he was to ever exorcise the demons that tormented his soul, if he was to ever overcome the dark clouds of depression that engulfed his being, if he was to ever rid himself of the anxiety that gripped his body and scrambled his mind with nightmarish dreams that pushed him to the edge of the emotional abyss. Reluctantly, but with determination, he opened the door and boldly went where he had never gone before: back in time and space to face the devils from his past to vent a lifetime of anger, resentment, and frustration that had steamed within him like a pressure cooker.

Walking slowly and confidently across the dusty floor, one by one, he made a quick survey of each room before making his way back to the living room. All the while, a search was made for some evidence of the presence of dear old Mom and Dad, straining to hear some sounds of battle vibrating in the walls. "Well, where are you? Come out and face me! Your little boy's home!" he challenged. Nothing but silence. Then, turning back toward the hallway, he saw them.

The reincarnation of his parents in the form of two gray figures loomed hauntingly before him. "Well, how about a few war games for old time's sake?" he taunted sarcastically. "A little rumble to make the old walls shake! C'mon, start one of those knock-down-drag-outs you're so good at and scare the hell out of me like you did when I was a kid."

But the gray-faced specters just stood there expressionless and unresponsive as if under a spell. "What's the matter? Can you pick only on a defenseless kid? Afraid a man won't take that kind of crap off of you?"

His blood began to boil; adrenaline rushed through his body. That timid, thirteen-year-old boy cowering in the corner, now as a man, was breaking free of the shackles of intimidation, casting aside the commandment to honor thy father and mother, embracing the freedom to admit that Mom and Dad are not always right and good but are sometimes wrong and bad. He pointed an accusing finger in the direction of the two pathetic figures.

"You were sorry excuses for parents!" he proclaimed angrily.

"Instead of home being a sanctuary, a place of refuge, you turned it into a living hell, a place I hated to return to because of the fighting and tension, because you were here. All you could do was raise hell with one another and cause me to stand over there clinging to that damn door trembling in tears. And, worst of all, you didn't seem to give a damn! You were so caught up in your own little war to see or care what it was doing to anyone else."

The apparitions stood in stoic silence, unmoved by his tirade.

"Well, say something in your defense, if you have a defense" he petitioned.

But the pale figures remained shrouded in ghostly silence.

"Tell me specters, from where do you journey today to this place? From what eternal abode do you venture? The halls of heaven or the bowels of hell? Oh, you played the religious game for all it was worth, didn't you? You went to church on Sunday; you'd get all 'spiritual' in the services, cry and shout like good evangelicals, read the Bible and talk the talk. Then, come home and immerse yourselves in your hate fights and spite games Monday through Saturday, then back to church on Sunday to display your 'religion' to all the other fine, upstanding church members. Can you really sing 'Oh, how I love Jesus' on Sunday and hate each other the rest of the week? Can you really be filled with the Holy Spirit in the church and have such an unholy spirit in the home? Hypocrisy!"

By now, Lincoln was literally screaming. His head ached, and his body trembled as the rage poured from him like a dike had burst and the flood waters could no longer be held back.

"And, Daddy dearest, I've had nightmares about you trying to kill me, you son of a bitch!" He pounded his fists against the wall and repeated, "Why? Why? Why?" He whirled back toward his antagonists, but the apparitions had fled this earthly scene, faded back into another dimension unrestrained by the fetters of mortality.

"Come back and answer my questions!" he demanded. "Give defense to the charges that have been leveled against you! Yeah, hide behind the curtain of death, you cowards! That's a flimsy excuse" he added sarcastically, "so go back where you came from...I hope you're burning in hell!"

Amidst a deathly silence, standing in the darkness of the old house punctured by shafts of filtered sunlight through the half-covered windows, Lincoln slumped to his knees physically, emotionally, and mentally exhausted. After a few minutes of unwinding, he arose and walked slowly, filled with mixed emotions, out of the house and into the bright sunlight.

There on the back-porch steps, he sat, basking in the warmth of the noonday December sun. In his mind, he replayed the scene that had just played out inside the house. He rehashed the words of the scathing indictment he had just levied against his folks. He recalled not only the things he had said, but also the anger and hostility with which he had said them.

He thought it strange that he, on the one hand, felt some guilt and shame at what he had said and done. After all, we're supposed to "love our enemies" and "do unto others..." and all that. Yet, at the same time, it was like a great burden had been lifted from his shoulders. He felt the freedom inside of a bird that has been released from its cage."

In retrospect, Lincoln determined that perhaps he had judged his parents too harshly. There were many times when homelife was bad, and it had had a profound effect on him, but it wasn't always so. After all, they did raise him, gave him a home, clothe and feed him, and send him to school. Looking at things from a more balanced perspective, they, too, were raised very poor, had little or no education, survived the Great Depression, and lived a hard life. They probably only knew what they were raised to know and did only what they were raised to know how to do. They had a very simple view of life and the world, but that's the world they lived in and it was all they knew and never dreamed of anything beyond its borders, let alone sought anything beyond it. Given the times and circumstances of their lives, they probably did the best they could with what they were financially, physically, mentally, and emotionally equipped.

This was not to excuse the situation they created for him to live in, but he was gaining some understanding of where they had been in their lives, that it wasn't intentional, and that the devastating effects that the interpersonal conflicts of two unhappy people were having on another family member was beyond their comprehension, and with that understanding comes truth and "the truth can set you free."

He finally sees who and what his demons are and why they have driven him to the brink of insanity for most of his life. They're no longer mysterious and frightful because they are recognizable and can be dealt with one day at a time. Will he ever defeat them and win the war? It won't come quickly or easily. Will he be successful? Only time will tell!

Chapter 85

Sheriff Cassidy, Deputy Crockett, and Deputy Willard Williams, who had recently been added to the force, for the past couple of weeks had been brainstorming on strategies for dislodging the Sugarman gang from the Lacy Hotel without coming to any satisfactory plan of action. The main problem was how to apprehend the bad guys (which would most assuredly involve gunplay) without endangering the lives of the hotel guests. They needed some way to lure the culprits away from the hotel and engage them in the open. But how? the gang seldom left the place, at least as a group.

Deputy Williams, a big, robust fellow of thirty who lived a couple of miles outside of town on Lakeland Road, which was also in his routine patrol area, reported that the trio of felons had apparently acquired a taste for trout, as they had shown up at the Trout House Restaurant on Steelhead Lake every Friday night for the last three weeks for the big fish fry. He also added that this brotherhood of malefactors was traveling in one of the large white vans in which they had transported the gambling equipment. Since the route they used to and from the hotel and restaurant put them in no-man's land and out of danger to the public for a significant amount of time, they would be left in an indefensible position and vulnerable to a surprise attack. This could be the lucky break the good guys were looking for and one that could lead to the downfall of the bad guys.

Since the revelations had been made concerning the circumstances surrounding his birth and the identities of his parentage, Lincoln had been moody without much to say. He had other things on his mind, other fish to fry. Now, he saw everyone and everything in a different light. He wasn't so keen on exterminating the rats from the Lacy and saving Miss Jessie's place of business from being turned into gambling casino. He had his own agenda to pursue with this woman, his "mother."

"Anybody got any ideas with this new scenario of Sugarman's boys at the Trout House?" asked Sheriff Cassidy.

"Why should I risk my life to save the Lacy?" Lincoln grumbled.

"Because it's not just Miss Jessie's place," said Sheriff Cassidy, "and we can't let people like these get a foothold in the town or soon there'll be others and the community will be ruined."

"All for the better good, right?" countered Lincoln.

"That's right. Say, what's wrong with you?" questioned Clay, "This don't sound like you, and you've always been for doing the right thing."

"This crazy man has threatened Miss Wingo's life," added Deputy Williams, "and it's our duty to protect our citizens."

"Well, don't look now, but he's also threatened the Sheriff and me!" growled Lincoln, throwing a pencil across the office.

"Settle down, Lincoln, settle down!" ordered Clay calmly.

"I don't know what's bothering you, but you need to go home and get a good night's sleep. We'll start this again tomorrow."

"Yeah! I guess you're right," said Lincoln contritely. "I guess I'm just a little down right now," he said as he walked toward the office door. He stopped in the doorway and half turned. "Hey, I just had a brainstorm about this thing with the van and the back roads," said Lincoln. "I'll show you tomorrow and see what you think."

The next day they reviewed the plan and, lacking any better proposals, decided it might just be wild enough to work. Working out the details, they determined to put the scheme into action the following Friday night.

Friday Night

Sheriff Cassidy, dressed in plain clothes, had been sitting in the parking lot of the Trout House in a nondescript automobile watching the white van for some time. About 9:00 p.m., he went inside where he found the four targets of their trap at a corner table quietly hogging down platters of fish and pitchers of beer. He went to the pay phone, dialed the restaurant's phone number, and asked to speak to one of the four men at the corner table. One of them reluctantly took the call.

In a disguised excited voice the Sheriff spoke, "Hey, you better get back to the hotel. The Sheriff's trying to arrest your boss and he's in the hotel lobby threatening to shoot up the place."

"Who is this?" the big man demanded.

"Your boss said to come a runnin.'"

The Sheriff hung up the phone.

Sugarman's cavalry stampeded out of the Trout House, piled into the van, and sped onto the road like a dog with its tail on fire with the Sheriff in hot pursuit.

The Sheriff radioed ahead to Lincoln and Willard and let them know that the quarry was on its way and to put the trap in place. The trap was two, two-by-twelve-foot boards nailed together with rows of six-inch tire-eating spikes driven into them. When Lincoln and Willard got the word, they were to anchor those boards to the highway with large spikes at Mile Marker 5 on the downside of Two Mile Hill.

When Clay topped Two Mile Hill, not far behind the van he saw Mile Marker 5. He looked at his speedometer: 80 mph. The van was getting close. He slowed down. Then he saw the van start swerving.

Lincoln and Willard had a ringside seat on a bank above the highway. They could hear the sounds of tires exploding and the crunching of sheet metal against guardrails. They had an unobstructed view of the vehicle flip-flopping and barrel-rolling for fifty yards down the road while gouging bucket-sized divots in the asphalt. Doors flew open, windows smashed, and sheet metal twisted and turned as the vehicle careened wildly out of control before the demolished carcass of the van finally came to rest in a pine thicket. Unbelievably, two of the gunmen actually survived the carnage but were in no condition to resist.

"Well, I guess your plan worked, Lincoln," said the Sheriff.

"Yeah, I guess it did, didn't it?" he answered somewhat mournfully.

But, as with many plans, if something can go wrong, it will.

"But, now we have the head of the snake to get," reminded Willard.

"He doesn't know what has happened here yet, so we could go back to the hotel and go in friendly-like and just arrest him," said the Sheriff, "but..."

"But, we have a mess to clean up here first," Lincoln finished his sentence.

The next morning

"Well, I say good riddance. It's just too bad that the Sugarman wasn't with them," said Miss Jessie on hearing about the wreck of the van from Sheriff Cassidy.

"You know he's the one who murdered Marge Henderson," added Jessica.

"Can you prove it?"

"I don't know, but he confessed it to me."

"Well, he should be easier to corral now without his gang to back him up," said the Sheriff.

"Don't underestimate him. He left here so mad he couldn't tell left from right and swearing vengeance on the Coldwater police department," warned Miss Jessie.

Chapter 86

Noon Christmas Eve

"Oh, what a tangled web we weave…when first we practice to deceive," said Lincoln. "Ole Sir Walter sure hit that one on the head, didn't he," Lincoln asked as he cast a small rock out into the vast space of the abyss below the rim of the bluff on which he stood. Ashley followed the stone's flight until it disappeared from sight, listening for its echo moments later as it clanked on the rocks somewhere below.

"Do you remember the first time we came here?" Lincoln asked.

"Yes. There was a ferryboat here then. This time we had to borrow a boat."

"Do you remember something else about the first time?"

"Yes. You told me you loved me. It took me some time, but I finally came around."

"We showed 'em didn't we…you know…a Millie and a Ridger," he said.

"Yeah. We showed 'em. What were the odds?" she agreed.

"And now this! What are the odds of this happening?" he asked, wondering.

"It looks like the cards were just stacked against us. It just wasn't meant to be," said Ashley shrugging her shoulders.

"So, what if we *are* half brother and sister! Why can't we be together as long as we don't have children?" Lincoln argued.

"It just wouldn't be right. We'd be a big joke. People would make fun of us. We'd be outcasts in the community," reasoned Ashley.

"I wish Doc Simpson had just kept it all to himself," said Lincoln.

"In one way I do too, but he didn't, and we have to live with it."

"So, where do we go from here?" Lincoln asked dejectedly, as if he didn't know the inevitable.

"My mother has refused to grant my father any absolution for his unfaithfulness to her, even though it happened many years ago, not so much for the sin itself but because of the party with whom he committed it. So, she's going to divorce him. She doesn't wish to remain in Coldwater and live with the family's shame, so she's going to relocate near some of her relatives in South Carolina. She should be able to live quite nicely on the handsome settlement I'm sure she'll receive for her share of the family business."

"Linc, fate, it seems, has drawn us into a situation not of our own doing. Our dreams have been shattered, but let's try to make the best of it we can. Linc, I love you and I'll always love you and I hope you can go along with this plan for my sake and the baby's. I don't want to stay here for some of the same reasons my mother doesn't, and I can't stay here because you're here. So, I want us to get a divorce. The baby and I will go with mother to live in South Carolina. We'll say that the baby's father was killed in some sort of accident or something."

"Sounds like your mother's plan to me. Everything works out great for her, you, and the baby, and I get left out in the cold. I never get to see my own child and you'll wind up marrying some tennis-playing, socialite junior executive with a country club membership."

"Linc, I don't want it this way, but please try to put the baby and me first."

"You could stay with your dad and raise the baby here."

"If we can't live together, I can't live here…running into you all the time…I'd go crazy! Mother and I don't get along that well, but it's the best alternative, the only one, really."

"I suppose you're right," said Lincoln with a tone of defeat in his voice.

"Mother wants to go ahead and get away as soon as possible, wo we'll probably be leaving shortly after the new year," she said, hanging her head. "This is certainly no Christmas Eve like I've ever known…no Christmas celebration at all. It seems so strange." Ashley sadly remarked.

"Yeah, it will be just another passing day," answered Lincoln. "I know I don't have any Christmas spirit."

He stared long into the depths of the valley like a soldier who had just laid down his weapon in surrender awaiting a march to the gallows.

It was far too late to try and rearrange the deck chairs on the *Titanic*; that ship had long since sunk and Lincoln wished he had sunk with it. He inched closer to the edge of the rim. He wondered what it would feel like just to step out into empty space like that stone he had tossed a few minutes earlier and freefall forever.

"Lincoln! Come back from there," shouted Ashley, "You could fall!" as she ran toward him. "What were you doing?" she asked fretfully, trembling herself.

He looked at her blankly. "I don't...don't...I don't know," he stuttered.

"Let's go back down to town," said Ashley softly, taking him by the hand.

They looked at each other for a long moment. They knew it was the last time they would be together.

Later that day

Following his meeting with Ashley, once he was alone, Lincoln's head ached from trying to understand what, where, when, how, and why his life, that was showing promise, had suddenly train-wrecked. Finding that you're not who you think you are, that your family is not really your family, that people you know are not who you think them to be, and that you're married to your sister, all are freakish concepts to absorb. How can you trust in anything or anyone as real?

The attendees at "The Meeting" (as it would become known) at the residence of Dr. Simpson's that fateful day shortly before Christmas, 1965, made a pact that all discussions related to it would be held in strictest confidence.

As to be expected, there was much finger-pointing and blame-laying of fault for the anguish that, out of nowhere, had hit them as suddenly and without warning as a snowstorm in July. Victoria, of course, chose to lay guilt at the feet of everyone except her own. Even though there was room enough for all parties involved in the debacle to bear at least some measure of responsibility, all parties, to a person, were of one mind and accord that the primary source of blame for this unlikely muddle of events should be laid at the feet of Dr. Jonas Simpson. There was one exception, however, that being Miss Jessie who chose to keep the entire matter at arm's length. Even Dr. Simpson blamed himself for the grief that had been caused by his action taken nineteen years ago (although at the time he thought it was a good idea) and by his recent action to make it known what he did, believing it was necessary for the well-being of all concerned regardless of the consequences, even for himself.

[354]

Lincoln began to tremble, to shake all over. Breaking out in a cold sweat, he became engulfed in the deepest and darkest black cloud of depression he had ever known. Damn Dr. Simpson! He always thought Doc had been his friend, but Doc had betrayed him. Miss Jessie had betrayed him! Old man Armstrong had betrayed him! Everyone had betrayed him! The world had betrayed him! Life had betrayed him! But those three individuals were the primary players in their little conspiracy. He'd dealt with his adoptive parents, now he'd have to deal with them.

"Damn! Damn! Damn!" He pounded his fists against the wall.

The seething pressure cooker of anger that had been held at bay so long only by the bonds of depression were now on the verge of gushing forth unabated like an oil strike bursting from the bowels of the earth.

Chapter 87

New Year's Eve

In spite of a couple of early-season storms that blanketed Coldwater with several inches of snow and ice, the inclement weather and cold temperatures had not deterred holiday shoppers in their quest to locate and acquire the season's must-have toys and gadgets. The small police force had been kept as busy as a woodpecker on a rubber tree. From dealing with a rash of fender-benders and minor disturbances between irate holiday shoppers, Lincoln had not had an overabundance of time to give serious consideration as to the ramifications the eye-opening disclosures that had been made concerning family relationships that, heretofore, had been held in strictest confidence.

Up until the present time, Lincoln had been trying to understand a lifetime of discontent with parents. Now, it had turned out, his parents were more accurately his "adoptive" parents. In addition to that revelation, unforeseen circumstances had brought to the light of day that he was, in reality, the bastard son of two prominent Coldwater citizens. The identities of these two adulterers and the results of their night of carnal lust kept secret had proven to have had profound effects on several lives. For Lincoln, this was too convoluted a mess to deal with. How was he supposed to feel about these people? Relate to them? Live with them? What was his true identity?

It was early morning—New Year's Eve morning, to be exact. With all that had been going on, it seemed that the week between Christmas and New Year's had just slipped by unnoticed. The sun opened a bright sunny day to the world. Lincoln sat in his recliner sipping a cup of coffee and staring at the pistol lying on the table in front of him. One day this week, while going through some of his father's things, he had come upon a box that his father had kept on a closet shelf that he had all but forgotten about. Inside the box, he had found a mint-condition Colt .45 revolver that his father had inherited from his father before him, or so he claimed. Lincoln had only seen it a time or two and had never shot it.

Turning the weapon over and over in his hands, softly stroking the cold hard steel, he could almost feel the power it commanded. The wheels had been turning in his head since he found it. Fumbling with a box of cartridges, he dumped the contents on the coffee table in front of him, sending them scattering hither and yon across the floor. Taking one of the bullets in hand, he slowly and deliberately inserted it into an empty chamber in the cylinder and gave it a spin. He smiled a devious smile. Those people had to pay. Their lives had gone on without skipping a beat according to their own choosing, but they had determined his fate. No, they had to pay, and pay they would!

11:00 a.m. at the Armstrong House

In his office at home, which he and Victoria had agreed that he could use until everything was settled, they met: Emerson Armstrong and Lincoln Crockett, holders of whatever family titles one preferred to use. On the outside, a bright sun had melted the last vestiges of snow from the streets and warmed the chilly air, but on the inside, the mercury dipped low in the thermometer. Both men were noticeably uncomfortable and the atmosphere formal if not a bit frosty.

"Mr. Crockett, I agreed to meet with you here today for you to say whatever you have to say. We're alone in the house so say whatever's on your mind, although I really don't know what you could expect from me or what I could offer you at this point in our lives. What happened all those years ago happened and nothing is going to change that. Sure, a number of people are upset about the situation, several people's lives have been affected by it, but what's to do but accept the facts and go on with life."

"So, 'Daddy,'" said Lincoln sarcastically, "that's what I am, just a 'situation?'"

"What do you want, boy? Everyone to turn their lives upside down for you?" asked Emerson. "Yes, technically, we're father and son, bonded by DNA. But, in reality, we're no more related than a dog and cat. We're products of two different worlds and that's the way it will remain."

"Man, are you sure Ashley is yours? You're a bigger S.O.B. than I thought you were," said Lincoln.

With a scowl on his face, Lincoln moved forward within a step of Emerson, pulled out the six-shooter, and waved it in Emerson's face.

"Now just what do you think you're going to do with that?" said Emerson in a halfway jest.

"Why didn't you ask yourself what you were doing nineteen years ago when you were committing adultery with your whore?"

"Not very nice words to be calling your *mother.*?"

"What kind of mother gives her kid away?" countered Lincoln. "What do you think public reaction will be when I reveal the sexual tryst that occurred between two of the town's business leaders. Even though it was nearly two decades ago, it will be shocking to most and will provide fodder for the gossip lines for a long time."

"That will hurt you as much as anyone," reasoned Emerson, not wanting to see their "family" business dragged through the social public press.

"But, you see, the difference between me and the rest of you snobs is that I don't give a damn!" snarled Lincoln.

"Why you sorry…"

"No! Daddy dearest, you're the one who's going to be sorry when I blow your nuts off with this .45."

"Wha…" His words fell short. Gazing upon the expressionless face of Lincoln Crockett, he was drawn to his eyes; eyes that burned with a fire that made Emerson Armstrong's blood run cold.

"You are crazy!" said Emerson almost whispering.

"Crazy like a fox!"

At the sound of the pistol's hammer cocking, Emerson grabbed the wrist of Lincoln's gun hand with both of his and spun around with his back to Lincoln's chest and the pistol pointing away from them just as it discharged a round. Thus, they went pirouetting around the room wrestling over the gun like two broken-legged geese learning to waltz. In their struggle to possess it, periodical discharges of the weapon, unfortunately, by fate or luck, managed to target one of Victoria's priceless heirlooms and other expensive treasures.

Finally, Lincoln lost grip of the gun which fell to the floor and was kicked aside by their scuffling. Face to face now, it became a fist fight, with the two exchanging blows and Lincoln getting the best of the older man. Emerson managed to get his younger opponent in a clinch by grabbing both sides of his shirt collar and pulling tight. Lincoln followed suit. Emerson began pushing Lincoln backward until the back of Lincoln's knees hit the edge of a glass-topped coffee table. Lincoln's knees buckled and, falling backward, he crashed through the table, taking Emerson with him. It took him a moment to recover from the shock of the crash and to now be lying in a pile of shattered glass. And, yet, something felt familiar. Hands! He felt hands!

Déjà vu! He'd been here before. It was Emerson's hands this time closing tightly around his throat and that same feeling of panic welled up in his chest.

"How about some of your own medicine, Millie?" growled Emerson. "Things were fine around here until you started messing around with my daughter. Well, I'll show you where you belong."

Every time Lincoln tried to move a shard of glass would jab at him somewhere. But, he would just have to grin and bear it to get free. He felt around for a long straight piece of glass that he could hold like a knife. He knew he would only get one shot for the glass would cut through his fingers denying him a second chance. All the time he and Emerson had been staring into one another's eyes. He was beginning to choke for air when he grasped the glass 'knife' as tightly as he could and swung for the man's neck. Bullseye!

Good or lucky, it didn't matter. He had struck the carotid artery. Blood shot from the man's neck like Old Faithful. Sitting up and grabbing his neck, Emerson tried in vain to stem the flow of blood with his hand. He stared at Lincoln and tried to speak but couldn't. A look of horror gripped his face. With one leg free, Lincoln pushed the man off the top of him and raised himself from his bed of glass. Upon closer examination, Lincoln found that he wasn't cut up as badly as he had felt there on the floor except for his "knife" hand.

He heard a car coming up the driveway. It was probably Victoria and Ashley returning. He knelt over Emerson. He wasn't breathing. He checked his pulse. None. He didn't have time to let grass grow under his feet; he had to make tracks. Retrieving the .45, he sneaked out the back and, when the women were inside, made his get-away.

Later on, the irony would strike him in the fact that he had killed both his biological and adoptive fathers and in the same way.

Chapter 88

12:00 noon at the Simpson Residence

Doctor Simpson answered the knock at the door. "Lincoln! Good grief! You look like you've been through a meat grinder."

"How observant doctor. I've been through a meat grinder for nineteen years, or haven't you perceived that in all the conversations we've had? Does it have to be as plain as blood for you to see or *care*?"

"Lincoln, I'm so sorry for everything that's happened and how it's hurt so many people. At the time, I thought it was a good thing to do. I guess I made a big mistake," admitted the doctor.

"Doc never intended to hurt you Lincoln," said Maggie who had just entered the room. "He's been your friend all your life."

"I'm not looking for your pathetic apologies. In fact, I'm going to give you a chance to redeem yourself from your sin," said Lincoln with a sinister smile.

"You're what?" asked Doc, not quite knowing how to react. "Well, if you could do that it would be greatly appreciated."

Lincoln pulled out the .45, put one cartridge in the cylinder, pushed doc into a chair, and placed the barrel of the gun to Doc's forehead. "Well, Doc, how about taking a spin of the wheel for a one-in-six chance of redeeming yourself from your sin?"

"Lincoln, this is crazy. I'm sorry for what happened, but, this is crazy."

"Everyone has to pay for their sins. I'm just giving you a one-in-six chance to do that."

"I'm not playing your sick game," he said. "I'm getting up."

He cocked the six-shooter and poked it back in the doctor's face.

"Sit down sawbones," he screamed, "or I'll blow your brains out right now!"

Maggie attempted to intervene but he warned her to stay put.

Trembling, Doc sat back down.

"Let's see if fate grants you absolution," said Lincoln.

He gave the cylinder a spin, put the barrel to Doc's forehead, and cocked the hammer.

Doc was trembling and sweating.

"Lincoln, please don't do this," begged Maggie.

Lincoln squeezed the trigger.

"CLICK."

"Sorry about that Doc. I guess you have to live with your sin." Turning to leave, Lincoln stopped halfway through the front door and looked back. "Take care of that heart, Doc," and closed the door behind him.

Doctor Simpson never heard him. The severe pain in his left arm was bending him double as he rolled out of the chair onto the floor. Outside of Doc and Maggie, no one knew about Doc's heart condition except Lincoln.

As Lincoln sped away he said with a grin, "Two down and one to go!"

1:00 p.m. at the Lacy Hotel

Miss Jessie always threw a big New Year's Eve shindig with live music, dancing, and party favors for the guests, and this year was no exception. The restaurant and lobby were bedecked with colorful decorations and, even though it was early afternoon, both were already beginning to fill with merrymakers. This jovial mood would continue until midnight when it would turn into sheer madness with the blowing of horns, ringing of bells, and the traditional kissing and singing of "Auld Lang Syne." Until then, there would be dance contests and drawings for door prizes to keep the patrons entertained, and, no one would ever know it was a dry county the way the booze would flow this night.

As news of the Armstrong murder was circulating through the ways and by-ways of the town, it was putting a bit of a damper on the holiday festivities, becoming the number one topic of conversation. Details of the shocking homicide, as they became known, were being bandied about (some with exaggerated amounts of blood and guts), accompanied by speculations of possible suspects at whose door could be laid the suspicion of guilt for such a gruesome crime. One prominent name on the "most wanted" list was one Lincoln Crockett who had been seen near the Armstrong residence that morning.

The afternoon hours were slowly drifting by and most everything that could be said about the murder had been said and the patrons were resorting to regurgitation of spent language for furtherance of the subject when a newsflash opened a new line of verbal dialog: Doctor Simpson had suffered a severe heart attack and was being taken to the big hospital in Central City. This report really did curb the partying for a spell, especially by the locals. Doctor Simpson was one of the most liked and respected people in Coldwater, both professionally and personally. For a few short minutes, the atmosphere was more like that of a hospital waiting room than the Lacy's short-term metamorphosis into a night club. It didn't squelch the talking and drinking for long, however. People just huddled in small groups, talking quietly for one reason and drinking for another.

No way could they have realized, or even dreamed, that by the very festive nature of the season and the heartfelt spirit of Christmas, they were lulled into a false sense of security. They did not know that in a matter of minutes all hell would be unleashed upon them. Laughter would turn into groaning, beauty into ugliness, toasts into sorrow, and party into massacre as lives were snuffed out like candles.

Chapter 89

Lincoln slipped unnoticed into the rear of the hotel and surveyed the layout. He determined that Miss Jessie and Clay Cassidy were being held at gunpoint in Miss Jessie's office by Sugarman, who had returned to exact revenge on both of them as he had promised. He had also learned that Deputy Willard was on call to Doc Simpson's residence. There was one significant figure whose presence he had not been able to ascertain, that being the hulking Bam Bam who was always lurking somewhere in the shadows and within spitting distance of Miss Jessie.

Damn Sugarman! he thought to himself. What mischief was he up to and where was he and his one remaining goon, who, by a twist of fate, had missed the trip to the Trout House and avoided being victimized by the assault on his compadres over on Two-Mile Hill? Whatever Sugarman's plans were, they were throwing a monkey wrench into Lincoln's.

Proceeding to the basement, he discovered that the kitchen area had been vacated and from the snakelike hissing sound emanating from the stoves, realized that the air was laden with deadly gas. He was sitting on a time bomb, and it was time to exit the premises! So, he made a mad dash for the outside door.

Momentarily, a thunderous explosion rocked the old building to its foundation. Floors, walls, and ceilings quivered and groaned, straining to hold fast against the force of the blast. In the restaurant and lobby, losing the battle with gravity, portions of ceilings and walls rained down on the floor which was beginning to crack and buckle. Terror spread through the crowd as the partiers, screaming and scrambling over the rubble and one another, stampeded for the exits. As if the explosion wasn't enough, suddenly, the place was ablaze. Tongues of fire licked and lapped their way up the large curtains that draped the windows in the lobby. Chaos ensued. The exits were jammed with hysterical people battling over escape routes.

Lincoln hadn't made it to the door. The concussion of the explosion had slammed him against a wall. Reeling from the impact of the blast, he stared unbelieving at the wreckage that lay before his eyes and cringed at the cries of the victims of a holocaust. Making his way upstairs he saw the guilty two lost souls on the road to perdition. Sugarman had hired them to do his bidding and they were tossing Molotov cocktails around the building with the obvious intent to burn the place and everyone in it down. He had to do something to stop these two angels of death.

Meanwhile, the explosion had caught all those in Miss Jessie's office off guard. That is, except for Sugarman; he was waiting for it. "Time to get on with business. It's payday," said the hood holding his gun at arm's length and pointing it at Miss Jessie.

Just as Sugarman pulled the trigger, Bam Bam leaped in front of his benefactor, taking the shot in his chest. Cursing, the gunman tried to steady himself on the quaking floor to pull off a second round when the wounded big man lunged at him. Just as Bam Bam locked his big hands around the man's throat, he felt the pain of Sugarman's second round burning a hole in his abdomen. Driving him down to the floor, the two of them lay there in a dying heap, both gasping for the last breaths of life they could suck into their lungs until they both were silent.

Suddenly, the office door burst open and Lincoln staggered in. "You've got to get outta here! The whole place is burning down," he ordered.

"Lincoln, I'm arresting you as a suspect in the murder of Emerson Armstrong," said Sheriff Cassidy, pointing his retrieved revolver at him.

"Well, I'll give you one in return, the murderer of Marjorie Henderson."

"Is that right?"

"Yes, she's standing right there!"

"You mean Jessica?" asked Clay.

"You mean ME?" snapped Jessica.

"Yes, YOU, Jessica," confirmed Lincoln.

"You see, that first night I was at her house she had had two or three glasses of wine and got a little loose-tongued and was going on something about us both working for Miss Jessie. She said Miss Jessie paid her to keep a secret. In other words, Marge was blackmailing Miss Jessie to keep quiet about something she knew about Miss Jessie that Miss Jessie didn't want to be public. The only hint she gave was that it had something to do with New Orleans."

"Shut up Lincoln. You don't know what you're talking about," snapped Jessica as she headed for the door.

"It was Bam Bam driving the blue van that almost ran over the cabbie, wasn't it Jessica? It was him that dumped her body in Town Creek after you shot her, wasn't it Jessica? You know, I came here to kill you myself, but, I think I'll just let the government lock your sorry ass up in a cold dark prison cell for the rest of your sorry life."

"I'll deal with both of you later, but right now we've got to get out of here," shouted a concerned Clay Cassidy.

"First, Sheriff, two of Sugarman's clowns are down there tossing Molotov cocktails around like it's the Fourth of July," warned Lincoln.

"Okay, let's get 'em!"

When the two lawmen reached the downstairs, they found the bedlam still underway with people pushing and shoving through the jammed exits. With guns drawn, Lincoln and the Sheriff sneaked through the burning, smoke-filled restaurant looking to ferret out their quarry.

Then, without warning, a shot rang out from somewhere in the blazing confines nearest Lincoln. Lincoln dropped to his knees and rolled over on the floor clutching his side. The bullet had struck him in the abdomen.

Hearing a noise behind him, the Sheriff spied a man trying to crawl through a window near the loading dock. He pursued him. After exchanging two rounds of fire, the man made a last futile attempt to escape via the space in the wall, but the Sheriff shot him out of the window.

The man's partner in crime had met with the same misfortune. He stole quietly, yet as quickly as he dared, until he was standing over what he assumed was the dead body of Lincoln Crockett. As he leaned down to take a closer look, Lincoln opened his eyes, shoved the Colt .45 right up to the villain's nose and blew his face off. Though badly wounded, Lincoln managed to get himself out of the building and into his car. He knew that Sheriff Clay would be after him. He had to get away.

Chapter 90

A chilling wind swirled around the bluffs, whistling through the crags and crevices of the face, carrying with it evidence of the coming night's predicted snowfall. Sitting on the edge of the precipice, Lincoln pulled his coat up tighter as a buffer against the piercing gusts that whipped about. As he surveyed the town below, he thought about the many times that he had sat on that very spot and marveled at the contrast between its postcard image and the reality of life there.

His thoughts were rudely interrupted by the searing pain from the wound in his side. It was bad. He had lost a lot of blood. The climb up the bluff had taken its toll. Getting weaker by the minute, he wondered if Clay had been able to follow him up the rock face. His answer was swift in coming.

"Lincoln!" came the voice of Clay Cassidy, who was a few yards up the bluff behind him.

"Well! The long arm of the law reaches out," answered Lincoln.

"Lincoln, I know you're badly injured. Let me get you down to the hospital."

"You think ole Doc will patch me up? I don't think so," answered Lincoln.

"Link. What happened? Why did you do the things today that you've apparently done?"

Lincoln struggled to his feet while holding his side.

"Hey! Old man Armstrong jumped me, had me down for the count by the throat. I've been there before. Only way I could get out was with a piece of glass."

"And ole Doc? I was just playing a game with him. Can I help it if he got upset about it?"

"And Jessica? I decided to just squeal on her and let you lock her up. She did kill Marge. You check it out."

"You can bet on that, but I believe the law might see things a bit differently than you do in your own case. You'll have to at least answer some questions. Come on. It's snowing harder and beginning to sleet. We need to get off the bluffs and back across the river before it gets worse," warned Clay. "Move away from the edge. The rock is getting slick."

"No! A Millie in a Ridger court? I don't think so. You know how that would go as well as I do. It don't matter anyway, I have been redeemed!" he shouted, throwing his arms up into the air in a jester of victory.

"Linc, I'm duty bound to take you in."

"I know you are, Clay, and I wouldn't respect you if you didn't."

Both men pointed their weapons in the vicinity of each other and fired. First Lincoln, then Clay. Each missed by a country mile. Then, Clay pointed his revolver directly at Lincoln and pleaded, "Linc, please don't make me do it."

"Okay, my friend, I'll make it easy for you. I don't think I'm going to make it anyway," answered a weak Lincoln still clutching his side.

Reeling backward from another stabbing pain, Lincoln's foot landed on the rock that he had been sitting on just minutes earlier; the rock that had served him as a perch affording a bird's-eye view of the vast expanse of space that loomed beyond the bluff's edge. This time, the rock, now ice-glazed, served as a catalyst to propel him *into* that space beyond the bluff's edge.

Sheriff Clay couldn't believe his eyes when he saw Lincoln disappear from the bluff's edge into the dusky, snow-blinding, late afternoon haze. Scrambling down to the cliff's edge where his friend and partner had gone over, he strained in vain to see anything below, but he couldn't. Due to the late hour of the day and the blustery weather conditions, he could hardly see ice-cold Little River, where Lincoln had gone in at one of the river's deepest holes. Although several attempts were made, Lincoln Crockett's body was never recovered from Little River. Few bodies ever were. That old man river had always been very stingy in giving up bodies once they had sunk into one of mythical watery abysses. Lincoln Crockett was never heard from again.

Chapter 91

Things were never the same in Coldwater after that. The town was like a punch-drunk boxer reeling from a barrage of blows that had left it down on the canvas ready to take the nine count. In its two-hundred-year history, the political, economic, and social upheaval in 1965 had been unprecedented. Reactions to the social deviations from the norm that had shaken sacred generations-old standards to their very foundations had resonated throughout all levels of Coldwater society. These reactions had resulted in some seeds of change being planted by choice, and others, merely by happenchance. These seeds bore fruit instrumental in transforming the town.

In the final analysis, however, one single factor emerged as the primary catalyst responsible for closing the doors to the Armstrong and Longworth empires and driving wedges between family members. It wasn't domestic squabbling, legalities, or political chicanery. It was love! Tragic love! It was the love story of two most unlikely star-crossed characters: a young man and woman from two different sides of town and from two different worlds. Theirs was an idealistic, ill-fated love that drove them to march to the beat of their own drums and stand united against family, friends, and the social system. The differences between what Coldwater was like then and what it is today, twenty-one years later, can be credited to Lincoln Crockett and Ashley Armstrong. They laid the groundwork, for they brought down the Walls of Jericho (so to speak) or, in their case, the walls of bigotry, fear, and injustice in Coldwater.

With the passage of time, the couple's reputations have grown in many people's minds as they have remembered them in hindsight or decided how they want to remember them, especially Lincoln. To the older generations, they recall a Bonnie and Clyde duo, a pair of disrespectful, immoral, troublemakers. The younger crowd has romanticized them into a Romeo and a Juliet, whose love held sway even unto death.

Lincoln Crockett has been immortalized in story, poem, song, and tall tale by local singers and writers of various genres. Not only has there been a concerted effort to keep him alive and well in memory, but also some lay claim to the notion that he could actually still be alive and kicking.

There have been incidences when hunters out in the swamps have reported the sighting of what appeared to be a wild-looking man running through the brush. Residents of Johnnytown have also claimed to have had glimpses of what could have been a shaggy-looking man. Some have been bold enough to speculate that this "wild man" might be Lincoln Crockett and that he might have survived the fall. Who knows?

Twenty-one years later

Racing down the interstate, keeping pace with the traffic, she glanced up at the interstate sign: Coldwater Next Exit. She felt the tingle of butterflies in her stomach. She wondered what the place would be like and what she would find. Questions keep running through her mind. How will she be accepted? Is she on a wild goose chase? She felt apprehensive. But she had come this far, and there was no need to turn back now. She grabbed the stick shift of the little red sports car, downshifted to third gear, and rolled swiftly down the exit ramp onto Main Street. Cruising slowly along, she scanned the store fronts looking for some familiar name.

Then she saw it. "Jessica's Antiques, now there's a name that has a familiar ring to it," she said out loud. She wheeled the BMW into a parking space in front of the store, climbed out, and hesitated a moment. She was tall and in her early twenties. Her long slender legs filled a pair of black leather pants complimented by matching heels. A mane of curly, coal-black hair that shimmered in the sunlight fell loosely down to her shoulders and onto the low-cut, red sweater that she wore. Sunglasses couldn't hide the pretty, tanned face of this beauty who strolled toward the shop door with the grace of a model down a runway.

"Hello. Welcome to Jessica's Antiques," said the proprietor.

The young woman approached the counter and removed her sunglasses.

"You must be 'Miss Jessie,'" said the young woman in an assuming tone of voice.

Jessica was taken aback by a strong sense of familiarity in the young woman's looks. She felt as if she had seen her before.

[369]

"Pardon me if I appear a bit speechless, but it's been quite a while since anyone has called me by that name," said Jessica Wingo.

"You also look familiar some way. If I may be so bold, just who are you young lady, and what's your business here in Coldwater?"

The young woman smiled and said, "Well, Miss Jessie, my name is Toni Jo Crockett, and I'm here to find my daddy!

ABOUT THE AUTHOR

G.W. Scott grew up in rural areas and small towns in East Tennessee near an entrance to the Great Smoky Mountains. With a degree in computer science from the University of Tennessee, Scott enjoyed a long career as a computing analyst in the business, aircraft, and government arenas. Scott enjoys writing, teaching, and speaking and is an experienced training instructor, Sunday school teacher, and presenter at technical conferences. *The Betrayal of Lincoln Crockett*, his second foray into the wide world of literature, is an exciting drama, action, and mystery novel. Now retired, Scott and his wife Peggy make their home in Lenoir City, Tennessee.

www.ingramcontent.com/pod-product-compliance
Lightning Source LLC
Chambersburg PA
CBHW051940240626
47153CB00005B/1572